SICK MAN

TEN DAYS INSIDE HISTORY

Book One of a Quantum Trilogy

Bülent Yavuz
Published by Novamerse LLC, Osprey, Florida, USA, 2025

Published by Novamerse LLC

ISBN: 979-8-9934676-0-3

Novamerse™ is a trademark of Bulent Yavuz. Application on file with the United States Patent and Trademark Office.

Cover design by Cheriefox.com

To the Unlived

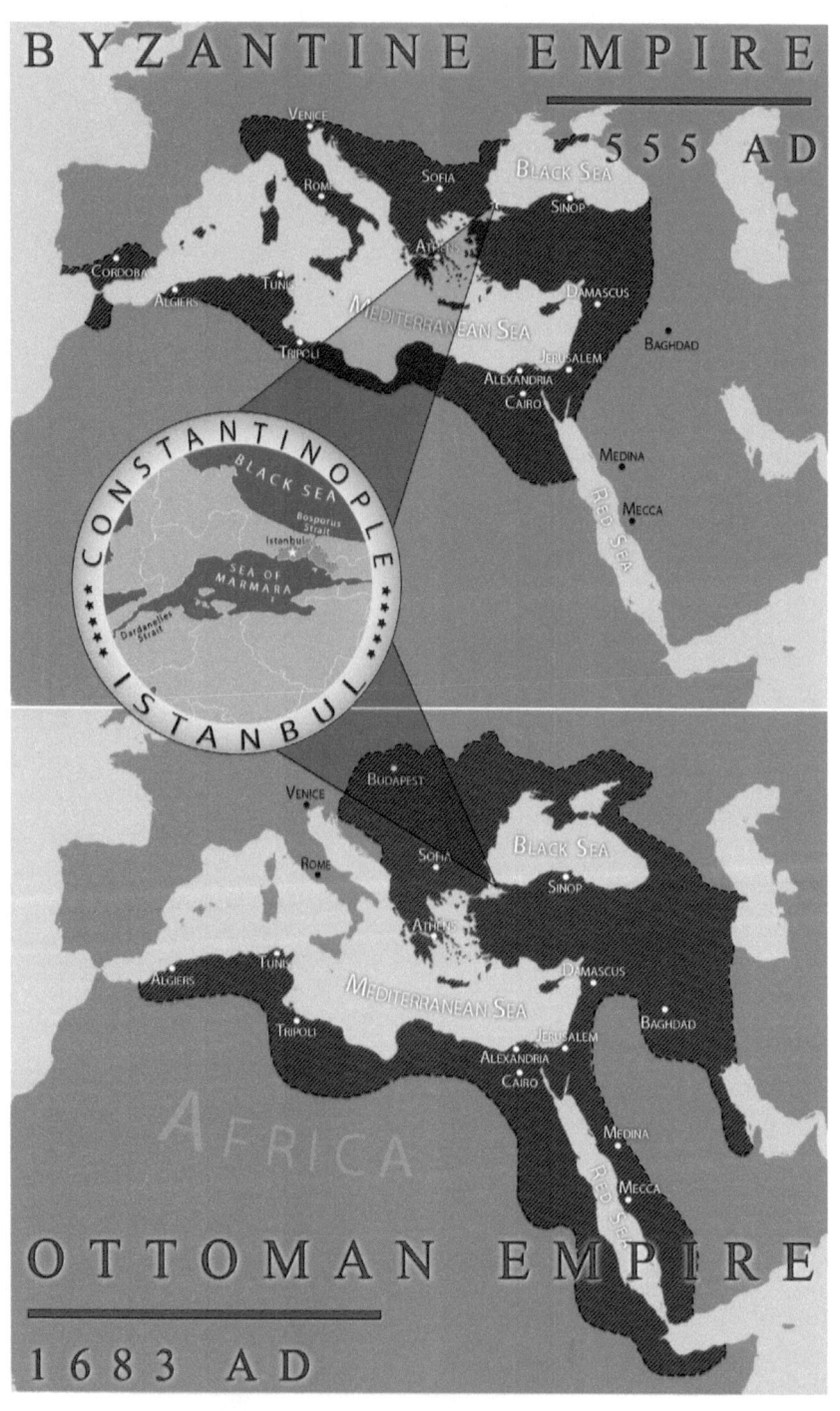

Map design by Cheriefox.com

I, who dare to think, reach the farthest thoughts, sculpted by them

Prof. Dr. Ahmet Arslan

DISCLAIMER

This is a work of historical fiction. While based on documented historical events and figures from the 19th century, all scenes, dialogue, character interactions, and personal behaviors are products of the author's imagination and dramatized for narrative purposes.

HISTORICAL FIGURES

Historical individuals portrayed in this work are fictionalized for dramatic purposes. Their depictions are based on public historical records, documented speeches, published correspondence, and period newspapers, but their personalities, private thoughts, emotional responses, and interpersonal dynamics are entirely imagined. All depictions of conduct and interactions are dramatized for narrative purposes, whether or not based on documented events.

SOURCES AND DIALOGUE

This work is based on research of 19th-century public domain materials, including government documents, contemporary newspapers, diplomatic correspondence, and historical records. Conversations attributed to historical figures incorporate excerpts from their public writings and speeches, adapted and placed in conversational settings for dramatic purposes. Modern scholarly works consulted for historical context are acknowledged in the reference section.

FICTIONAL CHARACTERS

Certain names of lesser-known historical figures have been fictionalized. Any resemblance to specific persons, living or dead, outside the well-known historical figures depicted, is purely coincidental.

NON-DEFAMATORY INTENT

This work is not intended to defame, disparage, or misrepresent any person, group, nation, or institution. Historical conflicts are explored as matters of public concern for educational and thematic purposes. The dramatizations, character interpretations, and narrative are original creative expression.

Contents

Preface And Acknowledgments

This book was written with the help, patience, inspiration, and encouragement of many remarkable people.

My deepest gratitude goes to my wife, Gülderen. Without her love, patience, unwavering belief, and editorial advice, this work would not have been possible.

To my daughter Suzanne and my son Ali, thank you for your understanding and support throughout this journey.

My special thanks to Caryn Pine, whose dedication and effort in content editing brought depth, coherence, and balance to the manuscript.

My heartfelt appreciation to the Dim Sum Ottawa beta team— Lâle and Suat Eskicioğlu, Zeynep Karaburçak, Hakan Tahiroğlu, and Madeleine Guindi—for their thoughtful and constructive review of the manuscript. Your insights helped sharpen both the story and its purpose.

Special thanks to Bruce Hurd, through his workshop guiding novice writers, and to Amber Meeker, for her encouragement when the idea was only beginning to take shape.

I appreciate the continued support of Jean-sébastiane Sardo, Andrea Esposito, and Kathy Camp.

My gratitude extends to my format editors, Refik Telhan and HMD Publishing, for their editorial expertise and commitment to excellence.

To Cherie Foxley, for designing a book cover that captures the essence and spirit of the story, and for her patience with me throughout the process.

And for the inspiration of countless, living and deceased, who had courageously contributed to the collective wisdom, by their life, work, example, poise—some recognized, but most unknown by the public, I feel my deepest gratitude. You drove me to walk on the path to the trilogy of *Ten Days Inside History*.

Finally, to those who believe true progress requires wisdom and wisdom matures within, I thank you for your presence.

"The book will write itself."

I vividly remember him speaking those words, his piercing light blue eyes locked on mine.

He was confident; I was not. Time proved him right.

I leaned over the food-stained, empty paper plate and murmured, "Finally, my friend."

I am the ghostwriter—but not in the way the word implies.

The air had thickened over the past hour, growing warmer by the minute. The empty room was a visual deception, filled with those silent incognitos—thousands of them, each eagerly clung to a page, ready to flee to the virtual cloud.

Before me lay the story that had shaken lives.

Whoever you are, wherever you live, I hope it will leave its mark on you, as it did on me.

I hovered the cursor over the "send" button on the publisher's website.

"For the unlived," I whispered.

I saluted the emptiness—and clicked.

1

THE RECRUIT

I checked the address on the wrinkled letter once again, hoping it might have magically changed, but it still read the same.

I was on the right path, but this wasn't the neighborhood I had anticipated. As excited as I had been that morning, woken by a chorus of cicadas welcoming me to a new day, I couldn't shake the nagging feeling that something wasn't quite right.

That familiar tightness. My hands grew clammy as I tucked the letter back into my pocket. I sighed, quickening my pace as if a brisk walk could somehow reshape the street ahead.

Thanksgiving was just a week away. Despite Covid lingering, New York City finally felt closer to normal than it had since the pandemic began, preparing for the upcoming holiday season. The streets buzzed with hustle and bustle—the usual noises mixed with the periodic screeching of those notorious critters in the background.

The holiday decorations on the busy sidewalk reflected the season's routine, but in 2022, they felt particularly convivial. Shopkeepers proudly displayed them as symbols of triumph, reclaiming their lives and fighting back against the invisible army that had besieged them for almost three years. The virus was no longer the main story on the front pages. The daily casualty figures in the war in Ukraine had already surpassed those attributed to the pandemic. The tabloids, their headlines visible from afar, reported a serial killer had claimed the life of another young woman in Brooklyn.

Nearly two months had passed since the Committee first contacted me, yet I still hadn't met its members face-to-face. Their enticing offer was hard to refuse: a ten-day, all-expenses-paid cruise—a fictional history tour featuring revolutionary quantum computing technology that simulated time travel. I would be one of the "novanauts"—astronauts on a mission to a virtual universe, tasked with answering the question: Can technology prevent World War III?

The offer letter noted that our focus would include the Crimean War of the 1850s. I would witness significant historical events that shaped today's world and gain a deeper understanding of Russia and the underlying causes of its invasion of Ukraine—insights beyond those of the expert pundits on screen.

They were drawn to me partly because of my family background and my fascination about the past. I'm no historian, though my father was, a respected professor of European geopolitics at Rutgers. However, my early interest in history was sparked by my grandfather, a gifted storyteller. My mother used to call him the "wise narrator." The Committee suggested each novanaut adopt a nickname for privacy and security, though it wasn't mandatory. I chose to take one. That's how mine became Narrator.

My cousin and I had planned a trip to the Bahamas during Thanksgiving week. He grudgingly agreed to cancel once he saw how excited I was about being chosen for this pioneering event.

He cautioned me. "This quantum stuff sounds too good to be true."

His concern made me uneasy, but not enough to change my mind. I told him this was a privilege I couldn't pass up. I could be the modern-day Neil Armstrong. His remark was, "Either him or Forrest Gump."

I would receive a daily honorarium, free meals and lodging, plus five thousand dollars for writing a book documenting the trip, payable upon manuscript submission. The money was nice, but it wasn't the deciding factor; the thrill was. This could be the adventure of a lifetime. Despite my excitement, the obligation to write a book kept me awake at night. I had never written one before.

If I agreed, I had to sign the enclosed contract. I did.

The letter included clear instructions requiring all novanauts to assemble at the launchpad at headquarters on November 18, 2022, three p.m. Eastern Time.

Just a block from my destination, I still passed many family-owned businesses lined up along this Brooklyn address. The area must have been zoned for residential and light commercial use. Doubts began to creep in. A launchpad? Here, of all places?

The letter included more specific instructions. "Bring no clothes" printed in bold. They would provide "suitable attire." I wore my jeans and sneakers, packed only the "bare necessities," and stored them in the backpack they had sent via UPS. The red bag, with distinctive yellow print, read, "Team Novanauts." They had planned everything.

I arrived at the address on the letter and checked it one last time. I had envisioned a corporate campus, but instead stood before an old three-story brick building, its party walls shared with neighboring structures. The ground floor housed a retail shop. Above the shop window, a rusty metal sign read, "Lata's Knick Knacks," with the tagline, written in cursive: "and more…" To its left, another store, also owned by Lata, sold used furniture.

Its shabby, unremarkable façade was far from what I'd imagined. It sharply contrasted with the professional interview process that promised an extraordinary initiative.

"Give me a break," I muttered. "This doesn't make sense." My cousin's warning echoed in my mind, a perpetual sound clip.

Sweat dripped down my back—wool sweater or panic, I wasn't sure. Pedestrians passed by, in front of and behind me.

I felt like Seymour in *Little Shop of Horrors*. Was I about to experience a life-changing event "in this seemingly most innocent and unlikely of places"?

I scanned the store window, searching for a peculiar plant in a tiny pot. Instead, I spotted a handwritten note taped to the bottom right-hand corner: "Launch Pad: Travelers Meet Inside @ 3:00 p.m."

I was in the right place.

Half an hour early, uneasy, and unsure of what to do next.

Then, a light switched on inside my brain. What if this was a ploy? Like the prank Tom and the "Gang of Four" had pulled on Jimmy, one of our coworkers.

Last year, Jimmy drove his family to their cabin in Maine for Easter. At the New Hampshire border, two officers pulled him over and asked for a visa to enter the Citizens' Free Republic of Maine.

"Sir, Maine is an independent country now," one officer said. "The state's agreement with the Union expired in March." The other officer, noticing Jimmy's confusion, muttered, "Every fifth grader knows that."

Jimmy had to exchange a hundred bucks for the Maine Pesoliras just to get in. His eight-year-old screamed in the back seat, certain it wasn't real. The hidden camera crew appeared, and the prank aired on cable that night.

Jimmy never lived it down. He stopped having lunch with anyone at work and left the company after his promotion fell through. Rumor had it that the VP told HR, "this idiot" should be paid in "effing pesoliras."

Jimmy didn't show up to his farewell dinner. I felt bad for him.

The Gang of Four was overly curious when I mentioned that my vacation involved a grand adventure. I couldn't share any details until I returned, having signed a secrecy agreement with the organizers.

Was I next in line for humiliation? Could this journey to the "quantum universe" be a grand setup for me? It's tough out there, no hiring. My career could end at any moment.

I began piecing things together, realizing the complexity of their scheme.

A delivery truck sat in front of the adjacent building. The driver kept his gaze on me, and the woman who stepped out didn't look away either. Why were they smiling? We were in New York City, not Sarasota. No one smiled at strangers in this town. Were there hidden cameras?

A terrifying sensation enveloped me, my heartbeat quickening—a full-blown panic attack. I was the fool on the hill, and everyone was laughing from their hiding spots. Another rush of sweat hit me, dripping from my forehead.

I called my cousin, but his phone was off. I texted him, "Urgent, call me back." Then I remembered he'd flown to Japan that morning and would be away for a week.

Mimicking time travel? Marching to the launchpad in my sneakers? I couldn't believe I'd fallen for this. Anger surged as I muttered, "What should I do now?"

I stood at a crossroads: retreat to avoid ridicule or embrace the risk promised by the letter, something I deeply desired. The real question was whether I could handle the embarrassment of becoming the office fool for chasing my passion.

I needed a place to gather my thoughts. A small pizza shop across the street caught my eye, and I rushed over. Cars honked as I darted through traffic.

Once inside, I ordered a slice of pepperoni without glancing at the menu. I took a seat at the bench along the front window, offering an unobstructed view of the building. Shortly after, the waiter served the slice on a paper plate. I gave him a nod without lifting my head, determined not to miss anything outside. I exhaled, trying to retrace the steps that had led to today.

It all began that day in early September, when Tom first mentioned the panel in his hometown.

2
THE MONKEY SCRATCH

"**W**hat does she eat?" Steve asked.

"Bananas, I suppose," Mike said. "Isn't that what they eat in the jungle?"

"Do they sell monkey food at pet stores?" Dave asked, raising a brow.

"They do." Tom twitched his lip. "Biscuits, worms, yogurt, grasshoppers. But thanks to the state, I don't need to worry about it for long. My wife cried her eyes out when she found out that pet monkeys are illegal in Pennsylvania."

Mike slurped his iced coffee. "What are you gonna do with the ape?"

"Find a buyer in a primate-friendly state. And for the record, she's a Japanese macaque, not an ape."

"What's the difference?" Mike narrowed his eyes. "They all have tails."

"No, they don't," Dave cut in. "Apes have none. Monkeys do."

"How long is her tail?" Steve mimed a ruler with both hands.

"She doesn't have one." Tom pressed his lips.

"So, she's an ape then." Mike grinned.

"Sure about that? Maybe hers is just a bud." Dave wiggled a finger.

Tom slammed the table. "I don't know, and I don't care!" His nostrils flared. "All I want is to get rid of the schmuck before a family crisis erupts. My mom can't wait until the critter's off the ranch. She saw her humping a deer in the backyard."

Laughter rippled around the table. Tom shrugged it off.

"Ever since my dad died, she has spent more time at the parish than at home. I'll probably hear some friendly advice from her pastor next."

These were snippets from cafeteria banter on the Friday before Labor Day. Lunch hour was our break from the grind of selling sophisticated products and engineering services in a fiercely competitive market.

The gang of four, named to fame, always claimed the round table in the corner, spacious for eight. Others, me included, sometimes joined them. Their post-lunch coffee ritual became a company routine. Politics was off-limits—wise. Topics stayed light: sports, golf, cars, fishing, home repairs, gardening, and horses, in which I had little interest. I usually stayed quiet, observant.

Our package included customer training, and clients rated me the best instructor in the industry. The VP credited it to my Chinese heritage, though it was only a trace, evident in my slightly upturned eyes. It showed more in my Aussie grandmother. Grandpa described her as a "breathtaking dishwater blonde with striking, slanted blue eyes." Her grandfather, Chou, a Shanghai gold miner, moved to Queensland in the mid-1800s seeking his fortune. He never found it.

I once sold our services at cost by mistake. The VP lost his temper. "I thought you were Confucius," he fumed, "but I forgot—you only have one-sixteenth of his brain."

That was when Conflake became my nickname at work, though not the only one. The Gang of Four rarely ventured into intellectually stimulating topics—that's when I spoke up, especially if it involved history. Steve called me Homer, after the historian. Mike stretched it to Homeroid, since history had been his worst subject in high school. I never knew when to stop, carried away, while my teammates sat with vacant expressions.

Rumor had it Dave was the first to suggest changing my title to "Senior Nerd Associate." Even the stiff HR manager cracked a laugh. It stung, but I didn't show it. A trait I carried from Dad.

I felt privileged to have a rich tapestry of background.

My father—a naturalized citizen—came to America for graduate school after his mother, my grandma Kathleen, died. Reserved and bookish, he looked like an Englishman, spoke like an Aussie, and showed no trace of his Turkish heritage from his father's side—neither in appearance nor behavior.

My Turkish grandfather was nothing like his son. Their relationship was distant, though Grandpa took pride in his son's achievements. I, however, was his cherished grandchild—the apple of his eye. He played a vital role in my upbringing. Every winter, he stayed with us in New Jersey; in the summers, my mother and I visited his farmhouse in Ephesus, outside Izmir. My father, a workaholic, rarely joined us.

My mother's roots run deep. Her British ancestors came over with the *Mayflower*, and her French lineage was Huguenot—the heritage she embraced most. That makes me nearly half English with a touch of Chinese, and ancestry from England and Australia, while the other half splits between Turkish and French.

Despite this diverse background, I am every bit American—born and raised in the land of the free, where lineage matters less than character. Yet, for all my pride in being American, I never fit the mold of popular culture. While my peers obsessed over batting averages, golf handicaps, and how many times the Giants had made the Super Bowl, I couldn't care less. These facts slipped away like writing in the sand, washed clean with the first wave. But if you ask me about *The Federalist Papers*, I can speak volumes. That is me.

Tom was the flamboyant leader of the Gang of Four. He often set the tone at the table. His family owned a sprawling estate and a horse farm in a charming Pennsylvania town near the New Jersey border. At one time, his ancestors nearly controlled the county where they settled.

"Don't you have a German Shepherd?" I asked.

"Oh, yeah, that's the other thing. My daughter complains she can't sleep at night. Rex barks at the primate until midnight. He was never like that before the monkey came into our lives."

"If Rex is anything like Fritz, you might have a disaster waiting at home." I gave a faint smile. "Tell your wife to keep them well apart."

"Who's Fritz?" Tom lifted a brow.

"The beloved dog of the late King Alexander of Greece."

"Here we go again!" Mike groaned, rolling his eyes. "Homer took the stage. I'm outta here."

"Wait a minute." Tom stopped him mid-exit. "I wanna hear this."

Tom's interest was rare. Usually, within a minute of my talking, he'd glance at his watch and say he had to get back to work.

I leaned back. "World War I, 1917. The Greeks ousted their Danish King, Constantine I, and replaced him with his young son, Alexander."

"I didn't know the Danes ruled Greece." Steve knitted his brows.

"They didn't. Their king was Danish."

"Couldn't they find a Greek guy to run the country?" Mike asked. "What about Zeus? Where was he then?"

Had I not known Mike, I would have thought he was joking. But he wasn't. He nearly cost us a major European contract when he told a potential client that, without dinosaurs, the Egyptians could never have built the pyramids. At first, Signor Pellegrino chuckled, but when he realized Mike was serious, he almost spilled his after-dinner limoncello at Gatto Nero. I quickly stepped in, framing it as a metaphor. Mike meant we shouldn't dismiss old methods; sometimes they prove more effective than so-called smart systems. That seemed to reassure the aristocrat from Torino.

On the way back, after the signing ceremony, Tom nearly kicked Mike when he doubled down, insisting it was true. He'd seen it on cable TV.

Thankfully, no clients were present when Dave claimed Jesus was buried beneath St. Peter's Basilica. That would have been harder to recover from.

I don't want to give the wrong impression—I wouldn't trade Dave, Mike, or Steve for anyone. They consistently delivered innovative technical solutions on the spot, impressing our clients. I'd long since recognized that humans are imperfect; no one excels at everything, but we thrive in what we do best. And there's no better place to do that than America, a country that offers unparalleled opportunity.

"Zeus was a god in ancient Greece, idiot," Tom blurted, then turned to me. "Keep going."

"After the war, the Greeks invaded the Turkish mainland, with Britain backing them. The Turks fought for their independence."

"Did the Turks win?" Steve asked.

"Eventually," I replied. "At first, though, the Greeks gained ground. King Alexander, a newlywed, delegated the war effort to his commanders, preferring time with his wife and his beloved German Shepherd, Fritz. When he added a few macaques to his collection, Fritz wasn't pleased and attacked one of the monkeys."

Tom parted his lips slightly.

"Alexander rushed in to break up the fight, but one of the macaques scratched him. He contracted sepsis and died a few days later at twenty-seven. The Greeks reinstated his father, Constantine, who replaced the commanders. Soon after, the Greek army began to lose to the Turks."

"Rotten souvlaki!" Dave exclaimed.

"Churchill allegedly said one monkey scratch had cost two hundred fifty thousand lives." I smiled knowingly. "I doubt he believed it. The Turks won the war, hands down, and he knew it."

"Winning independence is no monkey business," Steve quipped.

"Precisely."

Tom had drifted already. "I didn't know dogs attacked monkeys," he murmured.

"It's possible. Humans are social creatures, yet they kill each other every day."

"I'm glad you told me this story. I'll share it with my wife." Tom leaned toward me. "But it got me thinking. We have a historical society in our county. I'm on their advisory board."

"Really?" That surprised me. "I didn't know you had an interest in history."

"You should know me better than that by now—I don't. But my great-grandfather founded the county library, so I can't escape this obligation." He leaned closer. "Next Saturday, the society hosts a panel on Greece's bicentennial, its independence from the Turks. Supposed to happen last year, but Covid delayed it. We have a sizeable Greek community. Someone with Turkish heritage on the panel will enrich the gathering. Would you be willing to join?"

"That sounds interesting, but I can't even speak Turkish. I understand some and can read a little, but that's all. My dad was bilingual, though he rarely spoke it at home."

Tom nodded. "I know. Your old man was more English than a Londoner. God bless his soul."

"You'd be better off with a Turkish student or a recent immigrant. I know a few. Want me to introduce you?"

"You'll do a good job." Tom held my arm. "Just a heads-up, you'll be facing a tense crowd. Mostly bitter Greek Americans. But they won't bite. You'll have fun."

"Grease the turkey!" Mike blurted, then launched into his nerve-wracking laugh.

"Thanksgiving in September!" Steve chimed in. "I'll bring the pumpkin pie."

Dave smirked. "Conflake doesn't count as a Turk. He's only one-fourth, with a dash of Chinese."

"Quarter-pounder turkey burger topped with soy sauce," Mike quipped. Laughter rippled across the table.

I shrugged. I'd lost count of those tired nation-and-bird puns from self-proclaimed comedic geniuses.

I forced a wry smile. "I accept your offer."

Tom smiled back, softer. "Hey guys, the country's official name is now Türkiye. I heard it on the news."

"Too bad," Mike quipped. "Now they'll have to find a new name for the bird."

Another round of laughter followed, loud enough to turn heads in the cafeteria.

On Saturday, I drove to Pennsylvania.

When Tom told me the board had approved my participation, I spent the week buried in the region's history. My cousin said hardly any Americans cared about those old conflicts, aside from a handful of Turks and Greeks still bitter toward each other. He was annoyed that our weekend plans were off.

I agreed to this to honor Grandpa's memory. He would've been proud to see his grandson defend his homeland from a podium, like an ambassador. What I didn't know then was that the panel would ignite a chain of events that struck at the core of every American, if not every living soul.

That morning, Tom called to apologize. He had to drive to Ohio to deliver the monkey to her new owner. He assured me I'd be in good hands.

The audience was sizable for a small town, likely drawn by the promise of Greek food after the panel. American and Greek flags, balloons, and blue-and-white ribbons decorated the Victorian porch of the old library. Inside, a banner stretched across the stage.

GREECE - CELEBRATING 200 YEARS OF LIBERTY

Better a single hour of life that is free,

Than forty years of slavery and prison!

The moderator, Dr. Dennis Thompson, was a retired history teacher. Easygoing and friendly, he stood about six feet tall, with blond hair, light blue eyes, and a mustache that tilted slightly upward. After introducing me to the other two panelists, he gave us instructions.

Amid the rising commotion in the audience, I overheard a group of women debating whether Britain's new king, Charles III, could ever live up to Queen Elizabeth's legacy. It had only been two days since her passing. One woman, her wrists jingling with gold bracelets, insisted Princess Diana would have been queen consort had she lived. Most nodded, except for a woman in blue and white, who countered that Diana had divorced Charles long before she died.

Following the greetings, Dr. Thompson reminded the audience that the event was live and would be uploaded to the society's website.

"We gather here today to commemorate Greece's bicentennial of liberation from the Ottoman Empire. Before introducing our panelists, I'll give you the *Reader's Digest* version of history." He playfully warned, "There'll be a pop quiz at the end, and only those who pass will earn the privilege of savoring Auntie Ophelia's baklava. So, stay sharp." Laughter filled the room.

Two maps on tripods displayed the Byzantine and Ottoman Empires at their heights, both stretching across three continents, bridging the Islamic East and the Christian West.

"Anatolia." He paused, pointing to the Mediterranean shoreline. "This western Asian peninsula is home to the modern Turkish Republic, Türkiye. Its western region is often called Asia Minor."

The retired teacher went on, tracing early human migrations from Africa to the region.

I scanned the audience. A few wore masks. Some eyes drooped, some stared wide, and others were glued to phones. A message popped up on mine: a photo from Central Park. My cousin at the summer's final open-air concert, Dom Pérignon in one hand, a sign with an "S" in the other. I texted back. "*Stupid.*" He replied with a trophy emoji.

He had a point. Here I was stuck in a stuffy library, listening to the tales of Anatolian kingdoms since the Ice Age, while he sipped champagne under the September moon. Not my smartest choice.

Dr. Thompson finally arrived in the last millennium. "Muslim Turks and Christian Greeks have been rivals since the Turks entered Anatolia a thousand years ago. They conquered Constantinople in 1453, ending Byzantine rule. Over the next three centuries, the Ottoman Turkish Empire expanded into lands once held by the Byzantines, then declined from the 1700s until its collapse after World War I. Its successor is the Republic of Türkiye."

A table beneath the maps listed countries from the Balkans to North Africa.

"More than thirty modern countries emerged from the breakup of the Turkish Empire, beginning with Greece two hundred years ago."

Dennis gestured toward us. "Today, you'll hear its story from three panelists—two of Greek heritage and one with Turkish roots."

I jolted. None of us had grown up in the countries we were to represent, nor were we fluent in their languages. We were all Americans. Yet here we stood—like gladiators before a bloodthirsty crowd—a face-off, two against one. Cold prickles ran down my spine.

Dr. Thompson stepped forward. "For clarity, when I refer to 'Turkey,' I mean the Ottoman Empire." He let the words sink in. "I'm not reinventing history. Most documents from that era use the terms Turkey, the Turkish Empire, and the Ottoman Empire interchangeably. 'Türkiye,' on the other hand, refers to its successor, the modern Turkish Republic, founded in 1923."

I adopted the same convention.

He added, "In the Ottoman era, Constantinople and Stamboul both referred to today's Istanbul. Smyrna meant Izmir. Muslims were called Mussulmans, a term borrowed from French."

The first speaker was George, a man in his sixties, importer of Mediterranean food.

"My ancestors thrived in the tobacco trade in Asia Minor. This week marks the centennial of that dreadful day in September 1922 when the Turkish Army razed Smyrna. Americans rescued my great-grandfather and his family. They fled to Lesbos and eventually reached Ellis Island with barely a penny."

George skipped past the bicentennial we were gathered for and leaped to the 1920s. Greece had invaded Asia Minor, backed by Britain, to drive the Turks out. Many local Greeks welcomed the invasion. After three years of war, Turkish nationalists pushed them back and reclaimed their homeland. In the aftermath, Anatolian Greeks fled to Greece, and Turks in Greece emigrated to Anatolia. George's family was among them. The wounds of war made cohabitation extremely difficult.

George's voice crackled. "My grandfather was a boy then. He witnessed the Turkish atrocity in Smyrna and told his children never to forget. So, I remember."

Time freezes for immigrants.

Some might think a century should heal wounds. But many Greek Americans still carry that pain. The same is true on the other side. At Turkish food festivals in New York, elders recalled atrocities in Muslim villages during the Greek invasion.

Their stories, shaped by heritage and pain, passed down to American-born descendants, became legacies—cherished, never questioned.

My Turkish great-grandmother, Sidika Hanum, also endured horrors when the Greek army swept through her village. I only learned of it through my Australian great-grandmother, Deborah's diaries.

I stumbled upon them in Grandpa's attic. When I showed him, he warned me never to pass the stories to my children. Sidika had not wanted her memories retold. She believed they only bred hatred and vengeance, like fleas thriving on blood.

My father's words were crisp. "Learn the truth, but speak it with reason. Always be just, even to those who shout."

Next, a young man in his twenties spoke.

"I'm Rigas, a third-generation Greek American, with roots in Trikala, Thessaly." He was pursuing a PhD in sociology at Cornell. "My parents named me after the revolutionary Rigas Feraios, executed two hundred years before I was born."

I introduced myself last. "I'm American, born and raised. My grandfather was a Balkan Turk. His mother's family came from Trikala, the same town as Rigas; his father's side, from Shkodra, Albania. His grandfather, a merchant, settled in Istanbul and brought timber from what is now Romania for the construction and gilding of the sultan's palaces."

Dr. Thompson asked the young man the first question. "Tell us more about Rigas, the revolutionary."

He didn't miss a beat. "Born an Ottoman subject, Rigas Feraios envisioned a united Christian Orthodox state in the Balkans. Inspired by the French Revolution, he ignited the fight for independence against the Ottoman Turks, who had ruled Greece for centuries."

He pointed toward the banner above the stage. "Those lines are his, taken from Thourios, his revolutionary hymn. Before his execution, he declared: *'I have sown a rich seed; the hour is coming when my country will reap its glorious fruits.'*"

Dr. Thompson cut in, "And that hour came in 1821, twenty-three years later."

"Ending four hundred years of oppression!" George burst out, jolting me.

Rigas shot me a faint smile. "It began with wealthy Byzantine expatriates and merchants from Odessa and Constantinople, known as *Phanariotes*. They formed the *Filiki Eteria*, the Society of Friends, which sparked the revolts. At first, they lacked a national ideal. Thanks to Lord Byron, once they embraced Hellenism, the Greek cause shifted from religious freedom to nationalism."

I nodded. That was history without emotion, just the facts.

"Public opinion can be critical, but armies win wars," Dr. Thompson leaned toward Rigas. "How did the Greeks fare on that front?"

"They sought help from the West. England and France, at first reluctant, responded once they realized Russia's new czar, Nicholas, intended to liberate Greece, dismantle the Ottoman Empire, and seize Constantinople."

Dr. Thompson quipped, "Keep your friends close, but your enemies closer," drawing chuckles from the audience with the adage, famously revived in *The Godfather Part II*.

Rigas continued, "In 1827, the three powers formed an alliance and won a decisive victory at Navarino against the Ottoman navy. Greece established its kingdom in Morea and, over the next ninety years, gradually expanded its borders into the nation we recognize today."

"Who became the King of Greece?"

"A Bavarian nobleman named Otto."

"Why a Bavarian and not a Greek?" Dennis narrowed his eyes, drawing more giggles from the audience.

"No Greek wanted the other to take the throne." Rigas smiled bitterly. "And the three European powers that backed independence preferred a foreign monarch. Otto, a Catholic prince, was their convenient choice to rule the Orthodox Greeks. He reigned for three decades before being deposed."

"What legacy did he leave behind?"

"He brought beer to Greece." Rigas grinned, turning giggles into full laughter. I pressed my lips together. George stayed stern.

"Who succeeded him?"

"George I, a Danish prince from the House of Glücksburg. He ruled for fifty years and oversaw Greece's territorial expansion, including the annexation of Thessaly from the Turks."

That was when Sidika Hanum's family left for Asia Minor, but I'd decided not to bring that up.

"Let's turn to our third participant."

The hall's focus shifted to me. The banner above the stage loomed like a guillotine, ready to drop. I imagined my head falling before the Parisian spectators in the Place de la Révolution. Why had I accepted Tom's offer? According to my cousin, I loved searching for trouble.

"Why did the Greeks want to gain land from the Turks?" Dennis was blunt.

A new text buzzed on my cell. *"Have they shredded you yet?"*

I swallowed. "Some did. They believed in the *Megali Idea*. It means the great ideal in Greek."

Smiles and a few chuckles.

That was stupid—teaching Greeks an expression in their own language.

"A Hellenic vision of reviving the Byzantine Empire and reclaiming Constantinople." Dr. Thompson recited. "Did they ever pursue it?"

"Came close in the 1920s but failed. The Turkish nation, led by Mustafa Kemal, decisively defeated the Greek army that had invaded Asia Minor."

Dennis raised his arm. "Kemal Atatürk, father of modern Türkiye."

That was one man Grandpa wanted me to learn about in modern Turkish history. Mom became a fan too after reading Atatürk's biography. She was ecstatic when McLaughlin named him the Man of the Century on his Sunday morning show.

Dennis lowered his voice, eyes twinkling. "I'd like to share an intriguing coincidence I noticed."

The glint of mock gravity pulled the audience in.

"The Greek nation gained its independence two hundred years ago—a triumph for them but a disaster for the Turks. A century later came the *Great Asia Minor Catastrophe*—devastating for Greeks, yet winning independence for the Turks. Today marks its centennial."

Dr. Thompson leaned into the microphone and deepened his voice. "Are we on the brink of a new defining moment between the two nations?"

"Maybe what happened yesterday is a sign," I chimed in, grinning. Attention edged closer.

Dr. Thompson jerked his head back. "What happened yesterday?"

"Prince Charles became king!" someone called out.

"Exactly," I said, and launched into the monkey scratch story. Only a few had heard it before. The woman in blue and white was one. Most chuckled, some fell into thought. It helped me bond with the audience.

"The monkey's scratch restored Constantine to the Greek throne," I reminded them. "He was Prince Philip's uncle. A century after his defeat in Asia Minor, Philip's son, Charles, has ascended to the British throne."

The coincidence sparked a buzz. The woman with gold bracelets made a Greek cross as if she'd just heard a prophecy.

Numbers have a way of weaving themselves into history in mysterious ways.

Dennis pulled the conversation back on its track. "What did Turks say about these atrocity claims?" his gaze fixed on me.

I sighed. "Before I answer, may I pose a question to the audience?" He nodded.

"How many of you believe the Turks systematically burned Greek quarters in Smyrna?"

Most hands went up. The woman in blue and white kept hers down.

"I have reports from British and American authorities that may challenge your beliefs." I held up the articles. "You're welcome to review them after the forum."

I had come prepared.

"In his report, the French commander said allegations of Turks pouring kerosene on houses were unfounded. Instead, grenades thrown from Greek residences at Turkish soldiers contributed to the blaze. Unfavorable wind likely worsened it."

"I don't believe them," George shot back. "France betrayed the Greeks. They handed their weapons to Kemal's army and left."

I sensed I was slipping into a scoring match—tallying which side had suffered more. Yet silence might be taken as acceptance of unproven allegations.

I turned to George. "You said Americans rescued Greek families and helped them escape to Lesbos."

"Yes, they did. My family has always been grateful to America for that."

"I would be too." I smiled. "May God bless those who helped your families."

"Amen," came voices from the audience.

"Mark Prentiss was the United States rescue representative to the Near East. He likely helped many families." I leaned toward George. "Perhaps yours, too."

"Know the name. He is a saint!" someone shouted.

"I agree." I nodded. "On September 27, 1922, the *New York Times* published his report, written to the State Department. Would you like me to read a passage?"

"Sure."

"With the help of two hundred Turkish soldiers, American sailors rescued fifteen thousand Greek refugees, sending them to Mytilene on Lesbos. Turkish officials showed remarkable forbearance and tolerance."

George shook his head sharply. "Our family mansion was reduced to ashes. My grandfather said it was the Turks! I believe him."

"I'm not disputing your late grandfather's hardship. My point is that we can't generalize from his unfortunate experience."

"Smyrna was burned. That was no fake news," George grumbled, pressing his lips together.

"No doubt it was real. But blaming only the Turks isn't fair and, according to Western government reports, it's inaccurate."

I turned to the audience. "History taught isn't always the reality lived." Dad's line on the first day of class.

"If everyone tells me every day that green is red, I might come to believe it, too. First, learn the facts. Ride them to reach the truth. Then uphold it, before drawing conclusions."

I pulled another article, hoping to bring George to reason. "This one is from British Viscount St. Davids, Greece's ally. It reports that Greek soldiers burned and pillaged Turkish villages during their retreat."

George cut in tersely. "Don't bother. More Turkish propaganda. Kemal ordered the burning of Smyrna."

Everyone has a breaking point. For my grandfather, like most Turks, it was hearing an insult hurled at Mustafa Kemal Atatürk.

I had no choice. Representing Grandpa, war became inevitable.

Like a general unsheathing a long-kept sword from an old trunk, I reached into my dossier and drew out an excerpt from Deborah's diaries, though it went against Sidika Hanum's wishes.

"I'm sick of these arguments. I've heard them since the day I was born!"

That was the woman in blue and white. Her voice echoed in the room.

She turned toward me. "If 'learn' is the magic word, then let's start by learning how to build a future together."

Her words stopped me in my tracks. A chill ran through me, as if Sidika Hanum had descended from the heavens and was speaking through her.

"Tell us, Ophelia, how are we going to do that?" a man in the audience challenged.

Rigas leaned toward me, whispering. "She's my aunt. That's her husband."

"Greeks and Turks must learn to work together." Ophelia was firm. "A future free of outside manipulation, built by us."

"Pipedream!" her husband scoffed. Laughter followed. I wasn't surprised. Most Turks I knew would have reacted similarly.

Ophelia didn't flinch. "I wouldn't be too quick to dismiss it, Nico." She clasped her hands at her waist. "Everyone knows Atatürk and Venizelos were wartime foes, but not many remember they became allies just a decade later and proposed the Balkan Pact, a peace initiative."

Dr. Thompson raised his brow. "I didn't know that."

Rigas jumped in. "It's true. Venizelos nominated Atatürk for the 1934 Nobel Peace Prize for this visionary peace plan. Unfortunately, the timing wasn't right. The Second World War crushed the initiative before it could begin. Looking back, it foreshadowed the European Union initiative."

Ophelia addressed the audience. "Venizelos is a hero to many of us, a revered figure in Greek history." She turned toward the panelists. "My dear George, why on earth would he nominate a grand arsonist for the Nobel Prize? A man accused of ordering the burning of a city where two hundred and fifty thousand Greeks lived."

George clenched his teeth.

"Auntie, that was back then," Rigas cut in. "Today, tensions run high in the Eastern Mediterranean."

"That's exactly why we need dialogue." Ophelia shot back. "If Greeks and Turks can learn to trust one another, the Eastern Mediterranean could once again be the envy of the world. Just keep the *monkeys* from scratching us."

Her husband snapped, "Get real, Ophelia! Greeks and Turks don't collaborate."

"They must, Nico!" she fired back. "It's not just a choice but a necessity."

I was a skeptic myself. "Lofty goals. How would you do that?"

She locked her eyes on me. "If you make peace necessary, war no longer becomes a choice."

I jolted.

"Can't you see the ticking time bomb?" she grimaced. "No one nation should dominate the Mediterranean. We must learn to share the sea for everyone's sake."

"Do you have an example of success?"

"The French and Germans fought for centuries. Look at them now— almost no borders. Why can't Yorgos and Mehmet do the same?"

"Because they never have," Nico cut in, blunt.

"You're wrong," Ophelia swung back at her husband. "The world recently saw a powerful example. A Turkish couple and a Greek man collaborating for the greater good."

"What example?" Dr. Thompson asked.

"The leaders of the two companies who developed a COVID vaccine."

I chimed in, "Uğur Şahin of BioNTech, born in Türkiye, and Albert Bourla of Pfizer, born in Greece. They kept a bottle of raki in the fridge to celebrate."

"Don't forget the woman!" Ophelia wagged her finger at me.

"My apologies. Özlem Türeci, BioNTech. Born in Germany to Turkish parents."

"She co-invented it. She's the driving force, like Madame Curie or Mrs. Einstein." She raised her arm, declaring, "Turks and Greeks! It's time to learn to share. Pipedreams can come true."

The room erupted in a cacophony. Small groups broke off, voices rising. Laughter tangled with protest. A classic Mediterranean scene.

"Quiet, please!" Dennis rapped on the desk but failed to silence the noise.

Ophelia beamed at her husband, radiating confidence in her blue and white dress. Nico, arms crossed and brow furrowed, stared at the Byzantine map.

"Huh. It'll take a miracle," he murmured.

"Hey, Nico, you've got the pipe you've been dreaming of," someone quipped. "Your wife says the miracle's in the blue pill." Laughter cracked.

The noise swelled. No one paid attention to us anymore.

"Doc, you lost your meeting," Rigas mused with Dr. Thompson.

Dennis stood, lifted both arms, and called out, "Let's follow Auntie Ophelia's dream to paradise. Gyros and baklava await us on the other side."

I slipped Deborah's memoirs back into the dossier.

If there was one thing I carried from that day, it was Ophelia's words, echoing in my mind: Make peace a necessity, not a choice. But how?

My phone buzzed. *"Should I send a rescue squad?"*

I texted back. *"Sidika did."*

3

THE MAGIC WAND

"Scrumptious," Dr. Thompson said, savoring a toasted sesame bagel with cream cheese, capers, red onion, and a slice of Jersey tomato.

"Tastes as good as the one I had in Norway." He sipped his coffee.

"Eating here has become a weekend tradition for me," I said.

We had grabbed the corner table before the Saturday rush at Bagel Chateau in Westfield, New Jersey. I was glad my pick earned his approval.

Two weeks after the panel, Dennis had called with an intriguing offer: a unique, all-expenses-paid history activity during Thanksgiving week. I had tentative plans with my cousin but was flexible. The esteemed teacher provided no details, only saying he wanted to meet in person. I was flattered he would drive to Jersey on a Saturday just to see me.

I thanked him for inviting me to the panel and for the warm hospitality. Ophelia's catering was terrific. She and Nico had to rush back to their diner. Rigas left early for Cornell. Later, Tom joked I'd earned extra points for surviving George's Greek offensive.

George and his wife—the lady with the golden bracelets—were kind at the reception. She insisted I try her moussaka. She was right, it was out of this world.

After most guests left, Dr. Thompson and I lingered, talking nineteenth-century history. On the drive home, I replayed a cheerful exchange with my late grandfather in my mind. He would've been proud of my conduct.

Now, watching Dr. Thompson eat his sandwich, eyes half-closed in satisfaction, I waited for his reveal. My guess was a Woodstock-style weekend packed with workshops for history buffs.

"I wonder who supplies the nova lox?" he asked.

"It comes from a specialty house in Brooklyn. I think they keep it secret."

"Secrets, oh yeah, we must keep them." He took a bite. "Same for this project. Mum's the word until it's ready for the world." That erased my workshop theory but piqued my curiosity.

I wanted to know more about him. "Did you grow up in Pennsylvania?"

Dennis nodded while chewing. "Altoona. Small blue-collar town outside State College. My best friend in high school was Kazuo Jawara. Later, we were roommates at Penn State."

My jaw dropped.

"Do you mean KJ-San, the Blasian tech billionaire?"

"That's correct," he replied, wiping cream cheese off his bagel.

KJ's company had revolutionized the gaming industry. I was floored Dennis knew him well.

"Smartest kid in school. He stood out in our mostly white, German-American town." He gave a brief chuckle. "Some thought he was an alien. I call him the double outlier."

My cousin, a die-hard gamer, would be thrilled to hear this.

I grinned. "I watched an interview with him. He talked about what drives him—making a difference."

"That's what his mother told him." Dennis slurped the hot coffee. "After being bullied, he came home in tears, asking why he didn't look like the other kids. She told him those who stand apart are meant to make a difference."

Her words must have stayed with him. In that same interview, KJ said he took after his parents—one, a math prodigy in Japan; the other, a friend of Nelson Mandela, a revolutionary.

"Do you still keep in touch?"

"I spoke to him a week ago."

"That's amazing. You sound so casual about it."

Dennis shrugged. "I advise one of his committees, a new initiative merging advanced tech with history."

"That sounds fascinating. Can you tell me more?"

"Not yet." Dennis finished his coffee. "But he asked me to reach out to you."

I lost my breath for a moment.

"How would he know me?"

"He watched the panel recording online. Afterward, he asked the committee to consider you for his pilot project."

"Why?"

"One of your comments caught his interest."

"Which one?"

"Learn facts before forming an opinion; always strive to uphold the truth. That aligns with his mindset."

I had borrowed that line from my late father, a piece of advice he gave his students and lived by in his private life.

It was surreal. The world-famous Gen-Z idol, a billionaire software guru, thought I could contribute. But what was this project? What role awaited me?

"The Committee wants to schedule a phone interview to see if you qualify for the journey. They'll explain more on the call."

"A cruise?"

He smiled. "I promise it'll be worth it."

"I look forward to their call."

A week later, I joined a voice-only teleconference. Four individuals were on the line—three men and one woman: Histo, Magyar, English, and Angela. They made up the advisory board—the Committee.

"This is Histo speaking," a male voice declared. "I chair the Committee. We all watched the panel video. Each member has some questions for you."

His tone was brief, commanding, yet serene. I drew a deep breath, like a rookie stepping up to the plate.

"My name is Angela." Her drawl was cheerful. "What's the most significant current event in the international arena?"

Too easy—a soft pitch right down the middle. "The war in Ukraine. It's tragic."

Next came a male voice with an Eastern European accent. "This is Magyar. The government of the Ottoman Empire had a name. What was it?"

I couldn't recall. A simple curveball, and I whiffed.

"Sublime Porte, or simply the Porte," Magyar answered.

I should've known. Like a game show contestant who'd just blown the jackpot, I was eager to prove it was only a lapse.

"The name is symbolic. It refers to the monumental gate to the imperial palace."

"Bingo!" Magyar laughed heartily. I exhaled in relief.

Anglish spoke with a British accent. Mom used to tease Dad with the same nickname—half-breed Englishman with an Aussie accent.

"The term 'Great Powers' referred to which countries in the mid-nineteenth century?"

That was a tough pitch, but I connected with a solid hit. "There were four: the British Empire, ruling a quarter of the globe; Russia, the most populous with vast lands in Asia and Eastern Europe; France with holdings on four continents; and the multinational Austrian Habsburg Empire."

"Were others rising?"

"Prussia would become a great power under a united Germany. The United States would emerge after the Civil War."

"The Ottoman Empire controlled vast lands on three continents. You didn't include it. Why?"

"The Turkish Empire had been weakening. Europeans no longer saw the Ottomans as equals."

"What caused their decline?"

I gathered my thoughts. "The Ottomans overlooked the European Enlightenment and stayed detached from the Age of Exploration, missing out on wealth from the New World, Africa, and the Far East. They banned the printing press for nearly two centuries, falling behind in engineering, capital, and military innovation. As their power waned, they lost revenue and territory."

"Brilliant observations," Anglish said.

"A powerful oppressor yet an inept imperialist," Magyar chuckled.

"I'm enlightened," Angela added. I wasn't sure if she meant my comments or Magyar's. Either way, it felt like a home run.

For the next hour, the Committee grilled me on nineteenth-century history, firing sharp, intriguing questions—each like a fastball. I connected with most.

Histo remained quiet until the end. Then, in a measured tone, he spoke.

"Thank you for your time. You'll hear from us in a few days."

I woke early on the final interview day, torn between excitement and unease. I couldn't shake the thought that this might be a rejection call.

"Why would they bother with a teleconference if they were rejecting you?" my cousin reasoned, trying to ease my nerves. "They'd have just sent you a thank-you email and been done."

He reminded me that KJ-San had bought a digital tourism startup. Perhaps the committee wanted me to serve as a tour guide on a promotional luxury Danube cruise for affluent guests. I loved the thought. I visualized lecturing distinguished millionaires against a backdrop of breathtaking scenery, sharing photos and press clippings with the Gang of Four, and watching their envy.

I dialed in. Histo wasted no time. The committee leader wasn't one for small talk.

"Are wars necessary and inevitable?"

He caught me off guard. I needed a moment to think. The line went silent. I felt like I was defending my thesis before a jury.

"Not all wars are equal. Some are necessary—wars for survival or independence. Others are avoidable—wars of choice."

"Wars of necessity versus wars of choice," Anglish repeated. "I like that distinction."

Thank you, Ophelia, I thought. I borrowed her motto. The lady in blue and white had another supporter.

"Could you give us a few examples?"

I was quick in my reply. "The first and second Gulf Wars. Saddam's invasion of Kuwait in 1990 was a war of choice. Kuwait posed no threat to Iraq. For the United States, stopping a dictator from seizing Gulf oil was a strategic necessity."

"The second one?"

"By then, the United States was far less dependent on oil from the Gulf region. Al Qaeda had become the real threat. With no proven link to nine-eleven, President Bush still invaded Iraq. A war of choice."

"How did the administration rally support?"

"It claimed Saddam possessed weapons of mass destruction. The United Nations became the stage."

"Were they true?"

"Nope. The intelligence was wrong."

"The first casualty of war is the truth," Anglish echoed the old saying. "Was this an isolated case?"

"Not at all. Putin's invasion of Ukraine is the latest war of choice. Facing no existential threat, Russia attacked a country fighting for survival. A war of necessity for Ukraine."

Magyar cut in. "Remind us. What was Russia's justification?"

"Putin claimed Ukraine was always part of Russia and not sovereign. He spread propaganda that Neo-Nazis were slaughtering ethnic Russians in the Donbas region. State-controlled media pushed this fake reality."

"Fake reality," Magyar mused. "A useful oxymoron that consumes lives."

I added, confident in myself, "History has other examples. The Nazis claimed Jews controlled Moscow's communists."

"Fake it, fear them, repeat it every day—it works like a charm." Magyar chuckled.

Anglish interjected, "Russia is concerned that NATO is threatening its security. Isn't that legitimate?"

"The United States and Russia, together with Europe, can still shape a peaceful world order."

There was a missed opportunity after the collapse of the Soviet Union. My father and others in academia and government attempted to establish an institution for continuous diplomacy—one that could devise real-time strategies to prevent global conflicts before they arose. It failed for lack of funding.

"Vietnam? War of necessity or choice?" Angela asked.

"Choice."

"What was the justification?"

"Domino theory. The fear that if Vietnam fell to communism, the rest of Asia would follow."

"Did it?"

"No. The communists won, but the domino theory never materialized."

She kept firing questions.

"How about the war against Japan?"

"Japan bombed Pearl Harbor. We had to respond—necessity."

"Japan needed resources and sought expansion. Isn't that necessity?"

"After the war, that need didn't vanish. Yet within fifty years, Japan became an industrial powerhouse—without firing a single bullet. Their expansion was choice, not necessity."

"You mentioned Nazis. What's your view on them?"

"The Treaty of Versailles had harsh terms for Germany. It helped the Nazis seize power. Hitler's early moves—annexing Austria and the Sudetenland—had broad local support. He could have stopped and settled diplomatically with European powers, but once he marched into Poland, he crossed the line. Everything after that was Germany's *choice* and the Allies' *necessity*."

Magyar interjected, "Anglish thinks the British are as pure as the white linen airing in my grandmother's backyard. What do you say to him?"

"I've never said anything like that," Anglish shot back. Magyar chuckled.

Voices mingled over the line.

"Let's move on." That was Histo, calm but firm. It felt like the right moment to remind him about the purpose of the interview.

"I understand the Committee is planning a cruise. Could you tell me about it?" I bit my lip and held my breath. The lightness on the line stalled.

Histo broke the pause. "It's a crusade to uphold the truth. A fight to defend history from defamation. Humanity's story is under attack." I needed a moment to absorb that.

Angela picked up. "Truth is not self-evident. What color is a Christmas sweater knitted from multicolored yarn?" After a pause, she answered her own question. "Hard to say. Truth and falsehood often intertwine, making them difficult to tell apart. Uncovering them often demands a Herculean effort."

Her comment carried weight but little clarity.

She deepened her voice. "Beware of the manipulators. They have the loudest bullhorns. They construct their version of the truth and push it for public approval."

She might've meant media pundits, but I still couldn't see how this involved me. I pictured dark clouds gathering over the deck, heavy winds, and choppy waters on the Danube. Still, I played along.

"I hear you, but in the digital age, one person's hoax becomes another's truth. Opinions are one thing, but most people don't search for a universal truth. They don't question their version of reality."

Anglish didn't miss a beat. "There will always be sellers of hoaxes. We aim for far fewer buyers."

Magyar chimed in, "Welcome to flat-Earth society. Next door is the studio where the moon landing took place. Here's my selfie with the Martian who abducted me. Oh, did I mention my mother-in-law plotted against the Kennedys?" He chuckled.

I wasn't amused. "Setting aside the tabloid stuff, what makes you think people will ever agree on divisive issues like guns, abortion, or immigration?"

Angela's voice turned light. "Turn to history. She is fertile ground for wisdom—our lantern illuminating the way forward."

I pushed back. "History can be the narrative told by the powerful."

"That's why we must safeguard her, protect only the proven facts. Just as we wouldn't trust a faulty compass in a jungle, we should reject hearsay and distortion."

"History lies six feet under," Magyar cut in. "She can't defend herself from vandals—midnight gravediggers searching for corpses." His voice dropped, almost a hiss. "She is sacred. She needs protection."

Angela smirked. "That was gravely."

I pressed my challenge. "Current events shape each generation, not history. People forget. They move on."

Magyar didn't let it go. "History has a way of sneaking back. Sometimes, the past you thought buried claws its way to your doorstep— reemerging like a zombie's hand rising from the grave, surprising everyone."

Angela snapped. "Your metaphors are getting creepy."

Magyar burst into laughter.

With theatrical flair, Angela lifted her tone. "Current event or historical past—that is the question!"

"She's holding a skull!" Magyar quipped.

Laughter filled the line, but their humor didn't sway me.

Anglish picked up the conversation. "Seeing is the most powerful persuasion. If people could witness a war of choice firsthand, its supporters might think twice before justifying it."

"I love history, but I'm skeptical it can prevent future wars." I sharpened my voice. "Has there ever been a case where a history-conscious public stopped a war by learning from the past? I can't think of one."

Silence followed.

I pressed. "Protecting history from manipulation. Safeguarding truth. How exactly do these prevent future wars?"

Anglish offered a solution. "Imagine you had a magic wand that could."

His words drifted through the line like a quiet spell, inviting me into a fantasy. I half-expected Alice to step out of Wonderland. Still, I forced myself to give them the benefit of the doubt.

Maybe KJ wanted to create a fantasy tour for anti-war activists—a spectacle where celebrities in goggles swung phosphorus sabers, battling warmongers in the metaverse. Sean Penn might even be on the guest list. I'd read they were friends.

"That sounds poetic and fantastical." My irritation pressed through. "How exactly do you plan to achieve such an ambitious goal?"

"Using technology." That was Histo answering.

That explained nothing. Technology was everywhere.

"History is boring. Just ask my colleagues at work," I quipped. "Most would rather banter about pop culture."

"Then make history entertaining."

"Isn't that what Hollywood does?" I countered. "Movies educate, sure—but can you name one that stopped a war? What more can be done?"

"Living inside."

"Pardon me?"

"Go back and live inside history."

"How? Like time travel?"

"Something like that."

How did we get here? I placed my head in my hands, elbows on the desk, and sighed. My dream of cruising the Rhine alongside Meryl Streep and Bill Gates, sipping Petrus, drifted away like morning mist.

"This sounds like make-believe time travel." I let out a half-chuckle. "A fantasy."

"Yes and no." Histo's cryptic tone only deepened my confusion.

"Could you please tell me why I'm on this call? What exactly are you offering?" I spoke in an abrupt tone, on purpose, the way I did when my father ignored me.

"We're offering you the chance to witness history as if you were there. As a history enthusiast, we thought you'd appreciate it."

A teasing deflection. Not the answer I wanted. Cold, but not unkind. Just like Dad's. His calm stirred unease, the same guilt I felt with my father. I steadied myself. "How exactly do you accomplish time travel?"

Anglish broke the pause. "We don't board a spaceship that warps space or travels faster than light. There's no Scotty to beam you up. It's not a real cruise, either. You won't leave our headquarters for ten days. But it will feel like we rewound the clock, no different from time travel."

It sounded bizarre, like the hallucinations Mom described from her hippie days in France. I never touched any of that stuff. I was like Dad in that regard.

Anglish carried on, "You'll explore places virtually, interact with people from the past. Witness events—even participate in them. The sights, the scents, every detail authentic. Nothing like fantasy."

"In a computer-generated environment?"

"Exactly."

"Like a futuristic metaverse?"

"Beyond that."

I knew metaverse technology was advancing fast. I had my cousin's VR and AR headsets and immersed myself in virtual reality. Fun, sure, but spending my entire vacation playing them? Hardly worthwhile.

My voice tightened. "So, what's my role? Am I some augmented reality tour guide, wearing clunky headgear, leading history buffs on a virtual *Minecraft* boat, narrating the capture of Smederevo Castle by the Turks? Is this your 'ten-day all-expenses-paid cruise'?"

My sarcasm bled through the line. Whatever excitement I had left evaporated faster than Petrus spilling across my fantasy deck.

I slipped into Magyar's voice. "Ladies and gentlemen, welcome to Truthville-on-the-Rhine, an all-inclusive experience featuring a waterfront timeshare pitch. No purchase necessary."

Angela broke in, her tone softer, "That's an idea worth pursuing, but it's nothing like that. Histo can explain better."

The committee leader picked it up, his voice commanding. "KJ came up with a hypothesis."

Histo's words reminded me that a successful tech entrepreneur was behind all this. My inner voice nudged me to reset, wipe the slate clean, and remain positive.

"His idea is simple: when enough people repeatedly witness the same event firsthand, consensus forms."

My curiosity flared. "Does KJ have any real evidence to support his hypothesis, or is this purely conceptual?"

Anglish stepped in. "In 2020, a police officer in Minnesota killed a Black man by pressing his knee on his throat while he lay on the street. Have you heard of it?"

"Of course. Who hasn't? The victim was George Floyd. The courts ruled Officer Derek Chauvin had murdered him. He held his knee on Floyd's neck for eight minutes and forty-six seconds."

The memory was vivid. Outrage swept the nation—and the world—exposing the injustice behind Floyd's suffocation at the hands of law enforcement.

"You said, 'Who hasn't.' Why?"

"Because the whole country watched it."

"How did the entire country watch it?"

"A bystander recorded it on her cell phone and posted it on social media."

Anglish pressed in. "What if she hadn't?"

I hesitated. "Then it would've been harder to prove in court. Witnesses might not have remembered the exact time. And without public outrage, the hearings would've slipped by unnoticed."

Anglish carried on. "What if I told you that the whole thing was fabricated? That Chauvin only pressed his knee there for a minute?"

"I wouldn't believe you. The video left no doubt."

"Exactly." His voice warmed. "The truth was irrefutable because one young woman, Darnella Frazier, filmed it. Tens of millions bore witness."

Angela followed quickly. "Since then, we've seen fewer such cases. More than half of the country's largest cities have banned chokeholds. The change happened because the truth was laid bare before millions of eyes, sparking a demand for real reform."

It was a compelling argument in support of KJ's hypothesis. But could the same principle be applied to prevent wars?

"Vietnam War footage on the evening news shifted public opinion, but many still supported the war. What if those same citizens could have experienced the jungle alongside young soldiers without ever leaving their living rooms? Would that have changed their views?"

Before I grasped her point, Magyar cut in. "Picture this. You're on your couch, virtually leading soldiers through Baghdad in a Humvee.

The simulation is so real it's indistinguishable from combat. Then—boom! A roadside bomb. Everyone around you is wounded or dead. You're the only one left standing. Would you still support the war?"

I gave some thought before answering. "I can't picture how it would work, but if it did, I'd have second thoughts."

Magyar pressed harder. "Now imagine everyone reliving the scene dozens of times with no physical harm to themselves. Wouldn't that shift public view?"

I paused. He kept going.

"Drop something—it falls. Every time. Does anyone doubt gravity? Jump out a window."

Anglish regained the floor. "What he's saying is, if seeing is believing, living it is even more convincing. If people participate in a brutal battle firsthand, or share the suffering of a war-torn society, then maybe, just maybe, they'll stand against the next war before it begins."

Magyar hissed. "The big one. Number three."

KJ's logic was beginning to click. Books and films could teach, but nothing replaced experience. Reliving something—even virtually—multiple times would leave an undeniable mark. If enough people experienced it together, a consensus might follow.

"How do you plan to test this hypothesis? Time travel?" I asked.

The members paused, allowing Histo to proceed. "Time travel is still a fantasy. However, we now have technology that can reconstruct the recorded past, allowing people to observe—even participate."

"What kind of technology?"

"Quantum computing." The chairman's voice was soothing. "A fault-tolerant quantum computer capable of generating a virtual universe where history is reenacted with perfect fidelity, an experience indistinguishable from reality."

Anglish and Angela spoke in unison. "Bring the past to the present—and live it inside the quantum universe." Their voices carried reverence.

Their words sent a shiver down my spine. The phrase alone carried an air of mystery and boundless possibility. My understanding of quantum computers mainly came from my cousin. He once said what takes years to compute today would take only minutes. I also read an article comparing technology's advancement over the past seventy years to boarding a plane and speeding down the runway, with quantum computing marking the moment of takeoff.

Still in its infancy, a quantum computer capable of fulfilling its promise was supposedly a decade away, yet the Committee claimed KJ-San had already achieved it. If anyone could, this billionaire genius would be the one. It made sense. My excitement reignited.

I had new questions. "How do we know quantum computers can prevent future wars?"

"We don't," Histo replied. "But if KJ's hypothesis holds, governments will no longer be able to manipulate the public to justify wars of choice."

"That's the magic wand," I murmured. "How do we prove it's true?"

"We will test it in a pilot program."

"Now you know why you're on this call," Magyar added, chuckling. "Still wanna hang up?"

I felt like lightning had struck. Histo had just opened the *Pulp Fiction* briefcase, and I saw what was inside.

The quantum universe.

"What role do I play in this?" My pulse quickened, adrenaline surging through depleted reserves.

Histo's voice came steady, assuring. "You will embark on a ten-day journey through the quantum universe alongside your teammates, witnessing history firsthand. Afterward, you will document your experience."

"Document how? A travelogue?"

"Yes. A logbook of the journey, much like Madison's notes from the Constitutional Convention."

"Why me?"

"You have a strong grasp of history and a gift for articulation. This book will educate the public on safeguarding truth, prove that reliving history is possible, and inspire others to follow suit. Our ultimate goal is to reconstruct the past two centuries, protect it from distortion, and engage a billion visitors in the quantum universe within a decade."

I exhaled. "This is massive. Overwhelming." The Committee's ambition was staggering. I had never written a book, but I kept that to myself.

"Indeed, it is," Anglish acknowledged. "You will take the first step in a long journey."

Magyar added, "If perception is reality, truth must ye perceive."

Silence followed. The luxurious Danube cruise ship had vanished, replaced by an ancient wooden sailboat drifting into the unknown. Stars, my only lantern, guiding me.

Histo's voice cut through the quiet. "Will you embark on this pioneering journey into the quantum universe?"

A small voice stirred within me, urging me forward. The pull was undeniable—an invitation to become a disciple of truth on the adventure of a lifetime.

No longer a journey, it became an expedition.

Without hesitation, I answered, "Yes."

"Narrator, welcome to Team Novanauts."

4
THE GIGANUT

Seated at the pizza parlor, I forced myself to scrutinize every detail of the interviews, searching for any sign of a prank. I found none, yet the fear of becoming a laughingstock at work burned inside me, competing with my hope that all was real. My head spun, caught in a mental tug-of-war; the rope stretched so thin it felt ready to snap.

I hadn't touched my pizza. I was hungry, but the knot in my stomach dulled my appetite. As I reached for it, two pieces of pepperoni caught my attention. They looked like a pair of dark, affectionate eyes near the wider edge. A streak of tomato sauce closer to the tip curved into a crooked smile. From the paper plate, the slice stared back at me like a worried friend, trying to ease my discomfort.

I whispered to my triangular companion, "Come on, buddy. Give me a sign. Anything."

Nothing.

I lifted my head and looked outside at the retail shop. The delivery truck was still parked in front of the building to its right, unloading a mattress and some furniture. Lata's rusty sign looked even more pitiful from this angle. I couldn't believe I had fallen for this. A wave of sadness washed over me. I seriously contemplated heading back to my apartment, not falling prey to this elaborate gig.

Just as I was ready to quit, a young woman strolled across the street, her backpack identical to mine. I held my breath, willing her to step into the retail store.

She did.

I was lying helpless in a virtual ER. Like a nurse delivering a life-saving drug, she shot a surge of hope through me.

A moment later, two men with matching red bags approached from opposite directions. The gray-haired one slipped into the shop, while the tall man in black stopped by the moving truck. They had to be my fellow novanauts.

I exhaled.

Hope returned with fireworks, warming me from the inside.

"It is real!" I exclaimed to my newfound friend, his gaze still locked on me from the paper plate.

I checked the time—five minutes until the meeting. I grabbed my backpack and rushed out of the pizza shop, leaving the slice untouched.

Across the street, the woman in overalls marked items on a notepad while the crew hauled furniture into the two-story building beside the retail shop. As I waited for the pedestrian light to turn green, I spotted the man in black talking to the truck driver. The woman joined them. The movers nodded at him—the same ones who had smiled at me earlier. Then he shook their hands, shared a few laughs, waved at the woman and the driver, and stepped inside the shop.

My euphoria vanished, like water hissing off a hot rock.

They knew each other. Clear as daylight. The Johnny Cash mock-alike gave his final orders, then went inside to take his spot.

Sweat broke across my forehead. I kicked the light pole and scanned for more clues but came up empty.

The light turned green. I hesitated, but my feet took over, dragging me toward the shop.

Midway across the street, I saw it. The camera. Mounted above the entrance.

I knew it!

The whole thing was a staged play. My jaw clenched.

My mind raced faster than any computer could ever match, quantum or otherwise.

It dawned on me. We couldn't bring in Tom's high school buddy unless a position opened. That was the motive. They'd chosen me. This mockery was meant to push me out of the company.

Then it hit me harder. Dave's cousin owned a moving company. The man in black looked like him. It had to be them. The truck was rigged with a hidden camera, maybe another tucked inside one of the furniture pieces. A clever trick. A sneaky, giga-scale ruse.

"Of course," I muttered. "They'd lull me in, then yank the rug."

Everything snapped into place. This wasn't some holiday adventure anymore. It had turned into survival. My brain flipped into crisis mode. That's where I thrive. Even HR had attested to that.

I quickly devised a plan to turn their pathetic covert operation on its head and make their grand setup backfire.

Ten feet from the entrance, I locked eyes with the camera—the smoking gun.

"Listen up, everyone!"

The woman in overalls and the porters turned toward me.

I snarled at the camera. "Did you really think you fooled me?"

A woman in a yellow sari stepped out of the used furniture store, her eyes wide.

"Hate to break it to you, folks, but yours truly spoiled your game. I saw through it from the start. Guess what? That giga-scale gig was never on me—it was on you! Go on! Record it! Presenting—Yuri Gagaverse! Is that how you'll roll me out on cable tonight?"

I laughed, unhinged, then barked, "Hold your horses! I've got one better! The Giganut!"

An older couple slowed as they passed, staring with wide eyes.

"This is a war for survival." I grinned, leaning toward them. "Theirs is choice. Mine's necessity."

They averted their gaze and quickened their pace.

Nervous yet defiant, I stepped closer to the camera. "Now, let's see what surprises you've got waiting. A box of chocolates for Mr. Gump? Or a monkey biscuit for the astrochimp?"

I winked at the woman in overalls. She shook her head, pity in her eyes.

I shoved the door open and walked in.

5
TEAM NOVANAUTS

No camera crew was inside. Instead, a pleasant chime of bells greeted me. I caught a strong scent of gardenia from a burning candle. A young man stood behind the counter. The shelves were stuffed with used clothing, small wooden statues, framed photographs, and old books. No other customers in sight.

My heart pounded in my ears as I nervously mumbled, "I, uh—I'm here for the meeting. You know, the sign on the window. Launchpad!"

The receptionist widened his eyes and motioned toward a colorful beaded curtain in the back. I brushed my hand through the strings and stepped inside.

Still, no camera crew jumped out.

A row of chairs faced a wooden desk in a classroom-like setup. Behind the desk sat a middle-aged man with a shapely trimmed beard and heavily gelled blond hair slicked straight back. He looked out of place in a light blue three-piece suit and a flashy red tie.

The three people I'd seen enter earlier were already seated, each clutching their own backpack. The smell of fresh white paint was sharp. A shiny metallic door faced the back wall.

"Good afternoon." I forced a smile at the man behind the desk.

He sized me up, his piercing, glassy, light blue eyes locking with mine. His pale face showed no discernible expression, reminding me of a registration officer welcoming fresh army recruits.

"Have a seat."

I recognized his voice and took the only empty chair. I nodded to the participants. They looked wonderstruck, uncertain about what came next.

Scanning for signs of a prank, I found none. No hidden cameras either. My pulse eased from frantic urgency to a slow, sinking thud.

The room had no plants, no pictures, just bare walls, except for a live video feed behind the desk. The woman in overalls was directing her crew to unload a Queen Anne chest of drawers.

What if they had watched the solo stunt I'd pulled?

I held my breath at the creeping possibility.

The blond man exuded self-confidence. "Novanauts, on behalf of the Committee, I welcome you to the program. My name is Histo. I'm the executive director." His voice was steady and soothing, authoritative but without pretense.

He received everyone's negative PCR test results, the final check to qualify for the cruise. Then he asked us to introduce ourselves. Everyone opted to use the Novanaut code names.

Zena, in her early thirties, was a petite brunette with greenish-blue eyes. She was a graduate student at Columbia University, studying journalism, her lifelong passion. Born and raised in New York City, her father had Circassian roots, and her mother was a Christian Gagauz from Moldova.

Rocko, tall and in his late thirties, had slick hair. A staunch environmentalist, he had moved from Türkiye two decades ago after graduating from Robert College, a prestigious high school in Istanbul. Up close, he bore no resemblance to Dave but looked more like Clark Gable in all black Johnny Cash attire. A software specialist at a New York bank, he had recently gone through a bitter divorce. His ex—an Ashkenazi Jew—had little regard for his Sephardic roots.

Nakshi, mid-sixties, was fit, with silver hair and a trimmed gray goatee. He wore a warm smile. He was a Turkish businessman from Kayseri and introduced himself as a practicing Muslim. He spoke of his humble Anatolian roots. Recently naturalized, he was working to embrace his American identity—a challenge familiar to many immigrants. He imported dried foods, hazelnuts, and other Turkish products and co-owned a retail shop in Paterson, New Jersey.

I introduced myself as Narrator and briefly shared my blended roots.

Histo announced that the Committee had designated me to author a book documenting the team's collective experience and asked for everyone's support. There was no sign they'd watched my embarrassing show. I let out a sigh and shrugged.

The program director rose and paced before us, standing straight like a rigid post, his slight frame carrying no excess ounces.

"Tonight, you will embark on a journey to the quantum universe to spend the next ten days inside history. You will meet holograms. They are products of perfect fidelity."

Inside history. I liked the sound of it.

Histo scanned the team, all four seated in a row. His sharp, light-blue eyes pierced like a lance. His demeanor was that of a professor on the first day of class.

Zena raised her hand. "What is 'perfect fidelity'?"

"When the human eye, wearing specialty lenses, can't distinguish a virtual scene from reality, we call it perfect visual fidelity. The lenses block the real scene and replace it with the simulated one."

Rocko quipped, "So when I open my eyes, instead of this room I'll see a dinosaur grazing in a jungle. Am I right?"

Everyone smiled. Histo didn't flinch. "If we were exploring the Jurassic era, yes. But we're visiting the mid-nineteenth century. You'll encounter simulations of people who lived then."

Nakshi mused, "Could be President Lincoln. He won't bite."

The program director waited for the chuckles to fade. "Many of these holograms possess perfect cognitive fidelity."

"What does that mean?"

"They mirror human intelligence and communicate like real people. They can speak, think, and learn. You will meet and hear these holograms who resemble historical figures."

He held up the daily paper, pointing to the editorial page. "Separate from them, our imaginary characters will mirror the prevailing opinions of their time."

He let it sink in before continuing. "Pivotal events will unfold before your eyes, in perfect fidelity, visually and cognitively. All without ever leaving Brooklyn."

Zena raised her hand again. Histo nodded.

"Can I interview him?—President Lincoln?"

"We won't meet him on this journey."

Zena's lips quivered. "I'd have loved to see President Lincoln deliver the Gettysburg address. Live." Her emerald-blue eyes gleamed like marbles. "Did you reincarnate these people?"

"Not at all. They're not clones either. Just data, with limited knowledge of the characters they simulate. They speak the words their host character spoke or wrote. We may alter the occasion or the setting."

"Like in movies," Zena chimed in, "they say 'based on a true story,' not 'an exact account.' There's a reason for that."

"Same rule applies here," Histo replied. "The scenes may be theatrical, but the words reflect reality. We can't rely on hearsay."

"Safeguarding history," I muttered, recalling the debate with the Committee.

Before I could ask where the other members were, Zena snapped, startling me. "That's not fair! Some cultures pass down their history orally, like Native Americans. No written record exists." Her brows knitted in a glare.

Histo countered. "The Committee only accepts undisputed sources, such as newspaper articles, books, or other recorded material, but not unverifiable accounts."

Zena's gaze narrowed. "Written or oral, words drive actions, and actions make history." I wondered what was behind her passion for oral history, a mental note to ask.

Rocko asked, "So, shall we witness Mrs. Lincoln complaining to her husband at the kitchen table?"

Histo was unabashed. "Our simulated characters have no recollection of their host's personal lives."

"I'm moving universes. I'd like to forget all my ex's complaints." Rocko smiled faintly.

"No need to. Just ask Histo to create your intelligent hologram," Nakshi teased.

"It won't work. Her words are in public records—divorce court. Thick file. Nothing is hearsay." He winked.

The relaxed atmosphere made me feel more at ease. My mind finally drifted away from its harbor of anxiety.

Zena scribbled shorthand like a front-row student catching every word.

She pressed her pen to her lips. "How do you form such perfect live scenes?"

"Special qubits create them."

"What's a qubit?" Zena narrowed her eyes.

"We'll get to that later." Histo was curt. "You don't need notes. All exchanges are recorded and accessible on the intranet in the library upstairs."

I glanced at the ceiling and walls for a camera but saw none.

Everyone had spoken except me. I was still recovering from my panic. As my concern for a ploy faded, new doubts surfaced. My cousin's challenging looks lingered.

There had been chatter that artificial intelligence would soon be public. Perhaps it had something to do with our program. I raised my hand.

"I heard something big is coming. A system that talks, thinks, and responds like no other. Is KJ behind this?"

"He isn't, but you're not far off. The company you're thinking of is about to announce something major in AI. What we have here goes far beyond that. Our holograms possess quantum intelligence."

"How is it different?"

"Let me put it this way: while the industry's been racing to perfect autonomous cars, we built a self-flying jet. This is quantum technology."

"Wow!" Zena's jaw dropped.

Me? I had more doubts. He did sound too good to be true.

Histo shot me a glance before continuing. "Lastly, we have dummy holograms. They lack intelligence and only deliver preprogrammed words."

"Like extras in movies." Zena grinned. "At best, a 'day player' with a single line. My roommate was one. She played a waitress taking Tom Hanks's order. Ever since, Helga's been in love with him."

I couldn't look away from her bright smile.

Rocko leaned toward her. "Looks like we'll binge-watch movies for the next ten days."

Histo snapped, "Except, you'll be *in* them."

"Like playing inside *Jumanji*?" Nakshi wiggled his brows.

"It sounds like time travel." Zena's eyes widened. "Imagine meeting someone from the future without knowing it."

The idea thrilled me, though suspicion still lingered in my mind.

Histo moved on. "These holograms are no different. They don't suspect you're from their future. To them, you are a contemporary, living in the mid-nineteenth century. They retain what they learn from you. You must not reveal their future."

He let his words settle, then added, "If you tell them what's ahead, how they'll die, when the next war begins, they won't act like their true selves anymore."

"In what way?" Nakshi asked.

"If they know their future, their choices change. They will react to knowledge they were never meant to receive, warping our quantum-wise database of human history and defeating a key purpose."

"What purpose is that?" I cut in.

"Build and protect history in the quantum universe." He didn't look at me when he answered.

"Are there others?" I pressed.

Histo didn't respond. I wondered if my earlier behavior had irritated him.

Rocko asked, "Can't you erase the unwanted data entry?"

"We can, but if we're late or miss something, the error spreads, interacting with other holograms and passing along like a virus. One corrupted hologram can compromise the entire system. Our database is live. It breathes, constantly updating itself as it learns history."

Rocko raised his voice. "Team, if any of you bump into Napoleon by the water cooler, don't warn him about marching to Moscow in late fall."

Histo wasn't amused. I broke in to test the waters.

"We weren't alive when their hosts were. Wouldn't their identities distort when we communicate with them?"

"You will enrich the holograms and help them grow wiser."

His cryptic answer raised more questions than it settled.

Rocko scoffed. "Napoleon will get wiser just from talking to me?" His eyes narrowed. "How much impact could I possibly have on him?"

"Don't forget, millions—eventually billions—interact with some of these historical figures. All contribute to shaping the hologram's wisdom. You'll be among the first."

Rocko pushed back. "Who cares if he becomes wiser? He's gone, and history's already written. Why make holograms grow wiser?"

"Let's save that for later," Histo said curtly. His posture was firm, hands folded behind his back. "For the next ten days, you will witness the projection of a pivotal mid-nineteenth-century event: the Crimean War."

He reminded us of the program's core. "Russia clashed with an alliance of Turkey, the United Kingdom, and France—a conflict some historians call the proto-world war."

Rocko raised his hand. Histo nodded.

"The war in Crimea was significant, I get that. However, other conflicts had a greater impact on today's society. Like the two World Wars. Why focus on this one?"

"There are five reasons." Histo shifted into lecturer mode. "Our main question is: can technology prevent wars? In most conflicts, at least one party is belligerent by choice. The Crimean War had several. Second, it was the first media war. For the first time, people followed a conflict from their living rooms. War correspondents brought updates from the battlefield. We have undisputed records."

"There must be a lot more coverage for the world wars," Nakshi objected.

"True. But time matters. The older the conflict, the better it serves our purpose. That's the third reason."

"Why?"

"Because we want our simulated characters to grow in wisdom."

"Artificial intelligence knows it all," Nakshi probed.

"That's knowledge. Wisdom requires both experience and human exchange, both earned over time."

He reminded me of Dad.

Histo paced. "Our holograms don't age or die. They are *present*." He stressed the word. "As they engage in dialogue and gain knowledge in our universe, they remain timelessly present in the quantum universe."

Everyone exchanged glances. Mystery set in.

Histo moved on to the fourth reason.

"Russia's aggression against Ottoman Turkey in 1853 set off a chain reaction—a geopolitical earthquake whose aftershocks lasted a century and still echo today."

He turned to me. "Tell the novanauts what they were."

I felt myself shimmer. He honored me before my fellow novanauts. I had something to say on this. I had proofread my father's draft: Eastern Question—*A Geopolitical Puzzle That Defies Solution*. I could never get him to publish it. After Mom passed, he spiraled, losing his lifelong passion for his work. Within months, he was gone.

I swallowed, then began.

"The rivalry between Austria-Hungary and Russia over two former Ottoman territories—Bosnia and Serbia—led to the assassination of Archduke Franz Ferdinand in Sarajevo, triggering the First World War."

Zena cut in. "You should watch his lecture online. Very informative." Her eyes widened. "I hadn't realized how many global conflicts trace back to the unresolved Eastern Question."

I was surprised—and flattered. I hadn't even watched it myself. She touched my ego. My cousin once said I always strove to prove myself to win Mom's love over Dad—a textbook Oedipus complex.

"What does that phrase mean? The Eastern Question?" Histo, the professor, prompted.

Zena was quick. "How to divvy up the remnants of the Turkish Empire after its dissolution."

"Not far off. The borders in the Balkans and the Middle East have been shaky since the day they were drawn." Histo motioned for me to take over.

All eyes were on me. "Former Ottoman lands remain unstable from the Middle East to the Balkans. The Gulf wars, the Arab-Israeli conflict, the genocide in Bosnia, unrest in North Africa. More recently, parts of Ukraine. All were once part of the Turkish Empire."

I said it all in one breath, impressing even myself.

She clapped, grinning at me. Her emerald eyes unsettled me in an unexpected and exhilarating way. The applause left me euphoric, edged by a subtle bitterness, knowing the moment wasn't entirely mine. I shared it with Dad.

Histo added, "In short, to understand many of the conflicts of the past two centuries, we must go back to the dissolution of the Turkish Empire."

"What is the fifth reason?" Zena pressed.

"It helps us understand a current event—Russia's invasion of Ukraine, the defining issue on today's global stage."

In February of that year, President Putin claimed Russia had to protect its kin in the Donbas from ruling neo-Nazis, arguing that Ukraine was not a real country, had no true nationhood, and that Kyiv was 'the mother of all Russian cities.'

"I remember that day." Nakshi's words trailed off.

"Many do," Histo replied. "But few recall that on the eve of the Crimean War, Czar Nicholas I made similar arguments."

"What were they?"

"Russia had a duty to save its fellow Greek Orthodox Christians from the Turkish Muslim yoke and restore Constantinople as the capital of the Orthodox Church."

"Ottoman Turkey then, Ukraine now," Nakshi murmured.

Histo nodded. "Both Putin and Nicholas invoked the legacy of Peter the Great."

The resemblance between the two aggressions, separated by seventeen decades, was striking.

Zena read from her notes.

"In summary: Why the Crimean War? Five reasons. One and two: a war of choice and the Ottoman fallout—a geopolitical quake that still shakes the present. Three: parallels to the war in Ukraine. Four: well-documented, easy to fact-check. Five: far back enough to make the characters quantum-wise—whatever that means."

Rocko applauded. "All hail the power of note-taking."

"But why us?" Nakshi cut to the chase. "Why did the Committee choose us?"

"KJ required all participants to be Americans with Ottoman roots and diverse backgrounds."

"Why?"

"You'll have to ask him." Histo brushed him off. "But each of you fits the bill for the project."

"No one else qualified?"

"We evaluated over thirty candidates and selected seven," Histo explained. "Two declined. We ended up with five."

"Only four are here," Nakshi noted.

"We have an alternate novanaut as backup. He'll join if one of you backs out during the cruise."

"Back out? Now you're making me nervous." Rocko raised a brow. "I thought this was supposed to be a fun vacation."

"I believe it will be." Histo cracked a faint smile. "A memorable one, certainly. But I won't promise you'll enjoy everything you see. Not everyone can handle the truth."

Histo's stern tone quieted the room. Nakshi pressed on.

"You keep saying we must protect the truth. Politicians spin everything. What if someone we meet tells us lies? Do we protect their version?"

Histo was quick in his response. "Great question. If a deceit shaped history, yes."

Rocko barged in. "We have seen it many times. Like the Nazi claim that global Jewry masterminded Stalin's communism. It fooled millions in Germany."

Zena threw up her arm. "Fooling works. Bush justified the Second Gulf War based on false intel. There were no WMDs—the rest we know."

Histo kept his calm demeanor. "Protecting history means reminding people of the lies they were once told, so when the new deceivers come along, they won't fall for it." Histo paused to let his words sink in, then continued, "If someone tries to teach ten years from now that Saddam had those weapons, they'd be rewriting history based on a lie. But if people know their history, it won't hold up."

I recalled my father's commencement speech at my high school. Repeated lies can stick. Napoleon Bonaparte never admitted he'd lost at Waterloo. Some in France still believed he hadn't.

Histo echoed him. "Once the madness passes, those blatant falsehoods become part of real history. We teach them, so people remember. Because it could happen again."

"What if the falsehood becomes the curriculum?" I asked.

"The following generation must speak of the falsehoods that shaped history so they're not repeated."

"Should we say—" Zena checked her notes. "We should stand firm, speak the truth, and expose today's lies about history. But if those lies shape the present, future generations must not deny them, for they will become part of history."

"I couldn't have said it better." Histo flashed a smile. As brief as it was, this was the first time I'd seen him appear jolly.

Zena's words conveyed a complex idea with clarity and precision. She struck me as an observant woman with an analytical mind, destined to become an outstanding investigative journalist.

Her tone shifted, somber. "Unspoken truths are also part of history. We should know that. Are we also the guardians of the ugly silence?"

Histo stayed silent and nodded to Nakshi, who had several questions.

"People from different countries speak different languages. How will we understand them?"

"Unless we decide otherwise, we shall keep the dialogues in English, even if the original account was in another language, such as French."

"How will we know what to do?"

"I will be with you throughout this cruise. Any other questions?"

"Where do we stay and eat?"

"In the building next door. The movers were late with the furniture, but it should be ready by now."

The beaded curtain swung open, and the receptionist stepped in.

Histo gestured to him. "You've met Krish, our house manager and IT specialist. He'll show you to your rooms."

The young man grinned, revealing pearly white teeth. He was skinny, in a dress shirt with sleeves rolled up. His pants hadn't seen an iron in a while, held up by a belt on its last hole.

"Excuse me, sir." His southern Indian accent was distinct. "The mover lady wants to speak with you."

"Let her in, please."

The woman in overalls entered, ready to sign off after a hard day's work. "I want Mr. Rocko to know that we placed what he requested in his room."

Rocko thanked her, then explained, "I requested a specialty orthopedic mattress like the one I use at home. I have a back problem; otherwise, I'd be up all night."

Relief. That explained Rocko's chat with the movers. I couldn't believe how foolish I'd been to suspect a ploy. I sighed. The last doubt lifted. I closed my eyes, leaned back, and let my shoulders drop, waiting for more good news.

"Sir, I need to warn you about something," a heavily accented female voice cut in.

I opened my eyes. The woman in a yellow sari and leather sandals—the one I'd seen outside—stood behind Krish, her gaze fixed on me. She looked in her fifties.

"You know Farouq, the pizza man across the street."

Histo leaned forward. "What about him, Mrs. Lata?"

Krish gestured toward us. "Allow me to introduce Lata-ji. She owns this shop and the used furniture store next door. She is my amma."

"Hi, Mom." Rocko waved.

Mrs. Lata remained unfazed.

Krish went on. "She's been on edge lately. Farouq too. Get them in a room, they'll argue until dawn about who looks suspicious." He swayed his head. "You know—the news."

"The Brooklyn serial killer, right?" Zena jumped in.

Lata swayed her head.

Zena narrowed her eyes. "I know. Isn't that scary?"

Histo stayed calm. "What exactly happened?"

"A customer rushed out without paying Farouq," Krish said. "He shouted at people in the street, then stepped into our store."

My palms went clammy, heart pounding. Lata's brows furrowed as she watched my panic.

She turned to the woman in overalls. "You saw that too, right?" The supervisor cracked a silent smile.

Krish grinned. "Amma thinks the man fit the killer's profile. They now suspect he's a fugitive from the mental hospital."

Beads of sweat gathered on my temples.

"What did he shout, Mrs. Lata?" Histo asked.

Her gaze burned into me, daring others to join. "'I am Yuri Gaganut,' or something like that."

I wanted the earth beneath to split and swallow me whole.

"Anyway," Krish said, "I paid Farouq and calmed him down."

As a kid, whenever I was caught hiding something, Mom said, "*If you start digging, you'll keep digging until it heaps up over you.*"

I took a deep breath and exhaled. "I am so sorry. I'll reimburse the amount." A bead of sweat trickled down my neck.

Histo showed no emotion. "It's all right. Your pizza is on the house."

Rocko and Nakshi lowered their heads, their shoulders twitching. Zena couldn't hold back. She burst out laughing, hand over her mouth. "I'm sorry. I couldn't help it. But this is *so* hilarious!"

I avoided everyone's gaze. My face felt like hot logs pulled straight from a fireplace. Zena reached out and held my forearm.

"I must admit," she said, still laughing, "I had similar thoughts this morning. You weren't the only one who suspected a sting operation." Her reassurance only deepened my shame.

Speaking from one side of her mouth, the mover lady quipped, "Mrs. Lata, tell Farouq he got the name wrong. My crew thinks he's George Costanza—the original—from *Seinfeld*."

Laughter burst out—even mine, though nervous.

Rocko, tears in his eyes, said, "Double whammy, man! Yuri the Nut and Jack the Ripper wrapped in one. You've got no chance left, bud."

Nakshi leaned over and rested a hand on my knee. "This episode should be in the book."

Histo spoke calmly to Lata. "You don't need to worry, ma'am. We don't have a disturbed person here."

The Committee director rose as if propelled by a pogo stick to wrap up the meeting.

"Krish will show you to your rooms."

His chin lifted like a commander issuing final orders before an offensive.

"Team Novanauts, meet back in one hour sharp."

6

THE TAKE-OFF

Krish collected all our electronics.

"You already warped us back thirty years," Rocko quipped.

Krish grinned and pulled a white handle, opening a door seamlessly flush with the wall. Until then, I hadn't noticed the hidden entry.

We climbed the squeaky steps. At the top of the stairs, the space had transformed, no longer resembling a shop selling cheap collectibles but the elegant interior of a Victorian-era building.

"The kitchen stays open until midnight," Krish said as we passed a small dining room into the cooking area. "It's self-service. No microwave, no coffee pot. Just a stove-top percolator and a gas-fired cast iron stove—state-of-the-art in its day."

"No power outlets?" Rocko pulled a face.

"None, except in the library. We redesigned this floor to stay true to the 1850s."

The dining room opened into a hallway that stretched into the next building, with rooms on either side.

"Feels like an upscale hotel," I said.

"It is a hotel," Krish replied with a slight sway. "It'll be your home for the next ten days. Histo and I stay here too."

"Wow!" Zena's eyes widened. "These aren't reproductions." Oil paintings by various American artists lined the hallway.

Nakshi pointed at the fixtures. "Nor are the kerosene lamps."

"We've placed them in your rooms, too."

Next, Krish motioned toward the double doors at the end of the hall. "That's the library. A few desktops are inside, connected to our intranet only—not the web. You can use our in-house browser for research or to rewatch session segments."

His words reminded us we would be cut off from the world for the next ten days.

The first two rooms belonged to Krish and Histo, facing each other near the front of the hallway. Next came Nakshi's and Rocko's, followed by Zena's and mine. My room faced the street. Beyond ours lay two more rooms, with the hallway ending at the library like a cul-de-sac.

Two delivery workers stepped out of Zena's room after dropping off a piece of furniture.

Krish leaned toward her. "Lata-ji thought you'd need a makeup commode."

"How considerate. Please tell your mother I appreciate it."

"She is my mother-in-law, but I will."

Rocko chimed in, "That changes everything. High-stakes diplomacy. I've failed miserably."

Krish tilted his head. "How so?"

"My in-laws take my jokes at face value. Especially her. No sense of humor."

Krish pressed his words. "I have the opposite issue with mine. She thinks her daughter married the most boring man in Bangalore who doesn't know how to crack jokes."

Zena cut through the banter. "I can't wait to see my room."

"We've assigned you the executive suite." Krish grinned at her.

"So much for gender equality," Rocko teased. "But that's all right."

All the bedrooms boasted tall ceilings, but Zena's was the most spacious. Rich frescoes and intricate paneling embellished its walls. Tall mirrors, framed in gold leaf from the French Bourbon Restoration era, lined the room.

"I love it!" Zena's eyes went wide, her mouth agape. "Rosewood sofas, lounges, chairs, rockers, carved tables!"

The draperies and plush cushions complemented the classic bedframe. Goose-down comforters lay atop the bed.

"These rugs must be costly." Nakshi knelt to examine one. "High knot density."

"I believe you. With rugs, you can't fool a man from Kayseri." Rocko smiled wittily, then gestured to a tapestry on the wall. "This might be from Belgium. An original—not a reproduction. Could be Leyniers."

"If a Jewish man says so," Nakshi offered a faint smile.

"Everyone says my kin possesses those innate skills, but the traits must've skipped my DNA somehow." Rocko grinned. "Sometimes I think my in-laws were right to call me a social anomaly." The two men shared a chuckle.

I wasn't jealous, but admittedly envious of the two men already forging a bond. Mom was like that. She never said it, but I knew she wished I weren't shy.

"Oh my gosh! Check out these faucets!" Zena's voice carried from the bathroom. She was oblivious to the male camaraderie.

"One for hot water, another for cold." She twisted both polished brass faucets to fill the tub.

"Hold that cheer!" Rocko called. "Wait until you see what the department stores sent your way."

Her wardrobe boasted over two dozen outfits—nightgowns, robes, petticoats, hats, bonnets, gloves, and a dozen pairs of shoes and boots.

"It's all used clothing from old Broadway shows." Krish grinned. "You guys have plenty of choices, too."

"Impressive, but do we really need them?" I asked.

"The ten-day cruise will take you around the globe—day and night, summer and winter, battlefields and ballrooms. You'll need specific attire for each occasion." He adjusted the crooked dressing mirror. "Tonight, you'll be incognito, so what you're wearing is fine. Tomorrow, you'll need era-appropriate clothing for the journeys ahead."

Zena listened from the bathroom, sitting on the edge of a tinned copper tub resting on a black-and-white terracotta floor. She examined herself in a gold-framed hand mirror, gathering her hair up, revealing her graceful neck as steam clouded the glass. I couldn't help but notice—a swan.

Corrugated, shiny metallic covers sealed the windows. Modern, high-tech, jarringly out of place.

"Why these ugly panels?" I asked. "They block the view."

"Each room has those. You won't notice them once you're fully activated."

Everyone exchanged glances, unsure what he meant.

Krish waited until Zena turned off the faucets.

"I'll get you ready for this evening's trip." Krish's South Indian accent was gentle but carried quiet authority.

I had not anticipated starting the program on the night of arrival but kept that to myself.

Rocko, however, didn't hold back. "I thought we were just going to have a nice team dinner and hit the sack."

"We should get going." Krish's lips twitched. "Mr. Histo is strict about punctuality. He expects it from everyone."

"Back to the boarding school," Rocko muttered.

I checked into my room, similar to Zena's but smaller. The wardrobe held everything from nineteenth-century formal wear to robes and military uniforms, but I didn't have time to explore. I left my sack and hurried downstairs to the white-walled reception room to join my teammates.

Krish handed out a flexible patch and a pair of specialty lenses to everyone. He helped me fasten the cloth to my forearm. The fabric was woven with electronic circuitry, enveloping snugly like a blood pressure cuff and applying mild pressure. Then he guided me as I put on the lenses.

He repeated the process for the other novanauts. Irritated by the grip, Zena tried to adjust her patch.

"Give it a bit. You won't feel it," Krish said. "It's a smart wearable. It senses your tension and adjusts. Soon it'll feel like part of you. No need to take it off. Same goes for the lenses."

"I wear lenses," Nakshi said. "I take them out every evening before bed."

"Don't change your practice. Just wear your disposable over the smart one. Think of it as an extension of your eye—no cleaning or removal, good for fifteen days straight."

"How does that work?" Rocko asked.

Krish beamed. "Nanotechnology meets materials science." His eyes shimmered as he spoke, arms waving. "The nano-coating on the concave side binds to your eye's outer lipid layer—the tear film, produced by your meibomian glands, and—"

Histo cut in, "Do *not* take off the lenses or the patch for ten days. That's all you need to remember." His voice was sharp and final, more command than reminder.

"Can I shower wearing this gadget?" Zena asked.

Krish tilted his head. "The wearables are waterproof." His fingers danced across his iPad faster than I'd ever seen.

After a firm final click, the techie paused, eyes fixed on the screen until a soft beep sounded. Green lights flickered across the wearables. Krish grinned, giving his director a thumbs-up.

"Histo, party of six—your table is ready for dinner," Rocko called, drawing giggles from Zena. Her eyes warmed to him.

His sharp wit crowned Rocko's charm, another point of envy.

Unfazed, Histo addressed us.

"Tonight, you embark on your maiden voyage into the quantum universe. I'll accompany you. Krish will answer your technology questions later. For now, follow his instructions."

"Grab one." Krish pointed at a box of sweaters beside the shiny metallic door in the back. Everyone did—except Histo.

The young man from Bangalore opened the door and led us through.

A blast of sterile white light met us—clean, clinical, surreal—like a scene from a Stanley Kubrick movie. No hiss, no hum. Serene, like standing in a Nevada desert with no souls around.

Mirrored walls curved seamlessly into the domed ceiling, flowing down into a slick, eggshell-colored parquet floor of engineered material. The spacious, soundproof oval capsule seemed to have sprung from a science fiction book—a stark contrast to the shabby flea shop we had left behind the metallic door.

"Stunning," Rocko murmured. "Feels like being the yolk inside an egg."

Nakshi leaned toward me. "This must be the launchpad."

Krish motioned for us to take the cream-colored leather seats, six arranged in a crescent configuration like a *Star Trek* cockpit.

Zena shivered, glancing at the ceiling, her mouth still agape. The room was cold. My hair stood on end—not from the chill, but from the grandeur. We slipped into the wool sweaters. Krish settled us in. Histo, unyielding in his three-piece suit, took the seat on the farthest right.

Suddenly, the seats came alive, belts emerging from nowhere. Two straps crisscrossed my chest, pinning me like a toddler in a car seat. Once he confirmed we were secure, Krish left the room, leaving us fastened in place.

"I don't like windowless rooms," Zena said, breathing heavy. "Feels like a tomb."

"I'll rotate you folks clockwise," Krish's voice came through the surround-sound speaker. The seat tilted, my feet up and head down, until the footrest was at forty-five degrees from the floor, and my gaze fixed on the ceiling.

Nakshi's voice crackled. "Reminds me of the dentist's chair."

The Committee's letter had warned that the cruise would include intense simulated roller-coaster rides. This one had to be the opening act.

"Starting the countdown," Krish announced.

"Roger that," Histo replied from his seat.

The next minute was filled with a mix of nerves and excitement.

First, the lights dimmed, plunging the capsule into pitch darkness. After a brief countdown, humming began, followed by vibrations that swelled into tremors—like an earthquake high on the Richter scale.

My seat shot upward. My stomach dropped, lurching. I had no idea how high I'd risen until the pause.

Then came a mounting pressure—hot and crushing—followed by an immense forward thrust. I clenched my teeth and dug my nails into the armrest.

A fierce wind scraped my face, pushing my cheeks inward toward my mouth. Zena's screeching was deafening. The rest of us stayed silent—or maybe "stunned" was the better word.

The acceleration was beyond intense, eclipsing anything I had ever experienced at an amusement park. I felt dizzy, almost euphoric.

Then came the deceleration—and, finally, a complete stop. My heart thudded. Sweat clung to my shirt.

7

SICK MAN

First, a sharp mixture of kerosene and heavy perfume filled the air. Then the seats rotated flat against the floor. Our belts unfastened and snapped back into their slits like retractable cords, all by themselves.

"You can stand now." Histo's voice carried through the pitch dark.

I hesitated, uncertain how high we had ascended, gripped by the eerie sense that stepping out would be like unbuckling from a Ferris wheel stalled at its peak and meeting gravity head-on.

As light returned, relief came. I wasn't perched in the sky but inside a refined room. When we rose, our seats vanished, leaving me befuddled. The launchpad was gone too, as if we had been teleported into a secluded palace chamber. We huddled in awe, trading puzzled glances. Startling, to say the least.

Above us, a chandelier hung from the lofty ceiling, its lights casting shifting shadows. A large oval mahogany table, edged with silver, anchored the room. At its center, a grand vase engraved with Greco motifs rested on Belgian lace. Baroque furniture lined the walls. Blue velvet drapes cascaded from tall windows, tied back with gold cords. No one else was around, yet distant voices and faint laughter echoed in the background, mingling with a string melody.

Zena spoke first.

"Where are we?" Her eyes widened, hair still tousled from the plunge.

"Welcome to the quantum universe." Histo's voice was calm. "I trust your journey was pleasant."

"It was like Disneyland squared," Rocko mused.

"No kidding. More thrilling than any ride I've been on." Nakshi shifted, still unsteady.

Histo turned toward me, waiting.

"Best magic show I've ever seen."

His lips curled slightly, like a film director savoring a critic's backhanded punchline.

"You're inside history." He let the words settle before adding, "Grand Duchess Elena is hosting her traditional New Year's celebration at her palace in St. Petersburg."

"You mean in Russia?" Zena's eyes stayed wide.

"Doesn't look like the one in Florida." Rocko gestured toward the tall window, where snow blanketed the ground and torches flickered against the new moon.

"It's January 9, 1853." Nakshi pointed at a French calendar on the desk.

The double doors swung open. Two servants wheeled in drink carts, making everyone but Histo jump.

"They don't see or hear you." He didn't even glance at them.

"You mean they're not real?" Zena's voice wavered.

Histo shrugged. "Dummy holograms. Images, not people."

They looked indistinguishable from real people. To my surprise, no one questioned it. I didn't either—didn't want to be the sour thumb.

The servants parked the carts in the corner and slipped out.

Histo stepped forward. "Tonight's guest of honor is His Majesty Emperor Czar Nicholas and his wife. Soon, he'll enter the room with Sir George Hamilton Seymour, Britain's ambassador."

"We're in jeans and sneakers, totally out of place," Zena's eyes darted around.

"You'll be invisible to them. They won't hear you or sense your presence. Incognito."

Nakshi chimed in. "Ghosts from the past." He paused, then added, "I take it back. They're real, we're the ghosts."

I couldn't resist. "Traditionally, ghosts are from the past. We've arrived from the future."

Supposedly. But I didn't air my doubt.

Zena leaned in. "Or is it the past that's traveled to the present to become current again?"

Rocko snapped his fingers. "You got it!" Zena's eyes lit up.

I twitched. I don't like being outsmarted.

The double doors opened again. Framed by the servants, a tall, strikingly handsome blond man entered, chin high, moving with the poise of a Greek god who owned the universe. A thin mustache curled at the ends, and his uniform glittered with medals.

I recognized him from the paintings—Czar Nicholas I of Russia. Behind him came another man, also in his fifties, with round blue eyes, ruddy cheeks, and wavy gray hair parted down the middle. He had to be the British Ambassador.

"Feel at home, Chancellor Seymour." The czar offered his guest a drink and poured himself a glass of water.

"Your Excellency, I thank the Lord for granting me the honor of Your Majesty's audience."

The emperor nodded, a subtle gesture of appreciation.

"Amazing." Zena lowered her chin.

It truly was. Just ten feet away, the czar appeared as real as Nakshi beside me. Their voices carried no trace of mechanical tone. I'd seen cutting-edge holograms—impressive, but never completely convincing. Not like these two. The scene felt more theatrical than any virtual reality I had experienced, even the most sophisticated prototypes at my cousin's company.

"Unbelievable." Rocko shook his head.

I recalled the old saying: if it's too good to be true, it probably is. But I kept that to myself.

"I hear Her Majesty's Government is finally in place," the emperor said. "Please convey my sincerest wishes to Lord Aberdeen. We've known each other for forty years. Your press likens his multi-party coalition to a fragmentary mosaic—a challenge to govern." He lifted his glass. "I toast to the Aberdeen government's long tenure."

Ambassador Seymour offered a warm smile and raised his crystal glass.

The emperor sipped his water. "I also have confidence in Lord Russell as the head of the Foreign Office."

Seymour bowed in acknowledgement.

"You know my feelings toward England. What I have told you before, I say again." Seymour sat upright, eyes fixed on the emperor, listening intently. "Our two countries should remain in close amity."

The czar set down his glass and paced, hands folded behind his back.

"There have been a few disagreements between us. On nearly every matter, our interests are aligned." Nicholas smiled faintly. "Our difference in perspective—*manière de voir*—on the recent event in the West should not become an obstacle between us. The '*Third*' requires a longer discussion; I will not go into that now." Seymour lowered his eyes, avoiding the czar's gaze.

My teammates exchanged puzzled glances, unsure of the czar's cryptic reference.

I understood. I replayed the latest events in France, ready to explain later to my fellow novanauts. Just a month earlier, in December 1852, Louis Napoleon—Napoleon Bonaparte's cousin—had staged a *coup d'état* and declared himself Emperor of France, taking the title Napoleon III. The regnal "III" enraged Nicholas, for it implied dynastic legitimacy, as if this Corsican upstart belonged among Bourbons, Habsburgs, and Romanovs. Britain's tolerance of what he called a mockery deepened his resentment.

The czar lifted his hand halfway. "On the other hand, there is a question that requires an answer. I want you to call upon me some morning when I am free from engagements."

The ambassador leaned slightly forward. "If Your Majesty will be good enough to lay your orders upon me."

Their exchange and body language felt genuine. Nothing about them or their surroundings seemed artificial. But my suspicious mind snapped back to work. Was this really a quantum technology breakthrough, as Histo claimed? Or actors on a stage, cloaked in smoke screens—a David Copperfield illusion. Perhaps both—stagecraft layered with technology: high-tech mirrors, projections, an illusion woven into flawless reality.

Still, whatever the truth, stagecraft or a quantum marvel, my task remained the same: observe every instant and report it in a book. I silenced the Doubting Thomas in me, as my cousin would say.

I tuned back in.

The emperor walked to a tall window and watched the torches flicker against the dark sky, gathering his thoughts. Seymour's eyes followed, waiting for what might come next.

Czar Nicholas straightened. "I repeat—it is essential that the two governments—that is, the English government and I—should remain on the best terms." He paused to let his words sink in, each syllable pronounced. "And never has that necessity been greater than at present. I beg you to convey these words to Lord Russell." He strolled toward the double doors, signaling the meeting's end.

Hamilton Seymour nodded respectfully and followed.

Nicholas's voice grew firmer as he paced. "Unlike others, I am not concerned about the West."

Zena leaned in toward me. "West?"

"France." Her perfume tickled me.

"As to Turkey—that is another matter." The czar's voice thinned. "This country is in a critical state and may bring us all a great deal of trouble."

He paused before the double doors, then turned back to the ambassador. "And now I will take my leave of you."

Across from him, the ambassador pressed his lips together, holding composure though his eyes betrayed unease—aware he was leaving a vital conversation unfinished.

"Sir, with your gracious permission, I would like to take a great liberty."

"Certainly." Nicholas dropped his shoulders, relishing the turn. "What is it? I'd like to hear."

Sir Seymour collected himself before speaking. "I am confident Her Majesty's Government will receive well Your Majesty's assurances and the shared outlook. If possible, a few words on the recent developments in Turkey would help ease concerns in London. I would be honored to convey such reassurance on Your Majesty's behalf." He delivered it in one breath.

Czar Nicholas gave no reaction, unwilling to answer Seymour's question, though he held a pleasant expression.

"What recent development is he referring to?" Zena asked.

"Massive troop movements along the Danube, at Turkey's border," Histo said.

"Oh, right." She exhaled. "The Balkans then, Donbas now."

Nakshi leaned toward her. "Déjà vu." He winked. A hint at Putin's military buildup along Ukraine's eastern border before the invasion. It seemed to mirror the playbook of the 1850s.

Seymour pressed his lips and stepped toward the door.

"Stay!" The emperor's firmness pleasantly startled the ambassador.

Retracing his steps with intent, Czar Nicholas returned to the center of the room, Seymour trailing. The emperor paused before the mahogany table, hands folded behind his back. For a moment, he studied the flowers in the grand vase—buying time as he gathered his thoughts. Then, lifting his gaze to the ceiling, he exclaimed a single word:

"Turkey!"

He turned to the ambassador. "The affairs are in a very disorganized condition there. The country itself seems to be falling to pieces." Clenching his fist, he stressed in French, "*Menace de ruine.*"

Nicholas resumed pacing. "The fall will be a great misfortune. It is very important that England and Russia should come to a perfectly good understanding of these affairs." His phrasing—often literal translations from French—shifted his tone from a measured diplomatic warmth to bold confidence as he delivered his pointed message.

"Neither should take any decisive step of which the other is not apprised."

Seymour's brows lifted, eyes gleaming. I couldn't tell whether he welcomed the offer or questioned the urgency Nicholas painted around the Orient.

Then suddenly, the emperor's voice swelled, as if addressing the entire court.

"We have on our hands a sick man—a very sick man!"

He extended his arms, palms up, as though presenting a frail body.

"It will be, I tell you frankly, a great misfortune if, one of these days, he should slip away from us, especially before all necessary arrangements are made."

A shimmer sparked in Seymour's eye, as though he sensed a fertile diplomatic season ahead in the burning Eastern Question—a pressing concern of the century.

The emperor lowered his arms, miming someone slipping toward the floor. He shrugged, his tone softening. "However, this is not the time to speak on that question."

The ambassador's smile vanished. He seemed reluctant to accept the emperor's decision to end such a crucial exchange.

"Your Majesty says the man is sick; it is very true, but if His Majesty graciously allows me—if I may remark that it is part of a generous and strong man to treat a sick and feeble man with gentleness."

The emperor stood unfazed, gazing at the ambassador. George Hamilton Seymour's eyes widened, his cheeks flushing turnip-red as he held his breath, astonished by his own boldness. The czar averted his eyes, careful not to betray surprise at the ambassador's audacity, overstepping the bounds of his diplomatic rank.

"I will send for you on a future day," the czar said, in a distant but composed voice. Seymour bowed slightly and exited the room in haste.

The emperor plucked a red rose from the vase atop a Victorian cherry table, inhaled its scent, then set it carefully back in place before leaving the salon. The servants closed the double doors.

The lights dimmed.

The elegant salon was gone. We were back in the mirrored room, standing on the launchpad where our journey had begun—only now, the space felt smaller, the walls sealed in mirrored panels, the ceiling lower, braced with connecting rods.

The humming returned. The mirrored wall began to rise like a garage door, curving toward the ceiling and locking back into place, revealing the spacious launch room beneath.

"Look, we're elevated!" Zena pointed to the command console beneath, its seats flush with the floor. Like a hidden lift, a section of the floor had risen by one story.

Krish stepped in through the shiny metallic door and tapped a few keys on his iPad. The platform began to descend, lowering steadily until it aligned with the floor, restoring the room to its original configuration. The square tiles shifted vertically and independently, like Minecraft blocks coming to life, explaining the earlier lift, though not the strange sensations I felt during the ride.

"How was it?" Krish beamed from ear to ear.

We darted around like abductees reacclimating after being returned to Earth.

Rocko's voice carried expertise. "The launchpad separated during takeoff and ascended. Then the reflection-induced optical amplifiers kicked in, encapsulating the vessel to generate a perfect fidelity immersive environment."

I scoffed silently. What a show-off that was. A borrowed authority. A bank software specialist, hardly a quantum space engineer.

Krish swayed his head. "Not quite right—but hey, not bad. I'd say pretty close."

"Really?" Zena's eyes widened, her mouth slightly apart, sizing Rocko up as if seeing him for the first time.

Rocko smirked. I pursed my lips.

Krish clipped his words. "Basically, it's a quantum Faraday cage. It isolates optical qubits from feedback noise. A design concept we came up with."

"Royal we," Histo cut in, gesturing toward Krish. "He did it alone—good job. The system worked flawlessly." His voice was warm.

Zena shifted her admiring gaze to Krish. "I knew you were smart, but I didn't realize you were a genius."

The young man from Bangalore lowered his head, uneasy under the praise. "How did it feel, being inside history?" He was eager to deflect the attention.

"Wow!" Zena dropped her chin, mirroring the team's astonishment.

Histo had a faint smile, pleased by Team Novanaut's first reaction.

She turned to me. "Don't you think it was amazing?" Her green-blue eyes brightened.

Rocko intervened before I could reply. "In high school history, they teach the expression 'sick man,' in describing the state of the Ottoman Empire before its fall."

I shot Rocko a look. No one noticed.

Nakshi narrowed his eyes. "Is this the first time that anyone has used this expression?"

Histo's lips tightened before replying. "Not for certain. Nevertheless, Czar Nicholas I etched it into history."

Rocko leaned toward Zena, almost invading her space. "Put that in your CV—you were in the room when the phrase caught fire."

Zena flicked her head away, grinning. "Too bad I didn't record it on my cell."

Uneasy, I wanted to steer the talk back to substance. "Was the dialogue historically accurate?"

The program director lifted his chin. "What you just witnessed was a historic exchange between Russia and Great Britain. Others will follow. History will collectively label them as 'The Secret Correspondences.'"

"Why were they kept secret?"

Histo drew a letter from his jacket. "Seymour advised his foreign minister to keep communications with Russia under wraps—so Britain wouldn't end up between a rock and a hard place."

"How so?" Nakshi pressed, his brows knit.

"If the British government rejects Russia's offer, they'll have less standing to complain when the Turkish Empire collapses. But if they agree, they'll be seen as co-conspirators hastening the sultan's fall."

Zena stepped behind Histo, leaning in to read Seymour's letter to Russell.

She lifted a brow. "Heavy language. Etonian English, I suppose." She was needling the school of Britain's elite diplomats. "I can already hear the British pundits tearing into their government."

She slipped into a theatrical British accent: "Inferno in Europe! Russia proposed collaboration, but Great Britain rejected it!"

Rocko chuckled. "Now the second scenario."

Zena deepened her voice. "Stand up, Great Britain! You accepted Russia's offer, hastening the sultan's fall. You are the culprit of his demise." She gave a mock bow, grinning. Applause broke out.

Her flair was disarming—a fusion of intellect and elegance.

"You should've been the reporter, Zena," Rocko teased.

Zena smiled warmly. Jealousy struck me. The feeling came as a surprise.

Nakshi rubbed his beard. "No one else was in the room. How did the world learn about a conversation between two individuals?"

Histo replied without hesitation. "Seymour put it in writing and sent it to Lord Russell—top secret and confidential."

"Did we just read his letter in theatrical form?"

"Precisely."

Zena turned to me. "It felt so real. Would you agree?" Light caught her iris, revealing flecks of brown in a sea of green.

I nodded.

Histo cut in, jolting me from my trance. "Because it was. We brought the past to the present and played it out—live in the quantum universe. All authentic."

It was a moment of reflection, a wave of astonishment washing over the team. It gave me the chance to pull myself back into the game.

No doubt the experience was extraordinary, but I wasn't ready to buy into Histo's quantum narrative. For one, there were too many mirrors—one of the oldest tricks in a magician's kit. And a "Quantum Faraday Cage"? That sounded more like a flashy marketing pitch than science, something Tom would've used to lure new customers. I didn't mind immersing myself in the unfolding history, but part of me kept probing for cracks, searching for a way to test whether the spectacle was genuine.

Rocko's question snapped me from drifting thoughts. "How did the secret communications become no secret?"

"A St. Petersburg paper broke the story that both governments were secretly corresponding about Turkey, almost at the czar's direction. In response, England released the full series of correspondence."

"How many were there?"

"Ten in all. Seymour's letter among them—the one you just witnessed."

"Did the emperor get a reply to his questions?" Nakshi pressed.

"Eventually, yes. But first, Nicholas and Seymour met again."

Zena clasped her hands. "Let's hear them."

Krish showed us to our seats. The lights dimmed, plunging us into darkness. A low hum swelled, muffling the chatter behind me—Rocko, complaining of hunger, that he skipped lunch, Nakshi offering him the apple he had in his room.

Zena's warm hand found mine, sending butterflies fluttering in my belly.

"I'm scared," she whispered.

Krish came through the surround sound speakers.

"Liftoff."

Goosebumps rippled across my skin.

8

PORRIDGE IS THE CONTINGENCY

Zena's screaming blasted my ears. My hand was crushed in hers as the wind pressed our cheeks inward. The sensations blended—some pleasant, others not.

The brief ride dropped us into a grand salon. Two massive chandeliers filled the space. Tall windows framed by gilded pillars rose to a vaulted dome lined with cream moldings and gold motifs.

Histo led us toward the far-right corner. Krish froze the scene to upload a patch.

Czar Nicholas stood at a window, gazing over the courtyard. On the far side, Ambassador Seymour sat near a rosewood desk and carved fireplace. A red sofa and chairs with carved handles stood nearby.

This wasn't a computer screen. The curtain had just risen on a Broadway epic—a lavish mid-scene, waiting for the narrator's cue. I couldn't help but smile wryly.

Outside, visible through the windows, water shimmered. Sunlight streamed in. Bouncing off the gilded trim, it bathed the room in a golden hue. Crimson brocatelle curtains matched the rococo chairs. Small round tables lined the perimeter, revealing a floor spread with Victorian mosaic tiles.

The breathtaking view mesmerized Zena. "I always dreamed of living in a palace like this."

Rocko eyed her. "The czar is handsome, could pass for a Hollywood star. And loaded too. You're single, right? Here's your chance."

"Forget it. He's taken."

"But I'm not." The handsome novanaut flashed her a playful smile.

Nakshi leaned in from behind. "Beware. His ex already drained his coffers."

Zena chuckled, trading a gleeful glance with Rocko.

I could see it coming—they'd be dating before the quantum cruise was over.

Rocko scanned the room. "I recognize this place. The Gold Drawing Room of the Winter Palace in St. Petersburg. And that's the Neva River outside."

Histo nodded. I was impressed.

So was Zena. She squinted. "How do you know?"

Rocko shrugged. "I was here on my honeymoon. Anyone can visit. It's a popular tourist spot."

The scene unfroze.

A flock of deer darted along the river beyond the manicured grounds.

The czar gazed at his sprawling yard. "You know, Chancellor, Russia is blessed with nature's riches."

He stood tall, his posture perfect. "Empress Catherine was in the habit of indulging dreams and plans. They were handed down to our time. I inherited immense territorial possessions but did not inherit those visions." He swept his arm, smiling wryly. "Intentions, if you like to call them." He turned sharply and walked toward the liquor cabinet.

Nicholas clasped his hands behind his back. "My country is so vast, so happily circumstanced in every way, that it would be unreasonable for me to desire more territory or power than I already possess." He lifted a Waterford glass and poured the whiskey halfway.

Seymour rose and hurried toward him.

The emperor raised the glass. "On the contrary, I'm the first to admit—future expansion is a danger for this empire. Perhaps the only one we should fear."

Rocko leaned toward Histo. "You should invite Mr. Putin to the next workshop. Biggest landmass on Earth, yet look at the mess he's made chasing more in Ukraine."

Nakshi's lips curved into a bitter smile. "Maybe he found Catherine's plans in a dusty attic."

"Focus, please," Zena hissed.

The czar handed over the glass. "Highland Park. Smooth, with a peated balance."

"A regal choice—from Orkney." The ambassador smiled as he accepted it.

"Not that I'd know its taste." Nicholas laughed. We traded glances, unsure what he meant.

Histo clarified. "Emperor is a teetotaler."

A rarity in this vast land where liquor is a staple.

Nicholas grew solemn. "But I *do* know that close to us lies Turkey, and in our present condition, nothing better for our interests could be desired. The times have gone by when we had anything to fear from the fanatical spirit or the military ardor of the Turks, yet that country is still strong enough to preserve its independence and is respected by others."

Seymour rolled the drink in his mouth before swallowing.

"Please sit down." The czar gestured to the rococo chair as he paced. "I beg you to believe I am as desirous as one can be for the continuance of his life, but he may suddenly die upon our hands—*rester sur les bras*—as I said the other night." The emperor extended his arms, feigning the act of holding a body.

"If the Turkish Empire falls, it falls to rise no more. Nobody can bring the dead back to life." He smiled cunningly, pleased with his phrasing in both English and French.

"And I put it to you—better to prepare for contingency than to plunge into chaos and confusion. For certain, a European war will follow if catastrophe occurs before some ulterior system is devised. This is what I entreat you to press upon your government."

Zena leaned in. "Do you understand all this?"

I nodded. I'd grown up surrounded by diplomatic language. Dad used to play old State Department recordings on tape—many in what Mom called antiquated *Franclish*— while I built towers with my blocks.

"Can you give me the CliffsNotes version?" She grinned.

I leaned in, keeping my voice low. "He's saying Russia wouldn't swap Turkey for another neighbor. The Turk is no longer the threat he once was. But we must be realistic—he's dying, and we can't save him."

I paused. She stood staring at me with her emerald eyes wide open, waiting to hear more.

I swallowed. "Nicholas argues it's wiser to be prepared in advance than to face chaos and confusion afterward. A European war will likely follow if the catastrophe happens unexpectedly without any framework in place."

She smiled. "Thank you. That helps a lot." Being useful to her sent a tingle up my spine.

Rocko chimed in, lifting a brow. "No cheating."

George Seymour returned to his seat, listening intently.

The emperor quickened his pace. "The Turkish Empire has millions of Christians whose interests I am bound to protect, a right secured by treaties. At times, this duty forced me into disturbing practices, but I cannot escape it. Our Orthodox faith came from the East, and I must never lose sight of those ties."

Seymour nodded slightly. "His Imperial Majesty has spoken clearly. I will endeavor to match the candor."

The czar lifted a brow, waiting.

"Turkey's situation is dire." Calmness lingered in the ambassador's features. "If His Majesty allows me to say, in England, disposing of an old friend and ally meets with repugnance."

Rocko smirked. "I doubt the English public would be quick to come to Turkey's aid."

The emperor scoffed, as if he had heard the novanaut. "This must be a fine principle, especially in times of uncertainty and danger like the present."

Seymour bit his lip but pressed on. "With regard to contingency arrangements, as a general rule, Her Majesty's Government objects to entering engagements on possible eventualities and would perhaps be particularly disinclined in this instance."

The emperor squinted, walked over to the ambassador, and sat across from him. "Chancellor, now I desire to speak to you frankly, as a friend and gentleman."

I couldn't make out his voice. Candor, or a trace of annoyance?

The emperor planted his fist on the rosewood desk, unsettling the ambassador. "If England thinks of establishing herself one day at Constantinople, I will not allow it." His features stiffened, gaze locked onto Seymour. "I do not attribute this intention to you, but in these matters, it is better to speak plainly."

He leaned in. "For my part, I am equally disposed to take the engagement not to establish myself there as proprietor or landlord."

He flung his arms wide, leaning back. "But, if no provisions were made, or if everything were left to chance, circumstances might place me in the position of occupying Constantinople."

Seymour jolted.

The emperor raised a finger. "Not as occupier. I do not say."

Nakshi leaned toward me. "He's deliberately vague, yet unmistakably strategic."

I nodded. *That's Russia.* Its ruler had just signaled his readiness to take Constantinople by default—not by design, but by necessity. Not as a conqueror, but as a caretaker. For how long? He didn't say. Weeks? Years? Decades?

The czar shrugged, sipping his water. A faint smile tugged at his lips. "I must be the only man in Russia who prefers water over vodka. I have never acquired a taste for alcohol."

The ambassador feigned a smile, waiting until Nicholas set down the glass. "Her Majesty's Government is grateful for His Majesty's frankness. Open communication is the best safeguard against sudden dangers to which His Majesty alludes."

The czar leaned forward again, almost childlike.

Sir Seymour spoke softly. "Occupation of Constantinople—even with His Majesty's assurances that it would be temporary—would have unintended consequences for a country already weakened by financial crisis."

The emperor's brow shot up. The ambassador pressed on.

"We must anticipate two outcomes from the appearance of an imperial army on Turkey's frontiers: revolts by Christians against the sultan's authority and counter-demonstrations stirred by France."

The emperor jolted as if electrocuted.

"French?!" His outburst startled us. "Firstly, my army has undertaken no such maneuver, and I hope such preparation will never be necessary."

The czar's voice echoed in the Gold Room. He jabbed a finger. "On the other hand, if the French army entered the sultan's dominions, it would bring affairs to an immediate crisis. I would not hesitate to send my armies into Turkey without delay. It would be a matter of honor!"

Seymour gripped his chair, hoping for the flare to pass.

"Such an opening would bring about the downfall of *Le Grand Turc*, though the result would sadden me."

The agitated emperor rose and gestured for the ambassador to follow toward the grand salon's entrance, offering a farewell—polite yet unmistakably cold, in stark contrast to his earlier welcome.

He held the ambassador's arm mid-exit and spoke warmly. "If England and I can arrive at an understanding of this matter, the rest matters little to me." The two men locked eyes. The ambassador flinched. The czar's tone hardened. "You will report what has passed between us to the Queen's Government, and you will say I am ready to receive any communication they wish to make on the subject."

Seymour bowed and left the Gold Room.

The lights dimmed, then returned. We were still in the grand salon. No one was inside.

Histo stepped forward. "Next, Seymour reported everything you just saw. He also expressed his beliefs."

"And, what were they?" I asked.

His lips thinned. "If the two principal governments of Europe take precautions, the Mohammedan rule in the continent would be extinct without disrupting the peace. It would be a noble triumph for the civilized world."

Nakshi snapped. "Extinction? Does this man, Seymour, even hear himself? He's calling for the destruction of millions of Muslims in Europe and the expulsion of families from their homes in the Balkans. What crime have they committed?"

The room quieted, letting him vent.

"And he dares call himself civilized? He's advocating the erasure of an entire people!" Nakshi's voice rang through the chamber. "All because this so-called 'noble' Englishman disapproves of their faith?"

There was no stopping him now. "Learn your history before trying to make it!" He drew a long breath, avoiding eye contact.

I had not expected such an outburst from the man I thought the most composed of the team.

Nakshi reminded me of my grandfather—the kindest, most pleasant man I knew. When Mom first met Dad's family, Grandma Kathleen warned her never to cross the nationality line with Grandpa. My father was different. He didn't carry those sensitivities about his homeland. Perhaps he strove to be an impartial academic, or maybe it was simply who he was—more detached, less emotional.

No one spoke for a brief spell, remembering the starving faces. Bodies in shallow graves. Thousands of innocent Bosnian Muslims in Srebrenica reeled through my mind like old footage. Images from the former Ottoman lands in the '90s had infuriated many people, including my family, especially Grandpa, whose roots ran deep in the region.

Zena broke the silence with measured words. "The 'noble victory' this Sir speaks of is ethnic cleansing, dressed in polite language and passed off as diplomacy." She sighed. "It's familiar to me."

I wondered what she meant.

A brief flick of the lights—like a curtain falling and rising mid-act—boiled my suspicious mind, but I let it go.

The calendar on the cherry table read Monday, February 21, 1853. A month had passed. The emperor stood frozen at the tall window, straight as an arrow, chin lifted, hands folded behind his back, watching the snow-covered Winter Palace Square. It was a soothing sight—almost therapeutic.

Seymour's hologram, just as still, sat in the crimson rococo chair beside the crackling fireplace. A dossier and a Waterford crystal tumbler of scotch rested on the rosewood desk.

Krish's voice came over the speakers. "Bear with me a minute. I am patching."

I enjoyed watching these men, but their exchange didn't need quantum technology. They could be actors. The two reminded me of those still performers in Battery Park. My cousin and I used to sit on a bench, watching their flawless statue poses, living off tips from startled pedestrians when they suddenly came alive. One of them eventually made it to the big stage. Histo could have picked the czar and ambassador from that rich talent pool. If so, he nailed it. These men were worthy of Broadway.

Krish unfroze the scene. The czar sprang to life, pacing the room.

"Chancellor Seymour, don't mind me moving about. You may remain seated. I'd like you to read Lord Russell's letter aloud. I may interrupt now and then."

Seymour drew a letter from his dossier. "Her Majesty directed her government to reply with candor and courtesy, in the same spirit of His Imperial Majesty's frankness, moderation, and friendly disposition."

The emperor acknowledged with a subtle nod, signaling him to continue.

"His Majesty raises a serious question and urges that a framework of understanding be established between the two governments before the dissolution of the Turkish Empire, which, in his view, is likely soon, if not imminent."

"A contingency," the czar pressed, pacing.

Zena leaned in. "He keeps hammering that word. Why's that?"

Rocko smirked. "Make sure to have a plan before the poop hits the fan."

Zena's eyes narrowed. Her disdain made it clear that she disapproved of hearing the "s" word, which I sanitized here.

The emperor stopped before a window, watching the dancing snowflakes drift silently into the courtyard as he listened to the ambassador read Russell's letter.

"Her Majesty's Government is of the opinion that, as of today, there is no crisis severe enough to demand a solution to this broader European problem."

Seymour glanced sideways—no change in the emperor's calm stance. He went on, "If we examine the current tensions, we see disputes between Russia and France over the Holy Land—issues that don't involve the Turkish government. The situation in Montenegro is a border dispute between Austria and Turkey, and it does not pose a threat to the sultan's safety. In short, the sultan remains in control at home."

The emperor resumed pacing, eyes lowered, hands clasped behind his back.

Seymour continued, "The dissolution of the Turkish Empire cannot be assigned a specific date. This event could occur twenty-five, fifty, or a hundred years from now, but not today."

Rocko leaned in. "The Ottoman Empire dissolved in 1918, at the end of the Great War. How many years would that be from today?"

"Sixty-five," I whispered back.

"Wow, that's impressive." Zena's eyes widened.

"I'd call that a bull's eye." Rocko smiled, lowering his voice.

Nakshi added to the banter. "It's the British difference. Their foresight surpasses all."

"Focus, please." Histo's voice was firm.

Back to the performance. I let a smile linger.

The emperor interrupted Seymour. "I do not wish for Turkey's destruction any more than Britain. I alone saved the sultan's throne."

The czar referred to events three decades earlier. Sultan Mahmoud had called on Egypt's Ibrahim Pasha to help crush the Greek uprising in Morea. Britain, Russia, and France backed the Greeks and sank the Ottoman fleet at Navarino. Ibrahim then turned on the weakened Ottoman dynasty. The czar intervened, claiming credit for saving the sultan.

"Moreover, in 1829, had I not prevented General Diebitch from advancing to victory outside Adrianople, it would not be possible to speak of the sultan's authority today."

That claim I disputed. Sultan Mahmoud accepted Russia's peace offer in mid-battle, fearing the enemy seizing the city. Had he known that cholera had already ravaged Diebitch's troops, the sultan might have driven back the enemy—and history could have taken a different turn.

Seymour resumed reading the letter. "If England and Russia were to agree on a contingency that excludes Austria and France, it could trigger the very European war we both are trying to prevent."

He dabbed his forehead with his handkerchief. "Any contingency for Turkey's collapse must include a post-destruction strategy involving all the great powers. Neither Her Majesty's Government nor His Imperial Majesty would wish it otherwise. Therefore, in fairness, Austria and France could not be excluded from a contingency concerning only the pre-collapse."

The emperor didn't flinch.

Seymour's voice steadied. "History has shown that parties often breach agreements when new opportunities arise. Any contingency, even between our governments, wouldn't remain secret for long—and would likely hasten the very outcome it seeks to prevent: a European war."

Nicholas hastened his pace.

The ambassador smiled faintly. "Her Majesty's Government undertakes not to engage with other powers without first informing Russia. That should ease His Majesty's concerns."

Nicholas twitched but kept his composure.

Dad advised his students to invert the diplomatic phrases to catch concealed meanings. Perhaps Russell was hinting that Nicholas was dealing with other powers without informing Britain.

Zena leaned in. "It seems he hadn't thought about any of this before."

"I doubt that." Nakshi winked. "They think of everything. This is Russia."

Seymour, unaware of the czar's gaze, flipped a page of the long letter. "The mere knowledge of an agreement's existence would also alarm the sultan, alienate him from us, embolden his enemies, and escalate violence into prolonged conflict."

The emperor narrowed his eyes, his cheeks drawing taut.

Seymour shifted in his seat. "If rebels believe they can win, the sultan's generals may conclude that even victory won't save the regime. That could lead to the very anarchy now feared. The foresight of the patient's friends would prove the cause of his death."

The emperor paused mid-stride.

"Do you have a suggestion?"

Seymour looked up and pressed his lips together. "I'm afraid my idea may not suit Your Majesty—nor Her Majesty's Government."

Nicholas lifted his brows in anticipation.

Seymour sipped his whiskey. "What is good between man and man is often a sound principle between states. Suppose, in the event of a catastrophe in Turkey, Russia and England agreed that no power should lay claim to its provinces. The territory would remain sealed until an amicable arrangement could be reached for adjudication?"

Czar Nicholas laughed aloud. "Such a course would be challenging, if not impossible."

The ambassador reddened, realizing he had overplayed his hand.

The czar offered a smile, almost affectionate. "You'd see Mussulmans attacking Christians, Christians falling upon them, Christians of different sects quarreling among themselves—in short, chaos and anarchy."

Nakshi smiled bitterly. "He's right. Look at the Balkans, Syria, Iraq, Lebanon, Yemen. Even in our times. These are the lands the Ottomans once held."

Sir Hamilton Seymour returned a respectful smile. "If His gracious Majesty would permit me to speak freely, I wish to highlight a distinction between our two great nations."

Czar Nicholas offered an encouraging nod.

"His Imperial Majesty advocates contingency, anticipating Turkey's destruction. In contrast, we consider the measures needed to prevent its decline."

"Oh! Chancellor, you keep returning to the same point—but one day, this catastrophe will take us by surprise!" The emperor sputtered, swinging his arms.

"Turkey's destruction is imminent. I desire more than England that the catastrophes you mention not occur, but they are now all too probable, whether by external attack or internal unrest. Christians, impatient to shake off the Mohammedan yoke, rise against them. And then, the French." Czar Nicholas pursed his lips with a snobbish air. "A feud between the supporters of their new superficial 'reforms' and the Porte's old establishment could trigger collapse at any moment."

Their exchange reminded me of two renowned physicians consulting at the bedside of a gravely ill patient—aligned in diagnosis but divided in prognosis.

The emperor's voice tightened. "Everyone should have noticed my attitude toward the sultan. This gentleman—*ce monsieur*—breaks his written word to me and acts in a manner displeasing." His voice echoed through the grand salon, startling us. "I dispatched an ambassador to Constantinople to demand reparation. That was after taking advice to show restraint. Certainly, I could send an army there if I chose." He wagged a finger at Seymour. "Nothing could stop it."

He resumed his stride, still raging, "But I have contented myself with a show of force, to make clear I will not be trifled with."

Zena leaned close. "Wow! *Is-he-mad*? Who's the ambassador he's talking about?"

I shrugged.

Histo cut in, crisp and sharp. "You'll find out. So will Seymour. There's more coming."

"Only in the quantum universe." Rocko grinned. "Stay tuned."

Sir George Hamilton Seymour held steady. The timidness was gone. Ignoring the czar's anger toward the sultan, he flipped a few pages. "His Imperial Majesty has affirmed he does not aspire to annex Constantinople. Even as custodian, not owner, His Excellency would still face formidable pressure from the Russian people for failing to fulfill their long-cherished ambition."

Czar Nicholas drew back his chin. "What's that supposed to mean?"

Seymour's shoulders slumped, his poise transformed, as if freed of inner demons. He pressed on. "Your late brother, Emperor Alexander—still a legend in the hearts of your people—once said he was the only Russian who resisted anti-Turkey sentiment. His public stance cost him some popularity."

"That was thirty years ago." Nicholas's lips parted, his eyes narrowing.

Seymour was deliberate in his choice of words. "The passion remains the same among Russian people. Nations cling to long-standing aspirations. They would expect their emperor to be more than a custodian, and he—not someone else—should possess Constantinople and Hagia Sophia."

"C'mon. What people?" Rocko barged in, triggering a freeze. "Half of Russia was starving serfs back then. They had no say in governance. I'd say it was the St. Petersburg establishment that wanted Constantinople—not the 'people.'"

I recalled my father's final editorial, written from his deathbed. *Is it Putin or the Siloviki?*— Russia's "deep state." He argued the Russians and Ukrainians shared faith and roots and had no real quarrel with one another. The pro-war drive came from the establishment—a point that echoed Rocko's argument.

Nakshi shook his head. "Seymour implies Russians inherently hate Turks. I don't see that. If anything, it's the opposite, at least today."

Rocko flashed a thumbs-up. "True—and vice versa. Turks and Russians get along. Lots of people live in each other's countries. Intermarriages are common."

Zena perked up. "Oh, yeah. I met a few couples in Antalya last summer."

Histo cut in. "Save your social insights for dinner."

"Are we gonna have one?" Rocko rubbed his stomach. "I'm starving. Nakshi's apple won't do much."

"I've packed brown bags for each of you." Krish's voice echoed over the surround sound. "We'll chill in the lunchroom upstairs afterward."

"You can have mine. I don't feel like eating." Zena's lip twitched.

I leaned in. "Why? What's wrong?"

"Dunno. Stomach bug, maybe." She scrunched her face. "Not a big deal. I get it a lot." Her temples were damp with sweat. I kept quiet yet felt a tinge of worry for her.

Histo clapped his hands. "Let's move on if we're done with the sidebars."

I forced myself to focus on the scene.

Seymour resumed where he'd left off. "The power that replaces Constantinople controls the gateway to the Mediterranean and Black Sea. It will either support or restrain Russia. A victorious, ambitious state rising in place of the Sublime Porte could force Russia into war, turning efforts to preserve peace into a European conflict."

Realizing his contingency approach might not gain acceptance, Nicholas turned from Seymour, gazing at the courtyard.

The ambassador pressed on. "The new owners of this city might wield more power than the Turks ever did. Not the lazy, lethargic descendants of Mehmet II, but a formidable force—one that may oppose Russia's interest."

Nakshi chuckled nervously, triggering another pause. He wasn't enraged this time. He leaned toward Histo. "I'd have expected a more credible assessment from the British Foreign Ministry, not such a shallow view. The Turks ruled the Eastern Mediterranean for six centuries—the same lands the Eastern Roman Empire once held. How does that square with laziness?"

Histo thrust his hands, as if pushing back. "Don't look at me. You are inside history now. Like it or not, Seymour said what he said."

Krish resumed the scene.

The ambassador leaned forward. "Would His Imperial Majesty consider working with Her Majesty's Government to prevent Turkey's downfall?" His voice thinned, shedding a notch of ceremonial polish.

The czar didn't shift his gaze, still fixed on the courtyard.

Rocko wiggled a brow. "First, he shot down the emperor's contingency idea; now he's pitching the British alternative."

No longer hesitant, Seymour read from Russell's letter. "On resolving disputes around Turkey, we must engage the Sublime Porte and not exploit the sultan's weakness. Nor must we allow the sultan to turn our disagreements to his advantage."

The emperor silently waited for the ambassador to finish his pitch.

"These matters should be addressed in a spirit of friendship, not by imposition. Military maneuvers must remain a last resort. We must press the sultan to ensure equality for his Christian subjects and safeguard freedom of belief, in line with Europe's enlightened nations."

Nakshi scoffed. "Why not the same for his Muslim subjects? A just society endures—if the Brits really cared for one."

The emperor closed his eyes and tilted his chin up, basking in the sunlight that streamed through and bounced off the Byzantine mosaics. Outside, icicles dripped steadily—some faster than others.

Seymour hurried to finish. "The more the Sublime Porte embraces egalitarian and just governance, the less the Russian Emperor would feel compelled to resort to objectionable, burdensome, or extraordinary protection measures."

He glanced at the czar. Nicholas gave no reaction.

Seymour cleared his throat. "By maintaining the status quo, His Majesty would earn a more honored place in history than rulers who chased immortality through unprovoked conquests and left no lasting victories. No policy could be wiser—or better serve Europe."

He folded the letter, slipped it back into his brief, exhaled, dabbed his forehead, and gulped his drink.

"Pause, Krish," Histo called out, then turned to us. "What do you think?"

Rocko leaned in. "Britain just offered the Russian Emperor immortality—no battles, no mess. Nobel Peace Prize. Oops—just checked. Doesn't exist yet. Too bad." Laughter rippled through the room.

Nakshi piled on. "We'll build your statues, name boulevards after you, and write glowing tributes. Just follow our script."

Rocko pointed at Seymour, frozen mid-sip, tumbler hovering. "He offered a bribe. That's Britain's Anglo-Russian proposal in a nutshell."

"Hold on." Zena raised a hand, then turned to me. "It's overwhelming—too much, too fast, too heavy. What exactly did the British Ambassador just offer Russia in geostrategic terms?"

All eyes turned to me. Before I could speak, Nakshi jumped in.

"Keep Turkey alive, but keep her weak."

"Spot on." I nodded. "The Goldilocks strategy—not cold, not hot, just lukewarm. A British original." When I coined the phrase, Dad liked it enough to add it to his course notes—the only time he ever praised me in front of others.

Nakshi offered me a faint smile. "A porridge for the ages. Isn't it? It's the only contingency the powerful requires. It works to contain the weak. Foolproof. Cheap. Timeless."

"How is it implemented?" Zena didn't want me to go off on a tangent. She pulled me back—skip the analogy, stick to the facts.

"Economically, make sure they're never strong but not too weak either. Keep them at bay. Divide them in their minds: by religion, denomination, ethnicity—even lifestyle—secular versus faith-oriented, Western versus Eastern."

Rocko chimed in, "Internal conflicts. If there's none, create one." He snickered. "And if all else fails, there's always soccer. One club versus the other."

I nodded. "Sadly, it's not just the outside instigators stirring the pot." I let out a bitter breath. "People embrace division themselves— polarization, cultural splits, districts divided by invisible lines. That's how a country stays in perpetual disunity."

Nakshi offered a bitter smile. "It works. This strategy was first used against Turkey in the early nineteenth century. It hasn't stopped."

His tone turned brittle, as if old wounds surfaced.

Zena's gaze drifted. "Maybe someone's using this old playbook on us now. Look at America. We no longer talk to one another, follow opposing news, and live in different realities. My parents say they don't recognize the country they emigrated to."

Nakshi muttered. "Most divisions are self-inflicted." He sure had a story behind that.

Zena leaned toward me. "Goldilocks strategy. Brilliant summary in two words. You're good, Narrator." She beamed.

For a moment, I didn't feel the floor beneath me.

Pleased with the impromptu exchange, Histo signaled Krish to resume.

The scene unfroze.

The czar turned around and paced toward Seymour, pausing by his seat. The ambassador pressed his legs together, looking like a student caught passing notes.

Nicholas, supreme commander of "All Russias," stood at the center of the glittering hall, unabashed in his imperial splendor before Her Majesty's envoy. Towering at six feet, with an aquiline nose, square chin, and piercing blue eyes, reminiscent of a Greek god, he radiated the might of his empire.

The snowfall had ceased. As the clouds cleared, the setting sun streamed through the high windows, casting a golden halo around his head, like the mosaics of Hagia Sophia. Light shimmered through chandeliers, danced across Bohemian crystals, bounced off gilded walls, and spilled onto the mosaic floor. On that cold February afternoon, the Golden Room lived up to its name.

The czar spoke with a calm we hadn't heard before.

"The Turkish Empire is in decline. Any attempt to rebuild it must be avoided." He locked eyes with the ambassador. "I will object to such an endeavor."

It sounded as if he sniffed out a hidden agenda.

His voice stayed measured. "Rather than submit to such arrangements, I would rather go to war." He paused, watching the ambassador's eyes widen. "And as long as I have a man and a musket, I'll carry it on."

Seymour held his breath. Beads broke across his forehead. Russia—majestic and intimidating—had just challenged Great Britain.

As the emperor finished, the sunset dispelled the grand salon's magic. The glittering light fled behind clouds. He sat across from the ambassador, cloaked in shadow. The Golden Room was no more—majestic yet eerie, draped in gray.

Russia had spoken—the bear was no longer hibernating.

Seymour kept his poise, careful not to appear anxious. In a final attempt to avert what felt like an oncoming disaster, he spoke with measured calm.

"Her Majesty's Government aligns with His Majesty. It opposes any ambition over Constantinople. No power should seize the city. His Majesty should find comfort in this."

Read it inverted, as Dad would have said. Seymour just declared England would never permit Russia to seize Istanbul—temporarily or permanently. It was diplomacy at its best.

A heavy silence settled in the salon, broken only by the wind howling outside. The two men locked eyes. Neither blinked.

The emperor slowly rose. Thinking the meeting had ended, the ambassador followed.

"Please stay seated."

Russia wasn't done.

9

ASK NOT WHAT TO DO BUT WHAT NOT TO DO

Half-risen, the British Ambassador, Sir George Hamilton Seymour, sank back into his rococo seat. A faint crease cut across his brow.

Czar Nicholas loomed before him. "I beg you to understand. My commitments will bind my successor. Memorandums exist of my intentions. Whatever I have promised, my son Alexander will be as ready to perform as his father."

The ambassador cleared his throat. His knuckles whitened as his fingers dug into the armrest. This was no digital reenactment. A living, breathing man stood before us.

I shoved aside my doubts—as much as I enjoyed history, I wasn't about to swallow Histo's quantum fairy tales.

Seymour forced out his words. "It would hardly be consistent with the friendly feelings toward the sultan—"

"Chancellor!"

The emperor's nostrils flared. "I'm afraid Her Majesty's Government does not fully grasp my objective."

Seymour stared at the Russian Emperor like a bewildered farmer watching a tornado rise from a calm sky.

"The central question I've been asking is not what shall be done when the sick man dies—but what shall not be done when that happens."

Nicholas strode to the center of the salon and spun to face the ambassador. "It's not what to do, but what *not* to do! That's the question." His words echoed *Hamlet*'s famous lament.

Seymour offered nothing in return.

Nicholas stepped closer. His arms dropped to his sides. "I expected a declaration from Her Majesty's Government—even just an opinion."

Seymour struggled to hold his composure.

Nicholas resumed his stride, repeating himself, leaving no room for misunderstanding. "What ought not to be permitted in the event of Turkey's sudden collapse?" He exhaled softly. "That's all I ask." His sharp, emotional voice eased into a measured tone, his final words falling to a murmur.

Seymour placed Lord Russell's letter on the desk. "Perhaps Your Majesty would be good enough to explain his thoughts on this negative policy."

The emperor paused, taking his time, collecting his thoughts. He circled beneath the two massive chandeliers, tracing an invisible ellipse like a satellite orbiting twin planets.

Just as Seymour leaned in to speak, the czar broke his long silence.

"There are several things I will never tolerate. I begin with myself. I will not permanently occupy Constantinople."

He cast Seymour a quick glance, searching for a reaction. The ambassador did not flinch.

Nicholas lifted his chin. "Having said this—and I repeat—I will not allow the British to hold the city. Nor the French. Nor any other great nation."

Seymour kept his gaze fixed, alert not to miss a beat.

"And I will never allow the Byzantine Empire to be resurrected. That would make Greece too powerful."

Still circling, Nicholas wagged a finger high. "Another objection, perhaps less forceful, is the partition of Turkey into a few small republics."

He raised his voice, every word edged with disdain. "Otherwise, they will become sanctuaries for European revolutionaries, the Kossuths and the Mazzinis alike."

Zena leaned toward me. "You know them?" I shook my head.

The emperor stepped out of his orbit, stopped between the chandeliers, and faced Seymour directly.

"These are my thoughts." He gestured for the ambassador to respond.

Seymour steadied his voice. "Her Majesty's Government maintains that Turkey has the means to survive. No report suggests the sick man nears death."

Czar Nicholas let out a half-laugh. "If your government believes Turkey retains any element of existence, it has been misinformed."

Seymour's lips twitched. "We see no signs, no grounds to expect a sudden demise."

Nakshi leaned toward me. "Don't tell a British foreign officer his field guys are incompetent." We exchanged quick smiles.

The emperor shifted course, striding diagonally across the grand salon.

Sir Seymour leaned forward with a faint smile. "I have the sincere satisfaction of reporting to Her Majesty's Government that His Imperial Majesty considers himself even more invested than England in preventing a Turkish catastrophe. Her Majesty's Government will seek His Majesty's generous assistance in averting any circumstance that might provoke such a crisis."

The czar pressed on. "I repeat to you that the sick man is dying, and we can never allow such an event to catch us by surprise. We must come to some understanding."

Seymour fell silent. His poise was a deliberate act, a loud cry. Each man rejected the other's offer.

Czar Nicholas drifted away. "If I could speak ten minutes with your ministers—with the Earl of Aberdeen, for instance. The prime minister knows me so well and has full confidence in me, as I do in him."

Rocko nudged me. "If I heard it right, the czar just told Seymour he's not up to the task."

The ambassador's jaw clenched. He pushed back. "Countries do not die in such a hurry." He no longer resembled a seventh grader stuck in detention after the bell.

Sensing the edge of his innuendo, the emperor shifted to a measured tone.

"The British government and I must rely on each other's views. I don't concern myself much with the others." He offered a warm smile. "I'm not asking for a treaty or a protocol. All I seek is a mutual understanding between gentlemen. *La parole d'un gentilhomme.*"

The emperor had just lowered the bar—no longer a formal accord in print, but a verbal exchange between friends.

Seymour warmed in return. "If I may observe, perhaps the recent movements of France have unsettled His Imperial Majesty."

The emperor shrugged. A silent yes, I thought. More importantly, he had accepted Seymour's quiet offer to ease the tension.

Seymour continued, "Her Majesty's Government is as unwilling as His Imperial Majesty to tolerate a French presence at Constantinople."

"Blame the French. Smart move," Nakshi quipped.

"The 'Third' party," Rocko added, "no pun intended," referencing Louis Napoleon III.

The czar scoffed. "The French government is working hard to draw us toward the East."

Seymour brightened. The poking worked—the czar's earlier intensity was gone.

The czar swung his arms loosely. "Just last month, I told the sultan that if he asks for help resisting the French menace, I will be at his service!"

Nicholas halted in the farthest corner of the salon. Light from the embrasure behind him cast a long shadow across the floor.

"Their eyes are on Tunisia. Undoubtedly, the first among many." He paused, lifting his chin to bathe in the hues of the setting sun. "Personally, I care little about whatever course the French may choose in Eastern affairs."

He spun sharply and strode toward the ambassador. "When the Turkish Empire disintegrates, a satisfactory arrangement will be far easier than people think."

Seymour's eyes lit. He leaned back.

"He's talking about partition!" Zena's eyes widened. "Can you believe that?"

"Yes, I can," Nakshi murmured.

The emperor sat across from the ambassador. "Many principalities became independent once they came under my protection. Servia can follow the same model."

Seymour held his breath.

Zena turned to me. "What country is Servia?"

I was starting to enjoy being her go-to guy for questions.

"It's not a country, but a region in the northern Greek peninsula— most of it now part of modern Greece."

Nicholas pursed his lips. "I see no reason Bulgaria should not be independent."

Independence under his protection, of course, meant those lands stayed under his thumb.

Rocko leaned in. "He just claimed Bulgaria and Northern Greece." He snapped his fingers. "Just like that."

Nakshi knit his brows. "The big bear arrived. Suddenly. Out of the blue. Like bears do."

"As for Egypt..." Nicholas squinted in thought. "I understand its importance to England. I have no objection to Britain taking it. Same with Candia. Why isn't it already under British rule?" He grinned at Seymour.

Zena spread her arms, posing. "Welcome to holiday shopping! End-of-season blowout. This one comes free with the neighborhood you just bought."

"Candia is Crete—the largest island in the Archipelagos," Nakshi mused. "Go ahead and take it. I won't stand in your way, so long as you don't stand in mine."

The ambassador's eyes flickered, but as a British civil servant, he knew better than to indulge in partition talk before Russia's head of state.

Seymour straightened. "Britain's view of Egypt has always been limited to securing communication between the motherland and British India—nothing more."

Nakshi cracked a smile. "He didn't fall into the Russian trap. Held back his appetite."

"The man is smarter than that." Rocko wiggled his eyebrows.

Zena shook her head. "Nicholas offered a partition plan, like slicing a tray of baklava. Unbelievable."

Rocko winked. "I can see why Histo calls this a landmark conversation."

"Setting the stage for the next century across the Eastern Mediterranean and the Balkans," I said. "Plenty of baklava for everyone."

"Still going," Nakshi nodded. "Just more forks around the tray now."

Seymour leaned forward. "All these Eastern questions affect Austria closely. It must expect to be consulted."

The czar sipped water, rose, and began pacing—this time cutting across the salon's opposite diagonal like an admiral setting out to conquer the oceans before him.

Seymour colored his query. "Are there any discussions or understandings between St. Petersburg and Vienna?"

Nicholas didn't blink. "You must understand. When I speak of Russia, I also speak for Austria." He shrugged, lips pursed. "What suits one suits the other. Our interests regarding Turkey are identical." He quickened his pace.

Seymour's mouth parted as he absorbed the implication—that Austria acted under Russian directives.

The emperor spoke casually. "Take Montenegro. Austria supported my actions there."

He swung his right arm forward, the left tucked behind. "I could not allow ill-behaved Turks to kill Christians." He turned to Seymour. "It is impossible not to take interest in a people so deeply devoted to their religion, who long defended their land against the Turks."

"Both sides share responsibility for the injustices and atrocities." Seymour's gaze sharpened. "I am confident in saying that the Montenegrins—not the Turks—were the ones who provoked."

The emperor swayed his head in sync with his steps, a silent signal of agreement. His voice dropped, edging toward confessional.

"Both sides made mistakes, but those thugs—the crime-addicted mountaineers—angered me most."

The emperor's impartiality might have surpassed the ambassador's expectations, but their exchange struck a nerve, sending a chill down my spine.

I cut in tersely. "Scalped. Beheaded. The heads mounted on stakes."

Puzzled by my outburst, the novanauts waited to hear more.

"The deeds of his heroes seemed too gruesome even for the czar to bear—though they killed in the name of his faith."

Zena's eyes widened. "How do you know all this?"

"My great-grandfather's uncle's head was mounted on one."

"Did his grandnephew witness it?"

"He was ten."

"Oh my gosh! What a horror for a child. Is that where your roots are from?"

"Only my grandfather from my father's side." I sighed, my voice dropping. "His lineage traces back to the region. No one else survived; all were slaughtered."

"By those thugs they're talking about?"

"I suppose so."

Rocko cut in. "All in the name of a holy cause supposedly promising salvation." He tightened his brows. "No thanks, I'll pass."

Nakshi wagged a finger. "Don't blame the faith. It's those who exploit it for their ambitions."

"Quiet," Histo cut in. "You're missing the exchange."

But I had already drifted, thinking of my grandfather, whom I loved dearly. He always spoke about his roots with pride. They were Muslim Albanians, living peacefully among Christians until the revolt. Mountaineers stormed their village. No one from his family survived. Only his grandfather, who was ten. He fled across Lake Shkodra and eventually reached Istanbul, and merged into society, becoming Turks—like countless Muslim émigrés from the Balkans.

Through the din, I heard the emperor insisting both nations had already set a precedent in a case concerning Spain, while Seymour maintained their circumstances were different.

"An attempt by Omer Pasha against the people in the Balkan principalities will provoke massacres, sparking an uprising among the Christian communities." Czar Nicholas waved his fist. "This will likely cost the sultan his throne—permanently! We *must* settle on a contingency."

Rocko turned to me. "Omer Pasha. Who is he?"

"Dunno." The word slipped out as I tried to steady after hearing the czar on Montenegro. Then it struck me. Those massacred a few weeks ago may have included members of my own family.

The czar's voice cut through the fog.

"I want to support the sultan's authority, but he will disappear soon—and forever."

I lost focus and drifted back to Grandpa's stories. He once found a letter his grandfather had written to his son, congratulating him on becoming an officer in the Ottoman army and urging him to "kick a few butts" of those who had harmed his family—because he never could. Nor could his son. Before ever seeing action in the Balkan wars, he died of typhoid.

Suddenly, I realized the baton was now mine to carry out this unfinished task. An idea struck. Right before me, rambling on, stood the man in power who had just admitted he'd turned his back on despicable massacres to make ends meet. Who better to receive the booty?

The moment had arrived. I had a "great interest" in delivering my ancestral note. The feeling swelled—almost exalted.

The czar was approaching.

But one problem nagged me. What if he was only an actor? I even suspected as much. I wouldn't want to hurt someone just trying to earn a living. Better to test it first.

I stepped forward, planting myself in his path, to see if I was, in fact, invisible to him.

"What in the world—what are you doing?!" Rocko shouted.

I didn't answer.

The czar strode toward me head-on. If he were an actor, he'd notice and veer aside to avoid a crash. If not—a hologram blind to me, as Histo claimed—he'd march on. That was the plan.

Chin up, arms behind him, the emperor paced, listening to Seymour's counter-argument from his seat.

"The Treaty of Partition did not hasten the death of the Spanish King, but—"

As the czar drew closer, I realized his eyes stayed shut. With no chance of visual contact, he would never alter course. My plan had failed.

I quickly devised a new one.

I squatted, bracing for the crash—left foot planted, right stretched behind, arms locked tight across my chest—like a hornless ram, grounded and steady, ready to absorb the charging beast.

"Should I freeze?" Krish's voice crackled over the speakers.

"Let him face the reality." Histo's voice was calm.

I closed my eyes, clenched my teeth, and held my breath.

Nothing.

I didn't feel a thing. Not even a breeze—only Seymour's calm narration in the background, "—when a similar event happened in Tuscany—"

Then Zena's sudden screech tore through the air.

"We've got a problem." Krish's words came clipped through the speakers.

I opened my eyes and straightened, no longer squatting. No one stood before me. Across the room, Seymour gazed at me like a deer in headlights, his jaw slack.

I turned to the novanauts on the sideline.

"Whoa!" Rocko exclaimed. Nakshi froze, eyes wide. Zena covered her mouth, speechless.

Then I looked back at Seymour. No longer composed, he had leapt from his seat, staring at me in horror.

I spun around, ready to swing the golden kick, but found no one behind me. Just the back of the emperor's head, swaying loosely in the air, his body gone.

I looked down. I was wearing the emperor's uniform, heavy with medals across the chest.

"Oh, shhh—damn it!" Krish sounded unmistakably panicky. "I lost him."

"Oh my gosh! Oh my gosh!" Zena shrieked, staring at me like I was Frankenstein's monster.

I looked down again. This time, my body was gone—though I could still feel it. I didn't understand why.

Krish's voice came tight. "I'm taking the system down."

Nakshi gasped, pointing at me. "He became a chopped head!" All eyes fell on me in horror.

"Did I?"

Just ahead, the emperor floated—only a lone head drifting through the air. Unaware that his body was missing, he kept preaching to Seymour.

"We're headed into a catastrophe. Only *une parole*. That will do it. Nothing in writing."

Seymour's eyes nearly popped from their sockets. He bolted toward the exit, darting past the czar.

Disoriented, I turned toward the novanauts. The only experience I could compare it to was hitting "the wall" in the final stretch of the New York Marathon—numb from the hips down. But even that fell short. It was as if air had become an ocean, and I was adrift on a broken plank after a shipwreck, fighting to stay afloat.

As I neared my teammates, Rocko and Nakshi stepped back. Zena screamed again, her screech louder than ever, echoing through the Gold Room.

"Who are you?" I turned. That was Emperor Nicholas—a fellow talking head—staring at me, floating.

Krish scoffed. "Oh, darned! I can't keep him incognito anymore." Histo lowered his head, shaking.

I put on my best diplomatic façade. "Your Imperial Majesty—"

"Guards!" the czar shouted.

Zena dashed for the exit but smacked into an invisible barrier and fell back. The impact blinked the mirrored wall into view. In an instant, we were on the stage. The holograms were gone, along with the Gold Room.

"Back to the universe," Rocko sighed.

"Thank God," Nakshi exhaled.

To be sure I was whole again, I touched my arms, legs, and torso.

The mirrored wall ascended, humming like a garage door rising from the inside, while the stage lowered, steady and slow.

Krish stepped inside the launch room.

"It's a glitch in the code." His fingers twitched. "When two dissimilar masses overlapped, the system swapped their body parts. With holographics dominant, it reversed the incognito protocol."

He turned to me, avoiding my eyes. "The czar should've passed through you like a breeze. My apologies."

Unmoved by Krish taking the blame, Histo turned to Zena.

"You okay?" She had bumped into the mirrors. Her hair tousled, she looked rattled.

"I'm fine. But we need to understand better how all this works."

"That's what KJ says." Krish bit his lower lip, eyes fixed on his iPad.

He spoke to Histo, still keeping his head down. "He just messaged me. He wants to join us now. But the system is down. I need to fix it first."

"He can join bit-based while you fix the code," Histo replied, his voice calm. "But first—delete the last few minutes from Seymour's and the czar's quantum memories. What happened never happened."

Rocko raised his right hand. "Mum's the word. We won't tell anyone. Otherwise, history gets rewritten—Secret Communication Number Eleven—from Sir Hamilton Seymour to Lord Russell. Strictly Confidential. Revenge of the Chopped Heads. Czar's Winter Palace is haunted! Transfer me somewhere else. I'm freakin' gettin' outta here!" Nervous laughter followed—everyone but Histo.

Scowling, the program director stepped before me. I escaped from his piercing blue eyes. "Are you done with all of your circus acts?" His voice was stern.

I twitched a cheek, uttering no word.

His tone hardened. "We expect you to commit for the next ten days—not only what to do, but also what not to do." He paused to let his words sink in.

I nodded.

He leaned in, his face a few inches away. "Otherwise, leave now. I can fill your spot with an alternate. It's your call."

The room fell silent.

Like a kid who'd just broken a neighbor's window swinging a bat, I lowered my head and pressed my lips together, heat climbing to my earlobes.

Mom's motto chimed in my mind. "Happiness is arriving at peace with oneself."

I felt light, adrenaline still coursing, yet strangely soothed. My head was clear, like the sky after a hurricane—as if I'd been on a long and winding road and had finally reached my destination.

I was inside history, in the quantum universe.

I took a deep breath.

"I'm in."

10

MUBITS OF PETAMUNRA

"What does quantum mean?" Zena asked as we ate our sandwiches in the launch room. She passed her brown bag to Rocko and drank only water.

Krish swallowed his bite before answering. "It means discrete, not continuous."

"An example, please?"

"An elevator goes down floor by floor. That's continuous. In the quantum world, it drops from the ninth to the fourth in an instant, skipping in between. That's a discrete drop, a quantum change."

"That would cause more havoc than the spooky ride earlier." Rocko grinned.

Zena squinted. "Yeah, but that doesn't happen in real life."

"As a matter of fact, it does." Krish's eyes brightened. "Quantum mechanics governs nature at the atomic scale. As computer circuits shrink and become more powerful, additional progress requires engineering tiny clusters of atoms, pushing into the realm of quantum mechanics. The era of quantum computing is here."

"Quantum computers face serious challenges," I cut in. "Experts say a reliable one is a decade away."

Zena lifted her hands. "Sorry, no disrespect, but why a decade?"

"Current quantum computers require extreme cold to operate. Hard to scale, they're fragile and crash easily." I'd learned that from my cousin.

Histo stepped in. "This subject is too complex and not essential to our purpose. Those interested can find plenty in the open literature."

"What was your breakthrough?" Nakshi pressed, brushing off his statement. Histo motioned for his expert to answer.

"We developed the world's first 'fault-tolerant' scalable quantum computer, Petamunra," Krish stressed each syllable.

Before I could ask what the name meant, Zena jumped in. "What kind of person is he?"

"KJ? The most brilliant visionary I've ever met." Pride laced Krish's voice.

"I read his net worth is a billion."

"That's an old issue," he corrected. "He's worth billions now."

Zena's gaze drifted. "His time must be precious."

"Way more than mine, for sure," I joked, though I did wonder. "Why would he spend a Sunday evening with us?"

"Don't underestimate yourself," Rocko quipped. "He wouldn't be here if you hadn't severed Nicholas's head. You almost ended the Romanoff dynasty, decades before Lenin." Laughter erupted. I forced a smile.

Krish smiled. "When I first met him in Bangalore, the hotel manager said they'd installed a private express elevator just for his penthouse."

The anecdote only deepened my doubts, but I forced them down. I'd given Histo my word.

"Why did he want to meet with you?" Nakshi inquired.

"He offered me a position at his quantum computing start-up."

Histo stepped in. "The chairman is ready on the bit-based channel."

The young tech prodigy tapped a few keys on his iPad. Everyone held their breath as colorful square patches flickered on the stage. As they shrank, their details sharpened.

Eventually, a fit, handsome man in his fifties emerged—braided black hair, sharp features, and angular, dark eyes full of purpose. Unlike Seymour and the czar, the hologram lacked perfect fidelity.

"KJ-San!" Zena clapped. It was thrilling to see the celebrity, even as a projection. His global popularity was immense.

"Hello, novanauts." The hologram waved. A gentle halo in pastel shades edged him.

"Greetings from Redwood City, California." The holographic video projected him from his flagship company's headquarters in Silicon Valley. It might have been jaw-dropping, but we'd already seen the Winter Palace in perfect fidelity. Still, the artificial image impressed.

"I hope my hologram doesn't disappoint. It's not quantum. But I learned early I can't compete with emperors." KJ grinned, flashing his signature smile. His toothpaste advertisement earned him a nomination for an Emmy. He took pride in promoting children's health in sub-Saharan Africa.

"On the contrary," Nakshi waved at him. "This is the most extravagant video call I've ever been on."

Rocko joined in. "Feels like a night at the Oscars."

I forced a shy wave, still embarrassed from my head-on crash with the hologram.

KJ paused to survey the group. "Histo suggested I share a few thoughts. I understand some of you remain hesitant." The billionaire shifted his gaze toward me. "Some even suspect a sting operation."

A wave of warmth swept over me.

"I'll do my best to ease your concerns." His voice shifted to convivial. "First, welcome to our journey. Our goal is to explore: Can technology prevent wars? Global peace matters more than ever. Humanity's fate on Earth is at stake, and we are our own greatest adversary." He pursed his lips slightly, reminding me of President Obama.

"Anyway, tonight's not for philosophical debates. We'll save that for later."

Krish raised his hand. "Excuse me, KJ, I'll check the system. The reactor should be cooled by now." He walked over to a wall, tapped his iPad, and a doorway slid open. A hidden elevator emerged. He stepped in, and the door sealed shut, vanishing seamlessly into the wall.

KJ watched him leave. "I can't commend him enough." He shook his head, lifting his brows. "If you're wondering why this advanced technology sits hidden in an unassuming Brooklyn neighborhood, it's because Krish's wife couldn't leave her widowed mother, Mrs. Lata. She's in her sixties and agreed to relocate from India only if she could be near her relatives, two blocks from here, and bring along the family's generational knick-knack business."

That peeled off another layer of the puzzle. I sighed in relief.

Nakshi leaned in. "He must be outstanding."

"Undisputed king of algorithms," KJ shot back.

"You must have a sizable team."

"You'd be surprised, Nakshi. We have about a dozen engineers, scientists, and technicians, each a specialist in their field. We also partner with niche companies, some as contractors, others as collaborators, all eager to learn from your upcoming ten-day experience."

KJ's uplifting demeanor made me feel like a member of the Apollo crew, boarding the capsule while a top-notch ground team cheered us on.

"Why do you need a quantum computer for this project?" Nakshi pressed on.

"We're generating perfect-fidelity dynamic images. The characters are cognitive. The system is interactive with its users. These demands exceed the capabilities of today's most powerful systems. Even if they could, they'd consume immense power. Only an energy-efficient, high-capacity, fault-tolerant quantum computer can handle the load."

"How does it accomplish all that?" The dried food merchant from Paterson impressed me, asking the right questions.

"By using the principles of quantum mechanics and quantum algorithms."

"What are those principles?"

"The main ones are superposition, entanglement, and interference."

"That'll take time to digest." The novanaut grinned. "It's dense."

Zena held his arm. "Save a glass of digestif for me."

Nakshi gestured toward Rocko. "He should know—the software man."

Rocko cleared his throat. "Classical computers work with bits—zeros and ones. Like a light switch, they're either on or off. Quantum computers, on the other hand, use 'qubits,' or quantum bits, which can be in both states until measured. That's superposition, holding multiple potential values at once."

Nakshi gave a brief chuckle. "Now I'm more confused. How do you measure a qubit?"

"I'm on and off until I'm on *or* off," Zena quipped. "Sounds like my congressman. He's everywhere on the issues until he polls."

The billionaire clapped. "I love the analogy. Call him Qubit Joe, from now on." He surveyed the room. "Anyone else?"

I raised my hand to show off my knowledge. "In a restaurant, a customer with a bit-based wired mind starts at the top of the menu and goes down the list. Tomato soup? No. Coleslaw? No. French onion soup? Yes. He'll skip the rest and order the French onion soup."

Zena narrowed her eyes. "How about if you were a quantum customer?"

"Now I'm a qubit. I see all the menu items at a glance. Each is a possibility. Then I decide and order: French onion soup. Before that, it could've been any dish."

Krish jumped in, "You are in superposition!" His eyes widened. "In technical terms, the qubit is now collapsed into a single state."

"Kudos to Narrator. You explained it better than most." KJ gave a thumbs-up. "One thing to add: the quantum waiter knows you always order the dish your mother made, so he anticipated it, but wasn't sure until you did."

Mom used to make French onion soup from scratch on my birthdays. How could he know that? It was a bizarre coincidence.

"Where did you learn all this quantum?" Zena lifted her brows. "I thought you were a history major."

"I'm not," I shrugged. "I read stuff."

"That was a good analogy," Rocko leaned in, with no smirk, just a humble nudge. "I'll remember that." Fireworks went off in my mind. Earning someone's praise always made me feel good.

"If you thought superposition was bizarre, wait till you hear about entanglement," KJ raised his hand. "Anyone heard of it?" He looked like a professor.

Zena looked at me, expecting an answer. I stared blankly. My cousin had explained it once, but I never got it.

Rocko stepped in. "As he ordered the Frenchy dish, his date opted for the all-American tomato soup. A romantic pair, they always share and never choose the same thing. They are forever entangled."

"Is that true?" Zena turned to me, eyes wide.

"I don't have a girlfriend."

"That wasn't my question. Is that what entanglement means?"

As I fumbled for words, Zena perked up. "You know, Helga and I used to do that. One of us would order a beef, the other chicken, and we'd share." She pouted. "Not anymore. She's gone vegan. I don't like her choices."

KJ said, "In the quantum bistro, your choices would trigger someone across the room to order a veggie wrap. Might even impact a customer's falafel order in a diner on Jupiter, all at the same instant."

"Jupiter?" Zena gasped, her lips stretching. "I'm totally lost."

"Entangled particles can be worlds apart—but they instantly adjust based on each other's state."

"They must have a communication channel between them." Zena pulled her mouth askew.

KJ clapped. "That's what Einstein thought. Otherwise, it would be 'spooky action at a distance.' His words."

She raised her brows, lips parted. "Einstein and I agree on physics? I struggled with multiplication tables. Never excelled in science."

I leaned toward her. "You're a careful observer with an analytical mind." I meant it.

"You think so?" She squinted.

"It's evident." A spark lit her gaze, a subtle smile dancing on her lips.

"Don't get me wrong," I added, "Einstein helped pioneer quantum mechanics but grew skeptical as the theory evolved."

"So, he was a bit like you," Zena noted. "Always doubtful." I wasn't sure if that was praise or a veiled jab.

"What did your team accomplish that others couldn't?" Nakshi had more questions.

KJ stood firm. "We made use of a unique quantum particle."

"What kind?"

"Muons." He paused. Everyone exchanged glances. I'd never heard of such a thing.

"They're unstable and hard to generate, yet we've developed a scalable method to produce them in abundance. They fulfill two functions. Some act as qubits—we call them *mubits*. Others deliver the immense energy needed to power the quantum universe. Petamunra also uses optical qubits, but strictly within the dome."

The video game mogul bit his lip and let the novanauts breathe before closing. "Our approach defies conventional wisdom. While others chase zero kelvin, our qubits operate at temperatures hot enough to melt iron."

Rocko jerked back. "That's way out of the box!"

KJ nodded. "Krish will explain it—but beware, he can be overwhelming."

Histo stepped forward. "Perhaps, Novanauts should check the operation."

KJ spread his arms. His hologram blurred, colors overlapping. "Whatever the boss says. I'll stick around a while."

Histo turned to us. "This will be a technology exchange, nothing about history. You don't have to attend. You may retire and join us tomorrow morning."

None of us wanted to skip it.

Team Novanauts took the elevator down. Histo stayed behind with KJ.

"It's exciting." Zena squared her shoulders.

The doors opened onto a floor resembling a boiler room. At the center stood a plain, windowless concrete block, roughly the size of a shipping container. The nameplate read: *Nano-Fusion Reactor.*

Krish greeted us. "It houses the world's most powerful computer and produces the energy required to sustain the quantum universe. Also, the world's most potent power plant."

"This thing?" Zena gestured at the crude structure, her lips pulled tight.

My first reaction was no different. Unimpressive. But I kept my mouth shut.

"It can light up the entire Upper East Side." Krish's voice was thick with pride.

Rocko stepped forward, assuming the team's chief engineer role. "How efficient is it?"

"Eighty percent of the energy produced drives the quantum computing operations. Another fifteen percent rides on electron by-products, which we recapture to help power the muon reactor."

Zena pointed at two twelve-inch insulated pipes that jutted out before plunging into the ground. "The ugly dig I see from my bedroom window has them."

Krish swayed his head. "The last five percent becomes heat, which we vent through these exhaust pipes."

"Vent to where? We are sixty feet below street level," Rocko pressed.

"We couldn't harness the steam to power turbines. Petamunra remains secret. Waste heat is funneled into the Earth's mantle, vanishing into boiling rock."

Krish tapped keys on the wall. A hiss of hydraulics followed. Dark grey blocks shifted apart. After a second code, c-shaped arms swung outward like wings, revealing a shiny, torpedo-shaped vessel capped by domes.

"Meet Petamunra."

The word was etched alongside a symbol that resembled a pyramid and the Egyptian eye.

Krish motioned to the wing blocks surrounding the vessel. "Superconducting magnets suspend the positively charged cold plasma inside the nano-fusion reactor."

"How cold?"

"Two thousand kelvin. That will melt metals, but compared to the Sun, it's a freezer."

"Do you have plasma inside now?" Rocko seemed drawn in.

"The system is down. No one's allowed during the operation. The magnets would rip the metallic buttons off your jacket. Only non-metallic composite robots handle tasks."

The reactor was a twenty-five-foot-long double-layer composite vessel, with a vacuum pulled between the layers to minimize heat loss. Dozens of ports, varying in size and arranged in a checkerboard pattern, covered the vessel's tubular body at two-foot intervals, each sealed with bolted stainless-steel flanges.

"These guns cryogenically transmit microwaves to and from the reactor and the dome."

"What do the signals carry?"

"Quantum algorithm codes—instructions for the mubits. Their output is carried from the reactor to the tiles inside the dome and converted into optical waves, which serve as the quantum graphic interfaces."

That flew over my head, but I still wanted to show off my techno acumen, so I jumped in. "Do you lose information during signal transmission?"

"Zero loss. These composite tubes contain ceramic waveguides coated with microwave-conducive metamaterials—developed by one of our partner companies."

Zena exhaled with puffed cheeks. "I'm lost, nowhere to be found." She gestured at the vessel. "It looks like a submarine."

Rocko quipped, "Madame Nemo, enter *Twenty Thousand Leagues Under the Sea.*"

I slipped into a French accent—another show-off. "*Science possible*, as Jules Verne called his works. Time proved him right. Maybe we're witnessing someone else's dream coming true."

She turned to me, eyes narrowed. "Do you understand any of this?"

"Kind of." Truth was, not much.

She pressed her lips. "This is too much techno-dump pouring down my throat."

Krish leaned in. "Don't worry, you don't need to know any of this to enjoy your time in the quantum universe. Anyone can drive a car. One does not need to know how its engine works."

"Some of us do." Rocko arched a brow.

Nakshi's eyes darted around. "Where's the computer?"

"You're looking at it." Krish gestured toward the vessel.

"This tubular furnace?" Zena stretched her lips. "That's bizarre."

"Where's the CPU? The hardware?" Nakshi pressed, scanning for chips.

"It's the vessel itself." Krish grinned. "Petamunra is more than Zena's submarine."

Nakshi furrowed his brows.

"What happens inside?" Zena widened her eyes. "Wait! Go easy on me. I dropped chemistry and never took physics in high school."

Rocko smirked. "I thought you were done with all this techno-talk."

"I'm a journalist," she snapped. "I have my way of learning things. No subject is an exception."

The tension fizzled as fast as it sparked.

The young man from Bangalore grinned once more. "Let's start with the hydrogen atom."

"I know this much." Zena interrupted him. "All atoms have a nucleus with positive protons, neutral neutrons, and negatively charged electrons orbiting it."

"Good." The technologist nodded. "Hydrogen is the lightest atom, with one proton and one electron. Some versions include neutrons."

"Wait! I know that one, too." Zena snapped a finger. "Deuterium and tritium. They're hydrogen isotopes. Am I right?"

Krish clapped. "For someone who didn't take science, you know a lot."

She beamed. "There was a chem major in my dorm. We named her Queen Isotope. She'd given birth to triplets. Baby Hydrogen was a boy. Deuterium weighed less than Tritium." Everyone chuckled.

"Can hydrogen have two protons?"

Rocko answered, "It wouldn't be hydrogen anymore. It becomes helium."

I stepped in. "That's what happens in the sun. Two hydrogen nuclei fuse into helium, releasing massive energy—the light and heat that sustain life on Earth. It's called fusion."

"Is that what you do down here?" Zena lifted her brows. "Fusion?"

"Yes, but only at the nanoscale and using deuterium."

"Why not use regular hydrogen?"

"It requires the temperatures and pressures that exist in stars, and the high gravity they possess. We can't reproduce these conditions on Earth."

Zena chimed in. "It reminds me of my recurrent dream. A treasure chest is waiting for me across the room, but I can't move. An invisible force holds me back. I had to climb up to Mars and return to reach it. Then I wake up."

"Oops—close, but no cigar," Rocko quipped.

"It's like fusion with hydrogen." Krish brightened. "Nearly impossible."

"Krish does it with deuterium." Rocko leaned in toward her. "Now you only need to go up to the Moon. Now go back to sleep." Zena chuckled.

Krish nodded. "True. It'll be easier, but still very challenging. Imagine having a round trip to the Moon just to deliver a package."

"How much deuterium does it take for fusion?" I was curious.

"One gram powers thirty homes for a month."

"My gosh!" Zena threw up her arms. "Why don't people use it daily?"

"The technology wasn't feasible until recently. Our breakthrough finally makes fusion affordable."

Rocko cut in, his voice serious now, "Why mess with history? Climate change is an existential threat. Your innovation can put an end to fossil fuels."

I could've asked the same but held back; didn't want to sound like a skeptic again.

"You should ask KJ," Krish said, brushing off Rocko's question.

The conversation drifted back to the basics.

Nakshi gazed at Petamunra. "I've always wondered. Why doesn't the negatively charged electron just stick to the positively charged nucleus, like a magnet on a fridge? Opposites attract."

"That's too deep, man." Rocko wagged a finger. "I wouldn't go there."

Krish swayed his head. "I agree—it's complicated. One reason is their unequal mass. The electron is much lighter than a proton and behaves like a wave."

"How light?"

"As little as our hair contributes to our weight."

Nakshi narrowed his eyes. "But they're so close to each other yet still don't crash."

I stepped in. "Not as close as you think. Let's say we have a nucleus right here in Brooklyn, and it's the size of a soccer ball. The electron would be in Lower Manhattan. If it were the size of the Earth, it would orbit around Jupiter."

Everyone stared at me.

"I calculated it once over a weekend."

Rocko gave me the same look my cousin had, wondering if I had anything better to do with my life.

Nakshi moved on. "So, where do muons fit in?"

"A muon is negatively charged, like an electron, but it's over two hundred times heavier. Inside the chamber, it replaces the electron in deuterium's orbit."

"Rapunzel—still short on meat," Rocko joked. Zena broke into laughter.

Krish brushed off Rocko's innuendo and tapped a few keys on his iPad. "If your soccer ball-sized nucleus had an electron floating in Manhattan, the muon would be across the street at Farouq's."

His name jolted my earlier embarrassment, and I felt all eyes on me.

I took a deep breath. "My friend Muon: We have something in common. We both like pizza." Everyone laughed. I felt light. A wave of relief washed over me.

Zena leaned toward Krish. "Now that you've swapped the electron with a muon in deuterium's orbit—then what?"

"The muon's heavier mass shrinks the orbital diameter, enabling fusion with much less energy."

I piped up. "Now it only takes a ride over the hilltop to deliver a package."

Zena clapped. "Boom! Fusion, yay! Thanks to Rapunzel-the-muon. I no longer have to fly to the Moon to reach my treasure chest! We'll go out and have a ball."

"Unfortunately, she's no longer with us." Krish lifted a finger. "During fusion, the muon decays into an electron."

"Poor Rapunzel." Rocko lowered his head in mock solemnity. "She sacrificed all her hair. Now she's back to a crew cut."

I followed his line, slipping into a broadcaster's tone. "And deuterium moved on—now helium, not looking back." More laughs erupted. The warm reception made me feel even more at ease with my fellow novanauts.

Just then, the elevator door opened, revealing Histo. His brows lifted as he scanned the scene. He waited until the cacophony died down.

"Are you done touring the facility?" Everyone exchanged glances.

Krish gulped. "We haven't started yet, reviewing the basics."

Rocko smirked. "And having some fun. Rapunzel-the-muon leaned from her balcony, listening to deuterium sing below. One glance from her shifted the earth—and the rest became history, all recorded."

Histo disregarded the fusion metaphor and leveled his voice at Krish. "We've been waiting upstairs."

"They wanted to learn the physics—"

Histo's voice sharpened. "There's no end to quantum mechanics." Krish pursed his lips.

The program director quickly regained his composure. "They need to grasp how the images form, but only at a high level."

"I disagree," Zena barged in. "Without the basics, we have more questions than answers. Krish did great. You should be proud." She stood firm, chin raised.

Histo gave her a once-over. "*I am.* But my boss won't be proud of me if I keep him waiting much longer." The room fell silent.

He pointed at the torpedo-shaped vessel. "Who can tell me what happens in this unit?"

"Fusion," Zena's poise was steady. "It strips deuterium's electrons and replaces them with muons."

"Where do the muons come from? Supermarkets?" Everyone looked blank.

"We didn't get that far." She twitched her cheek.

Histo approached a smaller concrete block, the size of a minivan. "This is where we produce them." A nameplate read: *Muon Production Unit.*

"Can we peek inside?" Nakshi ventured.

The director shook his head. "Only a few are allowed. It's our core breakthrough. Without her, we have nothing. Nobody thought it possible—but here it is."

Histo stepped toward a laser gun vertically mounted above the chamber. "Variable-frequency catalytic electron sputtering on a proprietary target in the presence of a metamaterial bypassing pion production." He rattled it off in one breath, like a commander briefing his troops. Everyone exchanged blank glances.

Krish's feeble voice followed. "Quantum tunneling helps." His eyes had stayed wide since Histo's entrance.

"That's what I thought." Rocko leaned back. "Go figure."

Dismissing the insinuations, Histo gestured to two chambers. "All you need to know is we produce muons on demand here and transfer them to the nano-fusion reactor there."

Histo nodded to Krish to take over and explain the rest of the process.

The young man cleared his throat, strained, eyes still wide. "Transfer is done through superconducting wires operating at cryogenic temperatures. The muons decay in just over two microseconds and transform into high-energy electrons. They return to the muon reactor to recharge the laser guns and assist fresh muon production."

Histo hammered the keywords. "Closed loop. Efficient." He stood straight, like the gun behind him. The two would never intersect, not even in space. He stared at us, unfazed. "Any questions?"

"Crystal clear," Rocko teased. Nakshi smiled wryly.

Zena had already gone daydreaming. The beads of sweat were back on her temples.

"Let's head upstairs, Krish." Histo's voice was soothing. "KJ will take a few more before leaving."

Krish's eyes were back to their sparkle.

I raised my hand. "I have one." Histo gave me a nod.

"It's for Krish. The humming and wind during take-off?"

"Smoke and mirrors, man." The algorithm king grinned, swaying.

KJ scanned the team. "What are your thoughts?"

Zena lifted a brow. "I'm still looking for a computer screen."

"It's the scene you viewed in the Gold Room."

She turned to me. "Did you know you crashed a computer screen?" That caught me off guard.

Rocko gripped my arm and whispered. "When TVs were new, people broke the tube to see if someone was inside." He nudged me. "Don't feel bad. It's nothing new." I winced.

Nakshi piped up. "How does your quantum computer create those screens?"

KJ pursed his lips, Obama-like. "You saw two generators in the boiler room. One produces muons, the other receives them and uses some for power and turning the rest into mubits—the building blocks of Petamunra, our fault-tolerant quantum computer."

He let the words settle.

"Next step—turning mubits into a live scene. That happens on the tiles lining the Petamunra dome, your computer screen."

KJ motioned to the tech guru.

Krish stepped in. "The qubits inside the nano-fusion reactor generate wave functions. Microwave receptors capture and send them to the dome—every microsecond."

He pointed at the mirrored ceiling tiles. "These are the quantum graphic interface. Coated with a proprietary metamaterial, they compress incoming signals into millisecond packets, then convert them into optical qubits."

"Why milliseconds?" I asked.

"To match human vision. The eye refreshes a thousand times per second." Krish mimicked a pulse, hand flaring open and clenching shut in rhythm. "The optical qubits emit signals across the visible spectrum every millisecond inside the Petamunra dome. Think of the dome as a grid of voxels—three-dimensional pixels, each about the size of a red blood cell. Each signal fills one voxel."

KJ intervened. "The dome holds quadrillions of voxels, but only trillions matter for vision. The rest is empty air."

"That's still a lot," Zena jerked back. "How do the messages know which voxel to reach?"

"Entanglement," Krish smiled. "Each voxel is pre-entangled with an optical qubit."

KJ stepped in. "Think of yourself as an optical qubit, making a living delivering mail." The mogul was famous for vivid analogies. "You're handed a letter with no name or address. Billions of addresses exist. It could be for anyone, anywhere." He paused, biting his lips.

"The qubit is in superposition," Krish added. "It holds all possibilities."

"Nearby is a spray can that reveals invisible ink. You give it a puff."

Krish leaned in. "Spraying represents quantum operations."

KJ raised his arm. "The first pass reveals the country—the USA. That narrows it to three hundred million households. Next, the city: New York, down to fifteen million. Then the zip code, Midtown. Another puff. The name Jones. Finally, the full address. Now you know exactly where to deliver."

Krish took the quantum mechanics avenue. "The superposition collapses to a single outcome."

Zena squinted. "This is a weird post office. In real life, the right address is on the envelope. No spraying, no discovery. The mail just gets delivered."

"That's bit-based thinking, my dear," Rocko slid in.

"I get it—but it works. So why all this quantum stuff?"

KJ raised his arms. "Zena asks a fair question. Bit-based mail gets sorted one at a time. Fine for thousands of letters, but millions? It gets tricky. The quantum mailroom holds the world's mail at once. No sorting, no routing. Mail just shows up at the right address."

"How does that work?"

"If it's meant for France, it appears in that country instantly. Same for every country, state, and zip code."

"That's entanglement, minimizing churn," Krish grinned. "That's where quantum computing shines."

KJ jumped in, "As spooky as it sounds, it works—from photosynthesis to atomic structures, and now quantum computing."

He spread his arms. "When you look at the person next to you, do they appear pixel by pixel—or all at once? That's quantum. We take vision for granted, but it is miraculous."

Histo stepped in, saying, "That's what you experienced in the Gold Room. Each voxel got its mail—no errors—trillions of deliveries, every millisecond, for an hour."

Silence followed. The power of Petamunra had sunk in.

"Who wrote those letters?" Nakshi asked.

"Mubits," I ventured. "From inside the nano-fusion reactor?"

KJ nodded. "Want to hear a muon story? I tell it to my kids before bed." He grinned.

Zena clapped. "I'm all ears."

"Inside the muon reactor, a muon is born." KJ narrowed his eyes. "She lives briefly, only two microseconds, like all muons do."

"Muons are unstable particles." Krish played the physics tune. "They decay into electrons."

KJ inhaled. "Conceived in a special womb inside a muon chamber, she was born to loving parents—an electron and a laser pulse. Like her peers, the baby muon longs to reach the quantum universe and join a community striving for progress. She hops aboard the cryogenic superconducting train to Petamunra."

Krish kept translating the tale into science, though no one really paid attention. "Catalytic electro-sputtering produces muons. Superconducting wires cryogenically transmit them to the nano fusion reactor, where they meet the deuterium plasma and—"

Zena cut him off. "She reminds me of my roommate Helga, from Bavaria. She came to New York, her dream city."

"We'll call her Helga then," KJ beamed. "Her friends, Lucy, Max, and Billie, join her."

Zena cheered. "Four muons off to the promised land—Petamunra!" Everyone chuckled.

"Inside the nano-fusion reactor, they must choose. Sustain life or become qubits for its mission—a journey to progress. Billie chooses first, finds a deuterium, then vanishes in a burst of light."

"Fusion." Krish lifted a finger. "Once muons power quantum operations, they decay into electrons."

"Like Rapunzel, releasing energy as she falls," I chimed.

KJ pressed on, "The other three became mubits. Lucy's a gymnast, dreaming of Olympic glory in the Petamunra Arena built by Billie and countless other muons."

Krish said, "Flip, roll, and spin. They're like quantum operations, spin direction and angular momentum, that emit microwave signals picked up by superconductor sensors. The mubits also form 'logic qubits' to reduce quantum errors."

KJ added, "That would be Max. Helga runs the show, representing the 'logic gates.' She referees, sets the scoreboard, and runs the medal ceremonies."

Zena laughed. "That's my Helga, managing the household! I just study. She cooks, cleans, and pays the bills on time."

Krish went on, "The logic gates preserve integrity, prevent decoherence—"

Zena waved him off. "No offense, Krish. I'm sticking with the Olympics. Growing up, I only ate cereals if Mary Lou Retton was on the box. She was a perfect ten, like Lucy."

KJ carried on, "Mubit life is brief, but the races continue. Before she fades, Lucy passes her wins to the rookie mubit entering the chamber."

Krish said, "Continuous muon production ensures uninterrupted entanglement."

"Like passing a baton in a relay race," I said.

"Or streaming video packets to generate a 4K image," Rocko added.

KJ lifted his arm, eyes closed, as if preaching. "Quantum computation lives on. Entangled voxels form both scenes and voices."

Trillions of qubits—entangled, superposed, working together, reminded me of fire ants I once saw in Antigua, stacking into a meter-high tower to escape floodwater. None at the bottom got crushed.

Rocko raised a new question. "All this could create a still scene. How does Petamunra figure out the next millisecond?"

"That's Krish's magic." KJ gestured to the man from Bangalore. "His algorithm writes the next line of the screenplay. It uses another quantum principle: interference—selecting the most probable superposition as the outcome."

Krish cleared his throat. "The algorithm transforms each instruction into a microwave signal and sends it inside the nano fusion reactor. The mubits operate on them and send back their output to the dome, closing the loop."

"The quantum universe is now alive," Nakshi said with a knowing smile.

Zena hardened her voice, imitating Czar Nicholas. "*You know, Chancellor, Russia is blessed with nature's riches*. Lucy Jr., she just did another perfect act."

I smiled back. "You've got a good memory."

"I pay attention. Don't dilly-dally." I wondered if she was hinting at my occasional glances her way.

"Which voxel did she land on?"

Krish looked blank. "Could be the burgundy on the chair. Or Seymour's whiskers."

"I want her shine! Let her be a speck on Nicholas's emerald medal. The hue will carry her legacy."

KJ nodded. "Emerald it is."

"Matches your eyes." Rocko flashed a mischievous smile, leaning toward Zena.

I jumped in before she could respond. "No perfect fidelity can match that."

"Aww, that's sweet." Zena held my arm. Rocko's grin turned devilish. No idea which part of my superposed mind it slipped from, but it did. The best outcome.

Nakshi pressed, "Where do the specialty lenses and the wearables come in?" The quantum universe exists only when someone views it."

Krish said, "A metamaterial nanocoated on the lens fools the brain. Like a green screen, it blocks the real world and replaces it with the holographic one."

"I've seen that in a studio," Zena chimed in. "The weather lady points to maps that aren't there."

"Sounds like a psychotic trip without the drugs," Rocko said.

"I could still see Histo and the novanauts," Nakshi challenged. "They're real."

"Because they wear the wrap," Krish answered. "The device bypasses the subtraction."

The billionaire clapped his hands. "I hope we've convinced you that we are not a smoke-screen operation, and that the basics behind our revolutionary technology have answered your concerns."

I still couldn't ignore the white elephant in the room. Why history and time travel, but not inventing new drugs or discovering a cure for cancer? The questions were draining me.

KJ swung his arms. "In short, we've got workhorse qubits, logical qubits, and quantum gates, all powered by nano-fusion to create a universe delivered to view at every trillion nano-strides. That's Petamunra."

"What does the name mean?" Nakshi asked.

I ventured a guess. "Peta means a thousand trillion, the number of quantum operations each second?"

KJ gave me a thumbs-up.

"I can explain the rest," Zena jumped in. "It's Amun-Ra, the ancient Egyptian deity—the union of Amun, god of life, and Ra, god of the sun."

KJ clapped. "Exactly."

The same markings were etched on the vessel, just like on the dollar bill.

"Now I get it," Nakshi piped up, "Trillions of atomic-sized suns are born in the nano-fusion reactor, where mubits give life to the cognitive holograms."

"Bingo!" The billionaire video game mogul leaned toward Histo. "I knew the committee chose well." He sounded like Magyar.

"Any other questions?" He looked like a pharaoh who had commissioned the Great Pyramid of Giza.

I hesitated, but the urge won. "I have two."

KJ nodded.

"Why use it to reconstruct history? You could double your fortune with Petamunra," I said. "New drugs, discovery of winning financial strategies."

KJ turned somber. "There's more to history than it seems."

I lifted my brows, waiting.

"What good would that be if there was no one left to heal or nothing remained to call it wealth?" He paused and pursed his lips, letting his words sink in.

"Einstein once said he didn't know what weapons would be used in the Third World War, but the Fourth would be fought with sticks and stones. I tend to agree with those who say he was too optimistic. There might not be anyone left to pick up a pebble."

"And you think making history live will prevent that?"

"I don't know if it will. You'll tell me that. What I know is, for Intelligence, war may become its choice. For Wisdom, it will then be necessity."

Watching my teammates puzzle over his words, he raised his brows. "What's your second question?"

"Your hotel in India had to install a new elevator to save you twelve seconds."

"Yes. What about it?"

"The time you've spent with us adds up to hundreds of elevator rides. As a billionaire businessman, how do you rationalize that?"

KJ cracked a smile. "Do you *really* believe I am Kazuo Jawara, dropping in a fancy video chat?"

He paused for my response. Truth was, I did. But I was tongue-tied and couldn't say it.

"I don't mean to disappoint you, my friend." His smile turned wry. "KJ-San hasn't spent a microsecond with you today. I'm his cognitive hologram—humbly bit-based."

One could hear a pin drop inside the Petamunra dome. My mouth hung open, as I stood frozen. Had I been exchanging with an algorithm all this time? Blasian tech billionaire grinned ear to ear, flashing his award-nominated teeth, insured for a million dollars.

"Ladies and Gentlemen, on behalf of the Mubits of Petamunra, I welcome you to the Quantum Universe. Enjoy your stay over the next ten days."

Rectangular patches shimmered around him. Like a reincarnated mummy returning to his tomb, he faded.

11
HOTEL
METROPOLITAN

The novanauts lined up behind me in the library on the second floor.

"Tomorrow is a historic day. I hope everything runs smoothly." Krish couldn't hide his apprehension. His fingers fumbled with an electronic gadget, attaching it to my wearable communicator.

"How will it be different?"

"Mind will meet cognitive fidelity in the Quantum Universe." It was too late at night to press him.

He sent a signal from his phone, held his breath, and focused on the device.

"It's downloading," he exhaled. Once the light turned green, he detached it. "It'll activate at sunrise."

"Doing what?"

He didn't answer, eyes fixed on the rising bar on his iPad screen.

"Done!" He slumped his shoulders and beamed.

"You'll find out, trust me." He leaned back. "Next in line, please!"

I wished my teammates goodnight and dragged my feet to my room.

"Don't forget—breakfast is at eight down the hall," Krish hollered after me.

My room was a nice size and practical, though shiny; unappealing shutters blocked the street view. The dressing area was spacious and stocked with clothing. Too tired to try anything on, I dropped my clothes and sneakers in a laundry bag and left it outside.

I nearly fell asleep brushing my teeth. The exhausting day of highs and lows had finally ended. I rested on the pillow, fighting the adrenaline still coursing through me. Sounds of cars and distant sirens—a New York City hallmark—echoed around me.

Histo and the czar marched in formation; behind them, Rocko and Krish waved. The mover lady stood on the sidelines, checking off names. Last came the pizza slice, thumping a large drum on a cross belt, its two wide pepperoni eyes gleaming. They turned emerald green.

Faces blurred; noises faded.

Squeaky noises woke me up—missing were the usual city sounds. I glanced at the clock; an hour until the meeting. Still half-asleep, I sank into the soft bed, hugging my pillow as sunlight washed over my face.

A horse's neigh jolted me. I sprang from bed and looked out the second-floor window. The bizarre, depressing shutters had vanished, replaced by a street scene, unlike anything I'd seen the day before. The windowpane was plain, slightly wavy glass, its imperfections suggesting it wasn't modern.

Horse-drawn buggies with squeaking wheels rattled along a dusty macadam road. Young buggy drivers in colorful newsboy caps sat high behind pairs of horses pulling enclosed carts of men in black jackets and top hats. A buggy passed with a sign that read "Broadway Line." Solo riders in soft-felt hats trotted beside fast-moving carriages. Pedestrians strolled along the pavement; many seemed to be rushing to work. Women in long dresses wore bonnets, some carrying parasols.

It seemed I'd woken to the nineteenth century. I knew I hadn't, but it felt as if a night train had taken me to the past.

A knock on the door. "This is Krish. Are you awake?"

I opened it.

"I apologize. Plans changed last night after you left. We're starting earlier."

I gestured toward the window. "This doesn't resemble Brooklyn."

"That's because it isn't. It's 1851—Broadway, Manhattan. Video cameras record daily life in the quantum universe, like modern closed-circuit cameras placed around the city. Your windows are coated with a specialty metamaterial, projecting a near-fidelity feed of Petamunra's broadcast. Please dress era-appropriate and proceed to the launch room."

I washed up and scanned the wardrobe. It was organized with starched collars, shirts, pants, jackets, like those I'd seen outside.

I enjoy dressing for occasions. I chose a white shirt with a pinned collar, a burgundy floral puff tie, black tubular pants, a grey-white plaid vest, and a black jacket with a longer skirt.

Checking my reflection in a rusty mirror, the color coordination pleased me. I completed the look with black pointed leather shoes, grabbed a top hat, and hurried to the launch room, eager to compare my outfit with my teammates.

No one was inside. The launchpad seats sat empty. The floor blocks had already lifted the dome, now fully encased in mirrored tiles. Tubes jutted from the crisscrossed ceiling framework, aimed at the back of the tiles like guns, ready to transmit microwaves from the nano-fusion reactor.

One floor tile lit up. Krish's voice came through the speakers, instructing me to step onto it. The block rose like a service elevator to the control room one floor up. Krish was inside. He pressed a button, opening a narrow door and letting me into the dome.

All my teammates were seated around a round dining table. A rear door opened to the kitchen. Nakshi wore a dark green outfit with a brown tie. Rocko had a black jacket like mine. Histo sat alone at a far-right table, still in the same light blue suit and red tie from the day before. I placed my top hat on the hanger and took a seat.

"Good morning. Did everyone sleep well?"

"Like a log." Rocko gave a thumbs-up. "The mattress couldn't be better."

"I wish I could say that." Zena scoffed. "I woke up in the middle of the night to noises from the next room."

She wore a plain straw bonnet, her hair parted down the middle. A light brown silk curtain, stitched around the frame, matched her dress.

Two ribbons dangled from the wired buckram, forming a large bow as she tied them.

Nakshi studied her for a moment. "Krish keeps electronics and spare parts there. Maybe it was that."

"It sounded like footsteps." Zena twitched her cheek. "I couldn't sleep afterward. A serial killer is on the run, you know."

Rocko smirked. "He might come to your room tonight seeking asylum in the quantum universe."

"Will you stop it? You're making me more scared. I'll have a heart attack if someone knocks on my door at night."

"You can knock on mine anytime; I'll be all right." Rocko smiled mischievously.

Zena rolled her eyes, but a teasing glint followed. The verdict wasn't clear; playful attention or resentment of the unabashed flirting, especially with the whole team present.

Her dress, worn over a petticoat, displayed a light orange and white checkered pattern. Dark brown buttons ran from the neck to the waist. I couldn't decide if the garment enhanced her charm or if she made the dress look elegant.

Nakshi pulled back his chair a few inches. "Did you notice anything unusual?"

I glanced around. "The chair is very stiff." I shrugged. "Otherwise, nothing."

Rocko leaned in, "How come you're not falling on your butt?"

"Why should I?"

My chair gave off a subtle glow, but nothing seemed wrong with it.

Nakshi smiled. "They are supposed to be holographic, like everything else. We are inside the quantum universe, remember?"

Zena mused. "It's amazing how fast humans adopt everything."

Nakshi added, "The chairs and tables are carbon composites—light, sturdy, and mapped with voxels. They blend in with the quantum view."

"That's why they glow. That's smart."

"It's also smart that you slept while we prepared the stage," Rocko teased. "You'll unfold them when we're done."

Embarrassed, I apologized. "I misunderstood the timing."

Rocko nudged me, laughing. "I'm kidding. They're lightweight, easy to unfold and carry. I'll help you stow them."

As we spoke, a blonde woman in her fifties stepped out of the kitchen. A light pink bonnet, set over her parted hair, matched her plain, long dress.

"Good morning." She grinned as she approached. "Welcome to the Metropolitan Hotel. My name is Sarah." I greeted her back.

"What would you like to drink? Tea or coffee?"

"Coffee, please, black."

She cheered, "Four out of four—coffee for everyone!" and returned to the kitchen without asking anyone else.

Puzzled, I looked around.

"She took our order before you arrived," Nakshi explained.

"I didn't know the Committee employed support staff."

"They didn't," Nakshi smiled. "She isn't real."

"What do you mean? She just spoke to me."

Rocko shook my forearm. "She's a hologram, like the czar, but she sees us the way we see her. We're no longer incognito."

Zena leaned in, lowering her voice. "She thinks we're real."

I whispered back, "I thought we were."

"No, we're not. We're the aliens from another universe, remember?" She pressed a finger to her lips, then flashed a broad grin as I stared, dumbfounded.

"He needs his coffee first." Everyone chuckled, except Histo.

"I'd say you've already exceeded my daily dose of pranks." More laughter followed, though not from the program director.

Nakshi leaned in. "Histo is incognito."

I took a moment to gather my thoughts. "We're the aliens from another universe, but Sarah doesn't know that. She can't see or feel Histo, which makes him a ghost. That leaves Sarah as the only 'normal' person here, though in reality she's just a hologram, unaware of her own nature."

I paused, letting everyone sit with the thought. "Put yourself in her place, learning all this."

Zena grasped my arm. "What would freak me out most is realizing I wasn't human." She leaned closer and whispered, "Don't mention that to her." Her lavender scent drifted in, a warm sensation enveloping me. The moment felt otherworldly, briefly unsettling my balance.

"I promise I won't," I stammered.

A waiter wheeled in a cart with porcelain pots and matching cups, setting them on the embroidered white tablecloth. Each piece was eye-catching, hand-painted with an open-ended sepia wreath tied at both ends with a dark blue ribbon. The rich coffee aroma tickled my nose.

"Cream or sugar, anyone?" The waiter's voice was too familiar, though we had not seen him before.

"Krish? Is that you?" Nakshi squinted.

"He doesn't hear you," Histo said from his table. "Dummy holograms have limited communication capability. Krish slipped inside one to serve real food."

"How does that work?" Zena narrowed her eyes.

"The voxels touching his body are entangled with optical qubits. As the administrator, he's the only one authorized to do it."

Rocko leaned toward her. "Meet my friend Krish, the body snatcher."

Zena slapped his arm, scowling.

Sarah emerged from the kitchen, smiling. "Sam will serve your food shortly."

"The porcelainware is exquisite, Madame." Nakshi offered a smile. "Are they French or English?"

"Oh no, it's American—from Philadelphia. Tucker Ware." Her voice carried a humble pride. "We're a young nation, catching up with the old country."

"My room has elegant decorations like those in luxury European lodgings." Rocko smiled at her playfully. "I'm impressed."

"I'm glad you liked it." Sarah grinned. "Construction isn't finished yet."

She paused as Sam set down cream and sugar in silver bowls, then went on, "Management opened this small wing on the second floor—ten rooms and a modest kitchen—to gather feedback from select guests like yourselves before finalizing details for the grand opening next year."

I handed my cup to Sam for a refill.

"Our dining room will be magnificent." Sarah drifted away toward the horizon. "The kitchen can serve six hundred guests. Mr. Leland, our boss, is meticulous. He insists on advanced engineering and the finest materials. You should see the massive boilers and the steam engine. Hot water runs from the faucets, even heats the building."

She turned to us, eyes widening. "Isn't that amazing?"

She searched for awe but found none, unaware that she herself was the true marvel of technology, not the hot water circulating through the radiators.

"How many rooms will there be?" Nakshi's voice was soft, his manner polite.

"Five hundred on four floors!" Sarah beamed. "Fashionable stores will fill the entry level, spanning Broadway from Prince to Crosby."

Her voice brimmed with pride. "Did you see the construction? Once opened, the Metropolitan Hotel at 578 Broadway will be New York's largest—a landmark for our young nation."

Sam leaned over to refill Zena's cup. Sarah studied her outfit. "I like your coal scuttle. A perfect day to wear it."

"Thank you," Zena smiled. "I've always struggled with what to wear, so I brought a few bonnets."

Rocko chimed in, "You should've seen her luggage. We had to rent the room next door just to store her outfits."

"Really?" Sarah lifted her brows.

Zena waved him off. "Don't take everything he says too seriously." Then she bent closer to the maître d', her voice low with unease. "Do you know anything about the room beside mine? I heard noises there last night."

Sarah didn't answer. Her steady gaze only deepened Zena's apprehension. Instead, she turned to Rocko. "I hear an accent. Where is it from?"

"Turkey."

"My goodness. Welcome to New York!" Sarah threw up her arms. "Are you from the same town he lived in?" She squinted, searching for the name. "K…Konia? No, I remember now." She clapped her hands. "Kutahia!"

We traded baffled looks. How could anyone in New York know of such a remote place in the mid-nineteenth century? My mind flashed back. Grandpa once drove Mom and me through that small, sleepy Turkish town.

Sarah shut her eyes, forcing her mind to focus. "Let me guess—you're with the frontier team overseeing preparations before the big man arrives in town."

The mystery deepened. No one responded. I peeked at Histo out of the corner of my eye, searching for a clue. He sat quietly, eyes shut.

Rather than inventing a bogus answer, I decided to press the truth.

"I'm afraid we're not. But who is this celebrity coming from Kutahia?"

It was Sarah's turn to be appalled. "Kossuth. Louis Kossuth." Her jaw went slack. "The whole town has been talking about him."

"Of course!" Rocko jumped and smirked at me. "C'mon, how'd you forget the man?"

Zena shot me a glance, her brows knit, and a pang of apprehension ran through me. I was supposed to be the history expert of Team Novanauts.

Sarah said, "The papers have been covering his political views, his struggles in his homeland, and his whereabouts for months." Suddenly, she exclaimed, "Oh! I forgot today's papers. I have a few copies in the kitchen." Sarah set a basket of rolls on the table and hurried off.

Frustrated, I reached for a roll, only to watch my fingers sink through it.

"Stick with Sam's food in the Quantum Café." Rocko flashed a witty smile.

I flinched. Nothing I did seemed right.

Sarah returned with holographic copies of the daily papers. "I have the *Courier*, the *Herald*. Oh, and I forgot, we have a new one, just launched today. Mr. Raymond's paper. There's even an article on Governor Kossuth's departure." She set the papers on the dining table and went back to the kitchen.

Its front cover read:

New York Daily Times.

VOL 1…. NO 1

THURSDAY, SEPTEMBER 18, 1851. PRICE ONE CENT

The masthead typeface looked familiar. The paper ran four pages, each in six columns.

"Oh my gosh, this is history in the making!" Zena exclaimed. The journalism major from Columbia turned to the man at the far end. "You made my day, Histo. Thank you!"

The blond man responded with a subtle smile.

We had awakened in the quantum universe to the day the *New York Times* was founded, destined to become one of the world's most influential newspapers.

Sarah returned from the kitchen, Sam trailing behind with a tray of food.

"You're on the American Plan: johnnycakes, scrambled eggs, and beef sausage." Sarah headed back to the kitchen.

Krish, disguised as Sam, set down the plates and topped off our coffee one last time.

"You're not serving the boss?" Nakshi whispered, nodding toward Histo, who sat apart. Sam stayed silent, wheeling the cart past the director.

Zena swung her arm toward Nakshi. "Of course not. Think about it. She walks in and sees a fork and knife floating midair, sausage vanishing, eggs smashing themselves. I'd freak out—totally."

"The Phantom of the Hotel," Rocko quipped. "The place would shut down before it even opened."

Nakshi leaned in, eyes shifting from the hologram, "I can't believe we're staying at one of New York's most elite spots. Hotel Metropolitan."

As for me, I couldn't shake off the sting of being outshone in history by Rocko, my field of expertise.

"How do you know this guy—Kossuth?"

Rocko shrugged, chewing a piece of sausage. "I have no clue who he is."

12

THE EDITOR

Breakfast was over. The johnnycakes were finger-licking good.

"I'm glad you liked them," Sarah grinned. "My secret is buttermilk."

Zena barely touched hers, absorbed in the *New York Daily Times*. "They must have some secret sauce, too—impressive for a first issue."

"My daughter says it's Mr. Raymond himself. She calls him smart, ambitious, hardworking, and talented."

"What can you tell us about him?"

"He's also our statesman. One of his associates is downstairs talking with our engineers to get an update on the hotel construction. Should I have him come up and meet you?"

"That would be great." Zena smiled.

As she moved to the door, a handsome gentleman in his thirties entered.

"There he is!" Sarah exclaimed. "We were just talking about you." She grinned. "He always stops by. I think he likes my coffee best."

"Who wouldn't?" the man smiled.

"Mr. Voss, meet our distinguished guests visiting from the old country." Sarah gestured to us. "They're from where General Kossuth lived while under asylum granted by the sultan."

This much was clear: Kossuth was a prominent figure. Turks had shielded him from someone.

The young man's eyes widened at our team of four. "My name is Alexander Voss. Call me Alex. I'm an editorial writer and newsman at the *New York Daily Times*."

Sarah had introduced us as visiting Ottoman subjects.

Voss nodded. "Welcome to New York. What brings you here?"

As someone from New Jersey, I was used to being treated as an outsider by the New Yorkers, but this felt different.

"Are you from the Sublime Porte?" He leaned toward me. "Representing the sultan?"

I hesitated, but Rocko jumped in. "We don't represent the Ottoman Empire. We're investigative journalists, writers, and other professionals." I wondered what roles he had in mind for each of us.

"Aha, intellectuals from the Levant," Voss noted. "Any of you work for the *Times*?" He meant the influential British newspaper.

Zena stepped in. "We're not associated with any newspaper."

The tall man was briefly taken aback to see a woman speak in a professional capacity. He removed his top hat and nodded. She returned the gesture with a teasing smile. A spark flickered between them.

Sarah served Voss coffee. After thanking her, he sipped, then rested his hands on his lap.

"Congratulations," I said. "You must be thrilled to see the first issue out."

He tilted his head, then smiled. "I anticipate promising sales by day's end." His eyes slid to rival papers on the table. "Thanks to the noise stirred up by our competitors."

His smile turned sly. "Their attacks actually helped us."

"Who's behind this achievement?" Nakshi asked.

"One intellectual," Voss replied, earnest and quick. "Diligent, stubborn, self-made—Henry Jarvis Raymond. He made it happen." Pride rang in his voice.

"All alone?" Nakshi tugged his lips into a faint smile.

"No success comes from one person. He assembled an exceptional team."

Voss drained his coffee in three sips. Zena craned her neck at the empty cup, drawing the team's smiles. As Sarah refilled it with holographic brew, Voss continued his story.

"Henry spent ten years at the two leading papers—the *New York Tribune* and the *Courier and Enquirer*. He felt it was time to start his own paper. He shared his burning wish with me one day."

Sarah jumped in, "Mr. Voss knows Raymond well."

Alex grinned. "Not only my employer, but also a close friend. I've known Henry for many years. We met at Wesleyan Seminary when we were twelve. His father, a farmer from Lima, New York, of French descent, had modest means."

After finishing his second cup, the writer leaned back in his chair. "Henry's thirst for knowledge is boundless. He started reading at three and gave his first speech at five. Every night, he devoured books in the farmhouse. His father believed in his son's potential so deeply that he mortgaged the farm to pay for college at the University of Vermont."

Voss's narrative captivated everyone, yet Zena most of all. Eyes wide, mouth slightly parted, she was eager not to miss a word. An ambitious, self-disciplined young woman, she was a mix of purity, naivety, and intelligence all wrapped into one. Was her admiration for Raymond—or Voss? I couldn't tell. And why should it matter to me? It shouldn't.

"Henry Clay noticed him at a Vermont commencement." Alex paused as Sarah reached from the kitchen to refill his cup for the third time. "You may not know Clay. He's the former Speaker of the House, a notable statesman from Kentucky."

He sipped. "Your coffee keeps improving." He smiled at Sarah. I wondered how Krish's algorithm distinguished between brews. Sarah blushed at the compliment and sat beside Histo.

A hologram alive. A ghost in flesh. Bizarre, to say the least, though not in the quantum universe.

Alex went on. "The esteemed politician stayed alert with his snuff box through dull speeches, until Henry Jarvis Raymond took the stage."

Alex Voss leaned forward and drew us in with each word. "Clay told those around him to watch out for this young man. He'd make his mark."

Nakshi broke in. "I recall the late boxing champion Muhammad Ali, originally Cassius Clay, was from Kentucky. Was he related to Henry Clay?"

Histo called out. "Krish, freeze it!"

Alexander Voss and Sarah instantly turned into mannequins.

Histo approached our table and spoke softly. "You can't mention people not yet born."

Nakshi pursed his lips. "I forgot. I'm sorry. What now?"

"We can recover, but don't make it a habit. Be cautious. Cognitive holograms are as sharp as humans, with better memories. The knowledge they gain shapes how they interact."

Rocko quipped, "They must be related to my ex. She never forgot a thing."

Zena fixed her eyes on Voss, as if pulled toward the frozen man. "If they learn their future—which is our past—they might change their fate."

Did she fantasize about binding hers with his?

"Or corrupt history," Histo added. "In the quantum universe, history must stay factual. A corrupted database defeats the purpose."

Rocko turned to him. "Remind us of its purpose."

I jumped in before Histo could answer. "To preserve and protect human history. Not rewrite it."

Zena rolled her eyes. "That reminder again. Like a broken record. No verbal accounts are allowed in Histo's exclusive history club." Her frustration surfaced again, for reasons she kept to herself.

Squinting, she deepened her voice. "I'm Madame Zena, your Moldavian clairvoyant. I see the future. In ten years, civil war will shake up America."

She widened her eyes. "Hey, here's a thought. We could make big bucks reading fortunes. Can we wire the earnings back to real time?"

Histo, unamused, didn't flinch.

Zena pursed her lips. "I need to pay off my student loans."

I joined the banter. "If we don't behave, Histo will ship us back to prehistoric times and throw away the keys."

"Breakfast for dinosaurs," Rocko said, amused.

I chimed in, "That would be a real-life *Jumanji* experience. I loved that movie."

"Done. It's erased. It never happened." Krish's voice came through the speakers. "We're ready to roll."

"Before we resume—" Histo raised his hand. "Nakshi's point stands. The late Muhammad Ali was born Cassius Clay and was indeed related to Henry Clay. The Clay family was wealthy and owned many slaves."

Zena raised her notepad. "May I do the interview with Alexander Voss?"

"Of course." Histo's voice softened.

Zena beamed and reminded us. "I'm majoring in journalism."

Krish's voice rang out, "Three, two, one, action!"

Voss took another sip from his third cup.

"Henry worked with two prominent editors. In 1840, he joined the *Tribune* under Horace Greeley, helping it become a leading newspaper. Three years later, he moved to General James Webb's *Courier and Enquirer*, where he stayed until 1850."

Zena leaned forward. "I have a few questions, if that's all right."

Alexander offered a polite smile, glancing at her notepad. "I'm not accustomed to speaking with a female reporter, but please—continue."

Ignoring Alex's demeanor, Zena proceeded, "What prompted Mr. Raymond to leave the *Tribune*?

"Excessive hours and inadequate pay."

"And what led him to depart from the *Courier and Enquirer*?"

Alex Voss sighed. "Raymond and General Webb aimed to pursue politics through the Whig Party. Henry advanced quickly, eventually becoming Speaker of the New York Legislature, but the Whigs turned down the *Courier*'s chief. Henry's refusal to support him caused a personal rift."

"Why didn't he back his boss? Was it personal rivalry?"

Voss offered a faint smile. "Partly. But politics, too. Raymond supports abolition. The general opposes it."

"That's a significant divide for a daily paper." Zena's voice was sharp.

"Indeed, ma'am. Slavery has become a pivotal issue in American politics, dividing even families. When Raymond traveled to Europe this summer for medical treatment, Webb took it as a resignation."

Zena shot a quick follow-up. "What makes Mr. Raymond think New York needs a new paper?"

Voss pressed his lips sideways, thinking. "Americans read many papers, and with immigration nearly doubling the population in the last decade, demand for affordable dailies is growing. Existing papers aren't meeting it."

"What's lacking?"

"In 1843, low-cost papers replaced the old sixpenny editions. Today, three dominate: The *Herald, Courier and Enquirer*, and the *Tribune*. The *Herald* is pro-slavery, and its editor, Bennett, is self-serving. After Raymond left, the *Tribune* swung toward radical Fourierist socialism."

"What's that?"

"You know—communal living, shared wealth. Socialistic stuff."

"As un-American as it gets," Nakshi scoffed.

"That's right," Alex said, spreading his hands. "Readers are stuck between a rock and a hard place—one paper pushing socialist ideology, the other tainted by the unpleasantness of slavery. This town needs a fresh voice."

"Is Henry Jarvis Raymond the right fit?" Zena asked, not looking up from her notes.

"The investors think so. He's one of the most respected journalists in America. He excelled at both the *Tribune* and the *Courier*. Who better understands the competition than the man who once ran it?" Voss chuckled.

"What is the vision of the *New York Daily Times*?"

"To be the best and the cheapest daily family newspaper in the United States."

"What will set it apart?"

Nakshi leaned in, murmuring. "She leaves no stone unturned."

I nodded. Zena moved smoothly from one question to the next, showing why she was the most skilled among us to conduct interviews inside history.

The editorial writer raised three fingers. "Pure in tone, reasonable in price, and prompt in collecting the news." He gulped his third cup, then covered it to stop Sarah from refilling. Extending his other arm, palm open, he declared,

"New York has long been ready to embrace such a journal."

Zena paused, pen hovering. "Three P's—Pure, Price, and Prompt." Her eyes narrowed. "Could you elaborate on each?"

Caught off guard by her astuteness, Voss rubbed his chin. "Three P's. I like that. I'll keep that in mind."

Rocko leaned over. "Three B's: Bold, Beauty, and Brains. She's got them all."

This wasn't the setting to mix her looks with her sharpness. Zena twitched, pretending not to hear his flirtation.

Voss glanced between them, then fixed on me, as if he'd read all our minds. It was eerie. Were these holograms more than we were told?

Voss resumed. "Let's start with promptness. Eight years ago, before telegrams, reporters went to Boston to hear the Secretary of State, Daniel Webster. Henry Raymond, just twenty-three, covered it for the *Tribune*. While others partied on the way back, he worked in his cabin, equipped with a small printing office. By the time the ship reached New York before dawn, his transcript was ready for readers, crowning the *Tribune* the news king and proving his genius."

Rocko applauded. "That's ambition, creativity, and competitiveness." Nakshi and I joined in.

"How prompt can you be in bringing reliable news from Europe?" Zena challenged, ignoring the buzz.

"We'll be the first to access the news. We've placed correspondents at all the key junctures across the continent."

News from Europe reached Boston in five days if the voyage from Southampton went smoothly. Getting it to New York's presses took another day. By then, readers were seeing news at least a week old, not counting delays from continental Europe.

"Define 'affordable' for a daily paper?" That was the next "P." Price.

"One cent an issue," he answered swiftly. "Few sell at that price."

"How do you make money selling at one cent?"

"Advertisements and advance payments—that's the formula. Subscriptions cover the cost."

"What do you mean by 'pure in tone'?" Zena moved to the final point.

The hologram reached for his cup, then stopped, recalling he'd already had his daily quota. Fascinating. Like a human, I mused.

He raised his right hand. "The *Times* will be *conservative*." He stressed the word. "It shall best promote needful *reform*—mark that down."

He looked as if he expected she would publish the interview soon.

"Personal, social, and political improvement will rely on Christianity and republicanism. We will pursue the advancement of one and preservation of the other."

He paused, giving us time to absorb the keywords.

"We are dedicated to the Union and the Constitution, committed to the rule of law, and hold personal and civil liberties in the highest regard. We aim to ease—not incite—agitation, and to promote reason over prejudice."

He turned to Zena. "Did you get all that?" She lifted her right hand without looking up, still jotting with her left.

"Conservation and reform—conflicting paths. How can you uphold both?" Zena pressed.

Voss's voice brimmed with fervor. "Look, we Americans are conservative, yet rational. We never close ourselves to sensible changes that enhance our lives and liberties. Reform is welcome, revolutions are not."

Growing up in a household with a conservative father and a progressive mother, I connected with his words.

Voss pressed on, "We neither endorse Horace Greeley's Socialist Association nor the antiquated pro-slavery views of Bennett and Webb, who do not understand the evolution of society. As Thomas Jefferson noted, '*In matters of style, swim with the current; in matters of principle, stand like a rock.*'"

I was curious how Raymond managed the venture side of things.

I turned to Zena. "May I ask a question?"

"Certainly."

"Was there a eureka moment during fundraising?"

Voss clapped, laughing. "My favorite story. Raymond and his banker friend George Jones were on a ship when the lake froze. Everyone disembarked. The two crossed the ice for a few miles, and by the time they reached shore, George was sold on the idea."

He gestured to the first issue. "The rest is history."

It wasn't. It was only the beginning of a journey that would become a cornerstone of American journalism, one of the nation's premier media outlets, and ultimately a global powerhouse. Holding that back from Alexander Voss took effort.

Nakshi smiled. "Launching a start-up is like walking on ice."

"Sometimes, literally." Rocko leaned in, drawing a chuckle from Voss.

"How does the investment structure work?" I pressed.

"He and Jones convinced other bankers. Eight partners formed Raymond and Jones Inc. George and his partner Wesley put up most of the capital; Henry became editor."

Voss paused to sip, then continued. "The company issued ninety shares—seventy to the bankers, twenty to Raymond."

"That must've been a considerable sum. How did Raymond handle it?"

"Investors funded his shares. They trust his leadership."

"Why would bankers invest in such a risky business?" Nakshi arched a brow.

I agreed. The model sounded like modern Silicon Valley, except banks, not venture capitalists, funded the high-risk start-ups.

"Banking is losing appeal," Voss explained, "New York will soon regulate the industry. Bankers must diversify. Newspaper readership is expanding. Despite its flaws, the *Tribune* still turned a strong profit last year. Advertising dollars follow circulation."

His words echoed forward in time. A century and a half later, online readership and social media would pull the same dollars. Market shifts always redirect the flow of money. In the mid-nineteenth century, the stars were aligned for Henry Jarvis Raymond.

Zena resumed the interview. "Does he have people skills? Has he built a strong team besides you?" Alex beamed. She knew how to stroke a man's ego—hologram or in flesh.

"People in the industry not only trust Raymond, they like him. Once he announced the *Times*, several *Tribune* employees quit to join, including three editors and a dozen printers. Horace threatened to cut off distributors if they sold our paper, but none budged."

"What topics will the paper address?"

"Significant and reliable news from across the country and Europe, legislative updates, a strong focus on New York, national political trends, plus editorials and the arts."

"Where are you located?"

"113 Nassau Street. We're still in a mess. Once settled, visit us. The Turkish Empire spans a vast geography and is often in the news. We need talented people from every major region. You're sharp with shorthand and ask pointed questions. We lack female reporters."

Zena beamed. "I'm flattered. My colleagues and I would be delighted to visit." She shot a glance at Histo. No objection.

Alexander Voss thanked Sarah for the coffee, grabbed his top hat, and rose. We followed him toward the exit.

"You mentioned Turkey has been in the news. What's the story?" Nakshi asked.

The tall man halted and took a deep breath. "One word—Kossuth. It's the story of the year." His gaze drifted. "Turkey's courageous Mohammedan Sultan Abdulmejid has given the civilized Christian world a lesson in freedom." The curiosity inside the Petamunra dome deepened.

Rocko pointed to the journal on the table. "His name is in your paper."

"Another keen observer," Voss winked. "We needed standout stories in the first issue. The sultan's release of the Hungarian freedom champion was one. More will follow on him."

"Why is Kossuth significant to Americans?" Zena pressed, hoping to squeeze in one more answer before he left.

"I'd love to stay, but I must go. We'll publish an editorial a few days before his arrival."

"When will that be?"

"Probably early December. He left Turkey on the *Mississippi* to sail to Great Britain—that's all we know."

The gathering by the exit turned into a spontaneous press conference, like reporters tossing last-minute questions at a disembarking VIP.

"When can we see you again?" Zena fixed her gaze on the newsman.

Voss squinted, thinking. "The press is organizing a banquet in Governor Kossuth's honor this December. Henry is one of the hosts. I'll have him invite you as his guest." He smiled. "I'm on the event committee. I'll reserve a table for you."

"That sounds wonderful." Zena's eyes widened. "Perhaps we could meet with the governor."

Alex chuckled at the suggestion. "I can't promise that. Everyone will be lining up just to exchange a word with him. He's the Nation's Guest, like Lafayette was. The first since the Marquis."

That comparison elevated Kossuth's stature in my mind. The French aristocrat had become a combat leader and George Washington's most loyal companion during the Revolutionary War. Mom's family regarded him as a founding father.

Alex turned to Zena. "When and where will you publish this interview?"

Zena didn't expect a question from him. She glanced around but found no help. "In a future book. Maybe?"

Alexander Voss studied her for a moment, then tipped his hat with a playful smile and left. He didn't seem to like her answer.

Krish entered the room, beaming. Histo greeted him with rare warmth.

"Team Novanauts, you did well." Histo's words were crisp yet soothing. "This was the first true exchange between cognitive kinds in the quantum universe. The day is already a success."

"A selfie would've been nice for my social media pages," Rocko quipped.

Histo glanced at him, not amused. "We have two options this afternoon. A city promenade, or an excursion to greet Kossuth in England."

Rocko patted his stomach. "I am craving scones."

Zena raised her brow. "If we're going, secure us an interview with him, please."

Histo didn't answer. "Be at the launchpad after lunch." He stepped out, crossing paths with Sarah rushing from the kitchen.

"I heard someone say scones. I can make some."

"Thank you, Sarah. Maybe next time."

13

THE SOUTHAMPTON STAR

I folded the carbon composite chairs and table. They were light and sturdy, easy to move. Upstairs, a cozy dining room opened beside a small kitchen. It mirrored the Petamunra dome's breakfast room, or more precisely, the dome had copied it. A quantum cut-and-paste job, except for the heavy wooden table and chairs from Lata's used furniture store next door.

Rocko and Nakshi were at a game of backgammon.

"You're cheating!" Rocko threw up his arms.

Nakshi locked a six-point prime. "You must learn how to roll the dice," Krish grinned as he watched the chilling novanauts. Zena had slipped off to the library at the far end of the hall to prepare for her interview.

I went to check if she needed support. The library was cozy, its walls lined with books, mostly history and technology. Several desktops were linked to an intranet—not the internet—yet stocked with digital books, documents, and periodicals.

I found Zena was absorbed in a screen, taking notes.

"How's it coming along?"

Without looking up, she muttered, "Studying the Magyar," brushing off small talk. The clatter of backgammon checkers carried from down the hall, but it didn't seem to bother her.

In her bonnet and fluffy skirt, she looked like she'd stepped out of Eakins *Reading*—a knowledge-hungry woman lost in pages, though here it was a glowing screen.

She seemed in control. As I turned to leave, she said, "I appreciate you asking my permission to question Voss, though you didn't have to. You're a kind man."

A *kind man*. I liked that. Warmth spread through me. I decided not to leave and pulled a chair over. A few books lay spread across the table.

"I checked those out. Sometimes I can't fall asleep right away. Reading helps."

I skimmed through the pages. They were about Cherkess and Circassian history. One nonfiction volume was dense and well-researched.

"This will put you to sleep. Heavy stuff."

"Depends on the page. Some's eerie enough to keep you up all night. I have my copy at home. I just wanted to point out some details to Histo."

"You two seem at odds. What's the matter?"

She shrugged, leaned toward the screen, and jotted down notes. I felt stupid for asking a nosy question. I turned more pages.

"I woke up tired this morning," she said at last. "Must have skipped sleep phases. The noises next door bothered me."

"Maybe soothing music will help. I can ask Histo to bring power to your room and—"

She cut me off. "I'm not asking you to solve my problem. Just sharing it."

I didn't know what to say, so I stayed quiet.

"Never mind," she sighed. "It's a Mars and Venus thing. No one can change that."

I didn't understand what she meant and wanted to ask, but she was already back at her notes. I lowered my head onto the stack of books to rest my eyes. Before long, I dozed off.

A cacophony jolted me awake. The game had ended down the hall. Roars of laughter followed the cascading rattle of the checkers. I pictured Nakshi folding the board and tucking it under Rocko's arm, the mark of a crushing win. A scene I knew well, usually it was me carrying, rarely my cousin.

Krish entered the library, grinning. "We need to be at the launchpad in twenty minutes. Histo is a stickler for punctuality."

"He must hate procrastinators," I said. "I already scored one against him this morning."

"Boss never hates, only disapproves or dislikes." He headed downstairs to prep for launch.

"Don't forget wool," he called back. "Great Britain is chilly in late October."

The ride across the Atlantic was a thrill, compressed into a minute and colored by Zena's screams and Rocko's laughter. A cold wind hit me before the lights flickered on, carrying the scent of the ocean. The belts unlatched, the seats vanished, and we rose. Around us, a few dozen people cheered, unaware of our arrival.

Standing outdoors on a beach, inhaling the ocean breeze inside a flea shop. A sensation that defied telling.

The weather warning was spot on. We bundled into thick cloaks, except Histo, who showed no discomfort in his light blue suit.

"He's weird." Zena gestured at him, shivering as the damp cold cut like a knife.

In our costumes and top hats, Rocko and I stood out amid the mostly working-class crowd. Proud of his roots, Nakshi wore a fez that bobbed like a red buoy in a sea of flat caps.

Rocko tightened his blanket. "The Brits get around in short sleeves in winter. Their holograms are no different."

Histo led us to the protocol stand, pushing through the dummies. I stayed behind Nakshi and Rocko, watching parts of their torsos vanish inside holograms—first a side, then a shoulder—before reappearing. It felt like a thrill at Coney Island.

We pressed on until tall policemen blocked our way to the bleachers. Their dark blue wool tunics fit snug. Polished silver insignias gleamed on their chests.

Krish's triumphant voice echoed through the loudspeakers. "The new patch works. I'm locking it. Bear with me."

Rocko smirked. "No longer will body parts float around? That'll be boring."

"It's brutal." Zena shivered even under the thick cloak. "Does it have to be this cold?"

"Adjust the haptics, Krish," Histo called. The dome warmed, and the damp breeze eased in an instant.

The commotion grew louder. The holograms chanted the same slogans.

"Three groans for the tyrants!"

"The star of freedom!"

Histo pointed at the crowd. "They are just dummies. They only know a few words and don't respond."

A barefoot teenage lookout in overalls climbed a tower, as if it were a crow's nest, scanning the horizon for the long-awaited steam frigate. He stood on a wooden sign that read:

Southampton: Gateway to the World

Krish gave us a heads-up through the speaker. "I'll freeze the system to run a check on the patch."

The commotion stopped. The dummies stood motionless.

Nakshi leaned toward Zena. "While we wait, tell us what you've learned."

She gathered her thoughts. "1848 was a pivotal year in Europe, the 'Spring of Nations.' The working and middle classes demanded freedom of religion and the press, as well as universal male suffrage, fueled by nationalism and liberalism. The movement began in Italy and spread across the continent. Kossuth rose as Hungary's national leader and became Europe's symbol for freedom."

Nakshi asked, "Freedom from what?"

"Like Italy, Hungary was part of the Austrian Empire but governed as a separate kingdom."

Histo cut in, "Say 'is,' not 'was.' Today is October 23, 1851. Reset your mental calendars."

"Sorry, flipping centuries in a day can be confusing, but I'll try. The Austrian Emperor, Ferdinand I, is also Ferdinand V, King of Hungary, governing that country."

"Wait," Rocko said, "the same guy, same name, takes on a different number once he crosses the Danube from Vienna?"

"I know, it's confusing, but that's correct. Austria and Hungary have a complicated relationship."

"Cross the border, one jumps to five. That's a hell of a quantum leap, no pun intended." Rocko chuckled.

His remark didn't amuse Zena. "The teenage Franz Joseph took the Habsburg crown after Ferdinand abdicated. The Hungarian Parliament—the Diet—refused to recognize his authority and wouldn't support Austria against Italy's independence movement. Vienna panicked."

Nakshi smiled knowingly. "Empires don't like disobedience."

Zena surprised me again—first with technology, now with geopolitics and history. With no prior expertise, she proved a quick study—a priceless gift for a journalist.

"Two years ago, in 1849, Hungary's Diet declared full independence from Austria. Russia acted to support its Habsburg friend and ultimately crushed the Hungarian revolution."

Rocko creased his brow. "What's in it for Russia?"

Zena looked to me.

I stepped in. "To protect the Metternich order of 1815, the Concert of Europe."

Nakshi narrowed his eyes. "What was that again?"

"The principle of legitimacy." My knowledge came from Dad's notes. "Let empires rule their spheres. Suppress nationalist movements."

Zena lifted her hand. "The imperial camaraderie. Now I recall. Czar Nicholas told Ambassador Seymour, 'Turkey should not be a refuge for revolutionaries.' He even mentioned Kossuth by name."

I must have missed that, but Zena's radar had caught it.

Nakshi's mouth curled. "So, Hungary waits another spring. What role has Kossuth played in all this so far?"

"Lajos Kossuth came from a poor yet aristocratic Protestant Hungarian family. He began his career as a lawyer and journalist, gaining prominence through his powerful writing and speeches. He even spent time in jail for his activism supporting Hungarian independence from Austria. His growing popularity won him election to the Diet. He eventually became the finance minister in Hungary's first independent government."

Rocko tugged his lips sideways. "When did you learn all this? This morning, you didn't know a thing about this guy."

Nakshi cracked a smile. "When I was teaching you backgammon, she was studying history. You flunked both."

Histo lifted a hand before Rocko could respond. "Go on, Zena."

"Independent Hungary named Lajos Kossuth Governor-President. After Russian forces crushed the revolution, he fled into exile in the Ottoman Empire."

Histo stepped in. "That brings us to today." He nodded subtly in appreciation of Zena. "After two years in exile on Turkish soil, he's about to reach England's shores en route to America."

"Long live the revolution!" a hologram shouted, startling everyone. The pier roared to life.

Krish's voice crackled. "System secure. You can bump into anyone you want."

A well-dressed man stepped from behind the barracks. His vibrant eyes cut through the vacant, glassy stares. He was no dummy.

"Do you know this guy?" I leaned toward Zena.

She shot me a sly glance. "My ex-boyfriend from my old quantum days."

That was a dumb question. I puffed.

She waved back at him, then grinned at the towering officer to let us through. Once we reached him, the well-dressed man tipped his hat. "Miss Zena and her company, I presume?"

Zena nodded and introduced us.

The young man chimed in, "I'm Zgismond Wakey, the governor's aide-de-camp. Alexander Voss told me to be on the lookout for you."

Zena's mouth fell open. "He did that?" The realization unsettled me. The cognitive holograms could communicate with each other, bypassing Krish, the system administrator.

Wakey led us to the VIP bleachers, introducing Mayor Andrews of Southampton and Mr. Croskey, the American Consul.

The mayor gestured to Nakshi's fez. "The British press praises your country's bravery in standing up to intimidation by Austria and its ally, Russia."

Consul Croskey leaned in. "Are you all from Constantinople?"

Rocko squared his shoulders. "We're all Americans, arrived from New York to greet Governor Kossuth."

Zena asked the mayor. "Why is Lajos Kossuth coming to England?"

The two men exchanged glances—one pressed his lips, the other swallowed.

"I'm a journalist." Zena offered a nervous smile. The mayor gave her a once-over. Her smile faded.

The silence stretched. I stepped in. "Miss Zena is our chief editor. The rest of us report to her."

Croskey lifted his brows; Andrews furrowed his. As the two statesmen stared at her, Zena bit her lip, waiting.

Wakey leaned toward the mayor. "Sir, she's been recognized in New York for her work."

With a tilt of her head, Zena responded, "Reports say the dissident crisis cost the sultan eighty million piastres—about one and a half million US dollars."

That would be sixty million in today's money.

The mayor finally answered. "From the day Turkey accepted Kossuth until his release, Her Majesty's Government supported the sultan admirably."

"We'd love to meet the Magyar nation's illustrious hero for an interview." Zena flashed a smile.

Mayor Andrews scowled. "Excuse me, I'm needed at the pier." He walked off, murmuring, "The world is changing too fast for me."

Wakey whispered to Zena, "I'll see if I can arrange it while we're in Winchester."

He followed the mayor, stepping down on the protocol path to take on his duties.

Zena turned to the American consul, whose lips were clamped shut. "Sir, New Yorkers are eager to welcome Governor Kossuth. What insights can you share about America's fascination?" She locked eyes with him, and we backed her with silent stares.

A twitch tugged Croskey's cheeks, shifting his sideburns. The consul finally cleared his throat. "Americans are freedom lovers."

Histo pointed to a phosphorescent bench nearby. "It's the stool. Krish voxel-wrapped it."

She propped her boot on the bench, using her knee as a desk, and took notes. The gesture irked the diplomat. His eyes dropped to her stylish boots peeking out from under her skirt, then darted around searching for an escape, but there was none. I couldn't tell if he feared yielding to a female reporter or if he was simply struggling with a new reality.

The consul drew a breath. "Kossuth believes in republicanism, though not the radical kind, and is firmly opposed to despotism. Americans honor those who fight for the values our republic stands for."

Zena pressed. "Does the US government share the public's view?"

The American statesman gave a thoughtful pause before answering. "The US Senate invited Governor Kossuth as the Nation's Guest. President Fillmore sent the Navy's flagship steamer, the *Mississippi*, to bring Mr. Kossuth and fifty dissidents to the United States."

Zena read from her notepad. "Mostly Hungarians with a few Poles. The sultan treated them as guests for nearly a year. How would you describe Turkey's stance on this?"

"His Majesty Sultan Abdulmejid showed remarkable resolve. When Austria demanded reparations and the Russian Czar joined in, he didn't blink. He released Governor Kossuth and his comrades on the day he had promised, shouldering all the pressure the Sublime Court had faced."

Beads of sweat formed on Zena's temple. Given the mild weather, it couldn't be the heat. If it were anxiety—something I knew all too well— she masked it expertly. If anything, she came across as overconfident.

From behind Croskey, a man in his late twenties spoke. "I can explain why he's coming to England first." Zena smiled faintly, pleased at last to hear an answer to her lingering question.

The young man had wavy light brown hair and hardly any facial hair. He took a step down to level with us.

"On the day he left Turkey, Austria demanded his agreement never to return to Europe—right before he boarded. Good thing, the British Ambassador was present at his farewell. He objected, saying the governor is a free man, and like any other free man, he may go wherever he chooses."

"That's a bold one." Zena jerked her head.

"Governor Kossuth had already received a standing invitation to Great Britain. He accepted it on the spot and boarded the *Mississippi*."

"How do you know all this?"

"I was there."

"Who are you?"

"My name's Alan. I'm from Chicago. I write for hire for American newspapers, mostly the Tribune." That put him on the left of the political spectrum.

"When Captain Long fired the cannons of the mighty *Mississippi* to salute the sultan, no one missed it—Mussulman, Jew, Gentile."

Rocko cut in. "So, England became a stopover on the way to America? I can't wait to see the steamboat."

"Unfortunately, you won't." Alan gave a dry laugh. "Kossuth will arrive on a British frigate, the *Madrid*."

"Now I'm really confused." Zena shook her head.

"You oughta be," a middle-aged man called out from nearby. He wore a rough cowhide hat. "'Cause the Magyar's downright ungovernable. Acts like a firebrand."

Mr. Croskey stepped in to introduce the two men. "Sam and his younger brother, Tod—the Glasgow brothers—suppliers for the US Navy out of Georgia."

"Do you know Governor Kossuth?" Nakshi leaned in.

Tod eyed Nakshi's fez, comparing its flat top against his brother's wide-brimmed hat. "No, but we were on the *Mississippi*. We boarded the steamer in Egypt."

Sam broke in with a thick Southern drawl, "Those flairs ain't mine. They're Captain Long's. And he wasn't the only one. I heard the Navy commander hisself say worse. Said the devil done crawled up inside that gentleman, Kossuth." He let out a loud laugh.

"We got off in Marseilles." Tod Glasgow's cheek twitched. "Kossuth wanted to as well. He told Captain Long he'd disembark with his family and catch up with the *Mississippi* in Gibraltar." Tod's accent could've fooled me for a New Englander.

"Came outta nowhere, like a thunderclap on a clear day! Can ya believe that?" his brother added.

"To do what?" Zena squinted.

"He'd cross France, give speeches, then move on to England and do the same. After that, he'd sail to Gibraltar to meet the *Mississippi*," Tod said. "Captain Long told us the American Minister in Constantinople warned him Kossuth would jump ship anywhere to reignite his dead revolution, even at the cost of American neutrality."

"Reckon that prophecy came true." Sam chuckled. "Good thing the French turned him away."

"Reason they gave?"

Tod jumped in. "Officially? Passport issues. But everyone knew it was political."

Sam wagged his finger. "I reckon they didn't want no trouble brewin', damn socialist bunch hollerin'." He sputtered, "My brother here, he's smarter'n me. Got some fancy schoolin' up in Boston. He knows them kinds. They've got a whole bunch up there."

Zena sealed her lips, jerking her head back. Not satisfied with what she'd heard, she turned to the American Consul. "Why would the French reject him, sir?"

Croskey pulled his lips, thinking. "The reasons aren't clear. The French President might've wished to avoid upsetting the apple cart with the Russians and Austrians."

I doubted both explanations. Louis Napoleon, France's authoritarian president, had no reason to welcome a charismatic revolutionary like Kossuth, who could rouse public passions in his country. Within two months, he would secure an easy election victory and a year later dissolve the republic in a coup, declaring France's Second Empire. No one could have foreseen his true intentions.

Alan stepped in, his voice sharp. "Gentlemen, I disagree with you and the way you speak about the governor. He fights for the same freedoms and values we stand for. The best orator—dead, alive, or yet to be born."

"Yeah, sure, I heard your boss Horace Greeley run his mouth like that," Sam said, drawling. "He's one o' them Red Republicans."

"Kossuth is not," Alan pushed back. "You skipped mentioning the crowds gathered to greet him onshore. Of course, he'll give speeches everywhere he goes. Most of Europe is under oppression. He's a blessing. A gifted messenger. A disciple of freedom. The kind all tyrants fear, anywhere."

"Them bunch know not what freedom is." Sam brushed it off.

Tod's shoulder hitched. The hologram's involuntary tics didn't stop him from arguing. "If you'd seen the scene those Magyars caused on the ship, and heard their remarks, you'd have thought twice before being so sure about what you just said."

Sam mimicked an off-key Hungarian accent. "Ve escaped vun prison and govd't caught in anuzzer!" Switching back to his drawl, he added, "Ain't seen no blessin' in runnin' your mouth like that under a free flag. Pure disrespect, that's what it is."

Tod expanded on their stance. "My brother and I do business at all the major ports. We respect the laws of the land we're in. They ought to learn that and treat folks with courtesy."

Alan shook his head. "I've seen those men. Some may be rough, even vulgar, but they're warriors, willing to die for liberty. We ought to think about that and learn to show some respect. It's a disgrace that our government attaché in France called Kossuth a humbug and a demagogue!"

Tod's lips quivered. "Our country sent him its flagship. We bestowed upon him the nation's highest honor. Then, aboard, His Highness decides to take a little excursion through France, visit England, and tells Captain Long to wait in Gibraltar until he's done doin' business. What do you call this man?"

"Kossuth and his compatriots are heroes," Alan jabbed his finger in the air. "That's who they are. We expect Kossuth to be profoundly grateful for traveling aboard one of our finest ships, but can we not also understand his gratitude for the greater service he received from England?"

Caught in the midst of a conversational duel among three holograms—each possessing perfect cognitive fidelity, the first in history, in any universe—I watched them, breathless.

Rocko waved his arms, hoping to ease the tension. He seemed to forget they were only images. "The people of Marseille must've been disappointed not to hear from their hero passing through."

Tod wagged his finger. "The Reds may have been, but not everyone shared their frustration. The locals respect the US Consul in Marseille. He was furious when he learned Kossuth had managed to pen an article for the socialist paper, *Le Peuple*, saying, 'France's oppressive leader keeps me from embracing the people of Marseille.'"

Sam sputtered, his voice laced with passion. "He done all that while aboard our grand vessel, flutterin' our good ol' star-spangled banner, anchored in that there French port."

Alan took over. "Why aren't you talking about the hundreds of boats that surrounded the *Mississippi*, even at night, with people cheering, 'Vive Kossuth!' 'Vive les États Unis!' Does that sound disgraceful to the French commoner?"

He turned to us like a passionate lawyer addressing the jury. "Captain Long begged Kossuth to stay in his room until the crew finished charging the ship's banks with coal and not step outside to salute those men. To me, that's a shame."

Sam narrowed his eyes. "If he weren't under our protection, that'd be his own damn business. But like Captain Long said, if this whole mess had stirred up more, it could've compromised the American flag."

Tod spread his arms. "And what does Kossuth say to the captain? 'This vessel is a floating prison.'"

"Well, we don't know if he actually said that," Consul Croskey cut in. Until then, he had stayed out of the quarrel.

The diplomat turned to Zena. "Ma'am, this is what you should report. When the *Mississippi* reached Gibraltar, Kossuth honored Captain Long and thanked him. He decided to disembark and proceed to England before continuing to the United States. His compatriots stayed on board for New York." He paused, watching Zena note his every word. "He and his family boarded a British frigate and would soon be arriving in Southampton."

Consul Croskey dismissed the debate that was going nowhere, hoping Zena would publish his account to clear the air for a confused American public.

Alan, still smarting from the brothers' jabs, murmured to himself. "Without England's powerful intervention, Turkey couldn't have kept Kossuth alive. Why should Americans condemn a man for visiting the country that secured his freedom, just to show his gratitude?"

The barefoot youngster in the makeshift crow's nest waved his straw hat, catching everyone's attention. He hollered, "He's here!" The sun had just set, but the sky still burned scarlet.

Down at the pier, Mayor Andrews stepped onto a small wooden staircase, greeting constituents and waving his brown top hat. A mix of applause and boos erupted from the crowd. Constables formed a semicircle around him for protection.

Consul Croskey rose and tipped his hat to Zena. "My lady, gentlemen, enjoy the rest of your stay in England." He descended the platform steps to join the mayor.

A massive uproar erupted as the passengers aboard the *Madrid* came into view. Women waved handkerchiefs; men lifted brimmed hats. Young and old, workers and bourgeois, all seemed united, as if the entire nation had come together to welcome the savior they had awaited all their lives.

A bearded man appeared at the stern, waving his hat beneath the fluttering white ensign. The crowd roared.

"That's him." Zena pointed to the ship, her eyes shimmering. "He's right there." The thunderous reception mesmerized us.

"Do you hear the chants?" Alan shouted at the Glasgow brothers, then rushed toward the dock to join the surging crowd.

"Long live Kossuth!" The noise was deafening.

The two brothers stood quietly behind the bleachers, watching the reception, their lips curled in a sneer. Tod's jaw jerked sideways.

Zena leaned toward Histo. "Whose account is true?"

He locked eyes with her. "The truth is the accounts." He smiled faintly, reminding us of our task—to protect what was reported and steer clear of speculative conclusions.

Zena frowned but said nothing.

Constables lined the gates to clear a path for the dignitaries. Others formed a double line, pressing the crowd back. At the pier, Consul Croskey stood beside Mayor Andrews while Wakey nervously gave last-minute instructions to his team.

"A hell of a lot of qubits must be at work." Rocko looked down the bay at the hundreds of holograms spanning from the beach to the main road. "Petamunra must be heating up to capacity."

"Not even close," Krish's voice came through somewhere, barely audible but proud.

Amid fireworks lighting up the sky, cheers drowned out nearby conversations, all in celebration of the man millions of Europeans saw as the personification of freedom.

A subtle halo enveloped him, as if he had plucked the Northern Star from the sky, carried it from the steppes of Anatolia, and brought it to England's shores to raise it above the Great Alföld, the Hungarian plain.

"Amazing," Nakshi whispered, mouth ajar, pupils wide. Was his praise for the majestic welcome or the marvel of the technology? Perhaps both.

What a scene it was, the day Lajos Kossuth arrived in Southampton. I was there.

14

SULTAN AND THE TWO COUSINS

After a short break, we reconvened at the launch pad and set up the composite chairs.

Krish motioned toward the seats. "Once we release Petamunra 2.0, we won't even need these. You'll be able to sit on holographic chairs."

"You must be joking." Rocko lifted his head as he aligned the chairs into a crescent. "Brooklyn may have its own rules, but last I checked, gravity still applies here."

"You'll be standing, but it'll feel like you're sitting."

Zena's eyes lit. "That's bizarre. Can we try it?"

"Not until the new system is certified," Histo said. "It would be risky to use otherwise." He stood off to the side, not lifting a finger to help.

Rocko shrugged. "I thought I was going to be the next Neil Armstrong."

"That's for the next crew, apparently." Nakshi tossed a faint smile. "We are Apollo 10—a dress rehearsal for the moon landing. Snoopy got close but didn't land."

"He's saying you ain't seen nothin' yet," I mused, pointing at Krish. He swayed his head, grinning.

Histo waited until we'd arranged the chairs in a semi-circle, then clasped his hands. "A month has passed. It's November in England. Dress appropriately. You'll take long walks."

"I learned my lesson." Zena tugged at her skirts. "I've got four layers of petticoat on me this time. One of them even has horsehair."

"How can we take long walks inside the Petamunra dome?" I asked.

"Quantum motion looping," Krish stressed each word. "Basically, you walk around the dome in circles but perceive a straight path."

"Like inmates doing laps in the courtyard?"

"Not far off." Krish paused with a wide grin. "Except you won't notice the curvature and the scene changes as you walk."

"How does that work?"

Krish lifted his hand, sketching shapes in the air. "QML is quantum-spatial synchronization and eye-body coordination by your wearable, which—"

Histo cut him short with a raised palm. "You can explain the physics and engineering on your own time. Now it's time to march."

Our short ride took us to a local train station. Wakey was waiting for us.

"Welcome to Winchester." He beamed, arms spread wide. "It's a short walk from here. The sky is clear today, a rare treat on this island."

It was slightly chilly but warmer than expected, a pleasant mid-afternoon.

Nakshi leaned forward. "Thank you for accommodating us on such a busy schedule."

Wakey inclined his head. "You're the final group he'll see before sailing to New York. When he saw your names on the long list of people requesting to meet him, he told me, 'How could I refuse a delegation coming from Turkey?'"

No one corrected him that we had arrived from New York.

"The governor holds the sultan in high regard," Wakey continued. "Every banquet in his honor displays the Turkish flag alongside the colors of America and Hungary, and the Union Jack."

Kossuth's secretary walked briskly as he briefed us on what he had witnessed since the Hungarian hero landed.

"We expected crowds, but nothing like this. Hundreds, maybe over a thousand, stood shoulder to shoulder at the Birmingham and Manchester stations just for a glimpse of him."

Rocko and Nakshi walked beside him. Zena and I trailed behind.

"Where are the chairs?" Zena whispered, tugging at my sleeve.

I leaned closer and replied in a low voice. "They're at the center, and invisible until we're ready to use them."

"It's like circling the wagons, only you don't feel it." She stifled a laugh.

The young aide spoke loudly. "Governor's speech at Mayor Andrews' coach factory was a hit. He praised the workers' dedication to liberty and their sacrifice of time."

"I'd bet he charmed everyone," Rocko flashed a knowing grin.

"Not everyone. The *Times* criticized him for addressing the working class." Wakey's smile twisted. "But when twenty-four thousand showed up outside Copenhagen House in London to hear him, they backed off."

Nakshi clapped. "Bravo. You must have had a hectic month."

"It has been grueling—speeches, travel, banquets, interviews." He exhaled heavily. "But the hardest part has been last-minute changes. We had a few of those."

"It must be a challenge to keep up with a firebrand boss," Rocko smirked.

The young Magyar smiled bitterly, offering no words.

We strolled along what seemed like an endless trail, circling the dome multiple times, but its ever-changing view made it worthwhile. Most leaves had fallen, though a few still clung on. Sunlight filtered through the canopy, casting warm tones over the reds and browns. The mubits and qubits were at work, painting one scene after another.

Having Zena at my side, strolling in the woods, with no exchange, I filled my lungs with her perfume mingled with the scent of wildflowers. A peculiar lightness swarmed me. Nothing felt artificial.

Wakey gestured with his hands as he spoke. "Southampton's print shops are already selling Kossuth portraits. I wonder if even the British Prime Minister could pull that off."

Rocko mused, "Maybe your boss should run for office here, and you take charge in Hungary."

The aide laughed. "Clever idea. Let's keep that just between us."

Zena paused, and I stayed with her. She handed me her notes.

"Would you mind leading today? I'm not up to it." Her request flattered me, but I worried more about her than the pressure I suddenly felt.

"You okay?" She looked pale, short of breath.

"It's not that. It's the skirts. They're so heavy. But mostly, I miss my sneakers. Next time I time-travel, I'll pick a post-sneaker era." She tugged at the hem, chuckling.

We resumed walking, trailing the other three until we reached the iron gates of a stone mansion. A servant opened the heavy wooden door and ushered us inside. As we walked down the long hallway, I caught a glimpse of Mrs. Kossuth in the drawing room with her three young children. She looked fragile.

When we stepped into the study, invisible chairs came into view, arranged in an arc and upholstered in elegant holographic leather. Krish's algorithm must have borrowed from the best of interior design.

"He meets dignitaries daily, except Sundays," his aide said. "After sunset, he retreats here to prepare the next day's speech."

Stacks of handwritten papers covered the mahogany desk. Catching me glancing, Wakey leaned closer. "Governor is always working. These days, he reads a little—but mostly writes speeches and papers, then spends a few hours with family."

Our seating resembled a press briefing. A row of real chairs facing a single holographic one. Histo took the far seat, incognito to the holograms.

I skimmed the notes, realizing Zena had caught up on this man fast. She had skipped lunch and spent her break compiling an extensive list of questions, neatly organized by event and chronology—a testament to her thoroughness and determination.

"You did a good job." She didn't respond to me.

The side door suddenly opened, and Kossuth entered. Everyone rose. His presence instantly filled the room. After the introductions, Wakey left.

Louis Kossuth, as known in the Western media, stood about five feet eight, with a medium frame and slightly rounded shoulders. His straight black hair showed two bald spots, likely the result of a wound. A thick, dark brown beard covered most of his face except his chin, and a full mustache hid his lips. His green velvet jacket, worn and faded, paired with a red four-in-hand necktie and a white shirt, completed the Hungarian tricolor. His baggy trousers also looked tired, and his buckled shoes with square-tipped toes were rough. His weathered face matched his attire.

Governor Kossuth quickly sized up everyone. It was hard to escape his sharp gaze. He locked his gray eyes on Nakshi, the only man in the room wearing a fez.

"You come from the two great countries I am indebted to—and the third is hosting our meeting today." Nakshi mirrored the man's inquisitive look. "I have only fraternal sentiments toward Turkey. When one-half of Hungary was under Turkish dominion and the other half under the Austrian, the part under Turkish rule had more religious liberty, encouraging the development of Protestantism."

Nakshi beamed, melted by the kind words. Complimenting the Turks was always a weak spot for them, and the Magyar knew it.

I asked the governor the first question, reading from Zena's notes.

"Many call you the best orator of our time, the mightiest pen in Europe. You speak many languages as if each were your mother tongue. A lawyer, a journalist, a commander, a statesman—who is Lajos Kossuth?"

The governor was prompt. "A fighter for freedom." He turned his gaze on me. "Freedom is man's unalienable, God-given right. It is nature's law. And God created nature. Suppressing man's freedom is standing against the will of God. And when I fight for my people's freedom, I'm fighting for God."

Hungary's governor in exile summarized the revolutionary events of 1848 and his flight from his homeland. The novanauts listened intently. Zena watched with quiet confidence and pride, echoing what she had told us in Southampton.

I glanced at Zena's notes. "Why flee to Turkey?" She marked it as the second question.

"She is our neighboring country. When we reached her frontier with five thousand of my brethren, the Pasha of Vidin assured us that His Majesty the Padishah Sultan Abdulmejid had given his word that we would be treated as his guests."

Zena nudged me with her gaze, urging me to press harder.

"Strong words," I leaned forward, raising my brows. "Did Sultan Abdulmejid keep his promise?"

Kossuth did not hesitate, placing a hand over his chest. "Till the last day we breathed the Lord's air on his land." His voice mellowed. "The Turkish government treated us hospitably for weeks. Then the word came from Constantinople that the Cossack tyrant had made a new and despicable, inhuman demand."

Kossuth gazed out the window, his watery eyes piercing. His voice dropped. "Words fail me to describe the astonishing offer made to the fallen chief of a generous nation—suggestions that could hardly have been expected in the nineteenth century."

My eyebrow quirked. Kossuth sighed before continuing. "It was a letter from His Majesty the Czar to the sultan's court, stating that the five thousand Poles and Hungarians in my company should be surrendered unless they choose to renounce the faith of our forefathers in the religion of Christ and become Mussulmans."

Nakshi stepped in, furrowing his brows. "Either become a Muslim, and we will let you go, or we will slaughter you. Is that what the czar was saying?"

Kossuth inclined his head, not even a half nod, lips pursed. His cloudy gaze stayed on the windowpane, past the sparrows hopping on bare branches.

Suddenly, he sprang to life, swung around, and exclaimed, "Forcing five thousand Christians to choose between two terrible alternatives." He raised his arm. "Either take the scaffold or purchase your life by abandoning your faith!"

He paused, letting the weight settle.

Then, he touched his chest. "My fifteen million fellow citizens elected me to this high position. As Governor of Hungary, even in exile, I knew what I owed to my country's honor. My answer left no room for doubt. Between death and disgrace, my choice was clear. I leave no wealth to my children, but they will inherit an unsullied name."

A noble figure stood before us—unafraid, ready to sacrifice his life for his nation's honor.

He let out a breath. "I'm prepared to die, but I believe this measure is dishonorable and harmful to Turkey, a country whose interests I sincerely hold dear."

He returned to the window and spoke in a softer voice. "Feeling it my duty to protect my fellow exiles from a degrading choice, I wrote to Grand Vizier Mustafa Reshid Pasha. I also sought help from two great nations, France and England, to oppose this unjust demand."

He shifted from fearless revolutionary to shrewd diplomat, turning injustice to his advantage and aiming for a diplomatic victory. His theatrical style added color to his cause.

"The sultan declared he would not, under any condition, surrender the exiles or violate the laws of hospitality." He creased his forehead and nodded three times in gratitude. "He moved us to Kutahia, a town in western Asia Minor that became our home for the next eleven months."

I cut in, "The sultan's decision must have been a pleasant surprise, but it must have angered Vienna and St. Petersburg."

The governor's eyes narrowed. "Beyond any measure."

"How did you spend your time in exile?"

His shoulders eased. "I spent time reading, writing, gardening, accepting guests, and exercising. The sultan's government ensured we were comfortable and secure. I improved my English with Johnson's Dictionary and Shakespeare as my guides." His eyes lit—a rare gesture. I smiled back.

As I listened, it struck me. Grandpa once wanted to stop at the Hungarian House on our way to the Mediterranean coast. But I, an impatient sixth grader, had fussed in the car, demanding the sea before sunset. What I missed must have been Kossuth's exile home in Kutahia. Regret shrouded me.

Rocko chimed in, "Doesn't sound like a prison."

Kossuth shot him a cold glance, his gray eyes piercing. "Patriots were held against their will in detention."

Rocko forced a smile. "I meant, given the alternative. They were more like guests under the sultan's protection."

Kossuth's face eased. Rocko slumped, swallowing hard.

"Did anyone convert to Islam?" Nakshi asked, curiosity edging his voice.

"Several Polish and Magyar soldiers did. The late General Bem was one of them. He became Murat Pasha."

Kossuth's cheek muscles lifted his mustache, revealing his lips.

"General Bem was an exceptional Polish engineer and a brave soldier. He wasn't concerned with becoming a Musselman and told me, 'My only religion is being the enemy of Russia.'" He grinned bitterly, exposing his yellow-stained teeth.

"The Sublime Porte appointed him Governor of Aleppo, where he led Mussulman Turks and defended Turkey. He evaded the Russian musket all his life but couldn't escape malaria last year."

"May Allah have mercy on him." Nakshi was visibly moved. A devout Muslim, the merchant from Paterson, New Jersey, raised his palms and recited Al-Fatiha, ending the short prayer by passing his hands over his face.

Kossuth joined the impromptu interfaith memorial. "Born as Bem and died as Murat Pasha, he remained steadfast in rejecting oppression and left this world a free man. May God bless every soul in heaven and grant men their freedom on Earth."

We sealed the brief eulogy.

"Amen."

Conversion to Islam was common in the Turkish Empire, from the Balkans to Anatolia and parts of Central Europe. Many historical figures—grand viziers and ministers among them—had been born Christian Albanians, Bulgarians, or Serbians, and lived as Muslims under Turkish names.

Kossuth rose, motioning us to stay seated. "Religion is a personal choice. Take Omer Pasha, the Turkish general, one of the best military minds of our time. He follows his newly found faith, himself a Serbian Croat by birth."

I recalled Czar Nicholas mentioning the same name to Ambassador Seymour, praising his military skill. I made a note to learn more about him. For now, I didn't want to miss a single word from this extraordinary man before me.

Zena sank into deep thought, either handing me the wheel or losing interest. She removed her bonnet, revealing the beads of sweat that had dampened her temple. The rays of the setting sun seeped through the window, catching her blue-green eyes and shifting their color like a rare Brazilian jewel.

Kossuth drifted, gazing at the horizon. "Just as there are different ways to Heaven, there may also be—and there are—different ways to promote the happiness and welfare of the people; more than one way for a nation to achieve freedom and liberty. The question is not how a nation should govern, but does her governance make her the master of her fate?" Like Mozart, composing in his mind and setting the notes down in a single stroke, he expressed his views whole and unedited, all at once.

"England and the United States—two countries that are masters of their fate." He began pacing. "England seeks no change because she is governed by a constitutional monarchy where all classes enjoy the full benefits of free institutions. This must forever continue."

His deliberate choice to personify nations enriched his lyrical rhetoric, like an unexpected note that surprises the ear yet heightens the music.

"The United States, meanwhile, is a republic. Though governed differently, her people have no desire for change either, for they enjoy liberty, freedom, and have the means to develop their social structure." He smiled. "John Bull is proud of his young cousin, Jonathan, who built a great country under a glorious constitution. It must be gratifying."

Kossuth avoided mentioning America's growing divisions over slavery. I was tempted to press him but held back. The omission had to be deliberate.

"Not in every republic does freedom exist. I regret that among the great nations, one has people fit for liberty who still do not have it."

I sensed he was alluding to France. "What do you say to France's decision not to allow you on her soil?"

Kossuth halted, jabbing his finger toward the window. "It was the French government who rejected me, not the French people." He raised his arm. "I now live by a motto: '*There is no difficulty for him who wills.*' Words shouted by a Frenchman whose name I never learned, who leaped into the sea at Marseille and swam to the *Mississippi* just to deliver them to me."

"What do you foresee in France?"

He chose his words carefully. "It's impossible to predict what an hour may bring in that country. But I believe France will more likely not remain a republic six months from now. Military rule. A despotic regime upheld by bayonets."

He wasn't far off. Louis Napoleon would declare the Second Empire thirteen months later.

Kossuth clasped his hands behind his back. "Austria, Russia, and perhaps France—three of Europe's four great powers are ruled by authoritarians or absolute monarchs."

As he paced in small circles across the rug, I was reminded of Czar Nicholas, but I wouldn't stretch the comparison further.

He placed his palm over his chest. "Republic or monarchy is not the question; liberty is."

"You support the sultan," I reminded him. "He is a monarch, too."

His response was swift. "The Sublime Porte tolerates all faiths and allows them to self-govern. I've witnessed this firsthand in their civil court hearings."

"The common view is that the Turkish Empire is too weak to sustain itself. What's your view on that?"

"She is not. She is led to believe she is." The Magyar Governor did not hesitate. "Its integrity is paramount to the well-being of all Europe. Blood will wash over Europe if Turkey breaks apart. Turkey seeks progress, but the Russian menace stands in the way. The fates of Hungary and Turkey are intertwined, as is Europe's stability."

I hadn't expected such a strong stance.

Rocko cut in, "How do you compare religious liberties in these empires?"

"Compared to Russia and Austria, Turkey stands ahead of both. Austria has stripped the Protestant Church of its autonomy." He swung his arms as he paced. "Russia uses religion as a political tool, persecuting Catholics, Greeks, and Jews in ways that shock the conscience."

"I'm confused." Rocko shook his head. "The Balkan Christians have been crying out for help from Europe for ages, begging to be freed from the Turkish yoke."

"Freedom and liberty—they must have." Kossuth lifted a finger high. "But if the European powers believe these small states can remain free without their support, they are mistaken. Russia can engulf them, and Russia will."

"Out of the frying pan, into the fire," Rocko quipped. Kossuth stood unfazed.

I stepped in. "What is your remedy for the Balkans?"

"Autonomous nations, free in their administration, under the fair and just suzerainty of the Turkish Empire. The two mighty powers that cherish liberty above all else must protect them." Kossuth paused, letting his words settle. "The sultan and the two cousins—John Bull and Jonathan. All three respect religious freedom."

His vision for the Eastern Question was clear: the Ottoman Empire would retain suzerainty in the Balkans while granting each nation autonomy, with England and the United States guaranteeing their security.

My father's reaction would have been, "Holy intervention aside, not possible." That alliance never took root. What followed instead in the former Ottoman lands, from the Balkans to the Eastern Mediterranean, would haunt generations and still lingers today.

Nakshi's eyes narrowed. "Sir, your suggestion engages the United States in Europe's affairs. Doesn't that rub against America's vision?"

Kossuth straightened, both hands holding his broad lapels. "Washington's isolationist legacy is becoming increasingly difficult to uphold. Today's realities call for a more active US role in Europe. The American Consul, Mr. Croskey, suggested an alliance with Britain."

"Against whom?"

"Any alliance of tyrannical regimes that suppress liberty or impose absolutism."

That vision—a sustained ironclad alliance between the two cousins—would not materialize until ninety years later, after the attack on Pearl Harbor.

Impressed by his foresight, I grew curious about Kossuth's thoughts on our future. After all, there were no rules against gleaning wisdom from those we encountered in the quantum universe. So, I decided to ask him.

"Can humanity ever prevent wars?"

Kossuth narrowed his eyes in thought. "I don't believe it's possible to avoid war, given the ever-present forces of ambition, greed, and oppression that lead to despotism. War, though tragic, is often a necessary evil."

"Do you see yourself supporting one?" I followed up.

Lajos Kossuth shut his eyes and put his mind to work as if he were kneading ideas into a coherent dough of intellect. After what felt like more than a minute, he gazed at me sharply.

"I seek the friendship of nations, and I am a lover of peace. But if they must be purchased at the expense of independence and freedom, then I am for war. It is nobler to perish rather than to live under oppression."

Rocko leapt in. "What guides you in making such a hard decision? A faith? A doctrine?" Everyone held their breath.

"Ours is not the cause of one family, one party, or one faith; it is the fight of a people claiming those just rights to which a nation is entitled."

I pressed on. "Maybe humanity could form institutions that agree on a set of moral rules to decide when wars are justified. Possible?"

His answer was quick and firm. "I am no friend of codification because I am a friend of free, unarrested progress. Codification is an iron hand. It hinders the circulation of intelligence and fetters its development, which must go on freely toward boundless perfection—the destiny of humanity."

I didn't take his no for an answer. "What if, not rules, but laws, put war initiatives on trial before they began, judged by the universally accepted norms of justice?"

Kossuth shrugged. "Justice is immortal, eternal, and immovable, like God Himself. Law is man-made. It must hold pace in its development with the development of intelligence. But this law is—and must be—an object of continual progress."

"How would intelligence fuel the progress in a universal judicial system?"

He took a step forward toward me. "The progress in the development of law is only then a progress, when it is directed toward these immortal principles of justice."

Zena finally broke her silence. "What's the next step for intelligence?"

Kossuth showed no sign of surprise at hearing a question posed by a woman. "The spirit of the age is democratic."

"Democracy?" She raised her brows. "Is that your answer to progress?"

"All for the people, and all by the people. Nothing about the people without the people. That is democracy."

Lajos Kossuth ended the meeting. "Thank you for coming."

The lights dimmed. The grand orator's discourse bore a resemblance to that of a Shakespearean play, leaving behind profound words to contemplate. Humanity must strive to attain justice, guided by intelligence as its beacon, and intelligence is on a continuous journey to progress. What if it falls off the cliff before reaching the summit?

Looking ahead at the tragedies and injustices of the twentieth century, and beyond, aren't they all fueled by ever-advancing military technology, itself born of intelligence? Steering intelligence toward the path of righteousness requires wisdom. It won't do it by itself. Maybe I should have told him.

Krish led us along the same path back to the station, this time under the stars, the weather cooperating.

"Pleasant man indeed," Nakshi said. "But why Cousin Jonathan and not Uncle Sam?"

The director replied, "It would've been politically incorrect. During the War of 1812, American army supplies were stamped with 'U.S.' The soldiers turned 'U' into Uncle and 'S' into Sam."

"Who's Sam?"

"The arms supplier. His name was Sam Wilson." Everyone chuckled except Zena, who suddenly halted, out of breath.

"I'm exhausted," she gasped. Everyone stopped. "Do we have to walk to the train station?"

"Uber isn't into spaceships yet," Rocko quipped. "Want me to carry you?" Zena sighed, too drained to respond.

Histo called out, "Krish, let's cut the return short. Disengage the quantum motion loop."

"Roger that." The launch seats appeared.

As we latched in, waiting for the hum to start, the visionary Magyar's words still rang in my mind.

Kossuth's hopes hadn't shaped the nineteenth century, but his fears proved prophetic. The Balkans cracked. Russians advanced where Ottoman Turkey vanished. A world war erupted, then another followed. Tens of millions died. Nations crumbled. The continent burned. Then came nukes, followed by a cold peace behind a curtain of iron.

His principles? Still valid as world peace is threatened by the volcanoes of the twenty-first century—some erupting, from Ukraine to the Middle East, others simmering, like the South China Sea.

Kossuth saw the storm coming. We're still drenched in its rain.

Belts locked. Lights dimmed. Pressure built with the hum.

Histo sat beside me.

I tilted toward him. "He said we can't stop wars."

The director's light blue eyes glowed in the dark like a cat's.

"Did he?"

The wind surged. Vibrations swept my feet.

"Feels good! These rides are addictive," Rocko shouted.

The hum swelled, cheeks turned inward. I didn't hear Zena scream.

15
THE ARMENIAN

The middle of the night. A knock on my door jolted me awake. Three more followed, louder.

I jumped out of bed and opened the door.

"Are you awake?" It was Zena, half-wrapped in a blanket over her gown, eyes wide, pupils dilated.

"I am now." I swung the door open.

She looked over her shoulder to see if anyone was behind her, then stepped inside.

"I hear noises from the next room." Her chest heaved.

"Are you sure they're not from outside? Horses have been moving and neighing all night."

She shot me a sharp look. "I ride horses. I know the difference. It's a person. I heard footsteps. He must be hiding there."

"Who?"

Her eyes narrowed. "The serial killer, of course. Don't you get it? Where have you been living lately?"

"In another universe," I quipped, hoping to hold my own against Rocko in the smart-aleck category.

She rolled her eyes, waving me off.

Footsteps echoed in the hallway.

Zena jolted. "Did you hear that?" She backed into the far corner, clutching her blanket as if it could shield her from an attack.

I stepped out without hesitation. The hallway was dim and eerie. Flickering gas lamps cast wavering shadows. Krish appeared in his pajamas. His shadow loomed taller than him, gliding across the carpet.

"What's going on?" His eyes tried adjusting to the light. "I heard someone knocking."

Zena rushed into the hallway. "That was me," she blurted. "I heard noises from the next room. You told Sarah to stay out of that locked room. Who's in there?"

"Who's Sarah?" Krish rubbed his eyes.

Zena narrowed her gaze. "The woman who runs the kitchen."

"Oh! That Sarah." Krish grinned. "She's a hologram. You know that, right?"

Zena pressed her lips together.

Krish leaned in. "There's an auxiliary power unit in that room. I don't let cognitive holograms in there or the library. If they see the electronics, it'll mess everything up."

"How do you explain the footsteps?"

Krish scratched his head. "Could be the relays. The unit kicks on for test runs. I'm sorry. I should've told you."

Zena slumped, still doubtful.

"I can move you to the empty room across from the kitchen. It's the smallest one on the floor."

"No thanks. I need the space." Her lips jutted out a little.

Krish yawned. "It's almost four. Get some sleep. We've got a busy day ahead."

Zena lowered her head, dragged her feet to her room, and slipped the key into the lock. Krish and I watched, unsure if she was embarrassed or simply frustrated after hearing the explanation.

"Good night, Zena," I called after her.

"Good night," she muttered, keeping her head down as she shut the door.

Krish and I exchanged glances. He shrugged.

"I made these for you, Rocko." Sarah pointed to a tray of scones, half a dozen on a wide porcelain dish. A young woman stood beside her. "I used cranberries. You don't have them in the old country, but we grow them in New Jersey. You know, the state across the Hudson River."

"You're the best, Sarah." Rocko smiled.

"They know where New Jersey is, Mother." The young woman shook her head as she set down the warm biscuits. She looked to be in her late twenties. "Besides, they grow cranberries in Sweden. My beau says it's the berry capital of Europe."

"He knows everything except how to earn a living," Sarah muttered as they headed back to the kitchen. Her daughter didn't respond.

Rocko watched his buried fingers disappear into the aromatic dishes. "This is borderline torture," he said. They looked more genuine and smelled better than the real kind.

We'd already had donuts and bagels upstairs before settling inside the Petamunra dome. Not my top choice for a Sunday breakfast, but Krish had suggested we save our appetites for a surprise dinner feast.

Zena walked in, holding a cup of coffee. She looked pale and tired from lack of sleep, yet neatly dressed.

"Would you like some scones, my dear?" Rocko pointed at the basket, hoping to lure her in.

"No, thanks. I'm not hungry this morning."

The young woman stepped out of the kitchen. "Good morning, Ms. Zena! I'm Claire." Her grin stretched ear to ear. "I've heard so much about you from my mom. Welcome to New York!"

Zena returned the smile. "Hi, Claire, nice to meet you."

"It's rare to see people from Turkey in this town, let alone a female reporter. Two rarities in one."

"Make that three, my dear," Rocko chimed in. "The most stunning beauty in town." Zena shot him a sly glance. Why couldn't I ever come up with lines like that, no matter how hard I tried? I curled my lip.

"Oh, yes, she absolutely is," Sarah shouted from the kitchen.

Claire served her jelly. "Did you all arrive by the *Mississippi* with the Magyars?"

"No, not quite." Zena's eyes darted, latching onto fashion, grabbing it like a life raft after a shipwreck. "I adore your dress. It's so unique."

Claire wore baggy pants that trailed below her knees, fitting snugly at the ankles, paired with rabbit-hide moccasins in a Native American style.

"It's the Turkish pantaloon!" She twirled like a ballerina to show it off.

"It looks like shalwar." Zena's voice was full of awe. "Women wear them working in the fields. It's practical and simple."

"Amelia Bloomer introduced it to American women." Claire tugged at the pantaloon fabric. "Western women drag around heavy skirts while our Turkish sisters move freely in these. We're joining them."

"Speak for yourself, young lady," her mother called from the kitchen.

Claire threw up her arms. "I'm a proud Bloomerite!"

We novanauts exchanged glances. None of us had imagined the Turkish peasant dress, often dismissed as backward in Türkiye, had once been a symbol of women's liberation in mid-nineteenth-century America.

"Amelia's magazine, *Lily*, saw its circulation explode eightfold after she introduced bloomers." Sarah's eyes widened. "Maggie says men panicked. They don't like changes in women's society."

"Who's Maggie?" Zena lifted a brow.

"Simon Sarkisian's wife. They own the Osmanlee Café."

"His name sounds Armenian," Nakshi noted.

"He is, but people call him Simon the Turk. He's the unofficial Minister of Turkey. He's a sharp, entertaining storyteller. You should meet him. Maggie's lovely, too."

"I'd love that," Zena smiled.

"He hires unemployed immigrants and dresses them in Turkish costumes for his lectures." Claire counted with her fingers. "Janissaries with big mustaches, tall headgear, drums, timbales. It's unmissable on Broadway."

"He once pitched tents in Central Park to reenact the Turkish siege of Vienna," Sarah called out. "Even brought camels. The mayor fined him." Her laughter echoed from the kitchen.

"He's lecturing now," Claire leaned in, gesturing down the street. "It's just a few blocks away, an easy walk."

"Let's see him," Nakshi shot Histo with a look from the corner of his eye. The director nodded in approval.

On Prince Street, horse hooves clattered over cobblestones, blending into the city's din. We strolled on Broadway for ten minutes. Though I'd walked this avenue countless times, the perfect fidelity visuals made it feel new again on that sunny, chilly mid-October day in antebellum New York.

Women in hoop skirts with hand muffs peered into shop windows. Most passersby were white, except the coachmen ferrying men in top hats. The granite Astor House loomed on our right, Barnum's American Museum across the street. Grace Church's stained glass gleamed as it still does today—it's glamour defying time. New York's signature subway stench had given way to the heavy odor of horse manure, yet the city's familiar allure remained. A freckle-faced teenager balanced on a ladder, painting "New Arrivals from Europe" on a shop window, drawing a small crowd. Storefronts displayed furs and glittering jewelry. Across the street, a general store advertised carriage fittings.

We, the male novanauts, trailed behind Zena and Claire. Rocko and I wore formal coats, blending in—he in black, me in dark green with a red tie. Zena had chosen fewer petticoats that morning. Nakshi stood out in a burgundy fez, refusing a top hat in honor of his late father, who had rejected Western headgear.

Claire animatedly explained the female view at the Temperance Congress to Zena. Women passing by—many with parasols—shot her sharp looks. A few admired her, but all noticed her bloomer pants.

The lecture show had already started by the time we reached the Mercantile Library at Clinton Hall.

"Fifty cents?" Rocko furrowed his brows. "That's steep. A paper costs a penny."

Claire offered a knowing smile. "Simon donates most of it to orphaned children of our soldiers."

A woman in her thirties approached, waving.

"You're late, Claire. He'll be taking questions soon."

"I was with guests—the ones I told you about."

"Ah! You must be the Turks staying at the Metropolitan." The woman beamed. "I'm Maggie, Simon's wife. A Yankee original. My family traces back to the *Mayflower*, but Simon beats me by a few thousand years with Noah's Ark." Her laughter rang out. "I take it yours was the *Mississippi*, and you brought the Magyars to our shore."

"We're from another universe, visiting," Rocko smirked. After all, it wasn't untrue.

She leaned back, arms in the air. "You folks are the winners then." Everyone laughed.

"What makes you think we came from Turkey?" I asked.

Maggie pointed at Nakshi's fez with a broad grin. "My husband wears one of these." She leaned closer to Zena, dropping her voice. "We're sold out today, but he'd be upset if I turned away visitors from his home country. The show's ending anyway. You may go in, free of charge."

Before I could tell her we were locals, Zena nudged me. "Thank you," she said, flashing a grin at Maggie. As I stood befuddled, she shot me a glance, not to upset the apple cart.

Maggie's knee-length skirt and loose pants were much like Claire's. "I see you're wearing the bloomer outfit. I'm curious about the designer. Do you know her?"

"Join me next week, dear." Maggie winked. "There's a women's rally uptown. I'll introduce you to Amelia. She's among the speakers."

Zena glanced at Histo for approval. The incognito chief nodded. She beamed. "I'd be delighted. I wish I could wear pants like yours to the event. They look comfy and stylish. Where can I get a pair?"

Claire cut in, "I have an extra set. I'll bring it to you."

"Oh, honey, you're so sweet." Zena leaned in to kiss her cheek, then stopped short, remembering her lips would vanish into Claire's holographic face.

Rocko leaned toward me. "My friend, universe or another—women are women in every verse."

Clinton Hall was packed to capacity. We stood near the entrance, enveloped in smoke with no vent in sight. On stage, a tall man with bushy eyebrows and a slender mustache wore a black vest over a white shirt buttoned to the neck. His crimson fez set him apart.

"That must be him." Zena pointed, leaning in.

The man in front of us turned. "He's part showman, part scholar rolled into one." He glanced at Nakshi's fez. "You must be from the Orient."

"You probably are not." Nakshi smiled faintly. The man was tall, blond, a Nordic type. He craned his head toward us.

"Most of the audience isn't." He gestured to a group below. "But there are some from your part of the world. They're the most vocal." He grinned. "I call them the *neigh-sayers*, the opposition party. Fun to watch how they flare."

"This is our first time here." Rocko leaned in.

"I never miss his lectures. Turkey is important these days, a peculiar country to Americans. Simon explains it well and makes it simple."

A large banner read: "Lectures on Turkey by Simon Sarkisian." Another proclaimed: "Tanzimat—It Means Reformation."

Bearded men in turbans and veiled women sat beside a cardboard camel, flapping makeshift paper fans.

The Nordic man motioned toward them. "You missed the show-and-tell."

Maps on stage spanned six centuries of Ottoman history.

"Which century is he in now?" Rocko asked.

The blond man cracked a sly smile. "We've been through them all. Now it's current events."

Our attention turned to the man on stage. "Deeply Christian themselves, many Americans are confused, asking questions." The tall speaker raised his arm. "Why do the heads of the Church of England and Latin France oppose the august ruler of St. Petersburg, who claims he defends the righteous cross against the barbarous crescent? Did the Turk's saber convert the West to Mohammedanism?"

Someone shouted, "The news hasn't reached our shores yet." Laughter rippled through the hall.

Sarkisian grinned. "Everyone is trying to make sense of this impasse. But there is a reason behind it. And a good one. Before I explain, it's imperative to grasp the great changes unfolding in Turkey."

He paced the stage, passing *tableaux vivants* on portable tripods that depicted daily life in Stamboul—Constantinople, as captions named both.

"Once a world power, Turkey is no longer. Still home to the three great religions—Judaism, Christianity, and Islam—Turkey rules millions across three continents. The empire grew unmanageable under unenlightened, barbaric rule. When Mahmoud took power at the century's turn, he knew change was needed."

Zena craned her neck for a better view. Krish had tucked the wooden stool into the corner, its phosphorescent glow setting it apart. Rocko slipped through the holographic crowd and grabbed it.

"Very kind of you." Zena offered him a lingering smile. Rocko bowed and helped her step up.

Late again. I twitched, forcing out a sigh. Nakshi averted his eyes, pretending not to notice.

Sarkisian upped the fervor. "Sultan Mahmoud launched military and administrative reforms, standing boldly against the old guard. Only a daring sultan could."

Someone from the opposition party cut in, "Come on! During the Morea uprisings, Mahmoud hanged Greek subjects, including the patriarch, and left his body on display for three days."

Rocko leaned toward me, dropping his voice. "That's true. The Patriarch's iron gate has remained closed since that day, two hundred years ago."

Sarkisian nodded. "That's a fair point. Displaying the patriarch's body badly damaged Western perceptions, especially in England."

"Some reformist!" the naysayer snapped. "They say his mother was French. If true, she was no kin to Danton. Robespierre, maybe." The audience chuckled.

"Mahmoud is dead! Don't tell us old tales," someone else barked. "Abdulmejid is the sultan. Who's he related to? Voltaire?" More laughter followed.

Simon ignored the man. "Mustafa Reshid Pasha persuaded the young sultan to issue a reform proclamation, the Tanzimat, steering the empire toward the liberty harbors of the Occident. It changed Europe's view, offering hope that Turkey might survive and thrive."

"They only know how to make wars," the objector retorted. "But their swords are blunt and rusty now." Some naysayers leaped to their feet, clapping, a few whistling.

"I respectfully disagree, but it's true—the Turks can't run the empire without the Armenians." Sarkisian's passion swelled amid the commotion. "We are educated; they are not. We are skilled in trade and languages. Fusion is the only policy that can revitalize the Turkish Empire."

"Fusing whom?"

"Mussulmans, Jews, and Christians of every kind—Greeks and Armenians, especially." He lifted his chin. "All bound by a common vision: to preserve the Ottoman Empire with civil equality and full liberty of conscience for all faiths."

The Nordic man in front pressed back. "Many oppose the Tanzimat. How will reformists overcome the old guard? They still dominate the Sublime Porte."

Sarkisian ignored him. "Lecture is over. After a five-minute break, I will open the floor for questions." He pulled a handkerchief, wiped his brow, and poured a cup of water. The stifling hall and steady criticism had worn him down.

All ships rise. That was Sarkisian's hopeful dream—to lift the empire from the mud, heal the sick man, and place him on the pedestal of liberty. A second empire, perhaps secular like France, but multinational and interfaith. A beacon of justice and liberty for all, rolling into the twentieth century as one of the old world's mightiest states.

None of it happened, and Dad believed it never could—an unrealistic leap against history's flow. But why was it impossible? I never understood. Simon Sarkisian wouldn't, either.

Decades would pass. Nationalism would overshadow the empire's unity, as each millet sought its own destiny under a separate flag. The conflicts would turn Anatolia into a battleground among Greeks, Armenians, and Turks, setting the stage for tragedies yet to come. The Armenian optimist could not foresee them.

The same picture formed in each novanaut's mind—the foreknowledge of history. The promising future Sarkisian portrayed had not materialized in the Ottoman Empire. That truth weighed on Rocko. He'd lost some of his jolly spark. Nakshi, also in blues, sat deep in thought, both men under Histo's watchful gaze. Zena stared off, absent-minded, half-listening to Claire complain about the weak female participation in town hall events.

I drifted too, reflecting on Simon's words. No one spoke, but none of us needed to. We all shared the peculiar urge to change the course of history, as if we had any power to do so. It was all an illusion around us, yet it was becoming harder to believe it was.

Sarkisian opened the Q&A. "Introduce yourself, first name only, and where you're from." A few hands shot up.

"Vassilis from Astoria, Queens. The Turkish Empire will never be part of the civilized world. End of story." Vigorous applause rose from the opposition group.

"We all agree!"

"That's cutting into neighing," Nakshi scoffed.

Sarkisian managed a nervous grin. "As a Christian Osmanlee of Armenian extraction, I can attest that Turkish Mohammedanism does not impede progress." He paused, letting the words settle. "Europe was in darkness when the Muslim Abbasids created Baghdad, and the Arab Andalusians brought algebra to Spain. The East chiseled the pillars that built the modern West."

"They all learned from the Greeks!"

"I don't dispute that. But remember, all of this took place in the same part of the world. What I'm saying is, don't glorify the despotic regimes simply because they're Christian. Mussulman Turkey is more adaptable to civility. It's embedded in its soil. With Tanzimat, civilization will return."

"Yeah, if you can find it. It's buried deep." Applause, laughter, and whistling mingled.

Vassilis hollered, "You reformist Armenians are just as delusional as the Tanzimat Turks!"

Another man rose across the opposition stand. "We Greeks have our illusions too. After independence, some from Asia Minor moved to Morea. They later returned, disappointed by King Otto's despotic Hellenic government."

"Sit down, Stelios," another naysayer fired back. "How many piastres did the sultan pay you?"

A man with curly silver hair stood. "The Turkish Finance Minister fined some Armenian bankers. They thought it vindictive and fled to

Christian Russia, hoping for justice. But worse awaited them there. Most ended up returning."

Sarkisian raised both arms. "In both the Greek and Armenian cases, these Christian people became mere tenants in the lands of their dreams."

I could almost hear Dad saying, "The obstacle to Ottoman progress was the absence of civil liberties and fair justice." The West cared only about religious intolerance. Always, the lukewarm porridge.

"Now I'm opening the floor for questions on Russia," Simon announced.

More hands went up.

"Charlie, from the Bronx. Two questions. Why are England and France siding with Mussulman Turkey against Christian Russia?"

"Short answer. Europe's security. Stability in the Balkans and keeping Constantinople from falling into Russian hands. Both are essential."

"Why is the Turkish capital so important?" Charlie followed up.

"The great Napoleon wisely said, 'Turkey's imperial seat, Constantinople, is the key to all of Europe and geographically designed to be the world's capital.' Look at the maps. They lie along the path to reach the warm waters, which is the manifest destiny of Imperial Russia. The Russian bear has already clawed through Finland, Poland, Bessarabia, and the provinces of Circassia, and now has its eyes on Turkey."

A tap on my back. I turned. It was Zena, sitting on the stool, no longer straining to see the stage. "Where is Bessarabia?"

"Moldavia and Ukraine, pretty much," I leaned down. "Circassia is on the northeastern Black Sea, around—"

"I know where Circassia is," she cut in, shooting me a stern look. "I am Cherkess."

I felt stupid. My ignorance had irritated her. I turned back to the stage, twitching my cheek.

"John, from Brooklyn. Wouldn't it be better if Christian Russia ruled Constantinople instead of the barbaric Mussulman Turks?"

Sarkisian struck back curtly. "Czar Nicholas claims he is the champion of the Cross. His rhetoric should not fool us!"

He swung his arms, passion on his sleeve. "There is no Turkish threat to Europe, but Russia's despotic regime is casting dark clouds over liberty."

I heard Zena's feeble voice. "I don't feel well." I swung around. She signaled to Histo. "May I be excused? It must be the smoke and the crowd." Her forehead was damp.

"I'll walk you back," I jumped in.

"Krish, take Zena back to her room." The director motioned for me to stay.

"Roger that," Krish's voice came through. I wanted to speak to her, but Zena moved swiftly, weaving through the taller holograms until her body vanished.

An anonymous man rose to speak. "Are you saying all is well for Christians in the Turkish Empire?" He turned to the audience. "Many rayahs desire to escape and place themselves under foreign protection."

"Hear, hear."

The man in front craned his neck toward Rocko. "Who are rayahs?"

Rocko leaned forward. "Non-Muslim subjects of the Ottoman Empire, like me."

He twisted around, facing Rocko. "What are you?"

"I'm a Jew." The Nordic man stared at him, his expression hardening, then turned back toward the stage. Rocko shrugged.

Simon lifted his arms. "Christian or Mussulman—they both seek justice." His reply rang out. "What are their choices? Belong to the sultan or the august czar in St. Petersburg."

"I say, We the People!" a man hollered, waving an American flag. Applause erupted through Clinton Hall.

"Well said." Simon beamed. "That's why America is the greatest nation on Earth. Let's take one last question."

Nakshi shouted, surprising me. "Where do you see Armenians in Turkey's future? Nakshi from Kayseri."

Simon paused and looked our way, scanning the crowd. "Kayseri? Where are you, my Osmanlee?"

Nakshi waved his red fez, drawing a grin from Sarkisian. The audience turned toward us with curious looks.

A chant rose from the opposition group. *"Elefteria i Thanatos!"*

Seeing me befuddled, Rocko explained, ducking his head. "It means 'Freedom or Death' in Greek. My grandfather told me the same motto rang in the Jewish quarter when the Greeks took over Thessaloniki. Many Jews left. That's how we landed in Istanbul after abandoning our home of four hundred years since Ferdinand and Isabel expelled us from Spain."

Vassilis shouted, "Four hundred years of slavery!"

"That's another way of counting up to four hundred," Rocko quipped wryly.

It didn't sound humorous. My knees started to shake as I watched the rage in the naysayers' eyes. It felt as if George from the town hall meeting came to organize the holograms.

Vassilis pressed on, "The time has come for Greeks to rule Asia Minor again!"

"Hear, hear!" the naysayers echoed. The audience had a mixed reaction. Most watched—some staring with raised brows, others with mouths agape—while a few applauded, whistled, or booed.

Sarkisian raised his arm. "Quiet!"

Once everyone was seated, he spoke calmly. "Sadly, my Christian brethren, you can't rule the empire. Ottoman Christians are a house divided."

A commotion rose from the opposition. Sarkisian raised his voice. "Yes, we feel bitterness toward the Mussulmans. They've ruled unjustly for centuries. But who can assure us that a Christian rule would not be harsher? Besides, no Great Power, not even Russia, wants a new ruler in Constantinople. The revival of Byzantium is neither practical nor beneficial for liberty. The answer lies in fusion."

"You fuse yourself. Liberty to Greeks!" a naysayer shouted.

"Speaking of liberties," Simon grinned, hoping to defuse the tension. "Soon, New York will welcome Louis Kossuth, the bastion of liberty, her spokesman in modern times. How about we give him his first warm welcome?"

Applause and cheers rocked the hall. The entire room rose in ovation.

Maggie stepped beside her husband. "Thank you for coming!" she hollered. "Join us at the Café Osmanlee on Broadway and watch for the next announcement. Until next time!"

Simon Sarkisian concluded, "May Providence protect our Union! God bless, and long live the United States of America and those who uphold liberty."

Amid applause as the audience left, Simon Sarkisian climbed the stairs two at a time to reach us, Maggie trailing behind.

"*Hosh geldounuz, safalar getourdounuz effendum.*" He spoke in Turkish with an Armenian accent, offering a warm welcome.

Maggie chimed in. "Join us when Kossuth arrives. Simon is on the welcoming committee."

"We'd love to," Rocko and I replied.

She pouted. "I hope Zena feels better soon. I can't even imagine the fatigue she must be feeling after all that time across the ocean."

Simon stepped toward Nakshi. "I am hopeful about the future. Liberty and justice will be for all—Mussulman, Armenian, Greek, Jew—everyone. May God grant the sultan wisdom to keep competent viziers by his side—the likes of Reshid Pasha, not the fanatics of the old party."

Nakshi smiled bitterly. "Aren't you overly optimistic? Your Greek friends aren't."

Simon widened his eyes. "Who wouldn't want the empire as cosmopolitan as America, ranking among the most civilized on Earth. A model for all. Everyone's envy."

He sounded like Mom—an eternal romantic optimist. Dad held a different view. He believed the Eastern Mediterranean carried too much baggage for lasting peace. I never took sides in those family debates.

Vassilis overheard the chatter as he exited. "Come to Astoria, my friend," he called out to Nakshi. "We'll offer you a feast, just like in the old country." He smiled warmly. Nakshi lifted a hand in reply.

"He doesn't drink. I'll bring the raki," Rocko hollered.

"It's a deal." The Greek waved back. Pointing at Simon, he added, "Don't bring him. Simon is a sponge. He'd leave nothing for us to drink." They both chuckled, and Vassilis slipped away. Greeks and Turks. Argue in public, laugh together in private. Nothing new.

The gentleman who had brought up the Armenian bankers approached us, swinging a rolled-up newspaper. "You should read this." He handed it over to Sarkisian. It was a *New York Daily Times* issue.

Simon's grin faded as he read. "There's been a serious uprising in the city of Van, in eastern Turkey. The Armenian residents—about twenty thousand—revolted against the Mussulmans. They ransacked the place and set it on fire. If a Kurdish chief hadn't stepped in to restore order, it could've ended in a massacre."

Sarkisian lifted his head. "What caused it, Garabet?"

The man with the silver hair spread his arms. "The Armenians wanted to ring the church bells, but the Mohammedans didn't take kindly to it."

"That's strange." Simon furrowed his brows. "I'm familiar with this community. Locals have upheld unwritten social agreements for centuries. Everyone worships freely, but no daily church bells, except on religious holidays."

Garabet narrowed his gaze. "The writer suspects the Russian agents were behind it. They told young Armenians to ring the bells on weekdays, stirring trouble, inciting revolt, turning Christians and Mohammedans against one another."

I asked, "Are you suggesting the czar was behind this?"

"It might be any of the Great Powers." Garabet closed one eye knowingly. "I wouldn't trust any of them. Instigators, all." He jabbed at Sarkisian and Nakshi. "You two with the fezzes, be vigilant. They want you to be each other's enemies, not friends. Once the flames rise too high, you'll blame each other and forget who lit the fire."

As Sarkisian stared at the article, the wise man slipped into the departing hologram crowd. He was only an image, but his warning couldn't have been more real. In the decades ahead, such wise voices would grow scarce, warnings would fall on deaf ears, each event laying another stone on the path to disaster.

The Armenian sighed, murmuring with sorrow, "Since the dawn of time, human nature has changed little. Shepherds and sovereigns alike cannot escape the same demons." He froze.

Krish dimmed the stage. When the lights returned, we were at the center of the dome. The hall, the smoke, the sweaty odor, all gone without a trace, except for the old stool. The floor beneath us was descending, its soft hum blending with the hiss of the Petamunra tiles rising toward the ceiling.

Nakshi muttered the wise man's words. "Beware of the instigators." He sighed. "I didn't know it had already begun in 1851."

His words pointed to the animosities between Muslim Turks, Kurds, and Christian Armenians that culminated in the atrocities of 1915 during the Great War. Armenians call it genocide—over a million of their kin perished. The Turkish government rejects the term, acknowledging forced displacement with far fewer casualties. The word genocide is controversial. It means different things to different people. Grandpa rejected it. Mom believed otherwise. Dad never said a word, but I knew he thought it was.

Regardless, it was one of the century's greatest tragedies. Innocent people paid the price. Many from both sides perished, Armenians in far greater numbers, many during forced migrations across the Syrian desert.

My father believed powerful foreign nations had instigated this conflict, fueling rage and fear that hardened into hatred, blinding both sides to the instigators' role. In his view, aside from the loss of innocent lives, the deeper damage was the collapse of centuries-old harmony in Anatolia. That spirit of coexistence had contributed to Istanbul's skyline—from its mosques and palaces to its folklore, music, and cuisine. It echoed the Ottoman motto for Armenians: "the trusted nation." With no will left to build a shared future, the old brotherhood vanished.

I leaned toward Nakshi. "Do you believe it was?"

His eyes had moistened. He didn't say a word, staring at the wooden stool on stage, the simple piece of furniture that tied both universes.

16

MEN OF THE AGE

"I remember the day I first arrived in America." Sarkisian gazed at the crowd lining Broadway. "It didn't take long to know I had landed in a great country."

It was a sunny, unusually warm December day. We joined Maggie and Simon to greet Louis Kossuth as he made his grand entry into New York. The star-spangled banner and Hungarian colors decorated every windowsill and storefront along Broadway. We stood before a light brown Greek-style building with a triangular pediment and four Roman Ionic columns. A banner stretched across Broadway proclaimed, "Hungary is not lost," honoring the 1848 revolution.

Maggie knit her brows. "It's a pity Zena couldn't make it."

We told them she had business in New Jersey. In truth, she needed to recover lost sleep before the banquet. Rocko teased that she'd be safe—Sundays were the serial killer's day off.

"We woke up to gun blasts when the *Humboldt* first reached Staten Island, all thirty-one saluting the European hero." Sarkisian gave a dry laugh. "Maggie's grandfather thought the British were attacking and called for his gun and uniform."

Maggie straightened. "The government kept him in quarantine for three days." Her eyes lit. "Finally, the big day has arrived."

"Who's running the café?" I asked.

"We're closed today, like hundreds of businesses."

Rocko rose on his toes to scan the crowd. "I'd say the whole town's here to see liberty in the flesh."

Simon nodded. "The city predicts a record, one hundred thousand. Two out of every ten New Yorkers."

Southampton had been a big crowd, but this was something else. Krish told us later that Petamunra ran on eighty percent capacity.

"The welcoming committee chose a four-mile procession." Sarkisian gestured down Broadway. "It starts at the southern tip of Manhattan, moves up from Battery Park to Astor Place, then south on Bowery along Fourth Avenue, reaching City Hall Park's eastern gate."

Then came the roar, swelling from blocks away. Kids climbed lampposts, people filled balconies. An open buggy appeared, flanked by mounted officers. A cheer erupted behind me, rattling my eardrums. Police on horseback shouted, trying to hold back onlookers spilling into the convoy's path. Hats flew into the air.

Kossuth stood alone in the carriage, overwhelmed. Dressed in a long coat, he waved his top hat. Like swarming piranhas, holographic spectators tore through our bodies for a better view of the Nation's Guest. Nakshi, visible only from the chest up, waved his fez. Rocko, missing half his torso, glanced at me, amused. I must have looked just as awkward. Maggie and Simon cheered, unscathed by the holographic override.

The crowd's enthusiasm reminded me of the 1969 ticker-tape parade for the moon landing. My parents met that day. My dad caught my mom mid-fall as the crowd surged toward the convertible carrying the Apollo 11 astronauts. Mom used to call me Moondust, maybe because that moment made me possible, or as a nod to her hippie years in France's Dordogne Valley. Dad chased her relentlessly, even grew his hair long, smoked hookah, and took a year off from academia to live in Martel, ultimately winning her heart.

On December 5, 1851, Louis Kossuth arrived in New York. No spectator fell that day in the quantum universe, human or hologram.

In 1851, the Astor House was New York City's most prestigious hotel, the fitting venue for the Independent Republican Press banquet honoring the illustrious Magyar.

Our round table for six, glowing phosphorescent near the ballroom entrance, was reserved by Alexander Voss for the guests of the *New York*

Daily Times. A spacious dance floor stretched before us, with scattered tables set aside for press and dignitaries.

I wore a black tailcoat with wide lapels and a velvet collar, a satin waistcoat, and a mauve four-in-hand necktie tied in broad wings. Rocko and Nakshi chose classic pleated shirts with dark waistcoats. Zena would join us before dinner.

Krish had arranged real food. A French restaurant —one of Brooklyn's finest and a KJ favorite—recreated the original banquet menu.

Astor House lacked grand chandeliers. Its richness came from intellect, nothing like the czar's golden drawing room. Apart from Christmas ornaments—just a week away—there was little splendor in decoration. Humble, meritocratic Americanism downplayed the pomp of European aristocracy.

Simon wore a mulberry-black brocade smoking jacket with a velvet shawl lapel. Alongside Nakshi—two men in fezzes—they marked the Ottoman Empire's presence.

Rocko teased him. "Your outfit speaks louder than your statement."

Simon shrugged. "The man in the shabbiest clothes is the most influential here."

"And who would that be?"

He nodded toward a man with a balding head at the largest round table, bright with flowers. "Horace Greeley, the editor of the *New York Tribune*."

Greeley had thinning, unkempt white hair, wispy at the sides. With small, round spectacles, he resembled Benjamin Franklin—perhaps intentionally. Yet, unlike him, this powerful editor carried a stern demeanor, not a jolly expression. His high-collared shirt, waistcoat, and overcoat suggested an intellectual or politician more than a financier, though he embodied all these roles.

Across the empty floor, Alexander Voss sat at a round table for eight. He spoke to a man in his early thirties. Dressed in a high-collared shirt, bow tie, and dark overcoat, the man seemed to be the table's leader, exuding the aura of command, keenly absorbing his surroundings.

Before I could ask Simon who he was, hisses rose from the crowd. All heads turned to another man with thick, curly silver hair and white mutton-chop sideburns. His silk Parisian redingote outshone everyone.

Sarkisian leaned toward me. "General James Watson Webb, owner of the *Courier and Enquirer*."

"Why are they hissing at him?"

"The *Courier* cast Hungary's revolution as a racial struggle between Sclavonic masses and Magyars. The *Tribune* trashed Webb for his condescending attitude toward Kossuth and pro-slavery stance."

"He doesn't seem shaken."

"General Webb considers himself above the fray. His father was George Washington's aide-de-camp. He's never known humble beginnings, unlike Greeley and Raymond."

Just as I wished Zena could witness the media rivalry, she made a dazzling entrance, shining like a rare gemstone, overshadowing Webb. She wore a scarlet velvet dress with glass beads and burgundy ostrich feathers, reminiscent of Scarlett O'Hara from *Gone with the Wind*. A sheer silver shawl covered her bare shoulders. Her swanlike neck, full red lips, wavy chestnut hair, and emerald eyes outshone every beauty in the salon.

Most women sat at the far end of the hall. Zena took exception. Rocko stood and pulled the empty chair between us, flashing a Rhett Butler smile. Zena glanced playfully at the tall novanaut before taking the seat.

Rocko landed a soft kiss on her hand. "My lady, I never imagined a woman could be so charming." Zena returned the smile.

An iceberg bobbed in my stomach. Recognizing the fast-approaching danger of a head-on crash—a surge of one-sided emotions—I decided to block the thought and let the lovebirds chirp their sweet nothings beside me. Believe me, I speak from experience.

"How are you tonight?" Zena leaned toward me.

I forced a grin, avoiding her gaze, pretending to be oblivious to her breathtaking presence.

"Jubilant and dandy!" My nose surrendered to her intoxicating perfume. "Never felt better. I can't wait for a great meal." She jerked back, knitting her brows.

Suddenly, a burst of applause erupted.

Governor Louis Kossuth entered the grand salon to a standing ovation, accompanied by an older man wearing a ribbon rosette pinned to his lapel.

Sarkisian nodded at him. "Chairman William Cullen Bryant, America's poet."

I remembered the name. Dad kept his famous work, *Thanatopsis*, posing profound questions about humanity's place in nature.

The governor inclined several times, until the clapping faded, then took his seat at the VIP table opposite us.

Nakshi snapped his fingers. "Look, the governor noticed us."

Kossuth's gaze met mine. Zena waved with a grin. He nodded. Several eyes shifted her way, including Horace Greeley's. Her confident poise told me this wasn't the first time she had drawn public attention.

An army of servers rushed from the kitchen to begin the dinner service. Sarkisian excused himself and returned to his table across the floor.

Nakshi glanced at the menu. "How am I supposed to know what to eat?"

It was in French. *Suprême de Volaille aux truffes; filet de bœuf aux champignons; chartreuse de gibier à la chasse; ris de veau aux petits pois.*

"I'd wager most guests will pretend they know what to order."

I chimed in, "I may be able to help a little." Growing up, every year in September, our family "became French"—my mom's doing. During the week of *La Fête de la Rentrée*, she embraced the Huguenot heritage she'd learned to appreciate during her years in France. All week, we ate French dishes, some delicious—I mean out-of-this-world—while others grossed out my cousin and me. When Mom found the shriveled giblets under the couch pillow during the pre-holiday cleaning, she became furious, and my cousin and I each received a sack of coal for Christmas that year. To be fair, she made them arrive on toy trucks.

"The *volaille* should be poultry with truffles," I remarked. "I suppose the *gibier* is some kind of game animal, maybe covered in gelatin and prepared with *chartreuse*, an after-dinner liquor, but honestly, I've no idea how it's made."

"Gross." Zena stuck out her tongue.

"They'd probably taste pretty good." Rocko encouraged her. "The secret is picking the right wine with the dish."

Zena shrugged. "I'm gonna order rice with the veal with little *pois*, whatever that is,"

"If you meant *ris de veau*"— I leaned in—"if I remember right, that means sweetbread. Rice in French is *riz*, not *ris*."

Nakshi squinted. "A sugary bread dish with snow peas? Who would eat that?"

"Neither sweet nor bread, I'm afraid. It's probably the pancreatic gland of the cattle." I smiled wryly.

"Are you trying to make me throw up?" Zena narrowed her eyes. "Isn't there something normal on this menu for regular people?" She was jittery.

"You could try green turtle soup. That's American, for sure." I pointed at the holographic menu.

Rocko furrowed his brows. "Then I'll cross you off my favorites list."

"I can't believe they serve turtles," Zena shook her head, then leaned to Rocko. "But why would you cross me off?"

"We've gotta protect turtles, not eat them. That's why." Rocko lifted his chin, terse.

Zena jerked, taken aback. "I didn't know you were an environmentalist."

"A passionate one. It's practically my religion. The first thing you should know about me." Rocko's voice turned flirtatious. "Only if you're interested in learning."

Zena gave him a once-over. "Good for you." She returned to the menu. "I'll stick with the champagne beef. It's the safest bet."

"*Champignons* means mushrooms, not champagne, my dear." Rocko nudged her. "I know that much French."

"Oh, I hate mushrooms." Zena scrunched up her face. "They are so chewy."

Nakshi offered her a smile. "Go with the poultry dish. That's what I'll do, the least risky option. I eat halal."

Embedded in a server, Krish took our orders.

Next came a parade of confections. Chefs rolled out their masterpieces on green carts, with Franz Liszt's "Transcendental Études" on piano.

The candied statues included Kossuth's home in Kutahia, an Abdulmejid statue, the Blue Mosque, Hagia Sophia, Atlas lifting the globe, and the Grecian Tower.

"Emperor Franz Joseph wanted the governor's head," Nakshi quipped. "They should send his candy bust to the Austrian envoy."

Washington and Lafayette's busts drew heightened applause.

The dinner was excellent, but Zena toyed with her chicken, claiming no appetite. "I'll join Maggie and the ladies for coffee and dessert, *la tarte fine de perche*."

"That's not peach tart, it's fish." She didn't hear me. Her gaze fixed on Alexander Voss as he approached our table.

After greeting us, he knelt before Zena. "My lady, Mr. Raymond sends his best regards." Zena held her breath.

Voss dropped his voice. "I briefed Henry about our conversation. I told him you reminded me of the late Margaret Fuller. He dismissed it until Governor Kossuth mentioned your interviews, which impressed Henry that you could reach him."

He set a sealed envelope on the table. "I'm honored to present you with this generous offer."

The tall man straightened, spreading his arms. "Shall I say I've accomplished my mission?" He flashed a sly smile. "Mr. Raymond will counteroffer ten percent more than Horace. Knowing the old fox, he will."

Zena was speechless.

"Take your time to decide." Voss bowed slightly. "I wish everyone a memorable evening."

"What was that all about?" Histo muttered as Voss returned to his table, Greeley watching from afar.

"I've no clue," Krish's voice came over the speakers. "We can't restrict cognitive minds communicating."

This was a startling eye-opener. The quantum universe was more than a home for romantic nostalgia. It allowed inhabitants to act, unless checked by restrictive algorithms.

Zena reached for the envelope, but her fingers slipped inside.

"How do you open a letter in the hologramic world?" Rocko smiled. "Now that's a challenge."

I leaned toward Zena. "Congratulations, you just landed a job at the *New York Times*."

She beamed. "I wish I could carry this offer over to real-time."

Zena entered into recorded history, though the offer letter would remain unopened, buried in hologramic dust.

Rocko lifted a brow. "I think Voss wants you by his side." His voice was mischievous.

Zena's grin faded. "What do you mean?"

Rocko shrugged. "The man has taste. Obviously."

Zena's face stiffened.

I cut in. "She earned that offer. Her conduct at Southampton was exemplary. Kossuth knew I asked her questions as she wasn't feeling well."

Zena narrowed her eyes, waiting for more.

"Your mind surpasses your charm." I met her gaze. "But don't blame those who struggle to get it. Like perfect fidelity, it's not easy to grasp—visual or cognitive."

She fell into my face, her mouth half open. I drifted away toward the center stage, watching servers roll out carts of cheesecake topped with Hungarian tricolor toppings.

"Thank you," she whispered, her breath tantalizing me. I shrugged casually, without taking my eyes off the dessert trays, picturing tiny candy fairies tap-dancing on each slice.

Rocko smirked and threw me a wry smile.

My words were honest, though I had no idea where they came from. Perhaps my late mother was whispering from afar. She never let men overpower her. "*It's the Huguenot rebellion spirit in me*," she used to say.

Simon and Maggie returned.

"What a marvelous gathering." Maggie grinned at Zena. "Join us at our table. It's women only. You'll meet some from the female suffrage movement."

"I'd love that," Zena clapped. "Anyone knew Margaret Fuller?"

"A few," Maggie pursed her lips. "She's now a legend in suffrage and anti-slavery circles."

"I'm investigating what happened." Zena met Maggie's gaze under Rocko's bemused look.

Maggie sighed. "Oh, what a tragic loss that was. She was Greeley's most popular writer." Her voice took a solemn ride. "She and her family drowned on their way from Europe. That much I know." She spread her palms.

Zena filled her information gaps with measured charm, masking her lack of knowledge and shifting between naïve and assertive as needed. Keeping men at a distance made her formidable in the male-dominated media world.

"Oh dear, leave these roaches," Maggie chirped. "We keep only one—His Majesty the Sultan. He's sweet and huge!" She chuckled, gesturing to an oversized candy bust of Sultan Mejid in the center of the women's table.

"A harem! Genius!" Zena exclaimed. "But without a Cherkess, it's a garden without a rose." Their laughter vanished in the roar of the room.

She called to Histo, "I'll be with my concubine sisters."

The incognito director nodded.

Zena grinned at Maggie. "How about a belly-dancing party until dawn, after the men leave?"

"Splendid! The sultan would like that." Maggie giggled as they walked to the women's table, where laughter echoed off the tall ceilings.

Simon Sarkisian rolled his eyes and slid into Zena's seat.

After three pings on a crystal glass, the commotion faded. Chairman Bryant raised his glass for the first toast.

"Turkey, Great Britain, and the United States, the deliverers of the Nation's Guest. How just the cause, when nations so distant and different in government unite their sympathies and acts."

Nine cheers followed, three for each flag.

The chairman turned to the esteemed guest. "You—the fearless, eloquent, large of heart and mind. The free press of the United States stands with you and your countrymen."

He lifted his voice higher. "I give you the man of the age, Louis Kossuth."

The illustrious Magyar rose to a standing ovation that lasted a minute.

"My name is Lajos Kossuth. I stand before you as Hungary's rightful Governor."

The audience erupted again, applause rolling for another minute.

"My humble thanks to the independent republican press for this honor." He cracked a smile. "This occasion may decide the success or failure of my visit to the United States." The remark drew laughter.

Kossuth stepped to the center. "In America, several daily papers reach sixty thousand readers each morning, while the colossal *Times* counts no more than thirty thousand."

"Call that British paper a monster!" someone shouted.

The governor dismissed the heckle, raising a hand. "The reason is simple. In the United States, newspapers sell for one-twentieth the price of England's. Hence, the circulation of New York City papers alone surpasses that of the entire British Empire."

A joyous hum rose in the grand salon.

"Eighty years ago, Benjamin Franklin operated the only press in the colonies. Today, every American adult reads two papers a week. Four hundred million copies a year go into print."

Horace Greeley, champion of the one-penny paper, lifted his chin, pride etched on his face.

Kossuth stepped toward the editor's table. "The freedom of the press, to be practical, must benefit all, else it is no freedom, that is a privilege. It requires two ingredients: freedom of printing and reading. In England, there is no freedom of reading because economics hinders the possibility for the public."

Nakshi knitted his brows. "Why's that?"

Sarkisian explained, "High levies on printed matter make it a luxury for the British public."

The visionary Magyar shifted to education, continuing his comparison of the New World and the Old.

"America's true power comes from its free public education, not its ample land or resources. New York City alone has educated over one hundred thousand students. Free men armed with knowledge form the backbone of a qualified workforce in the military, finance, and beyond.

Since intelligent men shall always desire liberty, freedom is guaranteed in America."

Kossuth's prophecy did come true. Yet lately, America's public education—once thriving—now ranks low among industrialized nations.

The exiled governor deepened his voice. "America. What is your existence?"

He carried himself like a scholar addressing an Ivy League hall. "Once a baby, you were protected by yonder doctrine of non-interference. The great territorial cloak hung loose on your puerile limbs. There is nothing wiser for the protected infant than to grow. And growth, you did—and grow you still do." His arms lifted wide. "Now a giant, with one arm reaching Asia over the Pacific, another to Europe over the Atlantic, the dress, once loose, fits you no longer."

"So you are asking now." His oratory flourished. "Here I stand, in proud immensity—a world myself amid two great continents. Should I live the life of a mummy, like those distant nations of South America and Asia—and say, as Cain did, 'Am I my brother's keeper?'"

The exiled governor deepened his voice. "Is isolationism an eternal and sacred bequest from my father—or his was a wise strategic advice for a newborn in 1776, of merely three and a half million souls and thirteen states?"

He jabbed toward the editors. "And I now ask you, members of the republican press: Should a young man still sleep in the child's cradle and be lulled by the same lullaby?"

His chin lifted, fingers gripping his lapels. "The principles upon which your great nation was born, the moral and material interests it upholds, manifest one incessant destiny: intercourse with the world."

Kossuth swept his gaze across the room. "You are a power on earth—and you must feel resolved to be a power on earth!" His voice carried passion. "Fear not! There is no one who can intimidate you."

Applause burst out except at the *Courier* table.

The governor stepped closer to the opposition table, fixing on General Webb. "Neutrality is a policy, a matter of convenience, not of principle. Let foreign powers quarrel over ambition; you mind your concerns." His stare hardened. "Non-interference, by contrast, concerns sovereignty. Every nation has the right to govern itself. It's the common law of mankind, on which your own Republic stands."

Webb sat unfazed. A voice from the table objected. "Founding Fathers bequeathed us to remain neutral and not interfere in Europe's conflicts."

Kossuth lowered his voice. "To you, sir, I say: Great Washington counseled neutrality, never indifference to foreign interference against a nation's sovereignty. There is a mighty difference. I challenge anyone to find in the eleven volumes of his writings a single word counseling silence in the face of violated humanity's common laws."

He paced back to the center as stronger applause echoed through the chamber.

"Washington wrote to Lafayette: 'Give us twenty years of peace, and we shall be strong enough to defy any power on earth—in a just cause!'" Kossuth paused, then repeated, "In a just cause!"

The exiled governor slowed his stride. "Never was there a people more sacrilegiously, more treacherously, and by fouler means attacked than Hungary."

His voice rose. "Never has crime, cursed ambition, despotism, and violence been united in a more wicked manner, crushing down freedom and the very life! Never was a country more mortally offended than Hungary is."

He paused. Silence hung in the hall. His moist eyes drifted, then he resumed. "If the cause of my people is not sufficiently just to claim God's protection, then there is no just cause, and no justice on Earth. No new Abel will move toward Heaven." He shook his finger and cried, "Only the Cains of humanity walk proudly on Earth!"

Most applauded, though a few remained unmoved.

The governor continued, "Austrian Emperor Francis Joseph declared that Hungary no longer exists as a nation. We fight for the Hungarian language. Being Hungarian has nearly become a crime in our native land."

"Does that sound familiar?" Nakshi lifted his brows. Rocko smiled bitterly, recalling Vladimir Putin's claim that no Ukrainian nation or state exists.

A hand rose. Kossuth nodded.

"Austria and Russia violated your rights, and we condemn them. But we can't interfere in every injustice. Besides, Hungary is too far."

Kossuth smiled wryly. "What once took eighteen days to reach Europe now takes five—though the miles remain unchanged. The ocean, once a separation between us, has become a bridge of trade, connecting markets and the fruits of that most honorable labor your great nation cultivates. Agriculture."

The novanauts exchanged glances, wondering—visionary as he was—if Kossuth could have imagined a world where information travels continents in the blink of an eye.

"Commerce is the steam that powers the locomotive of republican principles. Absolutism strangles free trade. As long as your mighty country represents republican principles, absolutism will never sleep in peace. You symbolize all they fear. Make no mistake, absolutists hate you more than they hate me."

Applause erupted, some rising to their feet.

"Yes, your power is great, but do not grow too fond of it. Look to history. Ancient Rome fell. Mighty empires vanished." His voice, now grim, shifted. "If the absolutists unite and grow, they will one day become too powerful even for you."

Kossuth turned to Webb. "Not my words, but your government's warning: 'Tyrannies won't rest until they destroy every last trace of freedom—not only in Europe, but even in the United States.' Sir, without the restoration of Hungary and the liberation of Italy, you will not be safe."

The popular argument of our time flashed in my mind: If Ukraine falls, America won't be safe. Will it?

Someone hollered, "Don't let Europe fall to absolutism!"

Kossuth strolled toward the half-eaten candied Magyar house in Kutahia, where he and his comrades had spent a year.

He fixed his eyes on it, speaking softly. "I have a favorable bias for Turkey, and I won't hide it. In our darkest hour, the sultan vowed to sacrifice fifty thousand of his subjects rather than let a single hair on our heads be harmed. I will never forget that."

"Three cheers for the sultan!" someone shouted.

Louis Kossuth placed his right hand over his chest and raised his left fist. "I shall never join any arrangement, however promising, that might harm Turkey. I will champion her interests wherever I go!"

Another objector rose. "What are these foreign conflicts to us?"

Kossuth jerked his head. "'What is Hungary to me?' asks this gentleman. A fair question. President Fillmore has answered it. In his address, he said, 'Let every people choose for itself, and make and alter its political institutions.' That is Washington's principle—on which your Republic was built—still affirmed."

"Hear, hear." Applause followed.

Resolute, Kossuth added, "Your Secretary of State as well. I quote Mr. Webster: 'No one nation has the right to interfere in the affairs of another.' No cause has been more just than the cause of Hungary."

Kossuth leaned over and addressed the *Courier* table. "We must all understand the vicious endgame. It is the 'Russianism' of European lands and a quest for world dominance that reaches into the Ottoman and Austrian Empires. The Turks have escaped it so far, but the Habsburgs are now within Russia's sphere and an enemy of freedom."

A man beside Webb objected. "Sir, I don't rob, I don't murder, I don't burn. My duty as a citizen is to obey the law, not to stop others from breaking it."

Kossuth leaned back. "Suppose you see a man robbing, murdering, or burning your neighbor's home. Do you say, 'What others do is not my concern?'"

"He's not his brother's keeper," someone shouted.

"Next, it'll be his home!" another warned.

"Our Savior was not content to merely avoid evil," Kossuth pressed. "He drove the evildoers from the temple."

"Hallelujah!" Cheers erupted.

General Webb rose.

"Sit down!"

"Hear him!"

"Order, order!" The chairman banged the gavel. "It is our distinguished guest's wish that the gentleman be heard."

The uproar lingered until the gavel struck again and silence fell. The chairman nodded to Webb.

The silver-haired general surveyed the room, then turned to Kossuth. "Your cause is just, and you have our sympathy. But we cannot go to war for your country or furnish armies and fleets. We shall not fight your battle."

Hisses broke out, mixed with applause.

Kossuth placed his hand on his chest. "As the Lord said, 'To whom much is given, much will be expected.'"

Applause thundered.

He returned to the center, careful not to stir the tension.

"One final remark," Kossuth said. "The decisive question is what Great Britain and the United States choose to do. I wish these nations would unite behind a policy to protect freedom. I cannot cover so vast a topic in one speech before exhaustion sets in."

His wish for a lasting transatlantic alliance would wait nearly a century, until NATO.

A final ovation and nine cheers followed.

"What does Congress think?" I asked Simon.

"Selling goods and arms, yes. But participation? Doubtful. Henry Clay and President Fillmore remain distant. Kossuth seeks a loan. His best chance is media support."

"He's doing well on that front. What's next for him?"

"He'll tour the country and make his case. But in the end, it's Congress and the White House that decide, not the media, never the public."

I wondered how his quest would end. Kossuth's bust now stands outside the Speaker's office in Congress. It stared blankly as rioters stormed the halls on January 6.

Would he have seen them as insurrectionists, vandals, or fools manipulated by lies? Or patriots chasing hidden truths, heroes saving a stolen election? Americans split sharply over the same event. No technology could bring him back to clarify his stance.

Lost in these thoughts, I missed the chairman's toast and the introduction of the next speaker.

A medium-framed man in his thirties had already risen, scanning the guests with ice-blue eyes.

He lifted his chin. "My name is Henry Jarvis Raymond, chief editor of the *New York Daily Times*, a new paper in town."

His bushy, unkempt mustache clashed with his trimmed mutton-chop sideburns, framing a rugged face. A receding hairline broadened his forehead, hinting at a keen mind.

"Mr. President and gentlemen, sir, after such a lavish banquet and a historic speech, I'm afraid the toast you've assigned me is altogether dry."

Laughter rippled through the room.

"What was the toast?" I asked Nakshi.

"National independence, secured by international law, not left to the mercy of the strongest."

Raymond smiled on. "I'm not only a journalist but also a politician. The subject is better suited for a senatorial debate, yet I will nevertheless speak to it."

He stepped to the center for a clearer view of the guests.

"Gentlemen! We are not here for a convivial gathering. The purpose of this meeting is to aid Hungarian independence." His jaw tightened.

"Yes, sir!" came from the audience.

"Should we not respond to the downtrodden people of Europe, yearning for the political freedom and prosperity we enjoy? Or should we say, 'We have no sympathy; we are busy with our concerns. Fight your own battles.'"

Cries of "No! No!" rose from the floor. Speaker Raymond lifted his chin once more.

"A nation is responsible for its acts and its example because that example is among its acts. But, sir, if we choose selfishness or cowardice, we are doomed to lose self-respect, national greatness, and glory."

"What about neutrality?" someone shouted.

Raymond replied promptly, "Sir, our great Secretary of State, Mr. Webster, has defined neutrality."

"He is no expounder!"

"Sir, you may differ from me in that opinion, yet even you will admit Mr. Webster is a good authority—at least when his decision aligns with yours." Chuckles and clapping broke out. "He says, 'Our neutral policy protects neutrality, defends neutrality, and will take up arms, if need be, for neutrality.' Sir, that is a definition of neutrality I am perfectly willing to accept."

The majority applauded.

He lifted his arm. "I do not doubt we shall aid Hungary in her struggle."

The editor moved toward the tray holding the candied *Humboldt*, borne by English and American soldiers.

He raised his voice. "I do not doubt. Our government, in unison with Great Britain, will preserve the peace of Europe rather than break it."

"We do not doubt!" Alexander Voss shouted, joining the applause.

Gripping the lapels of his jacket, Henry Raymond stood firm, head high, and waited for the applause to fade before continuing.

"To those who say speaking of Russia makes war inevitable and ourselves ruinous—sir, I have an answer. Any nation that conducts its foreign policy in fear of war does not deserve the dignity of foreign relations. The United States must take counsel of its rights and interests, not its fears."

A rowdy commotion broke out. Raymond paused, waiting for it to fade. It didn't. He rose above the din. "And, sir, do we claim the mighty Republic of the West takes counsel of its fears?"

"No! No!"

The editor moved toward a foot-long confectionery statue of Sultan Abdulmejid on a cart.

"Tyrants demanded that the sultan surrender an honorable man."

He gestured to Kossuth. "This man. Champion of Hungary. Star of our admiration, and of his people who graced that chair tonight."

Swaying his arm back to the statue, he cried, "And what was the reply of this Mohammedan monarch?" Raymond's voice rose above the applause. "I respect your power, but I respect humanity's rights more." He lifted his fist. "He did not doubt!"

Kossuth nodded, pressing his lips together. He must have recalled those difficult hours waiting for the decision on his fate and that of his comrades.

"Russia and Austria amassed their armies." Raymond waved. "Millions of soldiers! Hovering on Turkey's frontiers, cannons aimed at the sultan's capital!"

Henry's voice swelled.

"Do your worst," the sultan said. "I shall do my duty and trust in God!"

"Hear, hear!"

He faced the tall candy. "Let us take courage. If you need courage, follow the example. If you need an example, look to the conduct of the Turkish Monarch."

Henry Raymond pointed our way and nodded. The audience applauded the two men in fezzes. Simon stepped forward, Nakshi behind him, both saluting. My grandfather's image flashed through my mind—smiling, proud of his heritage.

The editor paused, waiting like a tiger ready to strike. Once the assembly took their seats, he turned to Lajos Kossuth and rephrased his assigned toast.

"Don't leave national independence to the mercy of the strongest. Sir, this case needs no argument before the American people!"

He placed his hand on his chest like Washington crossing the Delaware and shouted, "I do not doubt!"

The Astor House roared as the esteemed editor of the *New York Daily Times* took his seat amid a standing ovation—Kossuth included.

The young editor matched the oratorical skill of the Magyar virtuoso before him. Fifty feet away, his piercing ice-blue eyes locked on mine, as if tasking me to report this dialogue between centuries, bridged by Russia, flanked by Ottoman Turkey and Hungary on one side, and modern Ukraine on the other. Goosebumps surged, and a heavy sense of responsibility sank into my bones.

Rocko narrowed his eyes, swallowing. "I didn't know sunny days were possible for the Sick Man in the nineteenth century."

"We missed it." Nakshi pressed his lips together, watching Sarkisian waving his fez at the guests, his grin stretching ear to ear.

"If only *we* could change history," I muttered.

"Mark the day, my friends." Rocko smiled knowingly. "This must have been the night the *New York Times* got ahead of the pack and never looked back."

"Two men of the age." Nakshi nodded, his eyes moist.

Lajos Kossuth and Henry Jarvis Raymond owned that night. I wished Zena hadn't left our table. Everything was perfect otherwise.

17
GRAND ELCHI

Monday morning. Day four in our journey into the quantum universe. We gathered in the Petamunra dome, sitting around the black carbon table.

"Where is Histo?" Nakshi looked around.

Krish sipped his tea. "He'll join us soon. Had some digestive issues."

"He didn't eat anything to digest," Rocko smirked. "That could be his problem."

"Just smelling those weird dishes could do that." Nakshi grimaced.

The sauces had been a bit too rich. Otherwise, it was a feast to remember, but not worth arguing over.

Krish had warned it would be chilly today. Everyone wore jeans and wool sweaters, sipping coffee from paper cups and munching on bagels and donuts.

Rocko eyed Zena's untidy hair. "Did you enjoy last night?"

"Enthralled. Captivating." She bit her donut.

"How so?"

She swallowed before answering. "I was with several transcendentalist women after everyone left. Learned a lot—Margaret Fuller, Ralph Waldo Emerson, and others." She gestured toward me. "I'm sure he knows all about their philosophy." She sipped her coffee.

"I do?" I knitted my brows. I didn't know about transcendentalism.

Her eyes brightened. "Every person carries a spark of the divine. God and truth are found within. Nature is sacred." That sounded intriguing.

"What else did you do with your soul sisters at the late-night soiree?" Rocko gave her a mischievous look. "Flip a quarter with your abs?"

She squinted. "What does that mean?"

"Last I heard, you suggested a group dance, letting them marvel at the harem's secret life."

"Is that what you think I do?" Her smile faded. "Belly dancing in the hammams?"

Rocko shrugged. "We do what we have to. I cleaned toilets to stay in the dorm for free."

Zena's lips tightened like someone in pain. "Oh! Did I tell you I pole dance in strip clubs after hours to pay for my student loans?" Zena scoffed, nostrils flaring. "I don't, but I've met women who do. I respect them, raising babies in diapers after their jerk husbands walked out on them. Honorable living isn't about what you do, but how you do it!"

She banged the table, jumping her half-eaten donut, then shoved her plate away.

Clenching her fist, she muttered. "Sometimes you have to dive deep to find a spark in people, if any."

Rocko stiffened, not saying a word. The room fell silent.

Histo entered in his light blue suit.

"Good morning. You'll be incognito at two events this morning. One in St. James, London, the other on a small island in the Aegean."

"What year did we wake up to?" Nakshi smiled faintly, easing the tension. "Last night's banquet was in December 1851."

"Early 1853."

It matched secret communications between Czar Nicholas and Ambassador Seymour in St. Petersburg.

"What's the occasion?" I asked.

"Britain's ambassador to Constantinople, Lord Stratford Canning, is returning from Europe."

The lights revealed a dock on blue waters. The trees had buds but no leaves yet. A British steamer, *HMS Fury*, was at the pier. At the stern, the white ensign billowed in the wind, marking her as a Royal Navy vessel on official duty.

A tall man with wavy dark brown hair stood on the dock. His silk suit looked like it had passed through the hands of a master tailor. He waved at a man stepping off the vessel.

"Welcome to Turkey, Stewart."

"Signor Sappini! Great to see you, Francesco."

"How did the chief fare?"

"Catching up on sleep. It's the first week of April, but snow is still on the ground in Europe. We're all exhausted but he the least." Stewart rolled his eyes. "Thank you, my good Lord, this is my final stop. I can't see myself doing this at his age."

"I thought I'd seen the last of the big man." Sappini smiled wryly.

"Never say never, my friend. Mrs. Canning thought they'd finally retire to their country estate. But St. James called the old wolf back to guard his henhouse in Constantinople." Stewart sighed. "Forty years in foreign service, most of them here."

"I found it strange that Prime Minister Lord Aberdeen insisted on working with him." Sappini raised a brow. "He is a political rival. Lord Stratford once told me that he would become the next foreign minister when his friend, Earl Derby, took office. But when he did, he gave the post to someone else."

"He later learned why St. James passed him over." Stewart winked. "When Russia's ambassador to London heard the name Stratford Canning, he said, *'quelle plaisanterie'*—how pleasant—then added, *'une mauvaise plaisanterie,'* yet a bad one." The two men chuckled.

Francesco leaned closer and lowered his voice. "Sending Lord Stratford to the empire's top foreign post would have been unwise while England was balancing relations with Russia. The czar despises him. The boss understood and didn't make an issue of it."

"But not when he was passed over again a few months later, this time for the ambassadorship in Paris." Stewart snapped. "Especially since someone less deserving got the position. That was unfair."

Sappini nodded. "Lord Canning lacks finesse. The royal couple does not befriend him, though Her Majesty respects his skills and experience and acknowledges his unwavering dedication to the Crown."

He caught his breath and added, "That was when Lord Stratford asked me to inform the Sublime Porte he was taking indefinite leave. I broke the news to the grand vizier and foreign minister that, in his absence, Colonel Rose would step in."

"How did they take it?"

"The Porte was taken aback. Their first reaction was, 'No one can fill his shoes.'"

"They must be pleased about his return."

"Not everyone." Sappini lifted a brow. "The sultan is, and that matters the most. But I'm curious. How did it happen?"

"We're going through extraordinary times." Stewart gazed at the horizon. "First Leiningen's arrival, then Prince Menshikov's. They rang alarm bells in St. James. Lord Aberdeen told Her Majesty he needed our toughest man at the Bosporus."

Sappini nodded once more. "He's right. Colonel Rose has skills, but it takes a rare person to handle that kind of pressure."

Stewart glanced around to check no one was listening, then dropped his voice. "Rumor has it Lord Aberdeen suggested to Her Majesty that Stratford Canning be awarded a peerage. Queen Victoria agreed and even invited him to choose his own title."

"Madonna mia! Is that right?" Sappini's eyes widened.

"Viscount Stratford de Redcliffe." Stewart nodded. "But Lord Stratford made it conditional. He would accept the title only if Her Majesty left no doubt he had earned the honor."

Sappini chuckled. "This man never stops surprising me. He's got guts, hasn't he?"

"Her Majesty complied." Stewart cracked a crooked smile. "Still, some at St. James doubted it was purely merit-based." He winked. "Passed over twice, then asked to return to your old post. Was it redress for exclusion or a noble act of volunteering? Either way, he earned the peerage."

"Who told him first?"

"Lord Clarendon, when he summoned him in February. Lord Stratford went thinking St. James finally approved his retirement request, but a surprise awaited him."

"I would've loved to see his reaction." Sappini smiled subtly.

The scene froze. The dome went pitch black.

When the lights returned, we found ourselves in a spacious office. The wall calendar showed February 25, 1853, forty days earlier. The moist, chilly spring wind had given way to a warm, stuffy odor rising from a crackling fireplace.

A tall man nearing seventy was reading the notes before him. Across from him sat a man in his fifties. A freshly engraved nameplate read: Foreign Secretary of Great Britain and Ireland: Earl of Clarendon, born George Villiers.

The younger man offered a faint smile. "These communications are for your eyes only, Viscount de Redcliffe."

The elderly man shuffled through them. "You may still call me Stratford, George. I'm still getting used to the peerage."

Lord Clarendon gave a brief chuckle. "I was born to it. You earned it, Lord Canning." Stratford Canning returned the smile, though tinged with bitterness.

Clarendon leaned in. "In a town filled with different opinions, there's rare consensus that no one else but *you* can manage the Turks."

Stratford Canning, unfazed, kept reading. Perhaps he was thinking he should be in Clarendon's place. The foreign secretary began to squeeze and release his fist as silence thickened.

"I need you, Canning." Clarendon's voice softened. "You and I haven't always seen eye to eye, but this time it's different. I ask—beg if I must—that you return to your post."

Stratford's features eased at the Earl's candor. "Czar Nicholas won't like this letter, perhaps even more than the one sent earlier by your predecessor."

The foreign secretary slumped back. "That's part of the point. Lord Aberdeen does not want to appear softer."

Clarendon pointed to the stack of papers on the table. "You've read Lord Russell's reports. My discourse won't change. Turkey's self-destruction is not imminent. Britain has made that clear to Russia."

Stratford leaned back in his chair. "Do you think Nicholas will go to war with the Turks?"

The foreign minister spread his hands. "He may have already decided."

"What makes you say that?"

"Three things. First, the Russian army has amassed troops in the Caucasus and increased activity along the Turkish border. Second, Czar Nicholas sent his envoy, Prince Menshikov, to Constantinople aboard a major steamship."

"What do you make of it?"

Clarendon sighed, his gaze at the window. "Czar Nicholas assured Ambassador Seymour Menshikov's trip is confined to the Holy Land crisis, a tug-of-war between Russians and French over church keys, particularly the Holy Sepulcher."

"Déjà vu." Stratford shook his head. "I managed a similar crisis two years ago. Latin Church or Eastern Orthodox? Trivial issues."

"The Holy Sepulcher may be the veil concealing the real reason for Menshikov's visit to Constantinople." Clarendon filled his pipe with tobacco. "Still, the consensus here is that this crisis won't escalate, despite the French Ambassador's rough play."

Troop movements along the border? Russia downplaying it. It all sounded familiar—like the buildup along the Ukrainian border in 2022 when Russia claimed it was just a routine exercise before launching the invasion.

Lord Canning twirled his fingers, thinking. "Colonel Rose could speak to the French Ambassador. Rose is an excellent soldier and a natural diplomat. He speaks French like a native and is fluent in Arabic and Turkish."

"France is run by an iron fist these days." Clarendon swatted the idea aside. "No roar is credible unless it comes from the lion's mouth."

"What's the third issue?"

"It's Austria. Count Leiningen came to Constantinople, threatened the Turks, and left with concessions in the Balkans, including Montenegro. His easy success alarmed Downing Street. The Sublime Porte lacks direction. Rose is a capable second fiddle but not suited for the limelight."

"Nicholas claims Austria is in his pocket." Stratford flipped through the notes.

"We don't know how true that is. It contradicts realpolitik. The two powers have conflicting interests over the Danube."

"The Danube should remain open to trade for all nations. Turkish administration is best suited for it."

Stratford's words echoed Grandpa's. Upset by Serbian aggression against Muslim Bosnians in the nineties, he often said Turks would have kept the Balkan nations in line as they had managed conflicts for centuries. Dad disagreed, arguing the Ottoman Empire relied on brutal oppression for false security. Geopolitical quarrels were common in my family.

"Keeping the alliance strong between Great Britain and Turkey benefits both parties." Lord Clarendon puffed his pipe, awaiting Stratford's response.

Stratford took a long breath, his mouth sealed. "My primary task has evolved over my years in Turkey." The ambassador hesitated as Clarendon leaned in, raising his brows. "The British mission in Constantinople has become the chief instrument for accomplishing reform within the Ottoman Empire."

Clarendon was quick to respond. "I don't see any conflict with that. Your return would only strengthen that objective." He exhaled, filling the room with a fruity-smelling smoke. "You have everyone's support at home."

Stratford puckered his lips to one side. "I'd like to hear from Emperor Napoleon and Minister von Metternich before embarking for Constantinople."

Clarendon slumped. "Your decision." He beamed, certain it was a yes. "I'll request Lord Aberdeen to arrange the meeting with the emperor. I'll handle the count in Vienna myself."

Both statesmen knew how to set aside differences in a crisis. Lord Stratford knew better than to press the issue of having been passed over. Clarendon was in charge, but he didn't impose on one of the Crown's most reputable diplomats. Realpolitik could forge unexpected alliances.

"As the Foreign Secretary, I should summon you." Clarendon offered him a blank sheet. "You write, I sign."

Lord Stratford took a deep breath, picked up the pen, dipped it into the inkwell, and began to write.

At this critical period in the fate of the Ottoman Empire, Her Majesty's Government has directed Viscount Stratford de Redcliffe to return to his post in Constantinople, entrusted with a special mission and charged with confidential instructions…

The scene froze in St. James.

We were back on the Aegean, sailing aboard the *HMS Fury*. Sappini stood on deck. The novanauts, incognito, wrapped ourselves in wool blankets Krish had handed out. Sweaters alone wouldn't suffice. Histo didn't bother with any.

"He must be former Navy." Rocko glanced at him. "Special forces."

Sappini spoke to a sailor in Turkish. His Istanbul drawl reminded me of Dad. Grandpa took pride in his son's flawless tongue. I felt a hint of resentment toward Dad for never teaching me his native tongue.

Rocko translated, "The captain says we'll reach Istanbul in less than an hour."

"I thought Sappini was Italian." Zena glanced at Rocko.

Rocko, still shaken from the morning quarrel, stayed silent, avoiding her gaze. Zena twitched, brushing off his dismissive attitude.

Nakshi chimed in, "He probably is, but he might be a dragoman."

I nodded. "That makes sense."

"What does that mean?" Zena squinted at me, holding her hand up as a visor against the sun.

"They served as translators and aides assigned to ambassadors and other dignitaries. The Porte had theirs, too."

A man in a wool vest and wrinkled pants stepped out from the cabin, grinning wide.

"Stephan Francesco Sappini! What a pleasure to see you."

"Charlie Alison!" Sappini spread his arms, smiling. "We expected you earlier. I hope you had a nice trip."

"The weather did not cooperate, but we finally made it with God's grace."

"You spent more than a month in continental Europe. How did it go?"

"We started in Paris. Lord Stratford dined with the French Emperor and Empress in the Tuileries."

"How was their chemistry?"

"Cordial and sincere. Louis Napoleon was open and candid in his views." The Englishman stretched his neck. "The emperor praised our Great Elchi. He said the Anglo-Turkish title the Turks awarded him didn't quite do him justice. 'Great ambassadors are rare, but they do exist,' he said, then proposed a Franco-Turkish version: *Grand Elchi, comme un grand homme.*"

"Grand Elchi, huh?" Sappini murmured. "I like the sound of it."

"Empress Eugénie excused herself in the final hour. Napoleon III invited the ambassador to his drawing room to discuss the crisis in the Holy Land."

"What's his view?"

"He aligns with the British. The emperor sees no imminent danger of the Turks collapsing and supports preserving the Turkish Empire's integrity." Alison arched his back, hands pressed on his waist. "But he hadn't expected the Turks to concede so easily to Austria."

"Leiningen came with an ultimatum to start a war." Sappini pursed his lips. "I doubt he'd have tried that if Lord Stratford were at the helm." The dragoman's curiosity grew. "How did Louis Napoleon read Prince Menshikov's arrival in Constantinople?"

"He didn't seem concerned. He thought Menshikov's mission was only about the Holy Shrine issue. He was eager to help resolve it. But he also believes the czar has a personal issue with him."

"What's that?"

Alison cracked a wry smile. "Czar Nicholas refuses to include 'Napoleon' in the European royal family registry. Nicholas calls him '*mon ami*' instead of '*mon frère,*' as tradition dictates, and privately mocks him as 'Ze Tird.'"

Sappini chuckled. "A friend, not a brother. Could be worse. Victor Hugo calls him '*Le Petit Napoleon,*' and he does it in public."

Alison joined the laugh, then fixed a stern gaze. "As we left Paris, we heard Colonel Rose had summoned Vice-Admiral Dundas to move the British Mediterranean fleet from Malta to Turkish ports."

Sappini shook his head. "Rose panicked. Menshikov's bluster in the seraglio halls pushed him to act too fast. Thank God the vice-admiral held back and asked London first. Then came Lord Clarendon's directive to stay put in Malta."

Charles Alison lifted his brows. "When he got the news, Lord Stratford wasn't pleased with Rose's decision. He feared that once the French Emperor learned of it, he would rush his fleet to Turkey."

Sappini's voice deepened. "He did. Diplomatic circles called it one of the British mission's worst missteps in Constantinople."

Alison cut in. "Read that, Lord Stratford Canning."

Sappini nodded. "I expect the Grand Elchi to drop Colonel Rose into a boiling *kazan*."

"It wasn't pretty inside the train, and it got worse when we missed our connection from Prague to Vienna." Alison smiled bitterly. "They didn't have enough water for the steam engines. The small German states lacked coordination."

"That sounds suspicious." Sappini narrowed his eyes. "More like a Viennese slow waltz."

"That's what Lord Stratford thought. We couldn't get word from Constantinople or London for days."

"That must have enraged him. How long did it take you to get from Paris to Vienna?"

"Six days. We checked into a hotel on the outskirts of Vienna, run by a single servant handling everything. A bell system linked rooms to the desk. One ring for the waiter, two for the chambermaid, three for the boots. None of it worked." Alison gave a dry laugh. "Lord Stratford asked to have his suit pressed for his meeting with the emperor. Three hours later, room service brought lukewarm goulash."

Francesco clapped, chuckling. "I can picture the proprietor. Did he know his guest doesn't like surprises?"

Alison held his smile. "Fortunately, Count Metternich postponed the meeting with Emperor Franz Joseph."

Sappini made a cross. "Thank you, Blessed Virgin Mary, for letting it be over."

"I wish it were." Alison leaned in. "The worst is yet to come."

Like Sappini, I held my breath.

"Vienna to Laibach was by train, slow but manageable, with stops. We cleared snow along the way, but the real challenge came in the last hundred kilometers to Trieste. Snowdrifts piled high and fallen trees blocked the tracks. The machinist told us to return to Graz by horse."

"Oh no! My Lordship doesn't like the word retreat."

"You know him well, Stephan. The machinist said there was nothing he could do but wait for spring. That's when he snapped." Alison chuckled. "A moment the poor man will never forget."

"What did you do then?"

"We walked to the nearest village, half-buried in snow, and hired a man with an ox cart to take us to the port. It took five days, but we finally reached Trieste. Everyone cheered when *HMS Fury* came into sight. She had been waiting for us for days. If there is one lesson I learned—oxen make the best snowplows."

The novanauts exchanged befuddled glances.

"Astonishing," Rocko broke the silence. "One day, you're dining with emperors; the next, you're riding oxen to catch your ship."

It was a moment to reflect. These events weren't so distant, just a few generations ago. Communication and transportation have leapt forward so dramatically that their story felt unreal. But what about us, our attitude, our morality? In that regard, we hadn't moved an inch.

Suddenly, the hallway door opened, and Stratford Canning stepped onto the deck, making his commanding presence felt. In his late sixties, he still looked fit and handsome with silver-blond hair. He wore a wool vest over a loose shirt; pants tucked into tall boots that reached his knees. An Irish and Anglo-Saxon mix, with Nordic traces in his features, his glassy blue eyes set off the sharp line of his aquiline nose and chiseled jawline.

"A joy to see you again, my Lordship." Sappini bowed slightly. "I wish Mrs. Canning had accompanied you."

"Not this time, Stephan. Not yet, at least. Someone with sanity must stay behind and teach the Foreign Office how to coordinate with the Orient." He smiled, giving him a once-over. "How is Helene?"

"She is fine. Thank you for asking, my Lordship."

"Your father sends his best regards. I spent a few days with Count Sappini—much to his regret. I presume Charles briefed you on our trip."

"He did, sir; he has been gracious." Stephan Sappini gestured to Alison. "I'm glad you survived the harsh weather, sir. Spring welcomes you in Constantinople."

Lord Stratford took a deep breath. "I didn't miss the city much, but I can't say the same for the sour cherries."

"You have been greatly missed, sir." Sappini's voice softened, though tinged with hurt. "Everyone at the embassy is thrilled to see you return. Everyone at the Porte has been waiting anxiously as well."

Lord Stratford pressed his lips, regretting his lapse of abruptness with his trusted aide.

"Pray tell me, Stephan. How did the Sublime Porte receive Prince Menshikov's arrival? For a fortnight I've been immured in white darkness, utterly cut off from all intercourse with civilization."

Sappini drew a big breath. "February 28 was a fearful day. I'll never forget the scene. Thousands of Greeks and Russians lined up along Tophane to greet Prince Menshikov. On his way, he visited the Russian fleet in Sebastopol, and rumor had it he ordered bakers in Odessa to bake only army biscuits."

"That must have caused more panic." Stratford's voice was dry.

Sappini nodded. "Menshikov bypassed protocols. He refused to meet with Fuad Effendi, the foreign minister, and insisted on visiting the grand vizier, Mehmed Ali Pasha, in civilian attire." The dragoman threw up his arms. "He raised his voice, almost cursing Fuad Effendi's labors in Wallachia."

Stratford furrowed his brow, barely concealing his puzzlement.

"Fuad resigned, and Rifat Pasha took his post."

Stratford Canning smiled subtly. "Rifat is a more able man and diplomat than Fuad. Menshikov's rage worked against him."

He took a few steps, head bowed in thought.

"His mission didn't rouse suspicion for belligerence in European courts. How did the Porte perceive it?"

Sappini tilted his head. "My Lord, in Turkey, we can smell a rotten egg long before it's cracked in the West." A bitter smile lingered. "You don't send a steam frigate just for church keys. The Russians anchored *The Thunderer* right beneath the sultan's windows."

"Did he have other demands?" Stratford paced, not looking at his aide.

"The prince handed them to Rifat Pasha in a note. He refused to show me, saying Russia would terminate diplomatic relations if he did."

"That's preposterous." Lord Stratford jerked his head. "How did the sultan take it?"

"Sultan Mejid is not himself these days. His mother is gravely ill."

"I'm sorry to hear that. What illness afflicts her?"

"Consumption, I suppose."

Her name was Bezmi-âlem Sultan. I heard her story from Grandpa. Once a simple bath attendant in the harem, her pale skin, soft hands, and reddish hair captivated Sultan Mahmoud. Beyond her beauty, she was strong and intelligent, a steadfast supporter of her husband's reforms.

Lord Stratford's gaze drifted to the horizon. "I remember when her teenage son, Abdulmejid, took the throne after Mahmoud's death. He followed his mother's counsel and defied the old guard by appointing Mustafa Reshid Pasha grand vizier. That took courage."

He turned to his chief dragoman. "Draft a letter to the Mother Sultan, offering my best wishes for her recovery."

Sappini exchanged glances with Alison. He was taken aback. Alison cleared his throat. "My Lord, I must advise against it. In the Porte's eyes, you are a *gâvour*, an infidel, addressing a Mussulman woman, and not just any woman, the sultan's mother. Nothing of the kind has ever occurred at the Ottoman court."

Stratford snapped. "Do you think I don't know that?"

He then turned to Sappini, speaking in a sharp tone. "You will deliver it to the harem. End of discussion."

"Yes, my Lord." Sappini bowed. Alison looked down at his shoes, his ears reddening. Stratford wasn't a man to cross.

Lord Canning seemed ill at ease after his sudden burst of anger. Without a word, he walked away, leaned on the rails, watching the wake as the vessel neared the Bosporus.

The steamer glided through the waters that had divided Europe and Asia since the Ice Age. Nature, raising the sea levels, has defined geopolitics since then. A sharp breeze reddened Elchi's cheek to a ruddy hue. The fresh air, fragrant with the seabed's brine, filled my lungs and set my head reeling. I wondered how Krish had managed to capture the Bosporus's unmistakable scent.

The magnificent silhouettes of the triple crown—the Topkapi Palace, the Blue Mosque, and the domes of Hagia Sophia—emerged from the morning fog. The crescents atop the minarets glittered. The city rose with the sun, saluting the morning with a symphony of sounds: the chirping of albatrosses, muezzins' call to prayer, the swoosh of waves gliding over opposing currents, one flowing from the Black Sea to the Marmara, the other in reverse. A pod of dolphins escorted the steamer, as if heralding the king's return to the strait after a long wait.

Stephan Sappini approached Canning from behind. Without shifting his gaze from the port side, the Englishman muttered, "Sheer magnificence. Every time feels like the first."

"It's a potpourri of aesthetics, sir. Nature's special gift to humanity." Stephan held his gaze on his chief as Stratford watched the dolphins vanish into the distance. "My wife tells her friends that Lord Stratford could no longer live without Constantinople. Should I tell Helene she's right?"

Lord Stratford sighed a half-chuckle with no words uttered.

"Everyone at the embassy thought we'd seen the last of you at your farewell party."

"That included me." Lord Stratford smirked. "A mysterious force draws me back. The more I try to leave, the stronger it pulls."

"Realpolitik, perhaps?" Sappini smiled.

Stratford Canning inhaled deeply, held it, then exhaled. "Had Napoleon Bonaparte seen this city in his youth, he might have ordered his conquests differently."

"If he had a *grand elchi* to his side to tell him that."

Lord Stratford flashed a crooked smile. "Charles told you that?"

Sappini did not respond, his smile lingering.

The ambassador's jaw loosened, his gaze fixing on the white wake trailing through the turquoise waters. He sighed, "Not everyone favors me."

Czar Nicholas despised him. They had met at the Congress of Vienna—Canning, a young diplomat, Nicholas, a prince. The

Englishman's air of equality had rankled the heir to the Russian throne. Years later, during Stratford Canning's short ambassadorship in Russia, Czar Nicholas treated him with open disdain—a slight Canning never forgot.

Cannon fire thundered from both flanks of the Bosporus as *HMS Fury* entered from the Sea of Marmara, hailing the white wolf's return to his den. He stood tall at the bow, undisturbed by the spindrift splashing his face. Like a lion on a ridge surveying the valley below, his posture exuded self-confidence, leaving no doubt in the minds of those watching him on shore, whether out of fear or reverence, but all with respect.

The captain sounded two short blasts, signaling the ship's docking on the European shore, portside. Muslims and rayahs erupted in cheers along Tophane.

Sappini stood behind. "Welcome home, my Lordship."

Tears welled in Stratford's eyes as Englishmen and women from the Levant and embassy staff stood apart, saluting their leader and waving the Union Jack. He spotted his beloved, skittish white horse.

The stage was set for a high-stakes diplomatic chess game unseen on these shores since the Siege of Troy. History would remember only one victor. Stratford Canning and Czar Nicholas both knew they alone could slice the Gordian knot of the Eastern Question. The rope would fall in one of two directions for the Ottoman Empire: resurrection or ruin, as Nicholas intended.

A sailor on the forecastle proclaimed, "The Honorable Stratford Canning, Viscount Stratford de Redcliffe!"

Grand Elchi filled his lungs with the Bosporus air once again and murmured, "The curtain rises."

As the vessel docked, two men boarded. The sultan's envoy in a fez, unsmiling, kissed Canning's hand—a gesture of respect. Sappini translated his brief greeting. The ambassador offered a polite wave, and the envoy bowed, stepped back, and disembarked.

Next came a middle-aged Western man, his eyes at odds with his smile. "Welcome home, Lord Canning."

"Thank you, Colonel Rose. How is your family?" Lord Stratford's demeanor was polite, his voice ice cold.

"All in good health, my Lord. Thank you."

"And the situation?" Canning was calm, deliberate.

"Turks are alarmed, wavering between fear and better judgment. Greeks are eager, expecting gains."

"And the Porte?"

Rose cleared his throat and lowered his voice. "The grand vizier has awaited your return. The Porte holds all dealings with Prince Menshikov in secrecy."

"Nothing remains secret in the Levant, Colonel." Lord Stratford fixed his gaze on Rose. "The skill lies in knowing how to unravel them."

"Welcome home, sir!" someone called, cutting in as Rose reddened.

Stratford beamed at the men approaching to take his belongings. "Hardy, Black, Hanson. Thank you for coming."

Black jabbed cheerfully, "Thank *you*, sir, for coming back! We heard it was a rough trip."

Lord Stratford gestured toward Charles Allison. "You should be thanking Mr. Alison. Without his resolve, we wouldn't have made it. He plodded a mile through knee-deep snow to fetch a carriage, while the rest of us stayed warm by the fire."

"Thank you, Mr. Alison, for bringing us our Great Elchi," Black waved his cap to the diplomat, who had stood quietly aside until then.

"Grand Elchi!" Charles Alison hollered back, grinning. "Time to liken the French, Mr. Black. We'll need them."

Lord Stratford shook his head with a lingering, faint smile.

Zena leaned toward me. "Didn't Alison say the oxen carriage was Lord Stratford's idea?"

"Apparently, it was Alison's." I remembered Dad's words. He considered bragging inappropriate. "*Learn to be patient. Acknowledgement could take time.*"

"Must be the British humility, I suppose," I muttered.

Hardy removed his cap.

"Let us pray to Divine Providence to inspire your lordship to serve the greater good."

With heads bowed, "Amen!"

The ambassador stood observant until Turkish security dispersed the non-Anglican crowd. He stepped onto a makeshift bench to address the remaining Englishmen and women.

"I am pleased and humbled to see the loyalty and candor before me. I shall have no cause to regret the great sacrifices I have made by absenting myself from my native country and my family to stand once again among you."

Applause followed.

"Unpleasant circumstances have transpired during my absence, but I believe we shall do better to occupy ourselves with the present rather than the past. England's policy leans toward the maintenance and independence of this great empire, which harbors us and our families as guests. Rest assured, there is no reason to despair over its future progress. I feel confident I may always calculate on your support."

"Grand Elchi!" Hanson cheered. The crowd echoed the chant.

Stratford Canning stepped down amid applause, declined his carriage, mounted his horse, and rode off toward the seraglio, Sappini trailing.

As the hoofbeats faded, I reflected on his words. No cause for despair. England would preserve the Ottoman Empire.

Had he brought a miracle pill to revive the ailing patient? Or was the Englishman merely a pretentious friend, offering hollow reassurances and false hope, angling for advantage when the empire collapsed?

Or perhaps he truly believed what he said—one of the few optimists at the Court of St. James.

Those questions lingered as the lights dimmed, turning the room pitch-black, warm air rushing in.

"You may pass me the wool blankets," Krish's voice came through. "Next stop: the Winter Palace in St. Petersburg. You won't need them inside."

18
THE
REVOLUTIONARY

Histo informed everyone. "Someone from the quantum universe will join you for the next session."

Rocko knitted his brow. "A hologram for a novanaut?"

"He'll be incognito like you, except I'll also be invisible to him."

"How would you correct him if he goofs?" I asked.

"He won't. He represents a reporter from the era, not a visitor from the future."

Zena beamed. "Like a guest star in a long-running TV show. Exciting."

Krish murmured, typing on his iPad, "He speaks his mind. Expect lots of freezes. Stop and go, like Friday rush hour."

An olive-skinned, stocky man stepped into the Petamunra dome.

"There he is." Rocko waved.

The guest looked to be in his thirties, with a broad forehead, wavy gray hair, and a full black beard. He wore a worn black frock and shoes like mine, though his pair needed a shine.

"Same brand, I suppose," I quipped, pointing at his feet and then mine.

The hologram shot me a sharp gaze with small, dark eyes. "Peals. Custom-made in London." A German accent cut through every word.

"Is that where you live?"

"Yes." His gaze darted around, assessing everyone, yet showing no interest in camaraderie.

Zena stepped toward him. "I'm Zena, a reporter from Brooklyn, USA. I understand you're also one." She grinned, hoping to warm the exchange.

"I've never been to America. Born in Trier, Prussia, but I've lived in various European cities."

We introduced ourselves in turn. The hologram surveyed us without a word.

"What's your name?" Rocko asked.

"Karl Marx. I write for the *New York Tribune*."

"Say that again?" Rocko narrowed his eyes.

It was the surprise of the day, another on the growing list since our journey began.

"You mean *the* Karl Marx?" Zena's chin dropped.

"Cut!" The hologram froze at Histo's call, leaving us astonished. "Yes, he's an intelligent hologram representing Karl Marx of Marxism." Histo paused at our confused faces. "Let me remind you of the rules: *do not* disclose the future."

Still in disbelief, I had to reconfirm. "Are you saying the creator of communism worked as a reporter in American media? For a newspaper that supported the Republican Party?"

The director nodded. "That's real history for you."

Karl Marx is one of the most recognizable figures in history, but most photos of him are from his later years. At first, the frozen young man didn't resemble him. No creases. The beard was there, but not the long, unkempt gray one. His hair was dark.

"That's him," Histo assured.

Zena prompted. "What has he accomplished so far?"

"He co-authored the *Communist Manifesto* but hasn't started writing *Das Kapital* yet."

Nakshi studied the man more closely. "Is he aware of the previous discussions between the emperor and the ambassador?"

"He was in the room while you witnessed their earlier dialogues."

"Incognito?" Zena's mouth slid. "We had an invisible novanaut all along?"

"Phantom of the Quantopera," Rocko quipped. "That might explain the noises at night."

Zena smiled, eyes widening. "Now it all makes sense."

"He's pulling your leg." Nakshi leaned in.

"You love it, don't you?" Zena pressed her lips, glimmering at Rocko, pleased he had forgotten his resentment toward her. Rocko returned a wry smile.

I wasn't jealous. In fact, I felt relieved that the two had made up. I never liked tension. Still, Rocko's joking remark stirred an idea that incognito souls might walk among us every day.

"Let's go, Krish!" The director was eager to stay on course.

Karl Marx unfroze.

"Who are you with?" he asked, startling Zena.

"I'm independent." She lifted her chin. "I have an offer from the *New York Daily Times*. I haven't accepted it yet, still contemplating."

Marx sized her up as if fitting her into some social equation. "I've heard good things about Raymond. He worked for Horace. My colleague Friedrich Engels writes anonymous commentaries in his paper." Another startling revelation, but by now, we were used to them.

"I didn't realize the authors of the *Manifesto* were reporters." Zena admired this hairy man, losing herself in his eyes, giving me a slight unease.

Karl Marx cracked her a bitter smile. "A man must make a living. Corporations don't fund the Communist League."

He looked ordinary, just another intellectual with limited means scraping by. Strange to think he'd come to shape the bloodlines of the century that followed.

Rocko cut in. "What else do you do besides cover secret intrigues for the New Yorkers?"

"Writing."

"On what?"

"Political economy, studying the relations between political and economic systems."

Krish froze Marx. "All right, team. We'll leave the maestro here to join him later. Go strap in for the final act of the secret communications drama."

We gathered in the far-left corner of the emperor's Gold Room in the Winter Palace. Marx studied Czar Nicholas gazing into the courtyard from a tall window. George Hamilton Seymour eased into the velvet armchair beneath the chandelier. The French calendar on the table read April 18, 1853.

"Two more weeks." Nicholas gestured toward the snow-covered trees. "Cherry blossoms will miraculously sprout from these frozen branches."

Nicholas began pacing. Seymour started to rise, but the emperor motioned him to stop.

"Please sit. I must keep moving. I may be the ruler of the greatest empire on Earth, but my back enslaves me. Spring is the worst season."

Folding his arms behind, he circled the room. "I place great reliance on *'la parole d'un gentilhomme.'* I may have said this before, but it bears repeating. A precise understanding leaves no room for misconception." Nicholas glanced at Seymour. "I feel obliged to recognize your contribution to this friendly *entente*."

Seymour rose halfway from his seat, gesturing acknowledgment. "Her Majesty's Government gladly complies with His Majesty's wish to continue this frank discussion in private."

The czar lifted his chin. "England has a new voice in the Foreign Office. Please express my sincere satisfaction to the Earl of Clarendon for his honest response."

Seymour inclined. "Lord Clarendon adheres to the same policy and principles laid down by the former minister, Lord Russell. Her Majesty's Government prefers His Imperial Majesty's words to any pre-agreement framed under any contingency."

Karl Marx let out a brief laugh. "Brave Earl. He thinks he can handle hot coals. I wonder if the freeborn Briton meant to remind the Russian ruler that the law advisors of the British Crown ended all past treaties with his country, all due to violations on her part."

Zena leaned toward him. "Once governments decide on war, no treaty is worth the paper it's written on." Marx smiled slightly. She beamed, savoring the moment with the legendary communist.

The emperor's voice dropped. "I would offer you a frank observation or two, but it might sound like a criticism of your lordship's dispatch." A subtle smile played on the ambassador's lips as he tried to match the czar's candor.

Nicholas slowed his pace. "Earl Clarendon states the fall of the Turkish Empire is an uncertain and distant contingency." He lowered his head in thought. "Uncertain and distant," he muttered. "One term excludes the other. Uncertain it is, indeed, but for that reason not necessarily remote. I desire not, but I am not sure it might prove."

Seymour leaned forward. "The British Government believes Turkey still possesses the elements of existence. No real crisis has occurred to render its realization imminent."

"And how did that belief come into existence?"

"Her Majesty's Government receives accurate reports on Turkey."

"Accurate?" The emperor furrowed his brow. "Some reports from British consular officers are erroneous and incorrect."

The ambassador straightened on the couch, lips pressed together.

Rocko smirked. "Here we go again. He mocks the British intelligence for bungling the job."

Marx leaned toward him. "Part of it must be the autocrat's resentment toward Stratford Canning. Earl's first act was to send Nicholas's dreaded enemy back to Constantinople."

"Why do you think he did that?" Zena asked deliberately, like any good reporter seeking multiple sources to confirm a story.

"It's a strong demonstration against Nicholas. That nobleman had long been one of Russia's chief antagonists. He is also the most effective tool to intimidate the sultan."

I would have said *influence*, but otherwise, he put it well. Burning to add my voice, I steered in. "As the British Ambassador to Turkey, he could inflict greater damage on the Russian ruler's aspirations."

I held my breath, confident Marx might acknowledge my insight. But the father of dialectical materialism ignored me as if I were the incognito in the room. I twitched, shooting him a slight glare.

Nicholas pressed, "Constantinople feeds London an overdose of optimism about Christian communities in Turkey. The Sublime Porte doesn't enforce the sultan's orders."

Karl Marx nodded. "The emperor makes a valid point. The British Embassy paints a bright picture of Turkey, but the *Times* holds a grim view of the country."

Zena lifted a brow. "What does it say about the Turkish Empire?"

Karl Marx's lips curled into a sly twist. "It is crumbling. Nothing remains of the Turk but the turban on his head."

Seymour countered, "No sufficient cause implies the sultan cannot maintain peace at home or friendly relations with neighbors."

The emperor paused, gazing at the ambassador and waiting for more.

"The Turkish Empire's decay is evident. However, it still holds vitality and wealth. Corruption, though rampant, does not possess a character that threatens the empire's existence."

The emperor pursed his lips, perhaps because he too suffered from corruption in his government, something he could not prevent.

Seymour was careful not to tread on the czar's toes. "Their treatment of Christians is not harsh. Their toleration might even serve as an example to governments that scorn Turkey as a barbarous power."

The emperor jerked his head back. "I disagree. Take Bulgaria, for instance. Without my constant efforts, they would have risen in insurrection." He quickened his pace. "Bosnia!" The czar clenched his fist. "Recent Turkish cruelties alone forced hundreds of Christian families to seek refuge in Austria."

Marx offered a clever smile. "The Briton should know the Cossack ruler is right on this point. The British press released a secret government dispatch stating the Porte is either weak or unwilling to address the grievances of Christians."

Depending on who held power at the Porte, both accounts could be true. Abdulmejid often reshuffled the Sublime Porte, alternating between the pro-Western faction and the old guard.

Turkey's divided identity has long puzzled the West. For two centuries, the country has grappled with a cultural struggle that still plays out in modern Türkiye. Grandpa used to say two veins feed

Turkish politics: liberals who look West and conservatives drawn to Islamist and Turkic ideals who look East.

Dad disagreed. He argued the tug-of-war was not sincere. To him, both camps leaned toward authoritarianism; neither was genuinely committed to liberal democracy.

The emperor cocked his head askew. "I doubt it's still possible to uphold Turkey's integrity."

Ambassador Seymour leaned forward, swallowing. "Her Majesty's Government believes nothing hastens Turkey's demise more than predictions of its imminent dissolution. Every European power wishes to avert this catastrophe. If the belief spreads, Turkey's downfall will come sooner than His Imperial Majesty expects."

Marx flashed a sardonic smile. "The Kalmuk, then, has only to divulge his opinion that the sick man is dying, and the next thing you know, the man is dead." He shook his head. "What an enviable vitality this is! No need for a blast from Jericho's trumpets. One breath from the emperor's august mouth, and the Ottoman Empire falls to pieces."

Noticing a few hollow glances, Histo decoded Marx's biblical allusion to the Israelites' conquest of Jericho, when the city collapsed at the sound of trumpets.

"Karl Marx is mocking the ambassador's idea that mere rumors of demise could bring down the Ottoman Empire."

The emperor paced, looking down, quietly framing his rebuttal as Seymour pressed on.

"But if the catastrophe did occur from unavoidable causes, Her Majesty's Government would entirely share the emperor's opinion."

"And what would those opinions of mine be?"

Seymour read from his foreign minister's dispatch. "The occupation of Constantinople by any great power would be incompatible with the balance of power, rendering peace in Europe precarious."

"Go on." The emperor clasped his hands behind his back.

"There are no elements for reconstruction of the Byzantine Empire, and Greece's misgovernment offers no encouragement for territorial expansion."

"Next?"

"There is no functioning provisional or communal government in Turkey. His Majesty's request could provoke intrigue and revolt among the Porte's Christian subjects. Anarchy would follow if Turkey's provinces governed themselves or splintered into republics, each power scrambling to secure its own interests."

"Hold that line for a moment!" Karl Marx exclaimed. The scene froze instantly. "This is a monstrous lie the ambassador keeps repeating—claiming Turkey lacks the elements to govern smaller republics." Marx's voice rose. "On the contrary! Its communal structure and provincial governments have helped Turkey withstand harsh external and internal shocks for centuries."

Marx was right. Ironically, after six centuries of peace under the Ottomans, many of those provinces began fighting the moment they raised their flags, and some battles still rage on to this day.

The scene resumed. Seymour elaborated on the Crown's perspective.

"England seeks no territorial aggrandizement. Nor can she be a party to any secret contingency. No prior arrangement, however general, can long be concealed from the other powers. Moreover, to withhold such knowledge would serve only to alienate them from us."

Marx laughed loudly, prompting another freeze, halting the czar mid-step, one foot half-raised. "Nicholas invites England to join a secret party, excluding France. Meanwhile, he had already entered into another with Austria. The Cossack autocrat didn't even inform England. So much for the parole of a *gentilhomme*."

I jumped in to show I had more to add. "Seymour might be hinting to the czar that Britain was aware of what he had done behind its back."

The revolutionary philosopher ignored me again and leaned closer to Zena, his tone warming. "When Seymour first learned of this secret alliance, he dispatched a frantic note to his government."

Zena met him with an equally warm glare. "The British Government must've become angry. Alienated."

Marx cracked a smile. "And what did Lord Clarendon do? Lover of the Turks?" He bounced away from her abruptly, raising a hand. "Upon hearing the news, he rushed to French Ambassador Walewski—Napoleon Bonaparte's illegitimate son—telling him Britain no longer trusted the emperor." He shook his head letting the words sink in.

I jumped in hastily. "He must then have inquired about France's position."

Marx didn't say a word. I wondered if Krish had made me incognito to him. As I silently worried about landing on the wrong side of one of the most influential figures of the next century—hologram or real—Seymour continued to read Lord Clarendon's dispatch.

"Every major agitation in the East sparks fresh discord in the West. All the more reason to uphold the Turkish Empire as the safeguard of Europe's peace."

The ambassador paused, casting a glance at the czar. The emperor, still pacing, gave a slight nod to continue.

"Moreover, every question in the West will assume a revolutionary character, compelling a revision of the entire social system. Continental governments are certainly not ready for this."

Nicholas stopped pacing and stood at a tall window, watching rabbits hop across the peaceful yard of the Winter Palace.

Sensing the ruler's drifting attention, the ambassador quickened his pace. "His Imperial Majesty must be aware of the forces bubbling beneath society, ready to explode. Firing the first cannon could spark disaster. The breakup of the Turkish Empire will lead to war, which explains Her Majesty's Government's concern to prevent such a catastrophe." He rushed the words in a single breath, then exhaled.

I cracked a smile. Neither man could have predicted that the mighty Romanov dynasty would collapse a year before the Sick Man of Europe. As Dad would say, history is shaped by surprises—like the Bolshevik Revolution in October 1917.

Avoiding Seymour's gaze, the emperor asked, "What will be Britain's course of action when the inevitable occurs?"

The Briton pulled out a handkerchief and dabbed his sweaty forehead. "With His Majesty's permission, I will reply by reading from Lord Clarendon's dispatch."

The emperor's eyes shifted to the birds chirping on the ice-rimmed branches.

"The sudden dissolution of the Turkish Empire could arouse jealousy among the powers, rendering their ambitions irreconcilable. For settlement, a European Congress would likely revise the treaties of the 1815 Congress of Vienna."

"Jealousies of European powers?" Marx squinted. "A more candid declaration would be that the fall of Turkey would spark a conflict between England and France, not with Russia."

Seymour, as if he had overheard Marx, pitched his tone toward convivial charm. "The imposing obligations of the Congress of Vienna have long been a source of irritation to France's national honor. She might even risk a European war to free herself from them."

Encouraged by the emperor's silence, the British diplomat slipped into the role of a pretentious salesman. "Her Majesty's Government desires to work with His Imperial Majesty to establish a firm and common European policy, thereby strengthening the alliance between our two countries. The interests of Russia and England in the East are perfectly aligned."

"Hear our conscientious Earl." Karl Marx spoke with biting wit. "The same Briton who misleads the European public into believing that England sides with France against Russia is now, in private, assuring this declared enemy that their interests are perfectly aligned!"

A virtuoso of dialectical materialism, Marx revealed the game beneath the words. His uncanny ability to expose contradictions and unravel the cunning undercurrents behind Britain's seemingly righteous stance was nothing short of awe-inspiring.

The emperor stood by the tall central window, admiring his courtyard while avoiding Seymour's eyes.

The ambassador's long discourse finally ended. His face had turned red, exhausted from his monologue. Afternoon sunlight stretched across the floor like a golden carpet, bouncing onto his face and making him squint. As the eerie pause deepened in the spacious salon, a bead of sweat slid from his temple and disappeared into his thick sideburns. He wondered if the czar's silence meant he had overstepped.

"*Erithacus rubecula*," the emperor uttered calmly, still gazing out the window. "They're the early signs of spring."

The novanauts exchanged glances, unsure of the words' meaning.

Seymour unclenched his jaw. "European robin." His shoulders slumped. "Aren't they beautiful?" His voice carried a nervous cheer.

The palm-sized birds, with their fiery orange breasts and soft, ice-blue feathers, chirped joyously.

The emperor drifted as his gaze deepened into the yard. "When I was a child, I would stand for hours beneath these frozen branches under the winter sun, like today, waiting for the ice to melt, drip, and fall into my mouth."

The joyous chirping sounds aside, there was no sound inside the room until a faint mechanical whir tore the eerie silence. The ambassador shifted, his eyes darting around the Gold Room to see where it came from. Suddenly, a mechanical clockwork perched in the corner sprang to life, startling us all. Zena let out a brief scream. The robins scattered.

Marx cracked a smile. Growing up in Central Europe, he had likely been familiar with such massive contraptions.

The automaton's wings twitched, then spread with metallic grace. Its beak opened, releasing a chilling chime that echoed through the grand salon.

The emperor, unfazed by the clockwork bird, advanced toward the British ambassador. Unsure which would strike first, Seymour stiffened, eyes wide, staring at the emperor and the eagle, both moving in sync.

The czar halted before him as the metallic bird clicked back to its housing. Seymour let out a breath.

Nicholas shot Seymour a sharp look. "The approach to the Eastern Question is one difference between our nations. I can name another." His voice was steady, cold. "We are far more patient than you."

The automaton's second chime echoed in the Gold Room. Its talons struck, marking the hour. The Russian Eagle had awakened.

The emperor leaned into Seymour's space, his words almost a whisper. "I mean much more patient." His gaze cut deep. Seymour dug his fingers into the armchair.

The chimes stopped, and the eagle fell still.

Nicholas stepped back and walked away toward the clock. "Prince Menshikov is on a peaceful mission to resolve the Holy Shrine issue. I sent him to the sultan. But you must already know this."

"I am aware, Your Majesty." Seymour straightened, composing himself. Nicholas's pale, upward-tilted mustache caught the orange glow of the setting sun.

The czar's voice softened. "The question of the holy keys grew far greater than it ever warranted. The sultan mishandled what was, in truth, a trivial matter." The ambassador dabbed his damp forehead as Nicholas paced.

The czar lifted his chin. "Prince Menshikov is a nobleman for whom I have deep respect. I approve of his acts."

Seymour leaned forward. "I received a dispatch today. French representatives have arrived in Pera to meet with their Russian counterparts to find a fair solution to the Holy Shrine crisis." His convivial tone was a mask he could not conceal.

The emperor dismissed Seymour's hopeful news. He pulled out a handkerchief, wiped a speck of dust from the eagle's beak. "It should be clear that I am prepared to go to war to protect my nation's honor and prevent hostile intrigues against all the Russias, such as the French-fomented strife in Turkey's provinces."

The ambassador stared back, brows knitted, unsure how to read the czar's shifting demeanor, like Jekyll turning into Hyde under a full moon.

Nicholas glanced at the dripping icicles. "It is melting! Time to celebrate." He strode to the liquor cabinet.

"But first, I congratulate myself." He lifted two goblets. "My views and those of the English government coincide. We both wish to avoid the extreme contingencies in the East and are equally committed to delaying the dreadful end for as long as possible."

Seymour jerked back, his stiffness giving way to puzzlement.

The czar knelt, opened the cabinet's bottom drawer, and drew out a bottle. He smiled softly. "I agree. The best way to prolong the Sublime Porte's life is not to harass it with overbearing demands or wound its dignity."

Karl Marx chuckled, shaking his head. "The emperor must be jesting with Seymour." The revolutionary leaned toward Zena. "His man, Menshikov, just wreaked havoc in the seraglio, insulting the sultan's brother-in-law with language hardly fit for a peaceful mission." By then, Menshikov's deliberate rudeness was in every major paper.

The emperor poured French brandy into one goblet under Seymour's watchful eyes, leaving the other empty. He carried both glasses and sat across from Seymour. The ambassador shifted uneasily in his seat.

Zena smiled bitterly. "He's crushing Seymour by serving drinks. Arrogance wrapped in humility." Marx nodded.

Rocko half-grinned. "So much for the pledge not to humiliate the sultan, huh?" Marx gave him a blank gaze.

The socialist's equal-opportunity obliviousness made me feel less small.

Nicholas set the goblets on the rosewood desk beside a crystal pitcher. "As great powers, we treat concessions from the sultan as weapons, pointing them at one another. We cannot continue like this."

He aligned the goblets evenly on either side of the pitcher. "There are matters on which we differ. Turkey's treatment of its Christian subjects, for one. But we must not let such differences hinder greater cooperation."

The Russian Czar broke into a broad smile. "I declare my willingness to work with England to prolong the Turkish Empire's existence, setting aside any thoughts of its dissolution."

Nicholas lifted the pitcher's soft Belgian lace cover and poured water into his goblet. "I trust the good intentions of the British cabinet, accept the evidence it presented, and the hope it brings. I am confident Russia's alliance with England will only grow stronger."

Seymour beamed. "I take great pleasure in informing my government of Your Majesty's decision at once."

The emperor handed him the brandy-filled goblet. A lifelong teetotaler, Czar Nicholas stood and raised his glass of plain water. Seymour rose with his drink in hand.

"Courvoisier." The emperor nodded toward Seymour's glass. "Some call it France's finest. I cannot attest to that. But none could say I failed to invite *mon cher ami* to our meeting."

Both men shared a thin, practiced chuckle.

Seymour raised his glass. "His Majesty honors me."

"*Za druzhbu*—to our friendship," the emperor toasted.

"*Za druzhbu!*" Seymour echoed. They drained their glasses.

Watching in silence, Karl Marx jabbed at Nakshi. "Never forget. Russia's policy never changes. It's world domination. Like the polar star—always above when you look up."

Nakshi murmured, "For the Russian, a generation or two is nothing. Everything else is *bear* tactics."

Marx smiled at Zena alone, then vanished.

We were back inside the Petamunra dome, no décor around. Krish walked in with a thermos and a cardboard tray of paper cups.

"Wow!" Zena exclaimed. "Where'd he go? I wanted to say goodbye."

"Krish will give you his e-mail," Rocko quipped.

Nakshi lifted his brows. "We mingled with one of history's most influential minds."

Krish broke in, "A hologram, not the real Marx. Still, theatrics aside, those words were his, written when he was alive."

"He's not very social." Zena pouted.

Histo pushed back. "He wasn't here to chat about his private life."

"Is there a Mrs. Marx?" Zena gazed at the Petamunra tiles as if searching for traces of the man.

Rocko choked, spilling coffee on his shirt.

Why did she ask that?

Nakshi stirred his tea. "Why would the Committee reincarnate Karl Marx into the quantum universe?"

"No one is reincarnated here," Histo said. "It's just a quantum hologram, pure data, projecting Marx's documented views."

"But he learns, doesn't he?" I pressed. It hit me—maybe the Committee wanted Karl Marx's hologram to study twentieth-century history. Would he revise his theories? Offer fixes for today's fractured societies? "If he were alive today, how would he see the world?"

Zena's eyes lit up. "I've got an idea. A bestseller in 2048. *The Communist Manifesto*, bicentennial edition, by Karl Marx, PFCH."

"What's the ending?"

"Perfect Fidelity Cognitive Hologram."

Nakshi chuckled. "Marxism, retooled for the quantum age."

Zena raised her arms, deepening her voice in mock drama. "Welcome to the hall of incognitos." She gestured to the air. "Sir, a lot has happened after you left. Remember your theory? It lit a fire. Lenin brought down the Russian Empire. His Bolsheviks followed your handbook. Did anyone tell you that? What would you say about the Soviet Empire and the communist regimes of the twentieth century? How do you rate their leaders—Lenin, Stalin, Mao, the rest?"

I quipped. "You do this interview. It'll win the mother of all Pulitzers."

Rocko cut in, "I wonder what he'd say about the climate crisis. That's what matters now—not the proletariat or the Chinese Communist Party's doctrine."

"Back to our mission." Histo cut off the Incognito Players Company and turned to me.

"Where do the talks stand between the two powers?"

I paused before summarizing. "Britain ended the round of secret correspondence as Russia agreed to its stance. The fall of the Turkish Empire is not imminent, but a distant possibility. A win for British diplomacy."

"I wouldn't jump to that conclusion. Nicholas just bought himself time." Nakshi winked. "Duplicity is part of the diplomat's toolkit, and no one wields it better than Russia."

"Speaking of keys." Rocko narrowed his eyes. "Did Menshikov retrieve them?"

"Only if the French agreed," I said. "We haven't heard from them."

"Let's find out." Histo nodded to Krish.

19

THE BONAPARTISTS

"**K**rish, could you please unlatch my seatbelt? I can't make it."
That was Zena. We were about to take off for Paris.

The humming stopped. The lights came back on. Everyone turned toward her.

"I think I have a stomach virus." She looked pale.

Histo gave her a once-over. "Stay in your room until you feel better."

"I'll be fine tomorrow." She got off her seat. "I've had this before. It's a twenty-four-hour bug."

"Drink plenty of water," I called after her.

"I will, Dad." She shot back, mocking my voice. "Stay hydrated, get vitamin C, and rest."

Rocko quipped. "He'll bring you chicken soup from Paris. They boil their feet, the best part."

"I don't want to hear about French food," she snapped. "I think I got this at the banquet. Histo is smart. He didn't touch any. He knows better." With that, she left.

The low hum resumed, and the lights dimmed.

When the lights brightened, the scene revealed a group of men around a large oval table covered with green cloth. Tall windows overlooked a courtyard blanketed in white pebbles with a shimmering pool at its center. The room held a mix of classical and rococo furniture—some plain, others carved with detail. A bust of Napoleon Bonaparte rose from a pedestal behind them. The wall calendar read March 19, 1853.

A man in his sixties with round features called the meeting to order. The sash across his chest marked authority.

"Messieurs, members of the state council, we face a rapidly unfolding situation in the Orient. This emergency meeting seeks consensus for our recommendation to the emperor. I yield the floor to the foreign minister, Monsieur de Lhuys."

A stocky man with heavy sideburns rose.

"Thank you, Chairman Abbatucci. I have received a dispatch from Constantinople. The British chargé d'affaires, Colonel Rose, has called on the admiral of the British Navy to deploy from Malta to Turkish shores."

He summarized Prince Menshikov's arrival in Constantinople and his inappropriate conduct before the sultan's cabinet, then yielded to the chairman.

"How should France respond?" Abbatucci turned to a man in his fifties. "Monsieur Fould, your thoughts?"

Fould rose. Despite his parted black hair, the lines on his face betrayed his age. "The final hour has tolled for Turkey. The French people do not want us to join Britain's futile effort to extinguish a hopeless blaze."

"I disagree with the state minister." The objection came from a man in his mid-forties. "Britain and France cooperated twenty years ago to help the Greeks gain independence, ensuring the honor would not fall to the Russians."

He wore a dark jacket over a vest. A dark mustache and sideburns contrasted with his receding hairline. The cursive card before his seat read: Duc de Persigny, Interior Minister.

Rocko jumped in, arms slicing the air. "Hey! I know this guy." His voice was too loud, freezing the moment with the speaker's mouth left hanging open.

"Count Persigny, born Victor Fialin." Rocko's eyes widened. "He played a pivotal role in the coup that ousted the Second Republic. Before that, he was jailed multiple times for failed attempts."

I was taken aback. I hadn't known about this obscure nineteenth-century French politician. "I admit, I'm impressed you know such a detail."

"I know squat about history, really. My interest comes from a book this man wrote in prison."

"About what?"

"Egyptian pyramids. He claimed a branch of the Nile once ran west but vanished long ago. Over the years, sand filled the riverbed—a process known as silting. Egyptians used the lost branch to transport heavy stones for building the pyramids."

"I don't remember reading this."

"Nobody paid attention, until recently, when researchers uncovered new evidence supporting a theory a militant French royalist proposed from his jail cell, a century and a half ago."

"And that's him?" I pointed to the frozen man.

Rocko nodded. "Amazing, isn't it?"

"How do you know all this?"

"The branch of history that interests me is how the environment has changed over centuries." Rocko's voice carried weight. "Environment is my passion. I've told you this already. But no one takes me seriously around here."

I pressed my lips, guilty I hadn't.

Histo brushed it aside. "Let's move on."

The scene unfroze.

Monsieur de Lhuys countered, "Count Persigny, back then the Briton and the Frenchman were both outraged. The Mussulman saber struck powerless Christians indiscriminately in Greece. Now the situation is different. Neither wishes to raise his sword against Christians to save Mussulmans."

"Britons want peace," Minister Fould affirmed. "Four thousand Londoners appealed to the French public, signing a civil alliance declaration—merchants, artisans, and intellectuals. Their message is clear. Forty years have passed since Waterloo. It's time to move on and prosper together in peace."

A low hum spread across the room, most nodding.

Persigny shook his head. "Swords build empires, not brush and palette." He surveyed the table. "Messieurs, I ask you. Without their navy and cannons, where would our islander friends be today?"

The commotion swelled into a heated debate, reviving the fiery Mediterranean spirit—arms flailing, everyone talking, no one listening. Dad used to divide Europe into two camps: calm, butter-eating Northerners and hot-blooded, olive oil Southerners; the French split between both, never predictable. *That's why I never had a dull moment with you*, he told Mom in his eulogy, referring to her Huguenot heritage that made everyone smile through their tears.

The argument lasted a few more minutes before Abbatucci called for a vote on the passive stance. It passed by majority.

Suddenly, the door opened. A medium-built man of fair complexion entered, and everyone rose. The cacophony cut off like a sword through silk, and the room fell silent.

It was Napoleon III. The French Emperor was unmistakable. His signature waxed mustache swept sideways as if defying gravity, paired with a pointed beard.

He quickly scanned the room. His beige military uniform was lined with medals and crossed by a blue sash.

Rocko motioned to the emperor's facial hair. "Czar Nicholas with a goatee."

Nakshi smiled. "He's making a statement: I am superior."

Rocko winked. "And stubborn." They let out a brief chuckle.

Born Louis Napoleon, he was Napoleon Bonaparte's nephew. After years in exile in the United States and London, he returned to France and became president in 1848. When his term ended, he still held majority support, but the constitution barred a second consecutive term. On December 2, 1851, his supporters staged a coup, establishing a Bonapartist autocracy. Just over three months ago, on the coup's first anniversary, Louis-Napoleon declared himself Emperor Napoleon III, ending the Second Republic and ushering in the Second Empire.

The emperor turned to the Corsican chairman. "Jacques Pierre, has the council reached a consensus?"

Abbatucci handed him the tally. "Your Majesty, all but one recommend that France avoid escalation and remain passive. Let the British take the lead."

Louis Napoleon didn't glance at the report. "Who is the dissenter?"

Count de Persigny raised his hand, leaning back in his chair, one hand at ease. His name tag might as well have read, *I own the Tuileries.*

The emperor nodded to him, then turned to his foreign minister.

"I didn't expect Lord Aberdeen to take Menshikov's circus act in the seraglio seriously. Sending the Navy to the Dardanelles is almost belligerent. He must know something we don't. What's your view, Drouyn?"

The foreign minister swallowed. "We're not sure if Lord Aberdeen authorized the move or if the British chargé d'affaires in Constantinople panicked."

The emperor furrowed his brow. "Are you telling me the summons was issued without the prime minister's approval?"

"Possible. Even likely."

Napoleon narrowed his eyes. "Where does the Grand Elchi fit into this?"

"We heard he's still buried under snow somewhere in Austria, Sire. The British diplomat may not be aware of the decision."

"Unless he concealed it from me." The emperor gazed at the courtyard, collecting his thoughts. "The empress and I dined with him here in the Galerie de Diane, on his way to Vienna." He dropped his voice. "I explained that our anti-secular *les parties-Prêtres* and the Montalembert school sparked this tug-of-war with the Russian Orthodox."

He shifted to a playful edge. "I love these priest parties! They're among my loyal supporters. But my passion for them does not extend to starting a war with the czar. They've become a headache lately."

His mischievous tone drew smiles.

"I hinted to Lord Stratford I'd be willing to pass the holy key to *mon bon frère* in St. Petersburg, so he could unlock every church in the Holy Land at dawn, before the serfs milk his cows. We French like to sleep late on Sundays, even the most faithful." Laughter rippled around the table.

Foreign Minister Drouyn de Lhuys slumped his shoulders, hoping the emperor would step back from the crisis he had wrestled with for months.

The emperor's demeanor suddenly turned solemn, drowning the jolly commotion. "I don't understand why the British would want to escalate the crisis." He shook his head.

I itched to tell him they hadn't. Admiral Dundas had refused Rose's directive. How marvelous it would be if we had the means to summon voices from the future to warn today's leaders before they act on false information.

Minister de Lhuys leaned forward, unflinching. "Your Majesty, I advise against deploying our fleet. The press and diplomatic circles may see it as a revival of France's Napoleonic ambitions."

Count Persigny cut in, slicing through the uneasy calm. "The czar won't stop until he reaches Constantinople. The Holy Land crisis is his Trojan Horse into Turkey. He seeks to fulfill Peter's dream of reaching warm waters." Persigny faced the foreign minister. "Monsieur de Lhuys, with all due respect, I beg to differ. Should France take a stand to stop Russia's march on Constantinople, Britain would not be anxious. On the contrary, they would welcome it." The silver chain of his pocket watch glinted in the afternoon light through the tall palace windows.

The confident minister kept his gaze on the emperor as he gestured toward a blond man in uniform. "Your Majesty, this brave man, Field Marshal St. Arnaud, commanded the troops on December 2."

The name Persigny was unknown to me, but not the commander. In a poem, Victor Hugo had called St. Arnaud a "jackal" for leading the troops and undermining the democratic spirit of the republic in a coup.

"The act he led was courageous for all who risked their lives that day." The minister's voice swelled with drama. "Each soldier earned an invisible badge of honor etched on his chest and wears it still."

He leaned toward the emperor with the familiarity of a close friend.

"Sire, next time you review your troops they may salute with somber faces, but silently disapproving underneath." He paused. The emperor gave no sign. He pressed on, "Knowing their emperor hesitated—despite the advice of his ministers."

His forceful poise matched his self-assurance as he used the plural form, though he was the lone dissenter. Turning to the council, he declared, "Messieurs, that glorious army would send tremors beneath our feet right here in Tuileries!"

Persigny stroked his chin, unabashed and unyielding. "Your Majesty, if it's a matter of national honor, risks should be taken."

The emperor flinched as if jolted by a current.

A heavy silence settled over the conference room, broken only by sparrows chirping on bare branches in the courtyard. Thick clouds loomed over Paris. Snow seemed imminent.

Louis Napoleon tapped his lips with his index finger, deep in thought.

After a pause, he turned to St. Arnaud. "Marshal, are you ready to fight the mighty Russian army?"

The legendary generalissimo looked pale and frail but replied firmly. "I require a few months of preparation."

The emperor rose. "I don't seek a domineering presence in the Mediterranean. It should be a grand European lake."

He paced, jabbing at the air. "But if England and Russia partition it, France will no longer be recognized as a great power. I cannot allow it."

Anxious glances swept the table. The foreign minister pressed his lips together.

The emperor nodded a few times. "Persigny is right." He spoke like a judge delivering a verdict after hearing both sides.

"But I want to send our fleet to Greek waters, not Turkey. We must signal to Russia that France cares about Constantinople, nothing more. That will encourage England to join us."

Persigny cracked a faint smile as de Lhuys dropped his head.

Fould made a final plea. "The people of both nations do not want war, Sire. The strongest opposition is in France."

The emperor slammed his hand on the table, startling everyone, even the novanauts. "Your job is to change the French perception!"

The interior minister flinched. The room fell silent.

Louis Napoleon held his fiery gaze. "Fould and Persigny, identify every newspaper, large or small. For those not Russophobic, give them a short warning. If they refuse to change their stance, shut them down."

He lifted his chin. "Messieurs, our mission is not to westernize Turkish headwear. I'll let Lord Palmerston handle that if he can." He paused, prompting a few forced chuckles from the council members.

"If the czar reaches Constantinople, his next stop will be Marseille. I want every Frenchman to understand the threat. Am I clear?"

Russians in Marseille? I exchanged puzzled glances with my fellow novanauts.

Nakshi leaned in, whispering. "Remember Saddam's weapons of mass destruction? The existential threat that never was?"

The emperor was no different, building a false case to justify a war of choice. But why?

Louis Napoleon raised a fist. "A show of strength will bring everyone in line!"

He answered my question as if he had heard me. The country is in danger. Unify around me. A war campaign will prevent an uprising against the leader. The narrative always works.

"Yes, Sire," many around the table replied forcefully. Persigny's smile lingered.

The French Emperor's authoritarian decisiveness stilled his aides, shoving their wisdom to the back of their minds.

Louis Napoleon spoke wryly. "If His Imperial Majesty engages in conflict with us, he should remember France has the best commander."

He gestured to St. Arnaud. "Marshal, list everything you need from the treasury."

The field marshal saluted.

The emperor next turned toward Abbatucci. "We'll set sail from Toulon to Salamis in three days." His eyes narrowed on the courtyard. "It will be a message from the new France to the world."

"Yes, Sire," the council chairman inclined.

The finance minister stepped forward. "Your Majesty, if we enter a long campaign, we must finance it with war bonds."

The emperor snapped. "Our citizens should also be able to purchase them, not just large financial institutions."

"I don't understand, Sire?"

"Issue them in small amounts so anyone can buy. No bank should exceed a set limit."

He waved off the puzzled looks. "If I'm asking citizens to sacrifice, it must come with a return."

Fould scratched his head. "That's never been done before."

The autocrat grinned. "I keep telling everyone I'm a socialist, and nobody believes me." He turned to his foreign minister. "Those alarmed by a Bonapartist empire should know the Empress is a Legitimist, my half-brother Morny an Orléanist, and Prince Napoleon a Republican. The only Bonapartist is Persigny, and he's crazy."

Seeing him chuckle at his own joke, everyone burst into laughter, but the levity didn't last. Napoleon's face hardened.

"Gentlemen, now that Menshikov issue is settled, I raise another matter." His sharp gaze silenced the room. "We must fight another war—a civic one requiring no hussars or lancers."

He raised his arm. "The enemy is the filth and decay of our streets—here in Paris—insidiously sapping prosperity." He stepped toward Persigny. "Victor, I want our ablest general to fight this war—audacious, relentless, incorruptible. A commander for the Prefecture of the Seine, master of his craft, he will redesign and beautify Paris. Her streets must breathe. They are suffocating now. Find him!"

Persigny inclined. "I will, Sire."

The emperor clasped his confidant's arm. "Paris must outshine every city, including London. He will wage war for life over decay, comfort over misery, light over darkness."

I raised my voice, deliberately freezing the scene, avoiding the spoil of the quantum database. "I know his choice—Baron Haussmann, creator of modern Paris."

Rocko lifted a brow. "Did Persigny discover him?" He shook his head. "The more I learn about this man, the more he amazes me."

"Join his fan club," Nakshi smiled. "*The Third* must be a member."

The scene unfroze.

The emperor raised his brows. "Is there anything else to discuss?"

A stocky man rose, Napoleonic hat tucked under his arm. "Your Majesty, we've uncovered several plots against you. We've removed the threats."

"Good work, Monsieur de Maupas." The emperor leaned toward the police chief. "I expect more to come."

Louis Napoleon strode to the door, the council trailing. He paused to thank the chairman. "Monsieur Abbatucci—"

A scream cut him short, jolting the emperor.

"Stop!" It was Krish shouting.

The door burst open. Everyone flinched.

Zena stumbled in barefoot, nightgown loose, hair wild, eyes wide.

Facing the emperor, she shrieked. "He's after me! The serial killer!" Her frantic eyes searched us—the incognito.

Napoleon recoiled. Maupas lunged forward. St. Arnaud drew his sword.

"Krish!" Histo barked.

The scene froze. Guards hung mid-stride.

Krish rushed in, clutching his cracked tablet. "She skipped steps downhill. I panicked, dropped it, couldn't stop the system."

Histo glared. "We drilled this. In a panic, hit the red button."

"Sorry, sir." Krish lowered his head.

For a perfectionist, nothing stung more than failing to hit a big red button. I felt for him.

Histo faced Zena next. "What happened?"

She panted. "I was asleep. Noises woke me—footsteps. Opened the door—saw a man in a black shroud." She shivered. "He was just like in the papers."

"Did you see his face?" The director kept his poise.

"Only his back. He was facing away from me. I ran. Downstairs." Her voice crackled.

Krish rolled his eyes. "That must be Prakash, Lata-jin's staff. I told him to restock coffee and eggs—we're out."

Histo soothed Zena. "Go back to your room. It should be safe."

She shook her head sharply. "I'm not going upstairs. Not alone." Her shoulders bounced. She clung to Nakshi.

The senior novanaut wrapped his arms around her. "Shhh, it's all right."

"I don't feel well," she cried. Sweat soaked her gown, clinging to her back.

Needles jabbed inside me. I wanted to comfort her but locked up, seething at my own inaptitude. I couldn't think of anything to say or do.

Histo instructed Krish. "Strike out this incident."

Rocko quipped, "We don't want tomorrow's headlines reading 'Lunatic Escapes Asylum—Fails to Assassinate Emperor.'"

Zena's sobs broke into nervous chuckles as she kept her face buried in Nakshi's chest.

"That would be reinventing history," Nakshi replied, stroking her hair.

"We're done in Paris," Histo declared, unamused. "Two-hour break. Next stop, Istanbul. You won't be incognito. Dress accordingly."

"I'm coming with you," Zena insisted, pouting.

20

HOLY KEYS OF DOSOGRAFA

Our first stop in Istanbul was the Sublime Porte. Histo kept us incognito for this session.

Stratford Caning and his chief dragoman, Stephan Francesco Sappini, sat in Victorian armchairs, sipping refreshments in a spacious drawing room decorated with paintings, calligraphy, and plants. Across from them, two scribes sat cross-legged on fluffy pillows beside their portable desks.

A guard announced: "Grand Vizier Mehmet Ali Pasha and Foreign Minister Rifat Pasha!"

Everyone rose. The scribes bowed. Two men entered. The one in front, with medals and a sash across his uniform, left no doubt he was the grand vizier.

"Welcome back, Lord Stratford. Or should I say, welcome home?" Mehmet Ali Pasha's smile revealed stained teeth between a walrus mustache and a streaked gray beard. Reddish-brown hair peeked from under his burgundy fez.

"Indeed, Your Excellency." Stratford returned the smile. "Her Majesty's Government commends your courageous stance against Prince Menshikov's unfortunate behavior. Insults have no place in diplomacy."

The grand vizier's hazel eyes narrowed, dark circles showing the strain of recent weeks. "As an admiral who has served the sultan for decades, I was appalled to see a fellow seaman misbehave." His milk-pale complexion made me wonder how he had ever commanded the fleet.

"I hope you understand why Rifat Pasha refused to pass Prince Menshikov's *note verbale* to Signor Sappini. The prince threatened to cut off diplomatic relations if the British were informed." The grand vizier swung his fist in the air. "Still, I took it upon myself to share its main points with Colonel Rose. He grasped the urgency and summoned the British fleet to our shores."

It was clever. He saved face for Rose and Rifat, gained Sappini as an ally, and showed Elchi he would not bow to Russian threats.

Lord Stratford kept his composure. "Without knowing the details of the Russian demands and what has transpired between your governments, it would be difficult to offer my counsel."

The grand vizier turned to his foreign minister. Rifat Pasha, a stocky man in his mid-forties with receding hair, wore a modest fez and dark tunic. "The prince has several demands. His top priority is the sanctuary keys in the Holy Land. Additionally, the Russians wish to build and supervise a church and hospital near Jerusalem and secure most-favored-nation status for their pilgrims."

"How was Prince Menshikov's behavior?"

"Amiable. Not abrupt, unlike how he treated my predecessor."

"These should not cause a crisis. Some are more reasonable than others, but none is unmanageable."

The grand vizier leaned toward Rifat. "You should present His Excellency the private letter."

The foreign minister pulled a handwritten note from a dossier. "Menshikov brought a personal letter from Emperor Nicholas to the sultan, proposing a Turco-Russian military alliance." He held the note out for Elchi. "Russia offers a fleet and four hundred thousand troops to defend the Ottoman Empire against any Western aggression."

Elchi furrowed his brow. "What is the *quid pro quo*?"

"The sultan must recognize the Russian Emperor as the protector of the Greeks within the Ottoman Empire."

The dragoman's widened eyes gave away the gravity of the news. Lord Canning read the letter—written in French—silently, while Sappini and Rifat Pasha exchanged hastily in Turkish. I understood only a few words. Rifat explained, in essence, what lay between the lines, and no meaning was lost in translation.

Stratford raised his head. "The czar demands exclusive authority over the Greek Church's administration. Russian representatives will control the Greek Church and appoint clergy."

Mehmet Ali nodded. "All thirteen thousand Orthodox clergymen."

Sappini dabbed his forehead. "My Lord, Russia demands His Majesty the Sultan obtain approval from their embassy before issuing any decree involving Greek subjects. The Porte must 'well receive' their orders."

Lord Stratford kept his lips pursed but stayed silent.

Rocko leaned in. "Finally, Igor is out of the box."

Nakshi's faint smile followed. "Once sprung, it hardly ever goes back in."

Lord Stratford returned the letter to Rifat. "What did His Majesty the Padishah say to this offer?"

Mehmet Ali smiled bitterly. "Menshikov might as well ask for the key to the seraglio." He paused to let his words sink in. "My sultan understands that by granting Russia these demands, he would hand over suzerainty of all his Greek subjects to the czar—ten million people, practically all of European Turkey, where the Orthodox are the majority."

Rifat Pasha added, "Prince Menshikov claims the Treaty of Kuchuk Kainarja granted Russia this right but says the Turks have failed in their obligation. He wants to amend the treaty to clarify Article Fourteen."

Sappini rolled his eyes. "The infamous church clause. Absurd!"

Stratford stood unfazed, his composure steady under the mounting pressure.

Mehmet Ali Pasha lifted his chin. "I told the prince I would resign rather than accept his proposal. It's disastrous."

"I agree, Your Excellency." Stratford forced a smile. "The Treaty of Kainarja should remain as it is. A revised treaty would invite new claims beyond the Holy Places in Palestine. The sultan would end up surrendering control to Russia."

"That would settle the Eastern Question, wouldn't it?" Mehmet Ali gave a bitter chuckle.

Lord Stratford closed his eyes, gathering his thoughts, then spoke. "Russia is within its rights in making claims about the Holy Places."

The two highest-ranking members of the Sublime Porte held their breath, listening to the wise old wolf.

"Regarding the Holy Places, a *firman* from His Majesty the Sultan will suffice to meet Russian demands."

Rifat pressed on. "He will not accept a firman."

Stratford shot back a sharp gaze. "He will. I'm optimistic France will cooperate."

The vizier lifted his brows, but we were not surprised. The French Emperor had assured Lord Stratford he would not escalate the Holy Keys crisis.

Stratford's voice turned flat. "The Russians, however, are mixing the reasonable with the inadmissible."

Rifat shook his head. "They're asking the sanctuary keys to unlock the seraglio gate."

Grand Elchi smiled wryly. "Jacob's voice and Esau's hand were never more skillfully combined."

Zena turned to Rocko for an explanation of the biblical analogy.

"Don't look at me. I was daydreaming in yeshiva."

I could explain. My mother taught Sunday school at the Unitarian Universalist Fellowship in Plainfield, New Jersey, and I had no choice but to attend.

"He means Russia is deceiving everyone, putting on one face while acting with another to reach a sinister goal."

Lord Stratford nodded to Rifat. "You took the right approach with the prince."

Rifat Pasha sighed, his eyes glinting, barely concealing a smile.

Grand Elchi's voice turned firm. "Next time you meet him, keep the issues concerning the Holy Land separate. If the Russians present a justifiable complaint, address it at once, but adhere strictly to existing treaty obligations. That is crucial."

The British Ambassador rose to pace, formulating his second recommendation.

"Prince Menshikov aims to erode the sultan's authority over his subjects. He may present new proposals, cloaking his true intention. You are within your rights to refuse to negotiate them until he fully explains their scope, how far they extend, and the reasons behind them. Always insist he anchor them to existing treaties."

Rifat glanced at the scribes to make sure they captured Grand Elchi's words.

Stratford's words brought back my father's advice: never counter an argument until you understand its full scope.

Lord Stratford returned to his seat and downed his sour cherry sherbet in one gulp. He pointed to his empty cup with a broad grin— rare as a fogless summer morning in Big Sur.

"This is why I'm back."

As the servants rushed to refill it, the hologram placed his hand over the cup and remarked, *"L'absence rend le cœur plus tendre."*—Abstinence makes the heart grow fonder.

It was a beautiful, clear day in early June, two months after the exchange we had just witnessed—a few minutes ago in the quantum universe. We stood in the courtyard of a well-kept mansion in Galata, just outside Pera. A plaque on the building marked it as the Sappini family's. A carpet of dried white and pink blossoms covered the ground, pushed out by the ripe cherries now seated on the branches.

Zena narrowed her eyes, "How does Sappini know us?"

Histo explained. "Alexander Voss wrote him. A team of American freelancers of Ottoman descent was visiting and wanted to meet him."

Team Novanauts, reporting from the Orient. I liked the sound of that.

A servant ushered us into the living room. As we walked, the wooden floorboards of the old kiosk creaked beneath our feet.

Krish, disguised as a servant, brought refreshments. We sat on rococo chairs in the living room, furnished with Venetian pieces on lavish rugs, waiting for our hosts.

While sipping our sherbets, Nakshi explained the knots per square inch and how dyes were made in the nineteenth century.

Tall windows stretched to the high ceilings, overlooking a manicured garden. The sloped yard, lined with trees, offered glimpses of the Bosporus. Rocko gave a crash course on mulberry and cherry trees while two holographic gardeners pruned the bushes outside. Ripened peaches hung low, making my mouth water, while cosmopolitan men and women—some in Western outfits, others in turbans and veils—strolled down the valley.

Zena asked, "Does anyone know about the treaty that made Sappini jump in his seat?"

Nakshi raised his hand. "Kainarja. It takes its name from the Bulgarian town where the Russians and Turks signed it after a war, but I don't know when. I used to visit the region to buy bulk dried food."

"Eighty years ago, in 1774," I cut in. "That's when the Turks lost Crimea to Russia."

Rocko leaned toward me. "That exchange made me think Persigny was right. The holy keys are just his excuse. Nicholas wants Istanbul. What do you think?"

He made me feel good by asking my opinion. Before I could respond, Zena broke in.

"Who is Persigny?"

"A visionary." Rocko lifted his chin. "He saw water where others saw sand."

"Where?" Zena wanted direct answers, no riddles.

"He solved the secrets of the Egyptian pyramids. They were built next to a riverbed that doesn't exist anymore."

"Well, he was wrong. They unraveled the secrets of the pyramids a long time ago. Aliens built them."

"Don't be ridiculous."

"You're ridiculous! There are books written on this. Bestsellers. That means it's recorded. And your job is to protect what's written." She turned to Histo. "Ask him if you don't believe me."

Histo didn't flinch, unmoved by her hostility.

I never liked tension. I jumped in to ease it. "Persigny's theory makes sense. The place was once vibrant, housing a wealthy community. A river flowed nearby—"

She cut me off. "So, this guy was in the desert, wandering, and saw a mirage. Timeshares in Giza. Waterfront properties." She narrowed her eyes. "And you say that makes sense? The greatest scam I've heard."

Rocko snapped before I could reply. "There's nothing ridiculous about environmental changes. They're real!"

As Zena readied her rebuttal, the floorboards creaked with approaching footsteps. Stephan Sappini entered with a broad smile, bringing the heated debate to a close. Tall and thin, with a well-trimmed goatee, he looked pale, the dark circles under his eyes betraying a lack of sleep.

He ran a hand through his dark, wavy hair, embarrassed.

"I'm sorry I'm late. My boss is demanding. Predicting when Grand Elchi will call it a day is always tricky. Some days I can't leave until midnight." The dragoman grinned. "Fortunately, your minister resident to the Ottoman Empire is dining with him tonight. He has just arrived from Egypt. The entire evening will be about the pyramids. I doubt the viscount will struggle to understand a Vermont intellectual speaking his tongue." He laughed at his own joke.

Nakshi leaned forward. "Pyramids? That's what we were talking about. What a coincidence."

"Well, you'll be in good company with Mr. Marsh then."

Rocko lifted his eyebrows. "Are you talking about George Perkins Marsh?"

"Yes." Sappini's grin widened. "Do you know him?"

"A name only, but I'd love to meet him."

Twice in a row. How could a man like Rocko, who wasn't even a history enthusiast, know people I'd never heard of?

"My brother-in-law will arrange a gathering for you. Alfred is the editor of the town's first Turkish-language newspaper, *Cerîde-i Havadis*, meaning 'daily news.' He's an Englishman, born and raised in Constantinople. His late father, William Churchill, founded the paper."

"We'd love to meet him, too." Rocko gestured toward Zena. "She'll be joining the *New York Daily Times*."

Sappini's eyes warmed. "I heard that."

"How?"

"Mr. Voss wrote to me."

"You must be well-connected."

Stephan returned Rocko's gesture. "Those who are better connected succeed more. My grandfather taught me that."

"Great advice. How long has your family been in Stamboul?"

"More generations than any Mussulman you'll find in this city. My ancestors were among the first to greet Mehmet the Second on May 29, 1453, when he entered Constantinople on his white horse and ended the Byzantine Empire. That was four hundred years ago last week." He gestured toward the Ottoman flags lining the shore, still hanging from the recent celebrations.

Francesco Sappini lifted his chin. "The sultan granted my ancestors privileges and raised them to special status among the rayahs."

Zena cut in, curious. "Who are your ancestors?"

Just as Stephan began to answer, the faint creak of the old floorboards returned, growing louder with each step until a green-eyed brunette walked into the living room.

"*Hosh Geldounuz!*" she greeted in Turkish with a broad grin.

"This is my wife, Helene." She was in her thirties, wearing an apricot-colored dress with embroidered sleeves and a lace turtleneck collar, a conservative choice for a summer day.

"Francesco tells me you've come from America."

"From New York," Zena emphasized, then began coughing. After a few sharp bursts, she stopped.

"Are you all right, dear? Marina can make you a honey-dipped *ihlamur*—linden tea from our yard."

"I'm fine, thank you. Just a long day." Beads of sweat formed on Zena's temple, barely visible beneath her turquoise-blue bonnet.

Helene looked us over. "It must've been a long, thrilling journey." She sighed. "Oh, America. Francesco says the future belongs to the New World."

"Do you plan to emigrate?"

Helene chuckled. "Oh no, dear! We'll be the last to leave this land. My husband is the chief dragoman for the British Embassy."

"Glorified translator," Stephan Sappini smirked.

"I take the 'glory' part." Helene's eyes sparkled. "Dragomen serve in every embassy and at the Sublime Porte. For generations, the Sappinis have been part of the diplomatic corps, a bridge between the Mussulman Turks and Christian Europeans."

"We are Levantines," Stephan answered Zena's earlier question. "Occidental Catholics and European families who call the Orient home. A small, close-knit community. Some of us are French, like Helene's family; some Austrian; most Italian, like me. My ancestors came from Venetia."

He lifted his head as if to display the bridge of his prominent Roman nose. "No ministry in Constantinople functions without someone from the Levantine community."

"What does Levant mean?" Zena pressed.

"It describes the lands of the Eastern Mediterranean. It comes from the French word '*se lever*,' meaning 'to rise,' like the sun in the Orient."

Helene chuckled. "We're the first to wake up and report the news."

Nakshi offered Helene a courteous smile. "And what did you learn when you woke up this morning?"

"The dawn heralded a day of peace," Helene threw up her hands, grinning, then turned serious. "No more roaring. The Russian bear has finally left town empty-handed, thanks to Lord Stratford's smart diplomacy." She turned toward her husband. "I wonder if your ancestors ever felt such a chill in the halls of the seraglio."

Stephan sighed. "Lord Stratford mediated between Prince Menshikov and the French Ambassador, surprising the prince by siding with him."

"How so?" Rocko knitted his brows.

Sappini cracked a witty smile. "Most visitors to Bethlehem are devout Russian pilgrims. The French are mostly secular tourists. During Easter, the Orthodox begin their rites earlier than the Latins at the Church of the Nativity. The French Ambassador didn't resist Elchi's logic."

It seemed the Porte had followed Lord Stratford's advice and kept negotiations focused on fair administration of the holy sites.

"Why would keys to the sanctuary cause a crisis?" Zena asked.

"It's been a centuries-old quarrel between the Latin and Orthodox churches. In the seventh century, when the Mussulmans took Jerusalem, they gave the Greek monks authority over the holy sites. It was a way to weaken the Latin Franks."

"There was never an official decree," Helene cut in. "The Greek bishop forged it!"

Stephan shrugged at his wife's claim. "When the Ottoman Turks conquered the Levant and Egypt in the sixteenth century, they exploited the rift between Orthodox and Catholics as a political tool, sometimes favoring the Russians, sometimes the Latins, granting guardianship to whichever side suited their interests."

"Playing one against the other," Zena flip-flopped her hand. "I thought only the British did that."

"They all do," Nakshi muttered. "It's a power play."

The dragoman spread his hands. "Lately, Turkish muscle has weakened, making it harder to sway both sides. At Easter, each faction demands the keys."

"Russians versus Latins? Aren't they all Christians?" Zena squinted.

Helene mused, "To the czar, only the Orthodox are Christians. Not Protestants and Catholics like us. When he speaks of protecting the Ottoman Christians, he means the Greek Orthodox."

"Not even the Armenians," Sappini added dryly.

"That's strange." Zena pressed a finger to her lips. "Possession of the keys wasn't enough for Menshikov. He invoked the old Kainarja Treaty. Why does that matter?"

Sappini smiled faintly, pleased to find a woman other than his wife who could spar over foreign affairs. He moved toward a wall where three texts hung side by side—Italian, Russian, and Turkish. The first two were typeset; the Turkish was handwritten.

"This is the Kainarja Treaty in three languages. Clause Fourteen grants Russia the right to build a church."

"Or *the* church," Helene broke in. "It implies an institution, not a building. The wording is vague, and each version, written in its own alphabet, says something slightly different."

Stephan ran his finger along the frame. "The Russian text states *Grekorossiykago*, meaning a Greco-Russian church from Byzantine times. The Italian reads *Chiesa Russo-Greca*, suggesting a Russian church in Greek style, something that never existed in Constantinople."

"It gets worse." Helene's lips curved in a thin smile. "In Turkish, the Latin word '*grek*' was misspelled as '*graf*,' which has no meaning."

"Why not fix it?" Zena pressed.

Sappini shrugged. "Because '*grek*' also means nothing in Turkish. Turks say '*rûm*' for Greeks, descendants of the Roman era. The scribe probably didn't know either word and settled on '*graf*'. No one corrected him."

Helene's grin widened. "Now comes the best part. Go ahead, Stephan."

Her husband pointed to a section in the Turkish script. "Read what it says here. Only the fourteenth clause."

He was asking me. Like a thief caught red-handed, I froze. Even most Turks today couldn't read Ottoman Turkish. The Turkish Republic abandoned the Arabic alphabet with Persian adaptations a century ago in favor of Latin letters. But Stephan Sappini rightfully assumed an Ottoman intellectual in America should be fluent in the mid-nineteenth century.

I stared at the script. It was gibberish. "As you know, Turkish calligraphy can be—" I cleared my throat, searching the room for rescue, "—confusing."

Nakshi leaned in. "His eyesight's worsened lately. He won't admit it. I'll try."

Relieved, I let him take over. A pious man, Nakshi could read Quranic Arabic. He squinted. "Not sure I'm reading this right. It says, Russia to build—" He hesitated. "Dosografa? Or is it Rosografa?"

The Sappinis chuckled. "Good enough. That's as close as any scholar gets."

Stephan pointed to the letters د and ر . "I explained this to Lord Stratford. The letters 'd' and 'r' look similar in the Ottoman alphabet, easy to confuse in handwriting." He chuckled. "He said Turks should build Dosografa only if they knew what it meant."

"Doso or Roso of the Grafa—that is the question," Helene quipped.

"And the answer is, who cares?" Sappini spread his arms. "Neither means anything."

Rocko smirked. "For the czar, it means one thing. Russia owns Turkey."

"Where is the sultan in all this?" I broke in.

Sappini didn't hesitate. "Elchi urged His Majesty Sultan Mejid to stand firm and appoint Mustafa Reshid Pasha as foreign minister." The dragoman stood tall, reassuring. "He's far more skilled than Rifat and better able to withstand intimidation."

"Did Sultan Mejid take the advice?"

"Not until Menshikov demanded the same change."

"Why would he do that?"

Francesco winked, smiling. "Reshid Pasha whispered to the Greek archbishop that Rifat refused to bow to Russian demands. Without him in office, the Porte might have yielded."

Helene added with a sly look. "The clergyman ran straight to Menshikov to report it!"

Rocko rubbed his chin. "This smells like a coordinated Reshid-Stratford operation. Menshikov made the same mistake twice, replacing less skilled diplomats with stronger ones."

Sappini clapped once. "Exactly how Lord Stratford described it. Not very smart of the prince."

Menshikov's bullying didn't help his nation. It only raised his archenemy, Lord Stratford, and the strongman Reshid Pasha to pivotal roles. The pressure drew France and England into an unlikely alliance. I saw echoes of Czar Nicholas in President Putin. Russia's aggression in Ukraine rallied the West against it, not long after French President Emmanuel Macron had called NATO "brain dead."

Does history repeat itself, or do those who write it not read the previous chapters?

Stephan carried on. "Reshid Pasha was firm but courteous with the prince. He praised Sultan Mejid's friendship with the czar, reminded him the sultan had already sided with the Greeks in the Church of the Nativity dispute, and argued a new treaty was unnecessary. As a last resort, the prince nearly begged for a verbal assurance. He got nothing. Enraged, he stormed out of the city and tore down the double-eagle Russian coat of arms from the embassy."

"Thank God he's gone." Helene exhaled loudly.

I wondered how others had taken it. "Did the local Greeks feel the same?"

Helene shook her head. "Marina, my assistant, swears the Turks seized the Nativity keys from the Greeks, not the Franks. The Muscovite emperor sent Menshikov to get them back."

Rocko let out a dry laugh. "That doesn't leave much room for ambiguity, does it? Greeks for Russia!"

Sappini's smile faded. "Now, the major powers are drafting resolutions and memoranda to preserve peace, but the czar may already have decided to advance into the Balkans under the banner of protecting the Orthodox Christians."

Helene's eyes softened. "Some days, I don't get to see Stephan. He's gone before dawn and back at midnight."

Stephan gazed out the window. "Because Lord Stratford is at the center of it all. Some say he's the most powerful man after the sultan."

"Why do so many people from different millets and faiths admire this Englishman?" Zena pressed.

The senior dragoman folded his hands. "He defends the wronged, rayah or Mussulman. Unfair taxes, theft by a local Pasha, he takes it to the Porte and pursues it until it's resolved."

"Does he have close friends?"

Helene shook her head. "Only his wife. She's his advisor, his confidant. Evenings, he writes to her. Lord Stratford knows many but keeps every tie strictly diplomatic. That's earned him respect."

Stephan's lips curled. "He influences England's foreign policy. Queen Victoria can't decide whether to admire or despise him. His temper irks those in power, but he won't bend when he believes he's right."

"But he can admit when he's wrong," Helene remarked with a knowing smile. "Sometimes he dines at the seraglio. Once, he lost his temper and swept the table clean, shattering plates because the food wasn't to his liking. The next day, he apologized to the Greek server in front of the staff. No one of his rank would've done that."

Stephan snapped his fingers, recalling. "He once challenged a ban on passing near the sultan's palace. The Porte relented. Locals no longer had to trudge miles uphill with their carts."

Helene touched his arm. "Do you remember his leisure sail over the Sweet Waters?" She straightened. "He's frugal and hates waste. He spotted a new palace foundation going up during a financial crisis and rushed to the seraglio to convince the sultan to halt construction, showing creditors fiscal discipline."

"But the biggest story is Carabet." Stephan gave a knowing smile.

Helene's eyes widened. "Oh, you must hear this!"

"One morning, people woke up to find a man's head propped on a chair in a public square. A Frank hat sat on it, with a note from the Porte detailing his disgrace. He was a poor, uneducated Armenian named Carabet."

"Awful!" Zena recoiled. "What crime did he commit?"

"Christian by birth, he converted to Islam, then soon after returned to his original faith. That made him an apostate, a Mussulman who became a Christian."

"Is that a crime?" Zena's eyes narrowed.

"Apostasy is punishable by death under the penal code unless the person repents. Carabet did not. The Porte executed him and displayed his head."

"I can't believe I'm hearing this! This is beyond barbarism." Zena's eyes bulged, bloodshot, her face damp with sweat, still blazing with outrage.

"You're not alone," Helene's voice dropped. "Grand Elchi stormed the Sublime Porte, demanding the sultan issue a firman banning such actions. He argued the Holy Quran supported his stance."

Nakshi jerked his head back. "How would he know that?"

Stephan lifted his chin. "Lord Canning has deep knowledge of Islam."

Helene nodded sharply, her eyes wide. "In Carabet's case, he challenged the ulema to show where the holy book justifies such punishment, knowing it doesn't. When they couldn't, the sultan amended the penal code."

Stephan Sappini recited the firman from memory. "Neither shall Christianity be insulted in my dominions, nor shall Christians be persecuted in any way for their faith."

Helene spread her arms. "His stand made Grand Elchi a hero in every Christian household from the Adriatic to Egypt. Everyone knew no other Frank held as much sway over the sultan. He became the hope of all rayahs and their Grand Elchi."

Histo pointed to his watch, pressing for time.

Ignoring him, Zena turned to me. "Did you know any of these?" She glanced at the Sappinis. "He's our in-house history guru."

Suddenly, I felt queasy. Why she put me on the spot, I'll never know. She knew I hadn't even heard of Lord Stratford before joining the program. As I scrambled for a response, I remembered what Grand Elchi had told the Earl of Clarendon.

"A few years ago, Lord Stratford solved a similar crisis in the Holy Lands."

Stephan nodded. "The cupola incident."

"Quite a showcase of diplomacy, wasn't it?" Zena pressed with a grin. "Francesco must know the inside story." Rocko shook his head, lips pressed.

The dragoman took her bait. "The dome of the Holy Sepulcher was leaking. Rain had weakened the stones, risking collapse. The Latins and Greeks blamed each other for stripping its lead cover. Though the Sublime Porte usually stayed out of Christian disputes, Lord Stratford urged an exception. Send a Turkish engineer to restore the cupola."

Helene added, "He argued that in the Turkish Empire, everything ultimately belongs to the sultan, even the holy sites."

"The Porte agreed," Sappini beamed. "The engineer fixed it. From then on, Turks would handle all repairs."

Zena motioned toward me with her thumb. "We heard the same account from him." She grinned. I lowered my head, blushing with a tinge of guilt and shame. I had never been a good liar.

"Oh, much more," Rocko waved his arm. "Don't forget the falafel recipe the engineer brought back."

"I never heard that." Helene's eyes widened, waiting for me to recount the story.

I stood there, mouth agape, before Rocko barged in. "We have a caique to catch."

Helene's brows knit in a glare. "Marina rolled dolmas for you."

"Next time, inshallah."

"Who holds the holy keys today?" Zena surveyed the team as we settled into our seats on the *Histoprise*.

Nakshi raised his hand. "The same Muslim family has held them for generations since the Ottoman era."

"What's the name of the holy site in the quantum universe?" Zena pressed on, turning it into an entertaining quiz show.

"You tell us." Krish grinned as he latched her into the inclined seat.

Zena raised her arm and deepened her voice, turning theatrical. "Pray, for the day shall come when Petamunra opens the gates of Dosografa. Let her holy encrypted keys lead every hologram to salvation."

"Amen!"

The lights dimmed. Giggles blended with humming.

21

A DAY AT THE PETERHOF

When the lights flickered on, they revealed a palace hallway and a grand marble staircase. Two Greek statues and two imposing guards flanked a tall wooden door. We stood nearby, incognito.

Three men climbed the stairs behind an usher. The eldest, a decorated military officer in his seventies, walked with quiet command.

"Field Marshal Paskevich," Histo told us. "Russia's most renowned military hero and viceroy of Poland, noted for his conquests of Nakhichevan and Persian Armenia." Our program director sounded as if he'd known him in person.

Behind him was a short civilian with a sharp nose. I didn't need Histo's cheat sheet to recognize him—Count Karl Nesselrode, Russia's longtime foreign minister.

The youngest was Count Orlov, head of the secret police. He had a fair complexion, a receding hairline, and a reddish walrus mustache.

At the top, the guards struck the floor with their weapons. The usher opened the door and gestured for them to enter. Histo signaled us to follow.

Inside was a spacious salon. Emperor Nicholas stood, his gaze fixed on a grand painting spanning the wall. Nearby, a middle-aged officer with plush epaulets sat at a round table. The name tag across from his chair read Prince Dolgorukov, War Minister.

"Where are we?" Zena asked Histo, admiring the pastel yellow frames around the tall windows, each trimmed with intricate white embroidery.

"This is Peterhof, Czar Nicholas's summer palace outside St. Petersburg."

Each guest greeted the emperor with a slight bow. Nicholas responded with a faint nod, not taking his eyes off the painting until everyone had taken their seats.

The painting's vibrant colors dominated the room, contrasting with the pastel walls. It captured a daring, staged nighttime naval attack. Fireships ablaze drifted toward enemy vessels anchored in a bay beneath a cloudy sky. Flames pierced the darkness as the full moon, half-veiled by thick clouds, cast eerie shadows over choppy waters. Black smoke billowed upward, deepening the night's gloom.

The emperor turned from the painting. "It's so vivid, so alive, like history grew wings and landed to tell its tale. Had I not known Ivan, I'd have sworn he witnessed it." He looked rested.

"It was July 1770." Paskevich kept his eyes on the painting. "The surprise attack destroyed the Ottoman fleet at the *Battle of Chesme*."

"This port is on the Aegean Sea," Rocko whispered to Zena. "Today it's a tourist town in Türkiye. The work is by Ivan Aivazovsky. I grew up with his paintings on our walls. My parents had several, mostly views of Constantinople."

Zena glanced at him from the corner of her eye. "Something you and the czar have in common."

"He has the original. We had reproductions." Rocko winked. "Small difference."

"You're real. He's the reproduction. You win." She smiled at him.

Winner? Was that an encrypted message?

Histo raised his voice. "Team, don't linger. Eyes forward."

Easier said than done, but I forced myself to pay attention.

The emperor stepped back a few paces, still studying the painting. "A true Russian hero from Crimea."

Nakshi murmured, "He was Armenian by blood."

I didn't even know the painter's name—embarrassing.

As servants moved about taking drink orders, Nicholas paced the room, arms folded behind. It had become a familiar scene. The Russian Emperor abstained from alcohol and preferred his guests to sit while he moved. Pacing eased his chronic back pain.

"Ivan captured your grandfather's triumph, Count Orlov."

The redheaded man inclined to Nicholas. "The greatest hero of that day wasn't my grandfather but his brother, my great-uncle. It was his idea to send the fireships into the Turkish port at night, catching them off guard."

The emperor lifted his chin. "Courage, genius, and above all, loyalty to the crown—that is the House of Orlov." The police chief beamed.

As His Imperial Majesty completed his inspection of the painting, I searched for signs of the nameless sailors whose lives had been cut short. There were none. Yet their agony and silent screams seemed to haunt the salon, carried by flames that soared high before vanishing into the thick clouds.

"I decided to order the troops to cross the River Prut." The emperor startled his guests. The war minister watched the three distinguished men with a faint smile.

Nesselrode spoke first. "Sire, we haven't exhausted all diplomatic means."

Nicholas twitched. "I sent my envoy. He returned empty-handed." He avoided his foreign minister's gaze.

Count Nesselrode was more than a high-level statesman. Alongside Prince von Metternich, he helped shape the nineteenth-century legitimist order, co-creating the Concert of Europe.

The seasoned diplomat measured his words. "Prince Menshikov is an admirable soldier. I fear involving him further in diplomacy may tarnish his reputation with the troops. I recommend Count Orlov, or someone of his caliber, take charge of future engagements with the Porte."

Nicholas snapped, "Count Nesselrode, I know you've had reservations about the Prince of Finland, but I had my reasons for sending him. He's incorruptible, far too rich for that." The czar's voice rose. "As a last resort, Menshikov sent a final ultimatum to the

Porte—eight days to meet my demands. They refused. The Turks have left me no choice but to cross the River Prut."

Paskevich leaned forward. "Once we step into their territory, the Turks may see it as a violation of their suzerainty."

"I can't control how they read it, Field Marshal." Nicholas's eyes flared. Paskevich looked away.

Nicholas swept his arm toward a tall window. "Christians are suffering under the Mussulman yoke. The existing treaties obligate me to protect their rights. I've tried everything to avoid a conflict. But let it be clear! I shall protect Russia's honor!"

He drew a deep breath, steadying himself under the watchful eyes of his ministers before resuming in a calm, measured tone.

"We've prepared thousands of pamphlets explaining our objectives. As we enter each village, we will distribute them to the residents. Prince Dolgorukov can read one."

The war minister retrieved a leaflet from his dossier. It featured the emperor's face beside an Orthodox cross, delivering a message from Russia's supreme ruler. He read aloud, "Russia does not seek war or the conquest of new territories. We demand a guarantee from the Ottoman government that the Emperor of All Russia upholds the sacred rights of the Orthodox Church. Should the Turkish Sultan refuse, we will advance and fight for our true faith with God on our side!"

Nicholas's voice turned cold and steady. "I anticipate the sultan will reject. We shall then blockade the Bosporus, seize Turkish ships in the Black Sea, and propose to Austria to take control of Herzegovina and Serbia. With Austria on our side, the Western powers will not risk declaring war against us."

The czar had made up his mind, bypassing the counsel of many senior staff in favor of a belligerent course. He nodded for his war minister to proceed.

Prince Dolgorukov cleared his throat. "We've already mobilized ninety thousand troops to advance into the Balkans, with another forty thousand ready to strike Constantinople at a moment's notice."

The salon fell silent, broken only by the faint murmur of the crowd gathering outside in the palace yard. Alongside the novanauts, I held my breath, the gravity of the moment pressing heavily on the room. Dolgorukov's subtle, lingering smile suggested a carefully guarded plan to shock Turkey by swiftly moving into the Balkans and destroying its naval forces in the Black Sea ports.

Nicholas stopped across from Field Marshal Paskevich, waiting for him to speak first.

"Sire, with all due respect, Austria may not support this plan."

The czar jerked back. "Franz Joseph will. He owes his throne to me." He tightened his brows. "Paskevich, you're the one who saved the Habsburgs by ousting Kossuth and his bandits from Austria."

"Your Majesty, I don't oppose a joint alliance with Austria." The field marshal was calm. "But Vienna might not support our troops entering the Balkans. The Habsburgs fear unrest could trigger Serbian and Slavic uprisings. Kossuth still haunts Emperor Joseph. And Western powers, especially Great Britain, might covertly fuel the chaos to plunge the region into disorder."

Nicholas pursed his lips and quickened his pace, mulling over what he had just heard. To my surprise, the czar did not dismiss the opposing view of his most senior brass. His demeanor grew calmer.

Dolgorukov raised his voice a notch. "In every Balkan village we enter, we'll find Christians from warring tribes, oppressed by the Turks, eager to rise and ready to join us in toppling the Turkish Empire."

Paskevich leaned back. "Neither the Bulgarians nor the Serbs will take up arms. They're peaceful country folk." His voice was steady.

The war minister pushed back. "That's because they haven't yet witnessed Turkish atrocities in their villages. Once the slaughter begins, those villagers will rally to our cause. The conflict will ignite a pan-Slavic revival against the Turks and establish our dominance over the Franks and the English."

The czar slowed his pace, bowed his head, and strolled with his arms still folded behind him. It was unclear whether he had detached himself from the debate or was weighing the arguments.

Count Orlov entered the discussion. "Our soldiers are poor peasants and serfs. They neither understand the dispute in the Holy Land nor care about pan-Slavic ideals." The police chief wore a knowing smile. "But every Russian understands God's calling. They will march into battle with a cross around their neck, ready to fight for Him. Our war must carry a religious banner against the infidel, not a national one."

Nesselrode spoke last, addressing His Majesty. "Sire, the combined lands of all the other European nations barely match ours—and that's counting only our European territory, not Asia." His voice was steady. "Yet our population is just one-fifth of theirs. We can't draft a third of our people. They're too short to carry a rifle, and half suffer from illness." He fixed his gaze on the emperor. "A long conflict in the Balkans will be difficult without an alliance with Austria. If we go it alone, Vienna might sever ties with us."

Nicholas paused, remaining unmoved. He could not dismiss Karl Nesselrode's warning, especially about Austria. No one in Russia knew the Habsburgs better. Nesselrode had helped forge the Holy Alliance with Prussia and Austria after the Napoleonic Wars, working closely with his Viennese counterpart, Prince von Metternich.

Nicholas resumed pacing, pressing his lips. Encouraged by the emperor's hesitation, Paskevich spoke. "Perhaps a better strategy would be a defensive occupation. We follow Your Majesty's orders to occupy the principalities but stop short of declaring war on Turkey."

Czar Nicholas stopped abruptly and fixed a sharp gaze on the field marshal, knitting his brows.

"Occupy, then pause." Paskevich gave a faint smile. Nicholas narrowed his gaze, his face staying tense.

"What would that accomplish?" The war minister's voice wavered.

Paskevich kept his poise. "The Powers will be alarmed and call for talks between us and the Turks. We will agree. That will buy us time. Meanwhile, we will train local Christian youth across the Danubian principalities under our control to raise a fifty thousand troops in a few years."

He paused, letting the idea settle. "Combined with our forces, that will be strong enough to launch a religious war against the Turks, who have long occupied Christian lands. We will no longer require Austrian troops to achieve victory."

Nicholas's eyes lit, a subtle smile lingering on his lips.

Like a skilled chess player seeing three moves ahead, Paskevich laid out his strategy with confidence. Time would prove it effective against Turkey, but not against history—the true grandmaster, seeing ten moves ahead. The plan would drive a wedge between the friendly Serbs and the pro-Austrian Christian Bosnians, setting in motion the events that led to the First World War, during which the Russian Empire would collapse into the Bolshevik Revolution.

As Dad used to say, one cannot engineer the future to create a desired history.

Orlov supported Paskevich's approach. "The Western powers will not interfere against such overwhelming strength. Their public will support a religious war of Christians against the Mussulmans to drive the Turks out of Europe."

Nesselrode narrowed his eyes. "The day we cross the river, Stratford Canning will call for a full-scale European alliance to save Turkey. He shall have Lord Palmerston's backing."

At the mention of the British diplomat's name, the emperor jolted and cut in. "Canning's actions won't deter me. Besides, I don't intend to cross the Danube—not yet at least—only the River Prut." He quipped, "That alone might be enough to bring down the Turkish Empire."

A few giggles rose around the table.

He quickly reverted to a serious tone. "Occupy, but don't declare war. I like that."

Paskevich slumped his shoulders. War Minister Dolgorukov blushed and bit his lip.

Nicholas placed his hand on his chest and sighed, his voice deepening. "No one can imagine how deeply these events sadden me. I have grown old. I wished to end my life in peace."

He lifted his chin, straightened, and raised his voice. "We shall cross the River Prut to occupy Moldavia and Wallachia, including the delta lands of Dobruja."

The czar awaited questions. None came.

"We are pressing for our rights, the protectorate of the Christians— but not proclaiming war. We wait until the Turks declare it against us. Our divisions will remain on a war footing." He smiled wryly. "The Turkish Empire's days are numbered. Turks and Mussulmans will no longer remain in Europe. St. Sophia has been yearning for her cross."

Everyone rose, applauding.

Nakshi clenched his teeth. "God told you that?"

Zena shook her head. "This isn't liberation. It's ethnic cleansing. Millions of Muslims have lived in the Balkans for centuries."

The grandfather clock chimed, as if announcing the arrival of the angel of judgment. From the balcony came a voice: "By the grace of God, the Emperor and Autocrat of all Russia—"

War Minister Dolgorukov leaned in. "Your Majesty, it's time for you to address the people."

Gazing at the boundless crowd gathered on the lawn, Emperor Nicholas drew a deep breath and moved toward the balcony doors, his eyes glassy.

He whispered. "Follow the path true to your faith. Fulfill your duty to protect Russia's honor."

It was as if some invisible force pushed him forward to take his place in history. Two cadets flanking the balcony flung open the tall wooden doors. The wind slipped inside, lifting the lace curtains as though saluting their august ruler. The Russian Emperor Nicholas I stepped onto the balcony to thunderous applause.

Count Orlov leaned close. "Your Imperial Majesty, Russia is at your feet."

When the lights returned, we stood in the courtyard of a stunning palace—a three-story Baroque masterpiece with interconnected buildings stretching for hundreds of feet. Its pale yellow and white façade, with pilasters and large arched windows, gleamed in the summer sun.

Behind us stretched a pond ringed with lush green lawns and walkways. A massive crowd of peasants, workers, and serfs filled the grounds, which sloped gradually toward the sea, ending at the shoreline a few hundred yards away.

"Wow! Where are we?" Zena asked, her eyes wide, gazing at the people standing shoulder to shoulder.

"Same place. Peterhof Palace, in the courtyard," Histo replied. "The emperor is meeting with his ministers and generals. He'll soon address the citizens."

"The same meeting we'd just witnessed?"

The director nodded. "Krish reversed the clock for an hour."

Rocko winked, "Only in the quantum universe."

"Be careful what you say." Histo raised a hand. "You are no longer incognito."

Zena gestured to the sculpted platform beneath us. "Check out these white and brown tiles. One giant checkerboard." She seemed absorbed in the architecture. "I like this place better than the Winter Palace."

Rocko leaned toward her. "Wouldn't you rather be up on that balcony?"

"I'd rather be in bed now. I'm exhausted."

He slipped an arm around her shoulder, flashing his Clark Gable smile. "You should meet with the czar and rewrite history."

"I'd like that." Zena arched a brow.

Rocko pulled her closer, squeezed her shoulder, and spoke into her ear. "Imagine you beside the emperor. The crowd prefers you as empress over Alexandra. The Prussian Princess doesn't hold a candle to you."

She chuckled. "You must be the royal matchmaker. Russian czars usually wed German aristocrats, not nameless Circassians."

Rocko pressed on, gazing into her emerald eyes. "Royal blood and wealth—he has those. You're the jewel he's missing. The czar would place a crown on your pretty head."

As he leaned in, his lips nearing hers, I gritted my teeth, a surge of painful emotion rising in me.

"Any king would—"

Zena jerked back, shoving his arm off with a snap. "Thanks, but no thanks. If I ever decide to become a gem in someone's collection, I'd pick old Nic, not a scumbag like you."

She shot him a sly look. He returned the smile.

"Is that where you're from?" A Russian officer standing to my left smiled at Zena, startling everyone. None of us expected to see an intelligent hologram among the crowd of dummies.

Zena was appalled. "What d'you mean? Where from what?"

"I heard you say you're a Circassian. Are you from Chechnya?" He was young, handsome, mid-twenties, about six feet tall.

"I am Cherkess on my father's side, but not Chechen."

"I spent a few years there." He grinned. "I admire the Circassians. Brave people."

"What's your rank, Officer?" Zena gave the tall man a once-over.

"I am a junker in the artillery brigade. It's a volunteer position. Lowest among the officer class, nothing impressive." He chuckled. "What brought you to Russia?"

Rocko slid between them. "We cover news for the American media. Freelancers." Zena's gaze soured, but Rocko didn't care. "We came to Peterhof, anticipating the emperor might make an important announcement."

"Me too." The officer widened his eyes. "His Imperial Majesty doesn't address the public often. Since he chose Peterhof as the venue, it must be important."

"It's a magnificent palace." Zena pushed Rocko back. "Do you know who built it?"

"Peter the Great," the junker replied. "One of a hundred palaces built during his reign. More came after, but Peterhof is special, the most splendid of them all." Pride laced his voice. "Our august czar had built St. Petersburg as a new city—Russia's window to the West—to transform Asiatic Russia into a European state."

Zena leaned in, absorbed in the officer's recounting of Russian history. His soft demeanor was telling. I wish I had that kind of talent. With half his charm, I could make history sound like a love song.

Rocko chimed in again. "I read it somewhere. Russians believe the city was built on the bones of thousands of serfs who died from cold, hunger, and sickness during its construction." He spoke with the confidence of a professor, eager to share his knowledge.

"Some Russians do." The officer was humble. "Some even fell prey to hungry wolves. It is sad but true. Peasants believe Peter built the city in the heavens and brought it down to earth."

"Any other reported miracles, Officer?" Nakshi barged in.

"No, unless you count the marvel of Russian engineering." The junker grinned, brushing aside Nakshi's wit. "Peterhof uses natural springs to circulate water through dozens of fountains without a single pump."

Zena shifted the subject. "Do you think there will be a war with Turkey?"

"We'll hear from the emperor soon, but it seems likely."

"Will you support his decision?" She slipped into investigative journalist mode, probing the Russian officer.

"I am a patriot. I trust whatever His Majesty decides. But don't let the uniform fool you. I'm not a soldier by trade."

"What do you do, then?"

"I am a writer—or at least, I try to be." He chuckled. "I write fiction."

"Really?" Zena chimed in, gripping my arm. "He is, too." I looked away, staring at my shoes, hoping someone would change the subject.

"You're wearing an officer's uniform," Nakshi noted. "How does that work?"

"I'm an officer reporting for the army paper."

"Are you famous?" Zena widened her eyes, slightly parting her mouth.

The young man let out a laugh. "I like the sound of it. Not exactly a household name—if that's what you're asking. I've only published one book so far, and that was last year."

"What was it about?"

"It's a work of fiction, inspired by my childhood memories." Zena's mouth parted. Her admiration for the handsome man's intellectual side was genuine.

The officer leaned toward me. "How many have you written?"

I twitched. "None. I've been commissioned to write one."

Zena jumped in. "He knows a lot about history. That's why they chose him." She stepped closer to the junker, brushing Rocko aside, signaling her discomfort with his advances. I felt much better.

The officer was oblivious to all this. "A historical novel, then. Ordered by a committee. I wish I had that kind of support." He exhaled, looking out toward the horizon. "I pay attention to details, but I also believe in articulating knowledge. Maybe you can teach me a few tricks. We should get together someday."

"I doubt I could teach you anything." I stopped short of admitting I hadn't written a single line yet.

"Don't believe him." Zena jabbed the air between us. "He's overly humble."

Her words warmed me. I smiled at the Russian man, feeling a lightness. "But getting together—that's a good thought. Over a cup of Russian tea, laced with vodka. I enjoy exchanging ideas. What's the title of your book?"

"*Detstvo*. It's in Russian, by LN. It means Childhood. It's the first one of a trilogy."

"LN? That's you?" Zena asked.

"They're my initials, Lev Nikolayevich."

A roar from the crowd cut off our conversation. A man stepped onto the balcony to make an announcement.

"By the grace of God, Emperor and Autocrat of all the Russias and Czar of Poland, His Majesty Nicholas, will now address his people," he proclaimed, bowing sharply before stepping aside to join the applause. Two cadets opened the tall balcony doors. The lace curtains fluttered in the breeze.

Moments later, Emperor Nicholas appeared, his all-too-familiar confidants behind him. The cheers grew deafening.

"Weren't we just there?" Nakshi narrowed his eyes. "Déjà vu."

"We still are." Rocko grinned. "Incognito."

I leaned in. "Being present in two places at the same time. Superposition."

Zena rolled her eyes. "A bunch of Martian smart alecks." The male novanauts flashed knowing smiles.

The balcony stretched beyond three tall arched windows framed by stucco, opening into the grand salon. A wrought-iron railing with intricate floral and geometric patterns jutted outward. At its center, the golden double-headed eagle—the Russian coat of arms—shone brilliantly, radiating grandeur.

The emperor stood poised as applause thundered on. He let it swell, then raised his arm. Silence fell.

"Our beloved and faithful subjects and all the people everywhere." The emperor gripped the railing above the double eagle and looked out over the crowd. "Maintaining our holy obligations is a duty inseparably connected to the throne. Our blessed ancestors always defended our faith." He raised his voice. "This sacred duty has been the object of my constant care and attention from the day it pleased the Almighty to place me on the throne of our fathers." The crowd roared.

The emperor raised his arm again to quiet them. "The treaty Russia signed with the Ottoman Empire eighty years ago, founded on the epic glory of our ancestors, obligated them to uphold the rights of our Church." He paused, surveying the sizeable crowd. "But to our extreme grief, the Ottoman Porte infringed upon these rights, and its many willful acts now threaten to overthrow the Orthodox discipline so precious to us." A wave of boos followed.

The emperor waited for the order to return. He turned to his right. "All our efforts to restrain the Porte from openly violating our rights have proved vain." His voice rose. "Even the word of the sultan, solemnly given to me by himself, was faithlessly broken!" More boos erupted.

Shifting to his left, Nicholas raised his pitch. "I exhausted every means to resolve our just claims through diplomacy."

He lifted his clenched fist. "I have deemed it indispensable to move our armies into the provinces on the Danube!"

The crowd roared and didn't stop even after the emperor raised his arm to silence them. He seemed pleased that, for once, his subjects refused to obey.

Once the commotion subsided, Czar Nicholas lifted his chin. "We do not seek conquests. Russia has no need for them. Yet the stubbornness and blindness of the Ottoman court have left us no choice but to act. I am compelled to defend the rights of the Orthodox faith."

"God is with Nicholas!" a priest shouted from beneath the balcony. The emperor nodded in acknowledgment as the roars swelled again.

The Russian czar extended his arms forward, like a pastor inviting his congregation to salvation. "We are calling God to our aid! We leave it to Him to decide our quarrel, and with full confidence in the right hand of the Almighty, we shall move forward!" Then he stepped back into the salon.

The crowd erupted in cheers, louder than before, tingling my eardrums. The holograms with glassy eyes waved fists, joining the emperor's call. It was a scene unlike anything we'd witnessed earlier. A nation mostly of serfs, with no freedom to their own will, yet allowed to vent their rage at those their master despised—people they had never met. It was a textbook case of declaring a war of choice.

"Does anyone remember the date?" Nakshi asked. "It was on the wall calendar."

"June 26, 1853," Zena answered. As always, she paid better attention.

Czar Nicholas's *Peterhof Imperial Manifesto* ordered Russian armies to cross the Prut River and invade Turkish-ruled Wallachia—modern-day Romania. A week later, on July 3, Russia would seize Bucharest, and by July 15, bring the Danubian Principalities under its control. Nicholas framed his campaign as a liberation of Orthodox brethren. The British press would dismiss those claims.

Fast forward to February 22, 2022. Following a televised address the day before, Russian President Vladimir Putin ordered troops into eastern Ukraine to protect their brethren—the Russian-speaking population in Donbas—and to "denazify" the Kyiv government. Once again, the West rejected these claims. A month later, in March 2022, the Kremlin formally acknowledged Russia was at war with Ukraine.

What would Dad say if he were beside me? I hadn't realized how much I missed him. Incognito, he must be somewhere. I smiled—bitterly.

The young officer joined in the crowd's enthusiasm, applauding. Setting aside my thoughts about the similarities between the two historical events, I asked, "Does this mean you'll soon depart for the front?"

"I'm not sure," he replied. "I will obey my orders, but please send me a copy of your book once you publish it."

"How do I find you?"

"Mail it to the Yasnaya Polyana estate in Tula."

"To Junker Lev Nikolayevich, and that'll reach you?"

"Add my last name. Everyone in town knows my family."

"I thought that was your full name. What is it then?"

"Tolstoy. Lev Nikolayevich Tolstoy."

I froze.

He leaned toward Zena with a mischievous smile. "Madame, Circassian women are renowned for their beauty, but your mysterious charm exceeds anyone's expectations."

Zena stood speechless, caught in his gaze. Admiration lit her face. I couldn't tell if it was his flattery, his charm, or the shock of meeting a future legend on the cusp of greatness.

Perhaps all.

Cheers wound down as Emperor Nicholas returned to the grand salon, met by the forceful applause of his ministers and generals.

"I must go now," the young officer said. "It was a pleasure meeting you all." He grinned and began to walk away, leaving me stunned. After a few steps, he paused, turned back, and called out, "Don't forget to send that copy! I learn from great writers."

"Of course," I stammered, my jaw slack and mind spinning as he disappeared. Writing a book no longer felt daunting. It felt impossible. The bar had risen beyond reach, hovering somewhere above the clouds.

"*Za Vera i Tsarya!*" screamed the holographic dummy behind me, making my ears ring.

22
THE REFORMIST

As I was still elated by meeting a great literary mind, Histo told us we would dine that evening in Istanbul at Reshid Pasha's mansion. He had invited Lord Stratford.

"Are we going to crash?" Nakshi asked.

"You'll be incognito. Krish will serve real food."

Rocko patted his stomach. "About time. I haven't had a bite since breakfast."

"May I be excused? I don't feel like eating." Zena pouted like a child. Seeing her drenched in sweat, Histo nodded.

Krish swayed his head. "Prakash stocked your room with plenty of bottled water."

"I only want my room and my pillow."

"Be nice to the boggy man," Rocko quipped.

"Shut up." Then Zena turned to me. "Save me a piece of baklava, please—will you?'

"I will." As she left the launchpad, a hollow space formed inside me.

We faced choppy waters at a wooden dock. The Galata Tower loomed behind us. We had to be on the European side of the city.

"I know where we are." Rocko pointed to a slender tower perched on a tiny islet in the Bosporus, a few hundred yards from the shore. "That is Maiden's Tower. Across the water is Scutari."

The crispness of early autumn lingered in the air, a cool breeze sweeping over fallen leaves scattered across the ground. The breeze stirred the long, multicolored canvas blinds, sun-faded and stained, that sheltered the storefronts.

Krish had handed out thick blankets before we got on *Histoprise*. He warned us humidity could cut like a knife in the Bosporus, even on warm fall days when the air felt mild. Petamunra missed nothing, simulating even the finest details.

A sixty-foot-long wooden caique, securely tethered to the dock by thick ropes, stood out among the other boats in the bay. Four cypress pillars supported a heavy cotton canvas canopy at the stern, its drapes tied back at the sides. A white ensign fluttered lazily at the bow, marking the boat as the property of the United Kingdom of Great Britain and Ireland.

A dozen sweepers sat in six pairs, facing the stern, each gripping an oar. They wore red shirts under black vests, pantaloons loose at the knee, and red caps tied snug beneath their chins. Every man bore a full mustache, otherwise clean-shaven. Nearby, a dozen bystanders—some in fezzes, others in turbans—watched the vessel and its oarsmen with quiet admiration.

We passed barefoot workers in dirty turbans and rags, unloading cargo from a commercial ship. A few quarreled over where to set the goods.

Histo still wore his light-blue suit while we wrapped ourselves in blankets. "How do you handle any weather, hot or cold? You always wear the same outfit."

The director brushed off Rocko's question and motioned us to board the royal caique and sit under the canopy. The boat wobbled as we stepped aboard. The sweepers pressed the blades flat against the deck to steady it.

Krish's voice came over the speakers. "The new patch works well."

Rocko winked. "Have mercy on us, Aladdin. Don't make us fall off. Bosporus is cold even in August."

Krish chuckled. "Histo promised me a lamp to replace my tablet."

Watching the baffled holograms peering into the water, thinking a big fish had caused the sudden chop, I wondered if invisible visitors were observing us in our universe with similar bemusement.

At last, Lord Stratford and Francesco Sappini arrived in the royal carriage and stepped off to board the caique. The ambassador and his dragoman took their seats opposite us. Moments later, twelve sweepers began rowing eastward in perfect harmony, effortlessly propelling the vessel across the Bosporus. They skillfully navigated around small caiques, shuttling passengers along the coast.

The setting sun cast a radiant glow behind us, warming the back of my neck and bathing the blue waters ahead in a tapestry of golden and fiery orange hues. Gentle ripples shimmered like liquid light in the breeze. Soon, the sky would surrender to the cool glow of moonlight.

A sizable construction site marked by heaps of sand and lumber came into view on the port side. Workers stood on tall wooden scaffolding, some climbing.

Sappini said, "They will name the new palace Dolmabahçe, and its mosque will bear the sultan's mother's name."

Stratford watched the construction silently. "I had an audience with the sultan a week after her passing to offer my condolences."

"How did he take his mother's loss?"

"Lost in grief, he mourned that she didn't live to see its completion." Stratford sighed at the sight of the majestic construction. "I wasn't sure he even heard my warning that his grand vizier was prone to compromise with the Russians."

"He must have." The dragoman spoke matter-of-factly. "He dismissed Mehmet Ali Pasha shortly after. He's now the war minister."

"I don't know which is worse." Elchi glimpsed a smile.

"My lordship, Bezmi-âlem Sultan wrote you from her deathbed to protect her son from the ill-willed seraglio ministers. You did just that."

Lord Stratford didn't respond. His eyelids grew heavy, his head dropped, and he began to doze. Sappini slumped, stretched his legs, and followed suit.

I watched porters unloading timbers from a commercial vessel. Noticing my subtle smile, Nakshi gave me an inquisitive look.

"My great-great-grandfather brought lumber from Dobruja, Romania, for use in the palace's construction." I smiled broadly.

"He must've left town just in time. We just heard from the horse's mouth."

Nakshi was right. The czar had listed the port city among his targets.

"Let's say hi to Grand-Grandpa," Rocko quipped. "He might be unloading as we speak."

That was intriguing. "Can we investigate? Seriously."

Histo declined, fizzing out my excitement. "The Committee declines such requests, unless the person of interest was a figure of history, or has an extensive biography or memoir."

No one in my family was a public figure. None left behind a biography, and apart from Deborah's, there were no memoirs either.

Histo pointed at three men supervising the workers. "They're the contractors your ancestor supplied with the timbers. The man in the black fez is Garabed Balyan, and the young man beside him is his son, Nikogos."

Nakshi jumped in, "The legendary Armenian family who shaped much of Istanbul's architecture. They built palaces, pavilions, mosques, and mansions."

I had heard much about them from Grandpa. Sultan Mejid ordered Dolmabahçe as his new residence, moving out of Topkapi, the palace where sultans had reigned and lived for four centuries. The Balyans extended the coastline with sand, creating new districts along the Bosporus and expanding the city.

Further along the Bosporus, a white mosque came into view, nearly finished. Its tall windows blended occidental and oriental styles.

Nakshi glimmered. "This one is my favorite."

The Great Mecidiye Mosque in Ortaköy, chalk-white, flanked by two slender minarets, was stunning at the water's edge. It was another Balyan work. Grand Elchi, now awake, silently admired it.

Rocko pointed at an older building behind the site. "That's the synagogue my family attended. A church must be nearby."

The Abrahamic meeting point symbolized Sultan Mejid's inclusive vision. A century and a half later, this landmark would backdrop President George W. Bush's speech after September 11, praising Türkiye as a secular democracy among Muslim nations.

Past the mosque, beneath a tall cypress, men sat cross-legged in its shade, eating grapes and bread as they waited for a day's hire. White seagulls circled overhead, chirping. One worker tossed seeds into the sea. The birds dived screeching at the splash, a Bosporus ritual between man and nature, repeated for millennia.

Along the strait, transporters lined up their caiques. One carried a group of young women, some veiled, all giggling. One trailed her hand in the water, splashing the rest. A man on shore watched.

The sight stirred Grandpa's tale. His grandfather had fallen for a jubilant beauty sailing in a caique at sunset. Her laughter carried across the water, and that alone won him as he stood on shore. It must have been a day like this. He chased her relentlessly and married her. She could've been that young woman. And the shadowed man on shore? The setting sun kept his face hidden.

Grandpa used to say he and I were both products of Bosporus love.

I caught Histo's warm gaze at me. Maybe he had replayed that moment for me, but I didn't ask. I wanted to believe my imagination was true.

Thanks to Petamunra, the excursion to Reshid Pasha's mansion felt priceless—worth trading my Thanksgiving week for time in the quantum universe. I wished I could share all this with my beloved Grandpa.

With Zena too, I must admit.

Francesco Sappini rubbed his eyes awake. "I'm counting on Pasha to treat us to a festive meal tonight."

Elchi's gaze drifted to a turbaned man puffing a nargileh on shore. "No doubt the after-dinner digestive will come as a generous overdose of smoke from Pasha's chibouk."

Sappini yawned, watching the shore. Merchants bustled under the gaze of lazy bystanders. "Life looks tranquil, but the plain truth is, everyone is anxious. Helene shops in the markets. She says people fear the Russians will tear down mosques and raise churches in their place."

"Stephan, life is anything but routine since the Cossacks crossed the Prut. The past three months have been one long war of diplomacy, unlike anything I've ever experienced."

Sappini shook his head. "I've lost count of the peace proposals. A dozen?"

Stratford's mouth curled faintly. "By the time one reached a capital, another was already fired off elsewhere."

"This last one from Vienna seems to culminate them all."

Elchi didn't reply at once. He watched dolphins racing them over the chop before breaking his silence.

"We have our work cut out for us tonight. Strict orders from Lord Clarendon: one last attempt to push the Turks to sign the Vienna Note as is. Nicholas has accepted. Let's not get sidetracked by Reshid's life story."

Stephan smiled at his boss's dry remark. "Pasha likes to reminisce about his Egypt days."

"Save the small talk for dinner. Pretend you're hearing it for the first time. Once the coffee is poured, it's business."

Sappini gave a wry shrug. "Helene says I should learn diplomacy from you, my lordship. She thinks I need it with my in-laws." The dragoman drew a thin smile from his boss.

The royal caique approached a three-story wooden mansion surrounded by several acres of land.

Rocko snapped a finger. "This is the Baltalimani district." He knew every corner of the city he grew up in. "The British and the Ottomans signed a trade accord here, favorable to the Brits. It raised duties on Turkish exports to England and lowered them for British goods coming in."

Nakshi leaned forward. "When was that?"

"Fifteen years ago," I said, eager to show off. "That makes it 1838."

"No wonder Britain sees Ottoman Turkey as a loyal ally," Nakshi said dryly. "Gold flows one way, from the Bosporus to the English Isles."

Dad would've agreed. He often told his students the Ottoman Empire had become Britain's biggest cash cow in the nineteenth century. Raw goods left Turkey cheap, returned as British products, undercutting and eventually crushing the local industry.

Perhaps Lord Stratford's real mission was to protect the goose that laid golden eggs. Something to think about.

The sweepers executed a surgical landing, first slowing the caique by lifting their oars on the port side, then, at a single command, pressing them down against the quay to bring the boat to a precise stop.

Reshid Pasha was a charming man in his fifties, short with a dark complexion, thick eyebrows, and a black beard. His broad-shouldered wrestler's build gave him quiet authority. His dark eyes brimmed with warmth as he greeted his guests.

"Surprise, surprise," Lord Stratford smiled, offering an elegantly wrapped box. Reshid accepted it with grace as servants rushed to collect coats and hats. Grand Elchi sat on an ottoman, struggling to remove his boots.

"You don't have to take them off," Reshid said, as two servants appeared with slippers.

"I spent so many years in your country, I adopted the culture," Lord Canning grinned. "Mehetabel Hanum even keeps a pair for me in London."

"Civilization takes time to adopt, one elchi at a time," the minister quipped. "After my years in London and Paris, I no longer eat on the floor." He took Sappini's arm. "Of course, it comes naturally to Stephan; he was born into both cultures."

"Don't make him sound more valuable than he is," Stratford teased. "He'll demand a raise tomorrow. Maybe this dinner's a trap you two cooked up." They all laughed.

Reshid unwrapped the gift.

"*Bleak House!*" he exclaimed. "How did you know I adore Dickens? I was just about to ask our embassy in London for a copy. Thank you, this is very kind."

Stratford gave a wry smile. "Never underestimate British intelligence, Mr. Minister. Though the Russians say we only send garbage to St. James."

Pasha's gaze shifted to the dragoman. "Signor Sappini, I must admit I was too casual toward you. I would've sent a formal invitation, but Mehmet Ali tells the sultan at every opportunity that I take orders from Great Britain."

Stratford's smile held no humor. "Sultan Mejid should know you're a tough nut to crack. If it's any consolation, they say the opposite about me in London."

"That's because you've lived with us so long, the Turkish spirit has grown in you." Reshid laughed, then leaned closer. "Since heading the armed forces, Mehmet Ali has been beating the war drums." He beamed. "But first—let's enjoy the evening. The ladies have prepared a feast."

Reshid led them into his study, which adjoined the dining room, its walls lined with mirrors and plaques. I recognized one: a copy of the *Edict of Gulhane*, in Turkish and French, dated November 3, 1839— the landmark proclamation that launched the Tanzimat, the Ottoman reform era. Mustafa Reshid Pasha had championed it.

Rocko leaned in, speaking in a low voice. "My ancestor Sholomo Effendi danced the hora at the foot of the White Tower in Thessaloniki that day."

Lord Stratford stood before the plaque. "I envy you, Reshid. You've carved your name into history. That was no small feat."

The ambassador must have read my mind. One spring break, my father took me to London and made me stand before Bryanston Square in Westminster. As a fifth-grader, craving ice cream and scones, it felt like hours. I watched Dad admiring a medallion on a building's façade. It stated Mustafa Reshid Pasha—a renowned Turkish reformer—had once lived there. Looking back, it was one of those rare moments when I saw pride in my father's eyes—the eternal anti-nationalist with mixed British-Turkish heritage.

Sappini chimed in. "Look who's here!"

A little girl with auburn ringlets descended the stairs, holding her caretaker's hand. She approached Lord Stratford, who knelt to meet her at eye level. His diplomatic façade melted like an ice cream cone under the August sun at the sight of the little girl in her silken dress.

"Melek, what a surprise! I've missed you so much."

Melek clasped Grand Elchi's hand. "I missed you, too." Then she pursed her lips, eyeing Sappini. "And I miss Mrs. Canning too."

Stephan knelt and brushed her cheek before handing her a tin of comfits in a decorative jar. Her gap-toothed smile lit up the room, instantly earning him a spot on her list of favorites.

The caretaker whispered for Melek to bid farewell.

"There's no love like the love for a grandchild." Reshid Pasha beamed as he watched her bounce jubilantly up the stairs.

Lord Canning leaned in, raising a brow. "I hear rumors of future festivities."

Pasha grinned from ear to ear. "His Majesty the Sultan has agreed to wed his eldest daughter, Fatma, to my son, Galip. You will soon receive the invitation."

"Should I congratulate or commiserate?" Lord Stratford cracked a wicked smile. "Becoming the sultan's in-law—personal gain or added stress?"

Pasha lifted his chin. "I am honored and humbled."

A server entered and bowed. Pasha announced, "It's time to feast."

He led his guests to the dining room, where a large round table stood draped with a Belgian lace tablecloth. Each place was set with fine English china, beside a bowl of strawberries, cherries, and cucumbers. Freshly cut tulips from the yard filled the central vase.

Pasha gestured to an officer in his twenties. "This young gentleman will be our scribe tonight."

The officer bowed politely. Lord Stratford nodded in response. Everyone took their seats, each marked with a name card. A servant offered ewers and towels. I didn't understand why. Nakshi explained cleansing the face and hands before dinner was a traditional Ottoman practice. For certain dishes, it was also customary to dip your hands into the ewer before eating with your fingers.

Krish led us to another table across the room, incognito to the holographs. Nakshi preferred an authentic experience with towels and ewers. Rocko and I passed, holding on to our forks and knives. The dishes were the same for everyone.

Rocko sniffed the air, his mouth watering, "Is this real, or just the haptics from the quantum kitchen?"

Krish grinned but said nothing. We would have revolted if the food wasn't real. When we spotted packaging from a famous Turkish restaurant in Manhattan, we cheered. Krish said it was also a KJ favorite.

The feast opened with samples of kebab and kofte, followed by an eggplant stew. Next came a parade of vegetables—spinach, artichokes, and more. For the next two hours, servers bustled around, presenting course after course: lamb, boiled beef, fried fish, and roasted liver, always served with a bowl of pilaf with kebab pieces stirred in.

Histo left before dinner to rejoin us later. I felt sorry for him he couldn't enjoy the feast. I wondered if his gastro problem was serious, but I didn't ask since Krish had warned us not to bring it up.

The servers draped fresh towels over the guests' shoulders, often replacing them. Nakshi synced with the ceremony. When the holographic staff replaced ewers and towels, Krish did the same for Nakshi, making us laugh. The ritual was delightful.

Finally, the dessert tray arrived: kadayif, baklava, and caramelized quince with crème—my favorite.

Krish served us half a dozen dishes before we tapped out. At the main table, I counted fourteen, and probably missed a few.

Lord Stratford was selective, sampling only a few dishes. Reshid Pasha and Sappini tried everything, while the young scribe devoured every course with gusto.

The dinner conversation was mostly one-sided, with Reshid Pasha recounting his career. Having served three times as grand vizier, nearly six years in total, twice dismissed and twice recalled, the Turkish statesman lived constantly on edge. Grand Elchi listened patiently, though it wasn't the first time he had heard it. Summarizing it all would take pages, but I've highlighted a few here.

Reshid Pasha plucked a handful of small strawberries and chewed them. Glancing at the young scribe with his mouth still full, he said, "I always remind him how important good notes are. That's what got me noticed." After swallowing, he added, "I had humble beginnings myself, son of a bookkeeper. But this young man speaks three languages, has a flair for literature, and even writes poetry! Still, Osman dreams of becoming an engineer—or was it a botanist? I always confuse the two."

The scribe, tall, handsome, with curly hair and a trimmed goatee, flashed a bright smile. "I have various interests, sir."

Pasha leaned toward the ambassador. "He wants to go to America. Thinks the next century belongs to the Yanks. He's memorized the biographies of all their founding fathers."

Lord Canning raised a brow, smiling. "Osman Bey, I should have had you as my aide when I served as Her Majesty's Ambassador to the States."

"Did you like it there, sir?" Osman asked eagerly.

Elchi, pleasantly surprised by Osman's outgoing nature, took a moment before replying. "To be frank, there's no place like home. I suppose that's true for everyone." He turned to Osman. "Do you have a favorite among America's founding fathers?"

"Yes, sir, I do."

"Don't tell me. Let me guess." Elchi paused. "Franklin?"

"Yes, sir. How did you know?" Osman Bey beamed.

"It wasn't too difficult. Engineering, poetry, botany, languages—you share much with the man. One difference, though. You're an officer; he was not."

Osman's grin widened, flashing his pearl-perfect teeth. "There are countless more differences, sir. You flatter me—too kind."

Reshid Pasha cut in. "Osman didn't have much of a choice. His father, a prominent pasha himself, insisted he follow the family path. I persuaded him that after serving the sultan for a few years, Osman should choose his own destiny. A luxury I never had."

Sappini smiled broadly at the young man. "Where in America?"

"New York, Inshallah."

"For now, we keep him as a scribe and dragoman, preparing him for greater responsibilities." The foreign vizier tore a piece of pita. "I was also a scribe in my early twenties, sent to Cairo. The legendary governor, Mehmet Ali Pasha, took notice and offered me a position. I declined, pledging loyalty to the Ottoman Sultan. He never ceased to resent me."

Reshid Pasha wrapped a piece of kofte in his pita and dipped his fingers into a copper bowl. A servant rushed in with a replacement, and another refreshed his towel.

"My stance caught Sultan Mahmoud's attention. He sent me to Paris to learn French and report on European affairs." He bit the wrap and chewed.

Stratford leaned forward. "You even managed to arrange an audience with Count Metternich. No small feat for any diplomat, let alone a young one."

"The Padishah rewarded me with an ambassadorship." Reshid Pasha gulped down water. "But years later, when I granted concessions to the same Mehmet Ali Pasha without consulting the Porte, His Excellency was furious—he even considered decapitating me." He gave a bitter chuckle. "Pertev Pasha saved my life, persuading the sultan I was fit to lead his reforms."

Lord Stratford bowed his head. "May God bless his soul."

"Amen," echoed the table.

The vizier speared a slice of eggplant. "That wasn't the only time my head nearly dropped to the basket. Grand Vizier Husrev first praised me before the Porte, then handed me a sealed note for the sultan. After reading it, the padishah—barely sixteen at the time—tore it up. Later, I learned the letter asked for my execution." He gave a nervous laugh.

"It was the Mother Sultana—may God have mercy. She had warned her son about Husrev, knowing you were the man to carry out her husband's reforms. She was right."

Reshid turned to Osman, who had been listening intently. "One last lesson. Never forget the ironclad rule of this land—*ab antiquo*—success poses risk. Higher authority doesn't guarantee your life. Quite the opposite."

He grabbed a piece of baklava and swallowed it whole. I saved mine for Zena.

Servants swept in, clearing plates and laying ladle-shaped spoons and copper bowls of sherbet made from raisins and dried apricots—the final act. He sipped then nodded. The chief server bowed and left the room.

Reshid smiled at the young scribe. "Osman probably thinks I'm an Anglophile. Many do, but they're wrong."

He leaned in toward Canning. "It's true, I support an alliance with England—for now." He paused and waited for everyone to taste the digestive. "I also supported Czar Nicholas when he blocked the Egyptian governor from seizing the crown. Does that make me a Russophile?"

He didn't wait for an answer. "I think not. My only loyalty is to the sultan. Reforms keep him standing firm." He slurped the last of his sherbet. "As ambassador in Paris and London, one thing was clear— true freedom exists only in England."

Stratford chimed in, "When you stood firm against Austria and welcomed Kossuth, you earned Britain's trust. Many now believe Tanzimat is real."

Reshid's gaze drifted. "I met many policymakers while drafting the edict. I told Lord Palmerston that only Turkey, not Egypt, can lead the Islamic world." He locked eyes with Stratford. Elchi didn't blink.

Sappini broke in. "Cairo's gift to Paris—the Luxor obelisk— blinded many. Certainly the French."

Reshid grew solemn. "Tanzimat stirred fierce opposition—not just Russophiles and zealots, but also Greek intellectuals, the Phanariots of Istanbul." His voice sharpened. "While Christians gained rights they had never dreamed of, some Greek landlords and tax collectors in the Balkans now resist. Freedoms created Muslim competitors, threatening their monopolies over their Christian brethren."

Sappini threw up his arm. "Who would've thought that? Fair taxes make it harder for a corrupt tax collector to skim off the top."

Reshid Pasha spread his arms with a grin. "I can't please everyone. But we can enjoy coffee and a chibouk." It was the signal. Everyone rose. Reshid led them to his study, gesturing Stratford ahead.

Through the dividing door, they left the Occident and entered the Orient, mirroring the empire's dual nature. Histo was inside, seated on a plush pillow. Servants lined others against paneled walls, inviting comfort. The chief butler offered long, white meerschaum chibouks, intricately carved. Lord Stratford politely declined, but others lit theirs, filling the room with fragrant smoke. Servants brought coffee in copper cups which looked like oversized thimbles. Krish served us the same. Lord Stratford requested tea with milk. Osman Bey knelt beside the lecterns. An aide delivered a dossier to Reshid Pasha, bowed, and left.

The time had come to address the urgent issue at hand.

Reshid Pasha spoke first. "We showed goodwill in preserving the peace."

Stratford Canning cleared his throat. "Her Majesty's Government commends your efforts and is pleased that the Porte has accepted the reasonable demands and pledged to address the others in the bucket."

Pasha offered a silent nod. The ambassador pressed on. "With the Holy Shrines issue behind us, it's time to see what can be moved from 'inadmissible' to 'manageable.' The Vienna Note offers us that opportunity."

Pasha, unfazed, set down his chibouk, pulled a letter from the dossier, and lifted it aloft. "Ten days after the prince left, I received this letter from Count Nesselrode. He fully endorses Menshikov's unabashed demeanor and demands even more."

He lowered his arm, brows knit. "Then we learned Russia had crossed the River Prut."

He pushed the letter aside, gripped his chibouk, inhaled deeply, and exhaled. A burst of fresh smoke spilled into the already cloudy room.

Elchi, undisturbed by the growing haze, locked his gaze on the minister. "Nesselrode's letter was arrogant and threatening. But so was your reply." His voice stayed even.

Reshid's eyes widened. "You find a man sitting on your sofa—uninvited. He refuses to leave. Do you ask him to break bread with you?" He stared at Stratford, mouth parted. "No. You tell him to pack and leave, or else."

He nervously drew on his chibouk and exhaled.

"Gosh, Krish, do you have to make it this real?" Rocko waved a hand through the smoke. "The alarm's gonna go off any second."

"No, it won't," Histo said. "There's no smoke. The haptics make you sense it."

We had long passed the point of distinguishing between what was Petamunra-made and what was real.

"They occupied but didn't declare war," Lord Stratford said evenly. "The czar left the door open for negotiation. That's the Russian way."

Nakshi barged in, citing Field Marshal Paskevich. "Russia is buying time to train the Balkan nationalists to fight the Turks. Somebody should tell him."

Pasha snapped back. "Two months ago, they crossed the river; now they're in Bucharest. This is an invasion."

"The ambassadors in Vienna fear a war in the Balkans could encourage Mazzini and Kossuth to incite rebellion. So, instead of forwarding your letter, they drafted one, the Vienna Note, incorporating the Turkish concerns and sent it—"

"And everyone cheered when the czar accepted it, didn't they?" Reshid cut in, arms flaring. "Without our consent, declaring our concerns?" He narrowed his eyes, voice turning icy. "The Austrians should be equally alarmed by Russia controlling the Danube. Their economy depends on river trade."

Stratford ignored the minister's sharp tone. "The Viennese are more concerned your response would worsen the crisis." He delivered Britain's stance, each word crisp. "Russia-did-not-declare-war." A sage smile followed. "Diplomacy remains alive until the first shot is fired."

"I wouldn't disagree." Reshid Pasha tried to mirror Elchi's calm. "To that end, the sultan reaffirmed the rights of his Christian subjects. Moreover, our Sovereign Padishah swallowed his pride and agreed to accept the Vienna Note—with a few modifications. He hasn't heard from the czar. What more can he offer?"

A servant moved to refill Elchi's tea, but he declined. "Emperor Nicholas has a valid point. He already agreed to sign the note." His voice deepened. "It is not diplomacy to propose further modifications once the language is settled, however minor they may seem to His Majesty the Sultan."

Reshid Pasha sipped his coffee, brows knitting.

Stratford leaned forward. "The door to peace is closing, Monsieur Minister."

Reshid Pasha squinted. "Russia claims it has the right to act as protector of the Greek Church. They don't. This should've been as clear as day to all the powers. The Vienna Note winks at this notion, implying Russia can intervene anytime under the pretense of protecting Orthodoxy, overriding the sultan's sovereignty."

"That's a matter of interpretation." Stratford's defense lacked his usual passion.

"Hopping from one vague treaty to another? What kind of peace is that? And who will guarantee the sultan's suzerainty over his subjects and lands?" The vizier leaned toward Lord Canning. "Menshikov asked for the amputation of a limb. The Vienna Note infuses poison into the body. Neither is acceptable." He exhaled a puff of smoke without breaking his gaze. "Nothing in the bucket could move from inadmissible to manageable."

Pasha told Osman in Turkish to stop writing. From then on, all would be off the record. The room fell quiet with the final screeches of Osman's pen.

Reshid chose his words carefully. "Acceptance may prove more disastrous than war. The incursions have stirred rage among Muslims and sparked Turkish nationalism. The Sublime Porte may not be able to contain such sentiments."

He swung his arm. "The ulema claim all troubles began with the Tanzimat, after the Porte granted rights to Christians. Tens of thousands of young men study under them."

Sappini intervened, "That shouldn't come as a surprise. The reforms threaten their careers. Now they're competing with graduates of secular schools."

"But hear this." The vizier leaned forward to Stratford and spoke in a lower voice, careful that the servants wouldn't hear. "Some religious leaders gave the sultan an ultimatum last week: declare war against the *gâvur*, or we shall abdicate you. Sixty thousand pious men petitioned."

"I'm aware. They want to end diplomacy. The sultan requested my assistance, along with that of the French Ambassador. We both pledged to bring up our fleets to suppress a revolution, if necessary."

Pasha drew a nervous puff. "The War Minister pushes us into war but won't claim we'll win, dodging responsibility if we lose." His animation drained, a shadow crossed his face.

"There is another angle to this."

Lord Stratford lifted a brow.

"Prolonging peace under these circumstances invites religious uprising. Instead of resisting the warmongers, I've decided to become the most belligerent vizier at the Porte. Otherwise, these zealots will overturn the Tanzimat, and everything I've worked for will crumble overnight."

Mustafa Resid Pasha leaned back, brows knit. Stratford Canning pressed his lips, seeming to acknowledge the vizier's stance.

"Mr. Ambassador, if the Tanzimat collapses, the empire will lose its sunlight. Its vitality will vanish." The reformist vizier's expression was hollow. "It will never stand on equal footing with Western nations. Not for a hundred years, if not longer."

Pasha searched Elchi's face for a reaction.

"What's next?" Stratford was as calm as still water.

"Tomorrow, the Grand Council will convene to advise the sultan to issue a final ultimatum to the czar. I expect a unanimous vote."

"What will it entail?"

"The aggressors must evacuate the principalities. The powers must guarantee that Russia will not invade again. If the czar refuses, our Sovereign Padishah will declare war."

Reshid Pasha held his breath. Sappini's eyes widened—both bracing for a strong reaction from the dinner guest. None came from the British ambassador.

Silence settled, broken only by the distant call of the muezzin summoning the faithful to Isha, the day's final prayer.

Grand Elchi raised his brows. "What does Omer Pasha think?"

Reshid let his shoulders drop, like a captain who had just steered clear of a storm. "Omer requested forty thousand troops for a Danube campaign and a couple of weeks to train them. He will deliver the Porte's ultimatum to Paskevich: evacuate the territories within two weeks or face war."

"Pragmatic commander." Stratford flicked a faint smile. "It gives the seraskier the time he asks for."

Omer Pasha's name had surfaced earlier, even from the czar. I decided to learn about the generalissimo, the seraskier.

Reshid Pasha studied the ambassador, as if searching for the man he had once known.

"Your Excellency, let's be frank. You came to persuade me to accept the Vienna Note. Yet I don't see you pressing. Why?"

Stratford shrugged. "Why waste my breath? You just told me you've already decided on war."

Pasha puffed in silence. Stratford was unassertive. That wasn't his characteristic poise.

As Dad would have said, this situation called for a geopolitical microscope. Only then did the complex relationship between these two men come into focus.

Their reasons differed, but their vision aligned. A progressive Turkey.

Stratford believed a modernized Turkey would become a stronger British ally against Russia. Many in Britain disagreed. Some saw Turkey as a land to exploit, others dreamed of a Christian revival to reclaim Rome's legacy, brushing concerns over Russian hegemony.

Reshid Pasha saw reform as the empire's only hope, with Britain as its best partner. Yet many peers rejected the Western path, clinging to Islamic principles or favoring authoritarian allies like France, Austria, and even Russia.

For both, Tanzimat was strategic. In short, the two men were in a forced alliance.

Pasha motioned for a servant to bring him a fresh chibouk. He drew deeply, puffing until the char settled. The two men sat in silence, watching each other with nothing more to say.

Was Lord Stratford implying sympathy for the Turkish case? Or quietly endorsing Pasha's reasoning despite his government's objections? Did he find Her Government's policy unjust, putting fairness—a sacred principle to a proud Christian—above loyalty?

Perhaps his reasoning was simply human. Some in St. James believed he had gone "too Turkish" to stay objective.

Or maybe his motive was darker. His hatred for Czar Nicholas had consumed him. The Russian Emperor had refused to recognize his ambassadorship to his country and blocked him from becoming foreign minister.

Whatever the reason, Elchi's silence spoke louder than volumes. Sentimental or rational, he forbade the words to voice his choice.

Reshid Pasha broke the silence. "Without a Western alliance, we may not win this war." He glimmered at the man he trusted his words.

"*Bakalum,*" Lord Stratford replied in broken Turkish—we shall see. "If Lord Palmerston were in charge, perhaps. It's unlikely the Aberdeen government will back a Balkan war. The press also opposes it. Public opinion matters in England."

"It sure does," Reshid's smile curdled into bitterness. "Better to die fighting than watch ourselves carved apart."

He drew on his chibouk, blowing the smoke away from Lord Stratford. Their eyes met, each carrying the weight of parents striving to save a prematurely born child—Tanzimat—clinging to life.

The grand vizier walked to the window, gazing into the dark courtyard. "We had a mild winter. The almond tree blossomed in early February. Yet the invisible snow hasn't left the seraglio since the man from the North arrived."

He lifted his chin. "We shall be victorious, inshallah."

23

MASSACRE AFTER MIDNIGHT

After dinner at Reshid Pasha's kiosk, everyone was curious about British hearts and minds. Histo proposed we attend a public meeting in London, which took place two weeks later.

The trip took only minutes. Rocko was pleased we would not be incognito. We faced a three-story building on Bishopsgate Street, its Georgian façade, with arched windows, rising in symmetry. A stone sign between the upper floors read, "City of London Tavern."

Inside, the tavern was packed, choked with thick smoke and the stench of cheap alcohol. Corinthian columns lifted the high ceiling. We edged sideways along the back wall, careful not to be swallowed by the dense holographic crowd.

Half a dozen men sat on stage. I noticed a familiar face staring at me.

"Do you remember me? We met in Southampton a few years back, on the day Kossuth arrived."

"Alan from Chicago! Of course I do. Good to see you." I grinned. "We're back in town to take the pulse of the English public."

"You came to the right place. They've got some prominent speakers tonight. Mostly Turcophiles, like many Londoners these days."

"Perhaps a better word would be Russophobes," a Londoner chimed in, his accent giving him away.

Alan gestured toward him. "Donovan is the nation's conscience in shoes. Ask his opinion, and you'll know how the country feels. He makes my life easy as a reporter." He chuckled.

A man stood on stage. The sash and rosette on his lapel suggested he was the chairman. He struck the gavel to silence the room. "The meeting is adjourned. Your presence is a testament to Londoners' desire to understand world affairs. I wish the room were ten times the size."

Alan leaned in. "He writes for the *Standard*, the London daily."

The chairman raised his arm. "I appeal to our government to hear us. This assembly resolves to uphold the nation's honor, defend England's interests, and earn the name of Englishmen."

Applause broke out.

"Our object tonight is to show London's support for Turkey against the Russian tyrant."

He outlined recent events in the Orient, from Menshikov's arrival in Constantinople to the Sublime Porte's ultimatum that Russia evacuate Moldavia and Wallachia. Russia gave no response. The deadline had passed. War was imminent.

Next, Lord Dudley Stuart, a member of Parliament, took the stage in a lavish silk jacket and bow tie. His square jaw and sideburns stood out. Nakshi remembered him from Southampton's welcoming committee.

Alan drew closer. "Lord Stuart convinced the government to welcome Kossuth in England."

Dudley Stuart didn't waste time. "What cause brings us here tonight?"

"To fight the tyrant!" Donovan called out.

Stuart pointed toward us. "The gentleman is right. The Russian Czar pursues nothing short of universal dominion—enslaving the world."

"He must be stopped!" someone bellowed.

"How does he fool the Russian nation?" he gripped his lapels. "By claiming grievances shared with Turkey's Christians."

"Don't believe he feels any!" Donovan's shout drew laughter and applause.

Stuart grinned. "Hear what the Cossack commander-in-chief told his troops before marching into Bucharest. '*The Lord calls upon Russia to annihilate the pagans.*'"

"A total hypocrisy!"

"Russia leads this so-called crusade with millions of armed serfs." Stuart raised his voice. "I ask you—is this faith, or aggression against the people of Turkey?"

"Want to fight persecution? Try Russia!" a voice called out.

"Or Austria," another shouted.

Stuart pressed on. "Or against the Protestants—like those executed in Estonia. Or Jews." Then he spread his arms. "Where are the persecuted nuns in Turkey? Someone show me!"

"Go to Russia! You'll find them in abundance."

"Your Majesty, I don't believe *zhese* Englishmen," Stuart mocked a Russian voice, drawing giggles. "Show me those pagans who suppress my Christian brethren. My sword will make them meet their Lord."

"Hallelujah!" A few chuckles followed.

He smiled at the cheers. "I rode from the Balkans to the Levant expecting to meet oppression by the infidels, but all I saw were Roman processions, Protestant churches, Catholic schools, and free worship everywhere. Even my horse was confused." Laughter rolled through the hall.

His voice turned solemn. "Why is it that in Turkey, ruled by infidels, all are free to follow their faith—unlike in Russia?" Hisses followed.

Lord Stuart was no longer sardonic. "And why have I seen a man on this platform more than once and not long ago, himself a living example of generosity?"

"Hear, hear!"

He raised his voice a notch. "A man who expressed deep gratitude to the sultan after arriving from this so-called land of oppression they call Turkey."

"Kossuth! Kossuth!" Cheers shook the grounds.

"He's still popular." Alan shifted closer so we could hear. "He's returned to England after a half-year tour in the States."

Kossuth had visited many states and received their warm support; however, he was unable to obtain any formal military or political aid from the White House and Congress for his fight against tyranny in Europe.

"Aye, Kossuth—the man the sultan and his brave Turks defended against the bloodhounds of Vienna and St. Petersburg." The crowd rose, applauding thunderously.

"Who're all these people?" Nakshi nodded toward the loud dummy holograms. "The cheers in Istanbul can't be any louder."

Alan smiled wryly. "Reshid Pasha funneled money through the Turkish embassy to rally support and sway the British press."

"Public relations initiative?" I caught myself—the term hadn't been coined yet. Histo lifted a brow but didn't interfere.

Alan didn't notice and went on. "As ambassador in London, Reshid saw how daily papers could shape policy and how public outcry could move governments. Don't you think that's remarkable?"

What Alan described wasn't common knowledge then. Mustafa Reshid Pasha was among the first to grasp the power of the media.

Admiral Napier stepped up next.

"You may recall when our admiral declined to sail to the Turkish straits, and rightly so." He referred to the Colonel Rose incident. "Russia had a strong fleet, and we had little to show in those waters. No longer the case."

The chatter subsided, showing respect for the high-ranking officer.

"Had the Cossack known he would meet our fleets on his shores, he would not have dared cross the Prut. We should have warned him. Now that he has, I ask you—how do we make him retrace his steps?"

"Not with Aberdeen. He must go!"

The admiral waved off the political cries. "Unless England and France act decisively, Russia will stay where she is."

"Do something!"

"Suppose France had blocked trade at the mouth of some German river. Would a man here not cry for war? If the Duke were alive, would the czar dare send his envoy to Constantinople backed by a squadron?"

"No! Never!" The crowd hailed the Duke of Wellington.

The admiral lowered his hand to calm them. Unlike a politician, he didn't need to stir.

"Don't think me friendly to the Turks. I care not if they were driven beyond the Bosporus tomorrow. But I will not see their place taken by Russia."

"Hear, hear."

"If Russia drags Turkey's Christians under her dominion, it will be disastrous for Europe. With one arm reaching the Baltic and the other the Dardanelles, she would block our naval routes and shut us out of the Mediterranean. And next? She will come after us in India."

That was the most honest explanation I had heard on this journey about England's passion for protecting Turkey.

Alan jumped in. "It's not only Lord Aberdeen. Many others are holding back, the queen included, protecting her friend, Nicholas."

The admiral heard Alan but ignored the American. "Meanwhile, the Turks must pay more attention to their Christian subjects and honor the promises they've made." Applause followed.

"But why only Christians?" Nakshi frowned as Napier stepped down. "Muslims in poverty suffer even more under the seraglio's suppression."

He had struck at a chronic flaw in Britain's fairness, common across the West. Never fair in the fight against unfairness, always selective. Mom used to say she would vomit at those lofty European ideals where race and religion were cloaked in disguise. A principle in gold required none in the pocket.

The chairman introduced the next speaker.

"The former ambassador to the Ottoman Empire. Honorable David Urquhart. He designed the flag of the Circassian tribes."

"Zena would have demanded an interview," Nakshi quipped.

"We wouldn't be back before midnight." Rocko smirked.

The diplomat scanned the crowd. "I'm asked here to make an announcement." The entire arena hushed. "Turkish forces, led by Omar Pasha, have crossed the Danube and reclaimed Kalafat from the Russians. Villagers joined them to oust Paskevich's Cossacks. The Turks march to Bucharest."

The crowd erupted.

Alan leaned in, voice raised. "War has started! Turks are beating the Russians!"

Urquhart waited for the cheers to fade. "But reports say the bashi-bazouks slaughtered Russia's supporters in Bulgarian villages—innocent men and women."

Hisses replaced the applause.

Rocko shook his head. "Russia's War Minister predicted that."

"I yield to the Honorable Dudley Stuart." Urquhart returned to his seat. A skilled politician would best deliver the cry.

The charismatic parliamentarian was back, surveying the hall. "Do you want cheap bread?"

"Aye! Abundant too," someone hollered.

"Where do we get corn but from the Danubian provinces—the granaries of Europe? Would Russia supply us?"

"Nay!"

"I didn't think so. Turks trade freely and take our goods. Austria and Russia? They bury us under tariffs."

Someone handed him a note.

Lord Stuart read it, then raised his voice. "I'm pleased to announce that, at the sultan's request, France and England have ordered their fleets to the Dardanelles."

"Hear, hear!"

"Must be a Lord Stratford difference." I smiled at Nakshi and Rocko.

Lord Dudley lifted his arm to silence the crowd. "Turks showed the world they won't be bullied. They gave a firm answer at Kalafat. Now, I call on our government to rise above the pleasures of office and the tinsel of life."

Applause burst forth.

"When the Cossack horses crossed the Prut, it was war against our ally. I expected us to send a fleet to the Black Sea. Did we?"

"Nay!"

"What did we do instead? Met in Vienna to 'discuss next steps.'"

"For weeks, still going." Alan cut in, his eyes widened. "Everyone knows the Vienna court is a Russian tool. Austria's Prime Minister, Buol, is the Russian ambassador's brother-in-law. They trade notes daily, leaving the sultan's minister stranded."

"He should've married the other sister," Rocko quipped. Alan chuckled.

On stage, Lord Dudley pressed on. "Russia hasn't moved an inch. And how did we fare?"

"Weak!" voices cried.

"The French had the dignity not to attend!" Donovan shouted.

Hisses and groans followed.

"I don't wish for war for the sake of it." Stuart was firm. "God forbid. War is a calamity, a crime, unless necessary. But we've reached a point—it's fight or accept dishonor. I ask you, who brought us here?"

"Aberdeen!" many shouted.

"If we had a bold, far-sighted leader—"

"Palmerston! Palmerston!" The cries shook the chandeliers.

Lord Stuart relished it. "—Russia would never have dared cross the Prut or touch the sultan's lands."

He raised his arm. "Securing the peace in the present at the expense of future safety is the root of all cowardice."

The hall thundered with applause.

The lights dimmed, leaving only the launchpad stage aglow. Alan was gone, so were all the holograms. A soft, white light brushed the curved ceiling.

Histo studied our tired faces, weighing our thoughts.

"I'd wager Kalafat made the czar upset," Nakshi said.

"Let's find out. Final stop of the day—quick excursion, I promise."

Czar Nicholas paced in his study, arms folded. Unlike the gilded Gold Room, this chamber was modest, overlooking a manicured yard. A carved mahogany desk stood at its center.

Across from it sat a man in his fifties, with a broad nose and a beard streaked in gray.

"The future belongs to the Slavs. It is Russia's providential mission."

Nicholas twitched, half-listening.

His guest pressed firmly, "How could a monk of the East accept the Turk's protection? That is absurd! Only we, their elder brothers, can protect them. The Church's duty is indivisible, not a prize to be split among Powers."

"That will be all-out war, Pogodin," Nicholas murmured.

"Let it be." The guest poured tea, calm, no stranger to court.

"Russia has not found its center. It was Novgorod, then Kyiv, moved to Moscow, and now here in St. Petersburg—a pendulum swinging north." He took a sip. "Can it remain there, so far from where it began? Is this city our center, or only the rim of a vast circle?"

Nicholas paused, gazing at him like a student before his professor.

"Alas, the pendulum swings back to Constantinople." Nicholas watched Pogodin's arm arc through the air.

"Not another rim in the South, but the true center longed for through the ages. Napoleon saw it from the Elbe. The center of the world."

He stepped closer to the czar, his voice low and almost secretive. "The East belongs to Russia. It always has. Since the Turk took the city, Greek prophecies have spoken. Russia will claim it. The time has come."

Pogodin returned to his seat and sipped his tea. His clothes were plain. His mind was too occupied for such details. He didn't need to impress anyone, only to persuade one man. And he stood before him.

"Your Majesty, our kin have waited too long for Russia to lead a Slavic empire. As Russians, we must claim Constantinople for our security. As Slavs, we must free millions of our brethren. As Europeans, we must drive out the Turks. As Orthodox Christians, we must restore Saint Sophia's cross."

"That sums it up." Rocko winked at me.

"A dreamer." Nakshi shook his head. "He must be from academia."

The emperor resumed pacing. He had likely heard such lines before.

"Omer Pasha came strong, more than Paskevich expected." Nicholas's voice was somber, his frown betraying displeasure. "The marshal got wounded. Minor, but it demoralized the troops. He's a living legend to them."

Pogodin smirked. "Kalafat was a skirmish, not a battle. See it not as defeat, but as God's reminder. The road to salvation is never easy. Remember—you hold a mandate from heaven."

"You believe that?" Nicholas turned to face his guest.

"History moves through chosen men. You are one."

The emperor's eyes gleamed. Mom used to say pompous words were never enough for men in power.

Pogodin closed his eyes. "Do you see the candles?"

The emperor raised a brow, unsure what to say.

"I see people in wooden barracks. The Slavs had kept them hidden in their sashes for generations until our horses crossed the Prut. Now they are lit, never to extinguish again."

Nicholas looked out the window. A reindeer and her two calves wandered the yard. "Your ideas are radical, professor, but I like them. Still, I've listened to Nesselrode—kept my distance from the Slavs so as not to alienate Austria. They're wary of a Little Russia in the Balkan plains."

"You desire Austria on our side. I pray they're not." Pogodin smiled wryly. "Only when all others stand against you will you know God has chosen you."

The two men locked gazes in brief silence.

"I don't understand why Europe is unfair to us." Nicholas's voice sharpened. "France takes Algeria from Turkey. Everyone accepts it. England devours Asian lands, and no one protests. Russia merely *considers* one city, Constantinople." He sharply wheeled on Pogodin. "And that, professor, somehow threatens the peace of Europe!"

"No European race sees us as family. Only the Slavs."

Nicholas spread his arms. "England declares war on China across the world and no one objects, while Russia must beg permission to confront a neighbor who breaks his word."

"Russia can expect nothing but animosity from the West." Pogodin smiled bitterly.

The emperor drifted away.

Pogodin stood. "Your Majesty—surprise them." He swung his fist through the air.

"With a bang!"

"I didn't know discrimination existed among the imperialists," Nakshi scoffed as the lights dimmed, and he left for bed.

Two faces of the same picture struck me. Aggression was one that the West knew all too well, as noted in Russia's approach to Ukraine in modern times. Unacceptance, however, came as a surprise. As Dad used to explain, the European West's enduring fallacy was its subtle discrimination of Eurasian cultures, framed by mistrust and fear.

Indefensible imperialist drives aside, not being seen as family must have been hurtful for those Russians who thought like Pogodin. His perspective was two centuries back, yet I wondered how many in Russia today felt the same unfairness.

Turks, too, are seen as the unwanted black sheep grazing in European grass. Russia, with its own sense of exclusion, had long been cast as a wolf in sheep's clothing. Perhaps it was never Russia's intention, never its desire, but Europe forced it to become a wolf.

A thought to ponder.

At any rate, it was eleven at night, too late to dwell on these things.

Rocko let out a long yawn. "It's way past my bedtime. I'll pass on the warm milk and cookies."

The lavish dinner and the long evening afterward had drained me. I wanted nothing more than to collapse into bed, yet I felt the urge to knock on Zena's door. I couldn't stop wondering how she was doing but dismissed the idea as foolish and intrusive. She was surely asleep.

Shuffling to my room, eyelids drooping, I barely managed to unlock the door.

When I stepped inside, I hardly recognized my room. An expansive balcony opened to a breathtaking view of fountains and gardens. A regal wrought-iron cage enclosed it, the double-eagle coat of arms at its center. Below, a sea of people filled the courtyard.

The interior had changed, too. It resembled the grand salon where we had watched Czar Nicholas meet his ministers just hours earlier, before issuing his ultimatum. My bed now sat in the middle, replacing the round table. It looked larger, fluffed with pillows of every color.

The Battle of Chesme still hung on the wall, now joined by other paintings—ships ablaze, others adrift, one beneath a Bosporus sunset.

The lighting was brighter, the colors no longer pastel. It felt like a set from a Stanley Kubrick movie.

As I tried to take it in, Sarah appeared in her work clothes. What was she doing here so late at night?

"The wedding is tonight." She pressed her lips thin. "The newlyweds are staying before flying off for their honeymoon. We're giving them your room. I need you to vacate immediately."

My blank stare didn't slow her. "Sorry, I'm behind. I told Claire to make the bed, but she slacked off. Now, I have to prepare it and hang another painting of—can't pronounce his name."

"You mean Ivan Aivazovsky? These are from Rocko's house. They're prints."

She scoffed. "Gospodin Ivan brought them here himself. Wedding gift."

I was taken aback. "Where will I sleep?"

"There is an old couch in the kitchen." Sarah gestured toward the door while laying clean satin sheets on the bed. Their edges shimmered with embroidered golden frescoes.

"It's their first night. You know how that is." She winked as she tucked the ends of the bedspread beneath the mattress.

Wiping her forehead, she exhaled. "The springs of the couch are busted, might not be comfortable, but you're too tired to feel it anyway."

Displeased, I began to pick up my belongings. Nakshi stepped inside.

"Thank God you're here. What's going on? Why are we back at Peterhof?"

He wore a long black wool robe, a cylindrical hat, and a silk stole draped around his neck. Seeing a pious Muslim dressed as an Orthodox clergyman was undeniably peculiar.

Sensing the edge in my voice, Sarah warned me. "Have some respect. He will officiate the ceremony."

Unfazed, I stood.

Nakshi handed me two jewelry boxes. "You have an important task to accomplish."

One box held a gold wedding ring nestled in a soft blue velvet. The other, a large diamond ring set against crimson.

As I tried to make sense of these glimmering pieces, someone tapped me on the shoulder. I turned to find Czar Nicholas beaming at me, dressed all in black, looking like Johnny Cash.

"It's a festive day, isn't it?" His wide grin was unwavering.

Agitated, I spotted Krish setting up a surround sound system.

"You're corrupting the data!" I snapped. "Electronics in 1853?"

The speakers began blaring the *1812 Overture.*

"You realize Tchaikovsky is barely a teenager? He won't compose this piece for decades."

Krish shrugged. "I brought the maestro from the future to DJ the wedding party."

Frustrated, I couldn't think of what to do next. Then came a roar from the courtyard. My room doors flew open. Two tall cadets flanked Zena and Rocko as they entered.

My jaw dropped. She looked stunning in a magnificent wedding dress, and Rocko was in Nicholas's uniform, decorated with medals.

Rocko extended his hand, palm open. She gave him hers.

The couple walked right past me, smiling, their steps perfectly in sync. They waved to the cheering crowd gathered beneath the balcony.

"Aren't they beautiful?" Sarah grinned from ear to ear as I stood holding the jewelry boxes. "The courtyard's been packed since last night."

Nakshi instructed curtly. "Place the rings on the tray."

"Do what Father says." Sarah nudged, motioning toward the gold-plated tray on a pedestal. "You are the best man, the Koumbaros."

I did. Nakshi blessed the rings and motioned me to pass him the golden band. He slipped it onto Rocko's finger. Next, he reached for the diamond ring and presented it to Rocko. The groom eagerly placed it on Zena's shapely wedding finger, flashing her his Clark Gable smile. She grinned like she had just fallen into him.

Father Nakshi signed the cross over the couple and blessed them with a short prayer. I couldn't understand the words.

Rocko held Zena and smashed a big kiss on her lips, sending the crowd into a jubilant frenzy. My stomach churned.

The cheers were deafening. I turned to Nicholas, waiting for an explanation.

"Don't look at me." He lifted his arms. "I decided to live in the future and left my throne behind. From now on, I'm incognito, living in the Bahamas." He smirked. "Your cousin asked me to join him. You should have flown there."

He called out as the couple passed. "Long live Czar Rocko and Queen Zena!"

Riding a white caparisoned horse, Histo descended from the sky. He wore a blue cloak, a helmet with a red plume, and carried a lance.

"Here comes St. George! Defender of the homeland!" Sarah made a quick cross and held her breath.

Glancing at me in disgust, Rocko the First ordered. "Slay him, George."

Two more heads popped from my shoulders. My legs reproduced, and my spine stretched into a tail. I lay helpless, transforming into a beast.

Histo approached with a stern look in his piercing blue eyes as the *1812 Overture* neared its grand finale. Real cannons fired in the glamorous yard, fireworks exploding overhead.

St. Histo's eyes darkened. His blue suit dissolved into black. A hood appeared, casting his face in shadow. He raised his sword, aiming to plunge the lance into my chest. I looked up to see my slayer's face— two large black eyes floating on a bright, flat surface, a flickering mosaic of black and white dots like an old TV with no signal.

"Goodbye, Zmey Gorynych," Nicholas whispered, naming the three-headed dragon of Russian folklore. "Losers have to go."

Pogodin appeared behind him. "Finally." He bared his teeth in a sneer.

I bolted upright, gasping for air. My heart pounded in my ears. It was dark. Unsure if the sword was still chasing me, I lunged off the bed. The cool wood beneath my feet reassured me. My legs were intact. I was in my room. The tangled sheets betrayed my restless sleep.

The floor shook with a distant blast. Was Pyotr Ilyich out there firing the cannons? I couldn't tell which reality I was in. Footsteps closed in fast. A knock at the door.

I grabbed the oil lamp, fumbling with the match tin, struck one, and lit the wick. The flame bloomed, shadows stretching across the wall.

Another bang—louder this time.

I opened the door. Krish stood there, giving me a quick once-over.

"Put something on. Go down to the launch room."

I stepped into the hallway in my boxer shorts, drenched in sweat. Nakshi and Rocko, groggy in their robes-de-chambre, stared at me.

"What's going on?" Rocko rubbed his eyes.

"An ambush." Krish darted to the library.

Rocko squinted. "Who'd wanna invade Brooklyn?"

I went back to my room, splashed water on my face, grabbed a sweater, slipped on my pants, and, with my boots untied, rushed downstairs.

The launch room was dim, with flickers of light barely illuminating the space. Rocko and Nakshi were standing; Zena sat on the stool, wearing a robe and slippers, her hair falling tangled over her shoulders. Reprints of English papers lay on the small desk beside her.

I was still shaking off the remnants of my nightmare, trying to focus on the present reality—whatever that meant. I usually forget my dreams, but this one was so vivid it lingered, like an unforgettable scene from a movie.

Histo was calm, his usual self. "Everyone's in."

"Roger that." Krish's voice came through the speakers.

Nakshi darted around. "Where is he?" Histo didn't respond.

"I'm upstairs in the control room. Enjoy the Black Sea. Don't fall in." Krish sounded refreshed.

Rocko puffed his cheeks and exhaled hard. "Mondays are always the hardest. I thought we already had the final stop of the day."

I barged in. "Technically, it's Tuesday, day five. It's past midnight." Rocko rolled his eyes at my nerdy response.

The platform beneath us began to rise, Petamunra tiles clamping down until we leveled with the deck. In an instant, it transformed into a ship, and we stood on its dock. A thunderous crack startled me, followed by a flash of light, revealing Histo standing at the stern of a warship. On shore, a garrison fortified the port, with a ridge of haphazard houses rising behind it.

Occasional bursts of gunfire lit the horizon, each flash exposing warships at sea and others anchored in the harbor miles away. Yet even at that distance, the tremors reached us, rumbling through the dock beneath our feet.

Histo handed around binoculars.

Zena narrowed her eyes. "Where are we?" she asked, still groggy.

"Sinop Bay, home to the Ottoman flotilla on the Black Sea." Histo scanned the puzzled faces. "No concern. We're anchored more than a mile from the fighting."

"I wouldn't mind feeling the action," Rocko scoffed. Histo waved him off.

An explosion shook the dock, jolting the platform beneath our feet. The warship took a direct hit.

"You sure about that?" Nakshi raised his brows, nearly tumbling.

The Russian blasts intensified. The Turkish garrison barely resisted, caught unprepared in what they trusted was a secure port. For every Turkish gun fired, at least five answered from Russian vessels. The cannonade was brutal. Nearly every ship was hit. Screaming sailors, some aflame, leaped overboard as Russian fire rained down on them.

"*The Battle of Sinope.*" Rocko nodded slowly, thoughtful. "We had that in my father's study."

Then it struck me. I had dreamt of that painting minutes ago. Some mysterious power had breathed life into the still image, projecting it with perfect fidelity in the theaters of the quantum universe. My dream had been its teaser. Watching the ships engulfed in flames, I wondered how it was possible.

The Russian fleet destroyed the Turkish flotilla in less than an hour. Some scientists believe the Sinop coast was carved by the great flood that followed the Ice Age. Now it was a tinderbox. Turkish ships blazed while the tall masts of the Russian vessels still loomed above the harbor, barely damaged.

Rocko glanced through the headlines in nearby papers. "Massacre at Midnight in the Orient! Three thousand killed. Queen now supports war."

Nakshi read another. "Sitting ducks at the harbor, a month after Turks reclaimed Bucharest."

"November 30, 1853." He smiled wryly. "Had they known the future, it would've read Pearl Harbor in the Black Sea."

"Do we know how this ambush happened?" I was curious.

Histo explained. "The Turkish vessels were to sail to the Caucasus to support the Cherkess under Sheik Shamil. Russian Admiral Nakhimov learned of the plan and brought in six warships in disguise to the Turkish harbor. The rest was history—inside which you've just lived." He shot a knowing glance.

Hearing "Cherkess," I stole a look at Zena from the corner of my eye. She was not herself, silent, lost in thought. I felt like I had to say something to her, but words never came.

Nakshi lingered with a bitter smile. "A small disagreement, born of sloppy handwriting and misspelling of some ignorant scribe, has now turned into a full-fledged war."

The weight of his words settled over me. That night, in Sinop— Diogenes's hometown—we saw absurdity unfold. It marked the beginning of the Crimean War, the "proto world war," as some historians call it. The renowned philosopher was missing. Perhaps he had wandered the alleys with his lantern, incognito, searching for an honest reason, only to return empty-handed. Maybe the soaring flames had carried it away, leaving behind only the cries of Turkish sailors, now frozen in the Aivazovsky painting, forever questioning the war's necessity.

Was it Russia's holy quest for Hagia Sophia? Britain's fear of losing its Asian jewels? France's hunger for prestige? The sultan's desperate bid to save his throne?

None required war. Diplomacy could have handled it all. But the fear of being left behind pulled everyone in.

Sinop was a cyclone. From it, a war was born. A war of choice, not necessity. No war like before: Christians fighting Christians to save Muslims.

Crimean War—the mother of all wars of choice. The very kind KJ hoped technology could prevent. A perfect laboratory to study why they happen. That's why he chose it—ten days inside history.

As I drifted, Rocko turned to the program director. "I appreciate you reserving me a front-row seat. But the Committee hasn't delivered on what they promised me."

Histo lifted his brows.

Rocko pressed. "You said we'd live in it. Remember? These were your words."

"Would you rather be on those ships?" Nakshi narrowed his eyes, his mouth slightly parted.

"That's why I signed up!" Rocko suddenly blurted out, startling everyone. "I didn't come here to watch a movie on a glorified screen. I want the flames to lick my face. Feel that heat. Smell the smoke. Suffocate—then jump into those dark, choppy waters, screaming like the guy next to me. Knowing my life is about to end."

I sure wasn't feeling the same. Like the others, I was taken aback, not expecting such a harsh stance from him.

Rocko straightened, fixing Histo with a stare, straining to contain his voice.

"Watching wouldn't be enough. Not if we want to stop the next one. You know that."

Histo didn't flinch.

The warmth of the burning ships was still in the air. So were the marching tunes, carried from the Russian boats heading north to Crimea.

Krish's soothing voice echoed over the speakers. "You must be tired. We can talk about this tomorrow."

Rocko stiffened and left. Nakshi followed, Histo trailing behind.

Zena wobbled as she stood. I moved to catch her, but she raised a hand to stop me. She headed up the stairs. I took my time, tied my shoelaces first, then climbed the steps alone, yawning.

I heard a thud. Down the hall, Zena had collapsed. The gas lamps cast long shadows across the walkway. It was blurry, but I caught a woman's silhouette in a green shroud sprinting toward me. She stopped when she saw me, then bolted back into the library.

A tall man stepped out of the small library next—dressed in black, hood pulled low, holding something shiny. A blade?

"Aaaagh!!"

Zena's scream tore through the hallway. She pressed her palms to the floor, kicking back against the wall, eyes fixed on the looming figure.

"Help!" she cried, eyes bulging.

The man and I locked eyes.

I jolted.

Two hollow eyes on a flat face, black and white, flickering like an old TV with no signal. Goosebumps crawled over me. He was just like the man from my nightmare.

Krish stepped out of the library as the shadowy figure darted past, nearly colliding with him. I chased the figure inside, but the room had no one.

"I swear he went in. Is there a fire escape?"

Krish jerked his head back. "What's the matter with you two?" He turned his wide gaze to Zena, still frantic on the floor, and helped her up.

"That was him—again!" she panted. "Did you see his face?"

"Saw who?" Krish's mouth parted.

"That man with the painted face. White. Like chalk—with dots." She spoke in bursts, her arms waving.

Shivers ran down my spine. Like chalk, with dots?

"I didn't see anyone," Krish said.

Zena narrowed her eyes. "He just passed by you. The same man I saw the other night. I swear!"

He shrugged. "I told you. I didn't see anyone."

Zena groaned, rolling her eyes.

"Why were you on the floor?" Krish asked as he frantically typed on his tablet.

Zena pouted.

"A woman in a green shroud pushed her over," I blurted.

"What?" Zena's eyes narrowed.

"What do you mean what? She must have bumped into you. I saw her running by you."

"I didn't see a woman. I don't know why I fell. Maybe a lapse." She sighed. "I don't feel well."

It was getting bizarre. I saw two people. Zena only the chalky man. Krish, no one.

"Excuse me," the young techie cut in curtly. "I need to shut down the launch room before the boss gets mad." He hurried past, forehead creased, lips tight. I had never seen him move so fast.

Zena turned to me, bloodshot eyes wide. "Don't tell me you didn't see the man." She was almost begging.

I was tongue-tied. "A woman, too. I think—" I swallowed, unsure of myself. She stepped forward, narrowing her eyes, waiting for more. "And a tall shadow—a man in black. But the hallway was dim."

She exhaled hard. "Thank you." Her shoulders slumped, hand pressing to her chest.

"I saw him in my dream." I let out an exhale.

Her eyes nearly bulged.

"Dream? Was he in Peterhof?"

"How do you know?" This time, it was my turn to be stunned.

She lowered her voice. "I had the same dream. He hosted festivities—threw an octopus into a bonfire. Each arm had a face, but I couldn't make them out."

Ice crawled up my spine.

"That was me, Zmey Gorynych." It felt like confessing a dark secret. "You must've seen my dream's sequel."

She ignored me and leaned closer. "You were right. We're trapped in something big. They're experimenting on us." Her gaze flicked around. "I think Histo's CIA."

She seemed past the serial killer fear, latching onto a more plausible conspiracy—if not a scarier one. Zena clenched her fists, curled in on herself, arms crossed under her chest, shivering.

"You said you're not feeling well. What's wrong?"

"I'm freezing."

I held out my hand.

She hesitated, then unclenched, reaching out. No ring. It was an odd relief. I held her hand. It was hot. Her forehead—burning.

"I think I caught Covid."

END OF BOOK I

Sick Man

TEN DAYS INSIDE HISTORY

A Quantum Trilogy

REFERENCES

The following works were consulted for historical context during research. This is a work of historical fiction, not an academic study.

EPIGRAPH

"Cumhuriyet'in İkinci Yüzyılı?—Second Century of the (Turkish) Republic," Prof. Dr. Ahmet Arslan, Prof. Dr. Celal Şengör, Fatih Altaylı Teke Tek 100.Yıl Özel, October 2023 https://www.youtube.com/watch?v=TE9AT2HviyY 00:55:50

THE RECRUIT - 1

Little Shop of Horrors, 1986, Theatrical, Roger Corman and Charles B. Griffith, archive.org/details/little-shop-of-horrors_1986_theatrical

MONKEY SCRATCH - 2

Gallipoli Sniper: The Remarkable Life of Billy Sing, John Hamilton, Frontline Books, 2008

"Public Meeting in Favour of Greeks," *The Morning Chronicle*, London, May 16, 1823

"Two Monkeys Bit King of Greece; Both Diseased," Wythe Williams, *The Brooklyn Daily Eagle*, New York, October 18, 1920

The Godfather Part II, based on *The Godfather* by Mario Puzo, Paramount Pictures, The Coppola Company 1974

The Ottoman Centuries, The Rise and Fall of the Turkish Empire, Lord Kinross Morrow Quill Paperbacks New York 1977

Rigas Feraios the Hero: Hero of the Greek Revolutionary War, Dimitrios Karamberopolulos, Hellenic Publishing, October 2015

All the Pasha's Men: Mehmet Ali, his Army and the Making of Modern Egypt, Khaled Fahmy, Cambridge University Press, 1998

"Actualities at Smyrna: Mark O. Prentiss, American Eyewitness," John Bakeless, *The Atlantic, January* 1924.

"Hasten Evacuation of Smyrna Hordes," Mark O. Prentiss, Special Representative of the Near East Relief in Smyrna, *New York Times*, September 27, 1922

"French Exonerate Turks; Foreign Office Denies Kemalists Set Fire to Smyrna," *Associated Press*, Paris, September 26, 1922

"Mustapha Kemal Pasha: Where is a Turk his own Master?" *Time Magazine*, March 24, 1923.

"Uğur Şahin and Özlem Türeci: German 'Dream Team' Behind Vaccine," Philip Oltermann, *The Guardian*, November 10, 2020

THE MAGIC WAND - 3

"War is *Not* Part of Human Nature," R. Brian Ferguson, *Scientific American*, Sept. 1, 2018

"The Political Testament of Peter the Great," *The Halifax Courier*, 2 July 1853,

War of Necessity, War of Choice, Richard N. Haass, Simon & Schuster 2009

"The impact of quantum computer to the sustainability of the future," Bulent Yavuz, https://genarturkiyeraporu.com/raporlar/agustos-2024/kuantum-bilgisayarin-surdurulebilir-gelecege-etkisi/ August 2024

"Bans on Chokeholds for federal officers latest in nationwide push to hold police to a 'higher standard,'" Emma Tucker, cnn.com September 15, 2021

SICK MAN - 7

"Communication respecting Turkey, made to Her Majesty's Government by the Emperor of Russia," *The New York Daily Times*, April 5, 1854

PORRIDGE IS THE LEGITIMACY - 8

"Designs of Russia Upon Turkey, Secret Papers," *The New York Daily Times*, April 5, 1854

"Sir G.H. Seymour to Lord John Russell," *The New York Daily Times*, April 5, 1854

Nicholas I and Official Nationality of Russia 1825-1855, Nicholas Riasanovsky, University of California Press, Berkeley, California 1959

"Lord John Russell to Sir G.H. Seymour," *The New York Daily Times*, April 5, 1854

NOT WHAT TO DO BUT WHAT NOT TO DO - 9

"The Earl of Clarendon to Sir G. H. Seymour," *The New York Daily Times*, April 5, 1854

"Design of Russia upon Turkey— General View of the Secret Correspondence," *The New York Daily Times*, April 5, 1854

MUBITS OF PETAMUNRA - 10

The Quantum Story: A History in 40 Moments, Jim Baggott, Oxford University Press, 2011

Einstein: His Life and Universe, Walter Isaacson, Simon & Schuster 2007

"Quantum Computing for Beginners," Kayla Riley 2023

"Transformative Impact of Quantum Computing on Social Science," Bulent Yavuz, Future of Digital Technology and AI in Social Sectors, *ICI Global*, 2024

"Quantum Computing: A Gentle Introduction," Elenor G. Rieffel and Wolfgang H. Polak, *The MIT Press*, 2014

"Evidence for the utility of quantum computing before fault tolerance," Kim, Y., Eddins, A., Anand, S. *et al. Nature*, 618, 2023.

HOTEL METROPOLITAN - 11

"Breakfast in America," *The New York Daily Times*, January 24, 1855

"A Word About Ourselves," *The New York Daily Times*, September 18, 1851

"Kossuth in Turkey," *The New York Daily Times*, September 18, 1851

THE EDITOR - 12

"Confinement of Hungarians at Kutahia," *The New York Daily Times*, September 24, 1851

Henry J. Raymond and The New York Press for Thirty Years, Augustus Maverick, A.S. Hale and Company, 1870

New York Daily Times; A new Morning and Evening Daily Newspaper, Henry J. Raymond, Raymond, Jones & Co. August 30, 1851

STAR OF FREEDOM - 13

125 Color Paintings of Thomas Eakins, Jacek Michalak, Amazon Kindle Edition.

The Life of Louis Kossuth, Phineas C. Headley, Derby & Miller, Auburn, England, 1852, p. 258.

"Louis Kossuth in America, 1851-1852," John Bartholomew St. Leger, Master of Arts Thesis, Univ. of Richmond, Virginia, June 1961

"Marsh to Long, US Congress, Executive Documents," 32nd congress, 1 Session, 8, no. 78, 49. September 6, 1851

"Morgan to Hodge, Senate, Executive Documents,' 32nd Congress, 1 Session, 8, No 78, 2. September 23, 1851

Kossuth, David Bogue, Fleet Street, London 1851

"Kossuth and Captain Long," *The Daily Dispatch*, January 20, 1852.

"Liberation of Kossuth," *The New York Daily Times*, September 29, 1851

"The Sultan and Kossuth," *The Miners' Express*, October 29, 1851

"News from Turkey," *The New York Daily Times*, October 9, 1851

"Arrival of M. Kossuth," *The Stirling Observer*, October 30, 1851

"Another Letter from Kossuth," *The Weekly Mississippian*, November 14, 1851

"Kossuth, The Bar Reception International Law," *The New York Daily Times*, December 20, 1851

SULTAN AND THE TWO COUSINS - 14

"Kossuth: Demonstration by the Working Classes of the Metropolis," *The Observer*, November 10, 1851

"American Interference in the Politics of Europe," *The New York Daily Times*, November 12, 1851

"Reception of Kossuth in England and the Magazine Punch in 1851," Thomas Kabdebo, *Hungarian Studies*, Akadémiai Kiado, Budapest 1985.

Kossuth House Museum, Ministry of Tourism, Republic of Türkiye https:// muze.gov.tr/muze-detay?SectionId=KKH01&DistId=MRK

"Biographical Account of Kossuth – The Hungarian Patriot," *The York Herald*, October 25, 1851

"Congressional Banquet to Kossuth, Speech of Gov. Kossuth," *The New York Daily Times*, January 8, 1852

"The Expected Arrival of Kossuth – His Service and Character," *The London Daily News*, September 25, 1851

"Kossuth, Events of Yesterday," *The New York Daily Times*, December 10, 1851

"Kossuth in England and America," Laszlo Solymar, https://www.thearticle.com/kossuth-in-england-and-america, December 23, 2023

"The Bar Reception," *The New York Daily Times*, December 20, 1851

"Kossuth at the Capital," *The New York Daily Times*, January 3, 1852

"Kossuth on Turkey," *The New York Daily Times*, January 9, 1852

"Political Aspects and Prospects of France and Italy," *The New York Daily Times*, November 4, 1851

"The Nation's Guest: Lajos Kossuth in America," George Boutwell, https://iowa-counties.com/kossuth/kossuth.htm

THE ARMENIAN - 15

The Sultan and His People, Christopher Oscanyan, Derby & Jackson New York, 1857

"Asia Minor," *The New York Daily Times*, October 9, 1851

MEN OF THE AGE - 16

"Arrival of Steamboat Humboldt," *The Baltimore Sun*, December 6, 1851

"Banquet of the Press to Louis Kossuth at the Astor House!!," *The New York Daily Times*, December 16, 1851

"Kossuth Speech," *The New York Daily Times*, December 20, 1851

"Kossuth Dinner, Magnificent Banquet, Kossuth's Great Speech," *The New York Daily Times*, December 12, 1851

"Kossuth Papers: Report on the State of Turkey," *The Daily News*, December 12, 1851

"Speech of Mr. Raymond," *The New York Daily Times*, December 17, 1851

The Life of Louis Kossuth, Phineas C. Headley, Auburn, England: (Derby & Miller), 1852, p. 258.

Daily Free Democrat, 23 December 1851, Milwaukee, Wisconsin

"Kossuth on Turkey," *The New York Daily Times*, January 9, 1852

GRAND ELCHI - 17

The Life of the Right Honorable Stratford Canning, Viscount Stratford de Redcliffe, Stanley Lane-Poole Longmans, Green, and Co. London, 1888

A Biography of Stratford Canning, Michael Warr, Alden Press Oxford, 1989

The Invasion of Crimea, Its Origin, and an Account of its Progress down to the Death of Lord Raglan, Vol. I, A. W. Kinglake, William Blackwood and Sons, 1890.

"British Heads of Mission at Constantinople 1583-1922," G. R. Berridge, www. diplomacy.edu

The New-York Daily Times, April 12, 1853

The History of Parliament; The House of Commons 1820-32 edited by D. R. Fisher, Cambridge University Press, 2009

"Family of Empires: The Pisanis in the Ottoman and British Empires," by Frank Castiglione, Ph.D. Thesis University of Michigan 2016

"On Brigham Young," *The New York Daily Times* August 12, 1854, September 8, 1854, *Deseret News* Utah July 23, 1854

"Etienne Pisani to Ambassador Lyons," 10 May 1867, 206-209 The National Archives, Foreign Office of Commonwealth

"Respecting the rights and privileges of the Greek and Latin Churches in Turkey, presented to both Houses of Parliament by Command of Her Majesty," No 94, v.8 pp 83-6 1854

History of Turkey, Volume 1, Alphonse de Lamartine, D. Appleton & Company, New York, 1855

Determining and Defining 'Wife': The Brigham Young Households, Johnson, Jeffery Ogden, Dialogue: A Journal of Mormon Thought. 20 (3) 57-70, 1987

"Arrival and Greeting of the United States Minister," *The New York Daily Times* April 3, 1854

"The Turkish Question," *The London Times*, May 26, 1853

THE REVOLUTIONARY - 18

The Secret Diplomatic Correspondence, Marx and Engels Collected Works, Volume 13 pp. 84-99, Progress Publishers, Moscow 1980. London, Friday, March 24, 1854

"Poland's European Mission, Karl Marx, 1867." https://www.marxists.org/archive/marx/works/1867/01/22a.htm

The Communist Manifesto, Marx and Engels Collected Works, Volume 6, pp. 477-519, International Publishers, 1976.

"The Secret Correspondences between England and Russia," *The New York Daily Times*, April 5, 1854

THE BONAPARTISTS - 19

"Mentchikoff arrives in Turkey," *The New York Daily Times*, April 6, 1853.

Prince Menshikov's Mission, The Life of the Right Honourable Stratford Canning, Viscounte Stratford de Redcliffe, Stanley Lane Poole Longmans, Green, Co., New York, 1888

Crimea, The Great Crimean War, 1854-1856, Trevor Royle, St. Martin's Press

The Crimean War: A History, Orlando Figes, 2011

"The London Press - Policy of Napoleon on the Turkish Question," Karl Marx, *New York Tribune*, April 11, 1853

THE HOLY KEY OF DOSOGRAFA - 20

"Departure of Menschikoff – Probability of War," *The New York Daily Times*, June 13, 1853

"The Shrines of the Holy Land," *The New York Daily Times*, December 20, 1852.

"History of the Possession of the Holy Sepulcher of Jerusalem by the Latins and Greeks," *The New York Daily Times*, November 29, 1852

"The 'Dosografa' Church in the Treaty of Küçük Kaynarca," Roderic H. Davison, Bulletin of the School of Oriental and African Studies, University of London, Vol, 42, No. 1 (1979)

The Ottoman Crimean War, Candan Badem, Brill, Leiden, Boston 2010

A DAY AT THE PETERHOF - 21

The Invasion of Crimea, Its Origin and an Account of its Progress down to the Death of Lord Raglan Vol I, Alexander William Kinglake, Cambridge University Press, New York, 2010, first published in 1863.

"La Turquie," *Journal des Débats*, March 16, 1852

"Ambassador Extraordinary from Russia," *The New York Daily Times*, April 12, 1852

"Attempts of Russia to Incite a Holy War," *The New York Daily Times*, June 1, 1853

"Parliament and Foreign Policies," *The New York Daily Times*, June 9, 1853

"Austria's categorical demands," *Trieste Zeitung*, March 7, 1853

The Washington Monument: A Technical History and Catalog of the Commemorative Stones, Judith M. Jacob, Wayback Machine, 2005.

"The Recent Crisis in Turkey," *London Morning Chronicle*, March 22, 1853

The Eastern Question, Karl Marx, ed. by Eleanor Marx Aveling and Edward Aveling Swan Sonnenschein & Co. 1897

Tolstoy: A Russian Life, Rosamund Bartlett, Profile Books, London 2010

"Revolution in Montenegro," *The New York Daily Times*, February 9, 1853

"News of the Morning," *The New York Daily Times*, February 18, 1853

"Prince Pays Cash for Each Turkish Head," *The New York Times*, February 18, 1853

"The Anglo-French Alliance," *The Bradford Observer*, March 31, 1853

"A Turkish War and Its Results," *The New York Daily Times*, March 11, 1853

THE REFORMIST - 22

St. Petersburg and London in the Years 1852-1864, Vitzthum von Eckstadt, Longmans, Green, and Co., New York, 1887

The Balyans: Ottoman Architecture and Balyan Archive, Buke Uras, Limited-HC-English Edition, Korpus, 2021

Bleak House, Charles Dickens, CreateSpace Independent Publishing Platform, 1852

Thirty Years in the Harem, Vol. I, Melek-Hanum, Elibron Classics Series 2005

Bu Mülkün Sultanları, Necdet Sakaoğlu, Oğlak Yayıncılık, 1999

"President Bush Discusses Democracy, Freedom From Turkey," The White House, June 29, 2004

Anti-Reformists and Mustafa Reshid Pasha: The Cost of the Tanzimat Edict, Ahmet Dönmez, International Periodical for the Languages, Literature and History of Turkish or Turkic 11/6 2016

"Ottoman Relations in the Nineteenth Century: Mustafa Reşid Paşa's Memorandum to Palmerston, 11 August 1839," Turgut Subaşı, International Journal of Human Sciences, 8 (1), 2011

Dangerous Gifts, Imperialism, Security, and Civil Wars in the Levant, 1798-1864, Ozan Ozavci, Oxford University Press

Diplomatic Study on the Crimean War, Russian Official Publication Allen & Co., 1882

MASSACRE IN MIDNIGHT - 23

"The Eastern Question: Great Meeting in the City of London," *The Standard*, October 8, 1853

"The America's News," *The New York Daily Times*, October 1, 1853

The Crimean War: A History, Orlando Figes, 2011

Nicholas I and Official Nationality in Russia 1825-1855, Nicholas Riasanovsky, University of California Press Berkeley and Los Angeles, 1967

Istoriko-politicheskiia pisma I zapiski, Mikhail Petrovich Pogodin, Moskva Tip, 1874

The War in the Crimea, Edward Hamley, 1855

"St. Petersburg's Tsar Attractions: Following in the Footsteps of the Romanovs," *The Times*, April 27, 2023

"Saint George and the Dragon," wikipedia.org

The Sinop Affair and its Aftermath, Andrew C. Rath, 2013

Interesting Details Concerning the Destruction of the Fleet, Die Triester Zeitung, Vienna, December 20, 1853

The Summons of the Fleet, The Life of the Right Honourable Stratford Canning, Viscounte Stratford de Redcliffe, Stanley Lane Poole Longmans, Green, Co., New York, 1888

The Accounts of the Sinope Naval Battle, Boris Yeltsin Presidential Library, #619768

"Sinope Particulars," *The New York Daily Times*, December 31, 1853

www.ingramcontent.com/pod-product-compliance
Lightning Source LLC
Chambersburg PA
CBHW022025120726
47901CB00008BA/2024